521 8

D0229800

That Girl From Nowhere

Dorothy Koomson, briefly . . .

Dorothy Koomson is the author of nine novels including *The Chocolate Run, Marshmallows For Breakfast, The Woman He Loved Before* and *The Flavours of Love*. She's been making up stories since she was thirteen when she used to share her stories with her convent school friends.

Dorothy's first novel, *The Cupid Effect*, was published in 2003 (when she was quite a bit older than thirteen). Her third book, *My Best Friend's Girl*, was selected for the Richard & Judy Summer Reads of 2006, and her novels *The Ice Cream Girls* and *The Rose Petal Beach* were both shortlisted for the popular fiction category of the British Book Awards in 2010 and 2013, respectively.

Dorothy's novels have been translated into more than thirty languages, and a TV adaptation loosely based on *The Ice Cream Girls* was first shown on ITV1 in 2013. After living in Sydney, Australia, for two years, Dorothy returned to England and now lives in Brighton. Well, Hove, actually.

While writing this book, Dorothy developed a bit of a penchant for making jewellery, drinking coffee and taking photos with a real camera.

For more information on Dorothy Koomson and her novels, including That Girl From Nowhere, *visit www.dorothykoomson.co.uk*

That Girl From Nowhere

Dorothy
KOOMSON

CENTURY

3 5 7 9 10 8 6 4 2

Century
20 Vauxhall Bridge Road
London SW1V 2SA

Century is part of the Penguin Random House group of companies
whose addresses can be found at global.penguinrandomhouse.com.

Penguin
Random House
UK

First published in the UK by Century, 2015

www.randomhouse.co.uk

A CIP catalogue record for this book is
available from the British Library.

ISBN 9781780893358

MIX
Paper from
responsible sources
FSC® C018179

Penguin Random House is committed to a sustainable future for
our business, our readers and our planet. This book is made from
Forest Stewardship Council® certified paper.

This book is dedicated, with love, to my dad – sometimes disapproving but *always* supportive.

*I've decided to say my thanks with KISSES (**K**eep **I**t **S**hort, **S**weet and **E**specially **S**imple). So . . .*

Thank you

to my gorgeous family who are everything to me
to Ant and James, my wonderful agents
to all the fantastic people at my publishers, Cornerstone (especially Susan, Jenny G, Gillian, Jen D, Richard, Charlotte, Natalie, Rebecca, Aslan)
to Emma D and Sophie, my great publicists.

A special thank you goes to those who helped with my research, particularly Sarah Marshall and Chris Manby, who also provided brilliant long chats as well as info.

And to E, G & M – thank you for being so amazing in every way. I love you.

As always, I would like to say thank you to you, the reader, for buying this book.

Prologue

With Her, sometime soon, Brighton

'You will help me, won't you?' she asks.

'If I can,' I reply. I wonder what she thinks someone she has just met will be able to help her do when she has a whole family down the hall in the living room who are at her beck and call. 'What is it you want help with?'

This woman, my grandmother, who has only really been in my life for the past hour, fixes me with a gaze that is determined and a little frightening; woven through with strands of defiance. Maybe I was mistaken; maybe those outside this room aren't as devoted and loving as I thought. Whatever it is that she wants to do is clearly something they're unlikely to agree to. She says nothing for a time, and the longer she stares at me with her brown eyes, the colour dimmed by age, the more a feeling of dread meanders outwards from the pit of my stomach. I should not be sitting here having this conversation with this woman. I should have brought her back here and left her to it. The longer I sit here, the longer things are going to go wrong for me.

Eventually, so eventually I thought she was planning on remaining silent, she speaks. Cautiously, haltingly, she says: 'My time has come. I am too old...too sick...too tired to carry on in this world.' She pauses but her eyes continue to drill into me. 'My time has come. I want...I want to leave this Earth. I need you to help me.'

Part 1

1

Smitty

'Miss Smittson, it's good to see you again.'

'You, too, Mr Wallace,' I reply. I smile at him and shove my hands into the pockets of my combat trousers to avoid having to shake hands with him. I've met him twice before – both times I've had to do it and both times his hand has been hot and clammy. The images of what he could have done to get it that way were a horror movie that played constantly through my head.

Mr Wallace, in a shabby, too-tight black suit, offers me his hand to shake. I hesitate. The rest of him seems dry and normal, I wonder if he'd accept a hug instead? It would get me out of touching his hand without seeming rude and it'd be altogether better for my mental health. He pulls a smile across his face, sticks his hand out a little bit further. Defeated, I offer up my hand to be encased in his moist, sweaty palm. The touch of him sends a shudder through me and I can't take my hand away fast enough, but not too fast in case he notices and his feelings are hurt. Maybe he can't help being sweaty-palmed, maybe he has a condition and it's not his fault. Maybe the horror movie in my head has got it all wrong and he doesn't do unsavoury things in his car before he meets clients.

Mr Wallace's attention strays to the older woman with wavy brown, grey-streaked hair who stands silently beside me. He smiles curiously at us both, waiting for an introduction.

Mum has obviously noticed how reluctant I was to shake the estate agent's hand so has taken to holding her bag in both hands, rendering them incapable of being shaken when I do the introductions.

'Mr Wallace, this is my mother, Heather Smittson,' I say. 'Mum, this is the estate agent who's dealing with renting the flat.'

Immediately, Mr Wallace's face does *that thing*. 'That thing' most people who don't know my family do: he double-takes, then rapidly moves his gaze from one of us to the other, wondering why the visuals don't match the words. After the staring comes the perplexed, suspicious frown and, right on cue, Mr Wallace's confusion develops on his face until he is frowning very hard indeed at us.

We're in the car park of a beautiful, reddish-yellow-brick, art deco block of flats on Hove seafront. This is going to be my new home, the place for my fresh start. Everything bad is three hundred miles away and in that place called 'the past' while everything good is here, and about to happen in that shiny new destination called 'the future'.

Except little snags like this, a man who is nearer to Mum's age than mine, giving us his version of Paddington Bear's hard stare because he doesn't understand why Mum is my mother and why I am her daughter. To him, it surely shouldn't be possible.

Mum suddenly needs something from her handbag, and she pops the black leather rectangle open and starts to ferret furiously through it. Clearly what she is searching for is so important the world might end if she doesn't find it RIGHT NOW. What she is actually doing is her version of 'Lalalalalala not happening', which she does every time she might need to explain our situation. If the handbag thing doesn't work, she'll simply wander off, pretending that she doesn't know we're in the middle of a conversation.

With Mum making it clear with every root through her meticulously organised bag that she isn't going to be forthcoming, Mr Wallace returns to me. It's now my job to explain. I'm supposed to say, 'I'm adopted'. To let him know that Mum and Dad did the whole white parents taking on black children thing well before various celebs made it fashionable. He stares at me, I stare at him – he wants answers to his unasked questions, I'm not giving them. I haven't got the energy.

As if someone On High knows I need rescuing, Mr Wallace's left, inside breast pocket begins to vibrate before the tinny, tiny sound of 'YMCA' joins it. 'Oh, excuse me,' he says and reaches for it. He checks the screen, grimaces, struggles with himself. 'I'm sorry, I have to get this. It's an emergency waiting to happen. Do you mind?' He's pressed the answer button and put it to his ear before I even have a chance to react. He wanders away from us, heading across the promenade and towards the blue-green railings that separate land from sea.

'Well, that was rude,' Mum states. She removes her head and her hand from her bag, snaps it closed again with a loud click as the brass clasp shuts itself tight. 'We were in the middle of a conversation.'

'*You mean I was*,' the person I am in my head says. '*You were going, "lalalala, not happening".*' The person I actually am says, 'It's fine, Mum. It gives us a chance to have a proper look at the place. So what do you think?'

This building is as beautiful as it is commanding. The bottom part of it is painted cream and looks from a distance like a short, satiny cream skirt, while the top half looks like it has been dressed in a blouse of russet sandstone. The corners of the building are curved instead of pointed and the whole of the top floor is apparently one penthouse apartment. My flat is on the first floor, and most of it overlooks the sea. I'd spent far too much money on renting it, even with the huge discount I'd got because it'd been empty for so long and the owners were desperate to fill it. It didn't matter about the money right now, it would come out of my savings, and it was only for six months before I decided what to do next.

Mum, who rarely shows if she is impressed, rotates slowly on the spot, stares at the sea, which today is a shimmery azure, and takes in the matching-coloured sky that is crammed with white, floccose clouds. While she looks, I retrieve my small instant camera from the left knee pocket of my navy blue combat trousers and flick it on. I need to take a snapshot of this moment so I can write underneath it: *With Mum, May 2015, Outside New Home (Brighton/Hove)* and stick it up on my wall. A reminder of the moment my new life began.

In my right knee pocket my mobile buzzzz-buzzzz-tings for probably the fiftieth time today. I ignore my phone and take the shot, capturing our proximity to the sea as well as the look of the building.

'Who is it that keeps sending you messages?' Mum asks. She can't ignore it any longer. She's held her tongue all day but this is the text that has sent her over the edge. She sounds so miffed anyone would think it was her who was being texted at least six times an hour all day. Mum becomes diabolically upset with people who use 'text' as a verb. (It's actually worth doing it just to see her nostrils flare and her eyes turn into hard blue lasers seeking to burn your tongue out of your head for such an evil act.) 'They were sending messages the whole of the journey and even now when you haven't replied. Who is it?'

'Who do you think it is?' I reply, a little more tartly than is necessary.

'Didn't you tell him that you don't want to see him any more?' she asks.

She says that like it was a casual fling – not a twelve-year, cohabiting relationship – that he should really be over by now.

'Well, didn't you?' she demands to my silence.

'Yes, of course I did.'

'Then why is he still sending you messages?'

For the same reason that I'm still reading them: I don't want it to be over; I don't want any of this to have happened; I want to be living at home in Leeds with our plans for the future and my eye on that shop in the Victoria Quarter. I want to be making jewellery, and arguing about my mess, and planning days out in our campervan. I want the life I was promised and thought I was going to live before all of this happened. It's the same for him, I'd imagine.

I can't talk about this with anyone, but especially not with her when she made it clear over the years how little she thought of him. 'I don't know why he's still texting, Mum.' Like clockwork her eyes harden and her nostrils show their annoyance at the text verb. 'Maybe he thinks if he sends me enough messages I'll change my mind.'

'Typical,' she mumbles nowhere near under her breath. 'I never did like the way he was so confident and sure of himself.'

'Really?' I reply. ''Cos I always loved that about him.'

'And look where that got you,' Mum says. Shocked, I take a step back. She's not normally that spiteful. Her words usually have a sting to them, but that was like a nasty stab from a vicious weapon and it's hit me square in the chest, right over my heart, right where everything seems to ache from at the moment.

Mum, even though she must have seen my reaction, and noticed that I have stepped away from her, is openly unapologetic as she observes me.

'*Oh, get knotted*,' teeters on the tip of my tongue, while huge tears are cramming themselves into my eyes. I take another step back and force myself to look away because I'm not sure if swearing at my mother or crying in front of her would be the worst thing to do right now.

With Seth & Dylan, November 1996, Liverpool

'Can I get you a drink?' The man who asked this question looked vaguely familiar, fitted right into this university world of distantly remembered, partially recalled faces.

He had come over and sat down on the stool on the other side of the table in the area of the student bar where Dylan, the absolute love of my life, had unintentionally annexed these last few weeks we'd been here. Dylan was like The Fonz in that people were drawn to him; they hung out near him like groupies around a rock star and didn't seem to mind if he didn't actually get around to talking to them during their time together in the bar. Today was one of those rare occasions where it was only Dylan and me having a drink after an additional early evening tutorial that only he and I had turned up for. Other lectures hadn't started or were about to finish, and in that lull I'd managed to get him all to myself. I was relishing every last second – until this guy appeared.

Like most of the people I met at college, I wasn't sure if this new bloke was someone I'd seen around – in halls, in the library, right here in the bar – or if I'd met him before I arrived at Liverpool University to study Political Science.

'I'll have a pint if you're buying,' Dylan replied to the new man.

'I wasn't asking you,' the new man said good-naturedly. 'I was asking your friend.'

I pointed to myself in surprise. 'Me?' Male or female, no one noticed me when I was sitting with Dylan. He was far too rock star-like.

'Yes,' he said.

'No. Thank you, but no.'

'Make the most of it while you can,' Dylan laughed. 'Seth's not exactly known for reaching into his pocket unprompted.'

'Think you're mistaking me for yourself there, mate,' the new guy, Seth, replied. 'Which is why I'm not offering to buy you a drink – you owe me a couple of thousand of them.'

Dylan laughed again.

'Does your mum like *Emmerdale Farm*, by any chance?' I asked. She may have had a special interest in Greek mythology but I was guessing modern-day TV was probably more her thing.

Seth nodded slowly. 'I got off quite lightly,' he said then laughed. When he laughed his pink lips moved back to show his perfect white teeth, while his hazel-green eyes danced with mirth and kindness. 'My brother's called Sugden. We've got Alans and Jacks in our extended family so Sugden he was named.'

'That's not true,' I scoffed.

'It is, actually,' Dylan said. 'I've known Seth since we were in nursery. Grew up near-ish to each other over the years. Now, apparently, he's transferred to do Political Science here, too. Can't get away from him, it seems. But yes, his brother is called Sugden. His family's dead posh and all, you'd think his mother would have some shame about it, but she's unrepentant.'

Seth nodded.

'Seth,' I said contemplatively.

'Yes?'

'Nothing, I was just turning the name over in my mouth. I don't think I've ever said it before.'

From the corner of my eye I saw Dylan's head turn towards me before he frowned.

'What's your name?' Seth asked.

'Clemency Smittson. I'm only telling you my surname because my friends call me Smitty. My dad started it when I was about twelve, drove my mum wild with annoyance, but it stuck.'

'I see.' He nodded. 'The question for me then is: are you a Smitty or a Clem to me?' It was Seth's turn to receive a small, suspicious frown from Dylan but Seth didn't seem to notice. Or if he did, he didn't care. Seth got to his feet, still staring intently at me. 'I shall ponder which one I think you are to me on my way to the bar. Are you sure you don't want a drink?'

'Actually, I think I will. Half a lager and lime, please.'

'A half with lime it is.'

Once Seth had left our vicinity, Dylan sat back in his seat, his body slid down a bit against his part of the corner sofa we'd commandeered and he stared at me with his head slightly to one side as though sizing me up. Eventually, when he'd watched me study Seth at the bar, he said to me: 'Don't go there, Smitty.'

'Go where?' I asked.

'*You know,*' he hissed irritably. 'Don't do it. Not with him.'

'Why not?'

'Just don't, all right?' He glanced over at Seth, which made me look at him too. 'We're all young, just starting college...don't be getting involved with blokes like him.'

'Why? Is he a complete bastard?'

'Nah...He's a nice guy. And if you do it with him, you'll fall in love with him or something equally stupid and he'll probably fall in love with you. It's too soon when you're still in college.'

'You are pulling my leg,' I said to him. I couldn't quite believe what I was hearing.

'No, no, I'm not. Not really. I just don't think...Look, being honest, I wouldn't like it. You're my friend, not his.'

Dylan and I had been 'friends' since the first week in college when I sat next to him in our Political Foundations class. I had turned to

9

ask him what time the lecture was due to finish and found my voice had abandoned me. He was simply the most beautiful man I had ever seen. With his dark olive skin, close-cut black hair, huge brown eyes, and easy, natural smile, I fell for him straight away. It was impossible not to. Over the next few lectures we'd discovered we had the same sense of humour and liked the same music and films so I rather easily slotted into becoming one of his groupies. For the most part I didn't mind because very few of the other groupies had all the same classes as him, so didn't get to spend as much time with him in and out of class as I did. What he was saying now, though, was that I was a cut above the entourage of good-looking women who seemed to draw his attention; I was different. He would be bothered if I slept with someone else.

'Are you seriously saying you wouldn't like me going out with Seth because he's a nice guy?' I asked.

'Going out?' Dylan said despairingly. 'Smitty, you've just met the guy. I'm only saying I don't think you should go there, all right?' He shrugged. 'Please. I've known him a long time, me and him are good mates. Me and you are good . . . well, whatever. Just don't.'

'It's nice of you to care about my feelings so much,' I replied casually. Inside . . . Inside all my internal organs were dancing: Dylan liked me enough to be jealous.

'I've thought long and hard,' Seth stated. He placed our two drinks on the table, ignored Dylan's grumbles about being left out and focused on me. 'I've decided you're going to be Smitty to me. Mind if I call you Smitty?'

My grin must have taken him by surprise. He had done me the hugest favour – he'd made me interesting *and* desirable in Dylan's eyes. Dylan wanted me. I never thought that would happen. Not ever. 'You certainly can call me Smitty. In fact, I'd be offended if you didn't.'

'Excellent,' Seth replied.

Really excellent, I thought as Dylan sat up, and with one hand picked up his almost empty glass and took a sip, while under the table, his other hand moved possessively on to my leg and stayed there. *Really, really excellent.*

Mr Wallace finishes his call and starts his way back to us. I am furiously blinking away tears, trying to sweep aside the pain from my mother's words and slowly the agony starts to recede while calmness takes over. Mum is still staring at me but I ignore her and focus on Mr Wallace, concentrate on not revealing how much she's hurt me. 'Many apologies for that, ladies,' he says. 'Now, if you'll follow me, I'll show you into your new home.'

Oh yes, like things aren't bad enough, my mother is also moving in with me.

2

Abi

To: Jonas Zebila
From: Abi Zebila
Subject: Purple Day
Monday, 25 May 2015

Dear Jonas,

Today is a purple day.

That's what Lily-Rose told me, anyway. Not quite sure where she got that from, or what it means, but when I came in from work earlier that was the first thing she said to me. It made me smile and it made me think of you. And I had to ask you what you think it means. Today is a purple day. It's also two years since you've been in touch and that's long enough now, don't you think?

Brother, dear brother, you've been gone from her for nearly half her life. You are her favourite uncle, she still talks about you. And I still think about you. We were a team, you and me.

I've read all this stuff online about how when a person decides to go 'no contact' with their family they have to cut everyone out, including the people you love because they're the ones who drag you back into the toxic mess, and I get it, I really do. But it's not fair. I didn't do anything. Remember? I'm the one you actually like.

I have no one here, apart from Lily-Rose and Declan, obviously, but no one knows I'm still seeing him – they all assumed we'd finished, which is why I moved back here. Yes, I came back to live with Mummy and Daddy. Really, I moved back in because Gran's seriously ill now and I decided to help Mummy with her meds and feeding her (most days she can't do that for herself) and other stuff.

So, what's new in the past two years apart from me living back here? Well, nothing much is the short answer. Ivor still lives here, and shows no signs of leaving – ever.

Mummy and Daddy are still the same. They don't argue, argue, but they do snipe at each other a lot still. It's definitely got worse since you left. Mummy blames him for you cutting us off but she won't say it, and Daddy pretends it hasn't happened.

The other bone of contention is that Mummy thinks Gran should be somewhere where she'll get specialist care. I hear them talking about it sometimes. Daddy's not having it. They talk quietly, but I swear, Daddy, when he speaks, raises his voice on words like 'duty' and 'loyalty' and 'respect'. 'Course, he can say all that because he doesn't have to do much. He talks to Gran whenever she makes it into the lounge, he goes in to say hello and goodnight to her most days. Yes, I wrote that right – *most* days he goes into her room. He has to pass her room to leave and enter the house but he doesn't even make it in to see her every day. Denial about how sick his mother is do you think?

And then there's Lily-Rose, Lil' 'Purple Day' herself. She's my entire world. You should see her now, she's so big. Tall, beautiful, funny. Remind you of anyone?! You never got to know how funny she was, properly. The other day she disappeared and after I looked in all her favourite hiding places in the house – I eventually found her in Gran's room, telling knock-knock jokes she'd made up. They were all pretty random, a lot didn't make sense, but some were hysterical. I could tell it was just what Gran needed.

Look, please get in touch. Two years is long enough. You used to think life was too short to hold a grudge, that you should let bygones be bygones. I know Gran was terrible to you and Meredith, and the results of what she did were devastating, but deep down, don't you still believe in *not* holding a grudge, especially against the people who didn't do what she did? Aren't you even a little bit curious about us, about Lily-Rose?

Today's a purple day. What does that mean to you?

Love,
Abi
xxxxxx

3

Smitty

I slide open the side of Lottie, my red and white camper van, and am greeted with a great wall of brown cardboard boxes. The suitcases, holdalls and bags have all been transported up to the flat in the last eight trips, and now I have the boxes to start on. I stare at them. I'm sure they've quadrupled in number since I stacked them in there last night.

Last night, he was out like I'd asked him to be so I could move the boxes into Lottie ready for today's trip, but I wasn't sure how long he'd stay out or if he'd be back to try to convince me to give us another chance, so I had shifted boxes without really noticing their number or weight. There were still some left in our flat, which is why I didn't want to tell him to leave me alone. I'd have to arrange a time to go and get the rest. Now, I don't really understand how I have so much stuff. It's not as if I have lots of clothes and shoes and bags, and the like. I took no furniture, I took no appliances, I left them all for him back at the flat, and yet... I have what seems like a million boxes.

They can't all be work-related. I read the words on the boxes as if I didn't label them myself: 'Tools', 'Old Tools', 'Wire', 'Polishers', 'Finishers', 'Rollers, Barrel Roller, etc.', 'Journals, Books, Swatches, etc.', 'Finished Pieces', 'Toolboxes', 'Findings', 'Beads', 'Resins, Glues', 'Samplers', 'Texturisers'. Maybe because I'd worked at Karina's Jewels for so long and I had a lot of my regularly used tools there and my other stuff at home, I didn't notice how much work stuff I'd accumulated.

I'm a jewellery maker, much to the upset and disapproval of my mother. With a good political science degree I was obviously on the road destined for Parliament, final stop Prime Minister. I had a different path to tread, though. We'd frequently rowed about it over the years (and I'm sure she still holds out hope for my great political career to emerge) but nothing gave me joy like making jewellery. From coming up with the initial design to handing over or displaying the finished piece, my job gave me real pleasure. My true love, though, was reloving people's old jewellery.

Nothing was sadder than jewellery that languished in a drawer or box, mostly forgotten, partially unloved, because it didn't fit into someone's life. I made people want to love their jewellery again. Unwanted things that used to be precious, could be precious again, were my speciality. I would do my best to make the jewellery fit the person's life, make them look at it again and see that they could love it, they did want it, they didn't want to forget it existed because for a time it wasn't quite up to scratch.

I sit on the edge of Lottie's footrest, momentarily defeated by the number of boxes I have to unload, by the task ahead of me. I have to start again. Establish my business down here, find new clients, set up my workshop, open my shop, all while living with my mother. I'd lived with her when I left my flat, and for the months before that, but I'd always known it was temporary so I could endure it. This is permanent. I close my eyes, allow the ebb and flow of the sea to wash over me. I can do this. I know I can. I need to believe that. It'd be easier, of course, with him. But, I can do this. Because I have to.

With Dylan & Seth, Xmas 1998, Liverpool (end of term party)
'How about we break with tradition this year and I kiss Smitty under the mistletoe first?' Seth asked.

We had all arrived separately at the Social Sciences department's end of term party in the dining hall, with me turning up last. Our department always went all out for their parties and waited until everyone had officially left so they could hire the dining hall and make it look spectacular. As soon as I walked in the door, Dylan and Seth both descended upon me – Seth was holding mistletoe. I looked from one to the other.

It wasn't as if I was going out with either of them, or that either of them didn't have girlfriends because I wasn't and they did. But for the last two Christmases, whenever they spotted mistletoe, I was their first port of call.

'How about we *don't* make this a tradition which could be seen as Smitty being a bit "free" with her affections around two men who have girlfriends?' I replied. Girlfriends who were probably in this very room, glaring at me.

Dylan snaked his hand around my waist, tugged me towards his body and kissed me full on the mouth, as he'd been doing for the last two Christmases, before anyone could say anything else. His lips, tasting of the rum-laced punch he'd obviously been drinking, lingered on mine. This was about to turn into a proper, full-on kiss where he would push his tongue into my mouth, he'd pull me closer to him and we'd forget anyo—. Abruptly, Dylan stepped away. As always his kiss was enough to tease me but not enough to promise me anything.

'You are such a git,' Seth complained. 'You don't even have mistletoe.'

'I've got mistletoe in my heart,' Dylan replied. He focused on me with his enormous black-brown eyes and I knew he was about to finish with his latest girlfriend. He always gave me that look, said something like that, when he was about to dump someone – it's not like anything had ever happened between us, or that he'd make a move once he was free, he just did this to let me know what he was thinking. And the only time he ever kissed me properly was at Christmas.

'Happy Christmas, Smitty,' Seth said. '*I'm still here, you know?*' he was actually saying.

I managed to tear my eyes away from Dylan, refocused on Seth. 'Happy Christmas, Seth,' I replied.

He held up the mistletoe, its white fruit unusually plump and large against its long, slender oval-shaped leaves. 'Any chance?' he asked. I hadn't even got my coat off or unwound my scarf.

I glanced at Dylan. He stared down at his feet, prodding at something invisible on the floor as though he wasn't bothered, his body language plainly broadcasting how bothered he was. I wasn't the one going out with someone else, I was single and able to kiss whoever I liked – no matter how chaste it really was. Seth, though... The mere idea of him and me bugged Dylan. He hadn't been bothered when I'd been out with or slept with other men, even with friends of his, but when it came to Seth, his jealousy was clear and evident.

'If you want to,' I told him.

Seth nodded in understanding. 'Next year,' he said. He tossed his mistletoe on to the buffet table, between the pile of greasy mini sausages and the large crystal punchbowl. 'I'll make sure that I get my kiss in first.'

Mum hasn't brought much stuff with her. *'I only really need my clothes and my photographs,'* she'd said, and she was as good as her word.

Considering her house in Otley was crammed with enough ornaments and knick-knacks to keep a small charity shop well stocked for a year or two, and she'd never shown any inclination to get rid of them, I was impressed that she really only brought her photo albums, clothes and beauty items. 'I won't take up much space,' she'd said during the conversation where I asked her to move in with me. That's how she tells it to anyone who'll listen – she even tells that to me and I was there for the conversation. *'Clemency was moving and she couldn't do it on her own, so she asked me to come with her. She's my only child, so I couldn't say no.'* What really happened was this:

'Mum, I know the timing could be better but I'm moving. I've got one more week to complete at work and then I'm going to tie up everything here and move to Brighton. Well, Hove, actually. That's where the flat I've found is. It's near enough to Brighton. I've got a workshop down there, too.' I decided to tell Mum I'd also got a shop space another time – too much information gave her too much to worry about and too much to mither me about.

'Oh, that sounds like a fantastic idea, Clemency. I'll get your uncle Colin to look after the house and I'll come with you. Thank you for suggesting it.'

'What?' I replied.

'Don't say, "what".'

'Wha— I don't understand what you've just said.'

'Or maybe Nancy and Sienna could move in?' she said to herself. 'They'll need a bigger space, I won't need to charge them rent and they're family so I know they'll take care of the place. Or maybe I shouldn't involve family? Maybe I should just look at renting it out through an agency.'

'What are you saying to me, Mother?'

'Your uncle Colin can help out. When are you going?'

'Two weeks.'

'Perfect. That's plenty of time to pack and have an estate agent value the place with a view to selling or renting.'

'But I'm moving on my own.' (I'm still not sure if I said that out loud.)

'This is perfect, Clemency. I won't take up much space. Just my photographs and personal belongings and clothes. I was wondering what I would do with myself now. I don't want to be here any more. Too many memories, especially from the last few months. But you've solved that problem for me.'

And created a whole world of problems for me. Mum and me in confined spaces, with nothing much to do . . . It is a bad combination.

'Clemency? Is that you?' Mum calls. I heft the first box through the front door. There are eighty-seven steps and three sets of doors between Lottie and this flat. I only noticed that while wrestling my way here with this box labelled 'Tools'.

'Who else is it going to be?' I call back.

'A simple "yes" will suffice,' she replies.

'What is it that you want, Mum?' I ask. Down the long wide corridor with large block, parquet flooring in a rich honey-coloured wood, I follow the sound of Mum's voice until I find her, in the second bedroom. Her bedroom. This was going to be my work-at-home place. It didn't have the sea views of the other rooms, but it had an en suite shower and loo, space for a desk as well as a (guest) bed and, most importantly, a large amount of wall space to pin up my designs and have a shelving unit to keep all the tools and materials – wire, beads, findings, bottle tops, trays, glues, resins, cords, etc., etc., etc. – I used at home.

'Yes, Mum?' I say. 'How can I help you?' I have sprinkled positivity, the type of sunshine drenching the outside world, into my voice because this is all going to work out. Everything is going to be fine. To make sure it is, I need to stay positive no matter what is sent to try me.

'This room is going to be fine for me,' she says.

'That's great,' I say.

'There isn't much natural light, though,' she adds, in case I get too comfortable with doing something almost right.

'I know. This side of the building overlooks the internal courtyard and because there are other parts of the building on all four sides, not much light comes in. Sorry.'

'That's OK,' she says.

Mum has eyes that are so blue they appear translucent in certain lights. When I was younger I was convinced she could use her eyes to hypnotise people into staying still, staying silent, while she said something important or cutting. I'm not one hundred per cent convinced she can't do that now because she is fixing them on me while she opens her mouth to speak. I want to turn away, to leave before I hear something that will be negative and draining; which will nibble away at the positivity I have been building up, but I can't move.

'Clemency, about what I said earlier,' Mum starts. She sighs and steps towards me. 'Don't take everything to heart so much.' She presses her hand on to my shoulder, reassures me with that touch that I am being oversensitive and what she said about the end of my relationship was completely justified.

20

Dylan stood beside me, our heads close together while someone took a picture of us in our black and purple gowns. I had a mortar board on my head, the tassel constantly hung just low enough to be an irritating distraction at the corner of my eye. The other distraction at the corner of my peripheral vision was Mum, glaring at me because, in her mind, merely standing next to a male was enough to impregnate me. 'We made it, eh, Smitty?' Dylan said.

I took my camera back from the person who'd snapped the shot, thanked them. 'Yes. Although it looked doubtful at times.'

'Don't just disappear now it's over, OK?' he said.

'If anyone's going to do a disappearing act it'll be you, don't you think?' I replied. 'Speaking of disappearing acts, what happened to Seth? I saw him in the ceremony but I haven't seen him since.'

'Maybe he finally got the message,' Dylan mumbled.

'What message would that be?' I asked. 'And can you clue me in on it?'

'Come on now, Smitty,' he said.

'No, you come on, Dylan. I've finished college, am I allowed to sleep with Seth now? Or is that still against the rules of being your mate?'

'Smitty...me and you...'

'Are mates, that's abundantly clear.'

'It's not that simple. Before you, I've never been friends with a girl without it being either purely sexual or purely platonic. It's both with you. And the longer we're mates, the more I feel for you. It's more than sex and more than just frienship with you.'

'Rhubarb, rhubarb, rhubarb,' I said in response.

Unexpectedly he stepped forward, our bodies now so close they almost touched. My breathing became quick and shallow; the pupils of his eyes dilated as he began to breathe quickly too. 'I'd love to kiss you,' he said, his gaze linked to mine, 'but I think your mum would probably lay me out with one punch. Meet me later? I've got a family meal, but come over to my house around ten o'clock?'

'I can't. Mum and Dad are taking me home after this. We're all packed up. We've got a family thing over in Otley. My cousin's having problems, too, Mum wants to get back for her.'

'Can't believe this,' he said. 'Are you going to come back any time soon?'

'Do you actually ever listen to a word I say? I told you, I've got a summer job, working six days a week so I can save up for my course to train to become a silversmith and jeweller. You can come and see me?'

'Will your mum smack me if I kiss you now?'

'Yes.'

'Your dad won't stop her?'

'Nope.'

'All right. I'll come over to see you.'

I knew he wouldn't. I desperately wanted him to, but I knew he wouldn't. It was easier for us both to pretend that he would.

Mum's stopped hypnotising me with her stare. She's instead focused on the butterfly pendant I wear around my neck. It is large and fashioned from silver, and one of the first things I made after I qualified as a silversmith. The pendant represents a lot of things to Mum, not only the fact I took no notice when it came to her career advice, but also that I still have an obsession with butterflies. And that obsession, to Mum, is hurtful. '*Try not to be so sensitive,*' I should say to her. Instead, I tuck it away under my T-shirt, out of her sight, out of her mind.

Now the butterfly is hidden away, she goes back to admonishing me while rubbing my shoulder. 'Clemency, you should know by now that you mustn't be so touchy about things,' Mum tells me. 'You should try to grow a thicker skin, so you aren't so sensitive.'

'OK,' I say to her, because it's easier than explaining that while I have normal skin like everyone else, I spend a lot of time pretending the snide comments, the sly digs and the outright vicious remarks about not knowing who my 'real' parents are don't bother me. Mum doesn't realise that I spend my life feigning the existence of a thick, impenetrable outer layer so that I can be seen to be able to 'take a joke', 'not be so sensitive', 'not take everything to heart'. She has no idea that for years I would cry alone because no one understood that every comment made me feel worthless and made me believe that those snipes were true.

And anyway, all this talk about not being oversensitive would be more credible if it wasn't coming from the woman who can't even bear to hear the word 'adoption', let alone talk about it in relation to her only daughter. That's why she has 'issues' with my butterfly obsession – it's a reminder of the fact I'm not biologically hers.

'Clemency,' she says, before I shut the door behind myself.

'Yes, Mum?' I reply tiredly. There's only so much I can take, only so much the positivity I've stretched over this new start can handle before it peels away, and starts flapping about uselessly like unsecured tarpaulin in the wind.

'Your father would have loved it here,' she says. 'He adored the sea. He always wanted to live by the sea again before . . . He would have been so proud of you.' She smiles. 'Even more proud of you than he was.'

I nod. 'Thanks, Mum,' I mumble, and leave.

I don't need her to tell me Dad was proud of me. I knew he was. He told me so all the time. Right up until he died.

4

Abi

To: Jonas Zebila
From: Abi Zebila
Subject: Please reply. PLEASE!!!!!
Friday, 29 May 2015

Dear J,

Another email from me where I hope all is well with you. You didn't tell me about your purple day. All is not well here, unfortunately. Gran was rushed to hospital while I was at work yesterday.

Daddy didn't even bother to leave work. Mummy had to call my office to get me to pick up Lily-Rose. I had to bring her back to work with me because I was up to my ears in client reports and billing, and the billing had to go out yesterday. Lily had a great old time, she was the centre of attention from all the residents. Mrs Lehtinen was the worst for it, practically adopted her there and then, showing her off as something as close to a great-grand-daughter as she could get.

Did I tell you Mrs Lehtinen is here at the home now? Do you remember her? She was from Finland and her family lived next door and she was great friends with Gran. Her family moved away when I was about five or six. She loved you, I remember that. She's not been here long but on the first day she recognised me even though I hope I've changed a little in twenty years. I didn't really remember her until she reminded me that it was her who had given Mummy the idea for those sleep boxes that we slept in as babies. And then, of course, she asked about you and it all came flooding back: how you were always her favourite because you used to wolf down those God-awful Jim bars she kept giving us. (I looked them up on the net to find out why they were so boak. Marmalade foam covered in chocolate. I can't believe Mummy let us eat them.)

Like I say, Mrs L practically stole Lily-Rose from me and kept telling her stories about what I got up to when I was her age. It would have been embarrassing if they didn't all show me as being the most amazing five-year-old!!

On the way home we dropped by the hospital to see Gran, Lily-Rose and I, but she wouldn't see us because she didn't want us to see her like that. Three days ago Lily's telling her jokes and now Gran won't see her. So much pride. So much stupid pride. That's what our family's problem is – too much pride, don't know when to swallow it. I mean, would it have hurt Gran to see Lily? I know it can be scary seeing someone looking frail, but she may not come out of hospital. We may never see her again because her pride makes her worried we'll see her looking vulnerable.

I'm gutted, Jonas, really gutted.

Tell me. Just tell me something. Anything.

I love you.
Abi
xxxx

P.S. Do you want some pictures of Lily-Rose? I may have a few (thousand).

5

Smitty

My bedroom in the flat is pretty incredible.

The main bedroom, my room, has panoramic views of the sea from the six, double-glazed sash windows. 'Triple aspect' I think it was called in the agency description. Triple aspect, three views of the sea, three chances to see the expanse of water while reclining in this king-size bed. I've made up the bed, I have unpacked my clothes, stashed my bags and cases at the bottom of the double wardrobes.

Now I'm doing what I do wherever I live: putting up my photos.

One of the first photos I have pressed on to the wall is from 1996. I am with Seth and Dylan. We are in the bar, in the booth where we were sitting when Seth first came over. I'm in between them, they've both got their arms around me, and I'm overwhelmed because I've never had so much male attention in my life. Under that photo I have scrawled:

With Seth & Dylan, Xmas 1996, Uni Bar. Mistletoe madness!!

Another photo:

With Dylan & Seth, Xmas party 1998, Liverpool (end of term party)
Dylan has his arm slung casually over my shoulder, Seth is standing beside us but a little apart, as though not really wanting to be there. I have my hand on his forearm, trying to draw him into the photo.

And another:

With Dylan, July 1999, Graduation Day

Dylan and I have our gowns on, I have a mortarboard, he doesn't. We've got our heads close together and are grinning at the camera. I'm looking pensive because Mum is off camera glaring at me.

With Mum & Dad, July 1999, Gradation Day

I'm in between Mum and Dad, grinning at the camera. Dad has plucked my black mortar board off my head and plonked it on his. He'd originally gone to put it on Mum's head but the look she fired stopped him. Seth had taken the photo but had only stopped by to say goodbye before he went off with his family.

With Seth, March 2003, Party at Seth's House (everyone's invited)

Seth was standing in the kitchen of his house, putting together a buffet for the party he was having. He turned and sort of smiled at the camera, just as I shouted, 'Say cheese'. I was staying with him at that time. I'd had a row with Mum that escalated into me sofa surfing for a few weeks with various friends and acquaintances. I was always careful not to stay for more than two days – three at the very maximum, so as not to wear out my welcome. The last sofa I washed up on was Seth's, a grey-black Muji put-me-up job that was easy to fold out and surprisingly comfortable – no metal bars or buttons in the wrong places. Dad had been on the phone almost daily trying to mediate between Mum and me but I wasn't ready to go back, especially since whenever I tried to leave, Seth kept telling me to stay and he never made a move on me, not once. That night he was having a party and it'd be the first time I would have seen Dylan in nearly a year. I was *so* excited that I didn't even mind when my cousin Nancy gate-crashed.

In my hand I hold the final photo from that sequence. There were others, of course, over the years, but those were the most significant, those were the ones that made it to the wall every time, move after move. And in my hand I hold the final one, the one that came after we got together. In it, it's the start of a new year, January 2004, I am sitting on his sofa, wearing his T-shirt, my hand in my very messy hair, beaming at the man taking the photo because we were finally together. I was finally happy.

With Seth, New Year's Eve 2003

I sat on the sofa I used to sleep on those weeks back in February and March when I stayed at his house, while Seth sat across the room at the dining table, warily watching me. Usually, he sat next to me, often I put my legs across his lap and he would rub my feet while we talked. But tonight, he'd been carefully avoiding being close to me. We ate dinner at opposite ends of the table and even cooking in his tiny kitchen had him keeping me at a noticeable distance.

I'd made all the right noises about the food, which was as delicious as I said it was, I'd drunk his wine and savoured it. I'd bought the bottle of expensive bubbly that was chilling on the first shelf of his small fridge, waiting for the chimes of Big Ben on telly. We'd talked, laughed, argued good-naturedly about the things we always debated over.

All the while, the clock was ticking down towards the end of the year. We were in the final hours of 2003 and I couldn't wait to see the back of it. It'd been one disaster after another, one lot of bad news after another, one falling out after another. When Seth had asked me over to his for dinner and to see in the New Year with him I'd jumped at the chance. I was looking forward to a quiet, uneventful end to this year and a respectful calm beginning to the next. It wasn't turning out like that, though, with Seth's pensive demeanour, which swirled around the room like invisible but choking smoke.

He'd never been like this in all the years I'd known him. Maybe it was because I hadn't called him much in the months since I'd left his sofa and had gone back to live with my parents, possibly he was feeling slighted that we'd gone from talking every night for hours to speaking once a fortnight.

'Have I upset you?' I asked him.

Seth shook his head, his face was cagey and his body was hyper-vigilant as he replied: 'No.'

'I'm sorry I haven't been in touch more,' I said. 'It's my training – it's taken over everything. I have to work doubly hard at everything because I'm not at all arty so even though I can see the designs up here,' I pointed to my head, 'I can't get them to look like they should on paper. The finished items are exactly what I saw, but the drawings don't work. I've been a bit consumed. I'm sorry for making you a casualty of that.'

'You've nothing to apologise for.' He sat back in the wooden-framed chair, stretched his legs out.

'Have I ruined your chance to go out on New Year by accepting your invitation? Did you want a big night out?'

'New Year is for people who don't go out the rest of the year,' he said.

'That's a bit harsh! I love New Year, usually. This year's just been a bit rubbish and I want to see a quiet end to it and to put it out of its misery, so to speak.'

'Come on,' he cajoled, 'it's true. If you went out and enjoyed yourself the rest of the year you wouldn't need to make such a big deal of nights like New Year's Eve.'

'Or maybe you simply want to see in the start of another twelve months in style?'

'Maybe.'

'Why are you sitting over there, Seth? What's going on?'

'I like it here. It's by the stereo.'

'Put a tune on then.'

He reached out his long fingers and pressed the square silver button with the green triangle. A whirr, an almost imperceptible click and the room was filled with Public Enemy's 'Welcome To The Terrordome'.

I stood up, determined to alter the course of this evening, get him to engage with me on some level. If I wanted to sit under the critical eye of someone who didn't know how to talk to me, I'd have stayed at home with my mother just as she'd practically ordered me to. I held out my hand to him. 'Care to dance?' I asked him. This wasn't dancing music, but needs must.

'How long have you known me?' he replied. 'You know I don't dance.'

'All right, let me see what's so great about that seat of yours,' I replied and moved towards him. He visibly tensed as though the idea of me being any closer was a horror he couldn't run fast enough from.

That stopped me in my tracks. 'Shall I leave?' I asked in frustration. I still had a chance to get home to the cream soda and Christmas After Eights before the chimes sounded so I could end the year as it started – with my parents.

'I don't want you to leave and there's really nothing wrong. I'm having a good time.'

You don't look like it, I thought.

I moved closer and he slowly slid up in his seat until he was fully upright. His eyes didn't leave my face as I approached him. I accepted then what was 'wrong'. I'd hoped I was mistaken, that I'd imagined it. The problem, of course, was he wanted to have sex with me. And he probably hated feeling like that when we were 'just friends', so he was keeping his distance until these feelings passed, just like a fleeting obsession with a pop band passed and you wondered what on Earth you were thinking. Seth knew, as well as I did, that sex would mean the end of our friendship. We couldn't go back to being mates if we went to bed together – we'd have to be together for the duration or not see each other again.

'About this seat,' I began. I slid carefully on to his lap until I was fully on top of him and we were face-to-face, my legs either side of his. 'I quite like it too.' Slowly, I took off my cream jumper, revealing my black bra underneath. 'Looks like I'll have to fight you for it.'

His breathing slowed and deepened, every muscle of his face was tense as though he was concentrating on staring into my eyes, trying to ignore how hard he'd become when I sat on him, while not wanting to stare at my breasts and my imperfect body on display to him. Seth suddenly smelt of a deep and startling desire, far more potent than I expected. When I pulled back a fraction, unsettled a little by how strongly he seemed to want this, his hands came up to rest on my back, then smoothed their way up and down my body.

As his fingers caressed my back, I reached for the top button of his jeans and suddenly his hands were on mine, stopping me from opening him up. I looked at him, his hazel-green eyes held mine.

'If we do this,' he said, keeping his hands in place, 'will it mean something to you?'

I knew what he was alluding to: in college and afterwards, I'd slept with quite a few people, more than a few of them were his friends from our wider group. To him, to anyone who wasn't me and wasn't privy to my mind and my heart, it must have seemed that none of it meant anything. To him, to anyone else, it must have seemed that I had sex and walked away without so much as a backward glance. 'Se—' I began.

''Cos this would mean *everything* to me,' he interrupted.

I paused properly then. *Everything?* I thought. *He wants me that much? Me?* I knew he fancied me but this seemed extreme. 'Everything?' I asked.

His face, topped with brown hair that he'd had shaved off to a grade one, was open and unwavering as he looked at me. 'I've waited nearly eight years for you, so yes, it'd mean everything.'

Of course it meant something. Sex always meant something to me but with him... Did he honestly think I would have risked rejection, our friendship, for nothing? That in eight years of knowing him I hadn't at least thought about it? It wasn't simply Dylan's objection that had put me off, it was the thought of wrecking what we had and losing him as a friend. I bent my head and carefully placed my lips on the smooth soft bow of his pink mouth. 'It means something to me,' I replied before I kissed him.

Seth immediately kissed me back, pressing his lips on to mine, our tongues meeting before slowly intertwining. The kisses grew deeper, more urgent, more desperate. Suddenly, almost painfully,

I wanted him. I ached for him between my legs, in the cavity of my chest, along the veins of my body. The longing for him was so fierce my breathing came in short bursts, I found it hard to keep air in my body.

'There are condoms in the bedroom,' he murmured between the urgent kisses.

I pulled away, looked him over again. '*We don't need condoms*,' I wanted to say. I always wanted to say that in the moments leading up to full sex. The temptation to be reckless, do something dangerous, personify stupidity for those few minutes, was powerful, instinctive. It was like a bright pink neon sign flashing in my head: **Have unprotected sex…and end up paying for it for the rest of your life**.

Unprotected sex with a virtual stranger was probably the reason I existed at all. I wanted to do it so I could validate my existence, prove that my being here wasn't the worst thing in the world to happen. Like I said: reckless, dangerous, stupid. But that instinct was almost overwhelming with Seth, I'd never felt it so strongly. I wanted nothing more than to be as unsafe as possible with him because he'd always been my point of safety.

'Have you changed your mind?' Seth asked when I didn't respond to his suggestion we move to the bedroom. 'Cos that's fine.'

Seth was here. My here. When I avoided looking backwards because the past was too painful to remember, and when I avoided looking forwards because the future was too terrifying to contemplate, I lived in the here. And here was where Seth was, too. He'd always been in my here. He was in my here and he would be in the future with me, and he would help me navigate the past if I wanted him to. Emotionally, Seth was here, in the same place that I was, at the same time. He was my here, and he was what love was all about. I could suddenly see that this wasn't about sex, it was about everything I'd ever wanted being on offer with this man. 'I haven't changed my mind,' I told him, the smile on my face even wider than it had been before. He grinned back at me.

Three days later he took that photo of me sitting on his sofa, grinning because I was with him at last. Giddy with excitement and joy and slight disbelief, underneath I wrote: *With Seth, finally!! January 2004.*

That moment the photo has frozen, preserved in a two-dimensional frame, is so clear, so vivid in my mind, I am almost there again. I can feel beneath me the material of the sofabed I'd slept on for six weeks. I can remember the effervescent excitement whizzing through my veins that bubbled up on my face as that smile. Then there was the touch of him, on my skin, on my lips, in my hair, inside my body. Tingles trilled through me every time another memory from those three days of being together wended through my mind. I am almost there, telling him the next morning that I didn't really want to go home. Him asking me if I was saying that because it was what he wanted to hear. Me asking him why I'd say that if it wasn't the truth. Him saying, 'Because you've never shown any interest in me beyond the effect it had on Dylan.'

'That's not entirely true, and you know I stopped feeling anything like that for Dylan a while back.'

'Maybe, but you'd also slept with a lot of my friends.'

'Does that bother you?' I replied.

'Not any more. At the time I never understood why it was them and never me. I liked you so much and I made it so obvious, and you never even looked in my direction.'

'You never tried it on, that's why.'

'All those guys tried it on with you, that's why?'

'Yeah, of course. I didn't sleep with all of them, no matter what they told others. But I was never going to make the first move – not if there was even the slightest chance of being rejected.' I'd been rejected from the moment I was born, from before I was born, probably. I avoided as much as possible being rejected as an adult – someone had to want me first before I would even think about wanting them. Except for Dylan.

'But you tried it on with me last night,' Seth said. 'I'm not imagining it, you made the first move.'

'Yes, I felt that much for you, I risked rejection.'

'So, all this really is about me?'

'Only you. These have been some of the best hours of my life. I've felt so wanted. So adored. You seem to understand me without me having to justify or qualify anything I say, or without having to censor myself . . . And I can't believe I just said that aloud. Please don't ever repeat that. Pretend I never said that.'

'Too late, Smitty, I heard you loud and clear.'

I need to stop remembering. I need to not do this now. On my bed is a large cardboard box decorated in hand-coloured butterflies that I've had since I was a baby and that I keep all my special photos in. The ones I can't put up because they're too painful to look at every day but are too precious to throw away because they're an important part of who I am.

I place the *With Seth, finally!!* picture in the butterfly box. I properly regard all the other photos tacked to my wall to form the tessellated wallpaper of my life, the collage of the people and times that make up who I am.

I always carry an instant camera to take photos of the people I make jewellery for, to capture on film things I see that inspire me, images I love. Yes, it's easier – cheaper – to take photos on my phone, but there's no feeling like holding a photo in your hand. Photographs are like crystallised moments of your history that you can't simply swipe on from to find the better shot, to seek a version that's more palatable to your sensibilities. Photos are the ultimate reality call as to how perfect or flawed you can be at any given moment in time.

These photos I put up wherever I live are like the crystallised elements of who I was, how I became who I am. There I am: with Seth. With Mum. With my niece Sienna. With Dad. With my cousin Nancy. With Dylan. With Karina, my former boss. With Primrose, Ayo and Clyde, my housemates in college. With all these people who made me feel real, relevant, as if I belong somewhere.

I continue to stare at the photos and see for the first time how many there are that say the same thing: *With Seth. With Seth. With*

34

Seth. With Seth. With Seth. He's everywhere. For nearly twenty years of my life he has been in my photos, been in my reality. For nearly two decades my life has been about this one person.

My fingers pluck the photo of me and Seth and Dylan, Xmas 1996, off the wall. I place it into the butterfly box on my bed. Next I remove *With Seth on the last day of exams.* Then comes down *With Seth after studying all night.* Then *With Seth, the town hall in Vilnius (Lithuania),* is removed...And *With Seth before our cancelled engagement party*... And *Seth the Starfish in new bed in our new flat!!!* Then *Me with Seth, new bed in new flat.* Then *Me & Seth & Lottie – finally finished the campervan refurb.* There are so many. So many. And I have to take them all down; I have to remove all these reminders and memories.

When I have finished editing him out, my wall of pictures is like Swiss cheese – there are holes everywhere. Now Seth has come down, I have to take *her,* my cousin Nancy, down, too. More holes, more Swiss cheesing of my life. And if I take her down, I have to take down Sienna, her daughter. And I have to take down Dylan because he is where it all began. And if I take down Dylan, there will be very few photos left. My life will be decimated.

I sit down on my bed, the firm mattress does not sag or give at all under my weight. The wallpaper made of photos has now become a latticework of photos – tenuously linked by my handwriting beneath or on the back of the pictures.

I know what I have to do. It's absolutely obvious. I have to start again. Totally. People say all the time that something is completely devastated, as though anything can ever be partially devastated. My life has been devastated, I can't partially reflect that on my wall.

I'm on my feet again, new purpose in my movements: I have to take it all down; I have to devastate everything and start again. That's what the rest of me has done, so why not my visual history, too?

35

6

Smitty

'A coffee, please.'

The tall barista who is displaying his gym-sculpted arms in a short-sleeved white T-shirt has his back to me when I stand up on the chrome foot rail and lean on the counter. Coffee, coffee, coffee. The perfect thing to get my body moving on my way to have a proper look at my shop. I haven't told my mother about the shop, I'm still working up to that. It's been a good four days, mainly because I have been holding my tongue, biting my tongue and swallowing my tongue. Actually, I'm surprised I still have a tongue left at all. But it's been worth it. The flat has been peaceful, we've unpacked most things, we've bought a TV, DVD player and Freeview box, a kettle and toaster, pans and crockery, cutlery and wooden spoons. Other bits and pieces have migrated their way into the flat, and we're waiting for the telephone line to be connected so we can get Wi-Fi, but it is a more than habitable home now. We can relax and enjoy it. Which is why I'm out early this morning. If I'm out before Mum wakes up, it's a million times less likely that we'll have a row about something stupid.

I'm surprised how quiet it is in this café, given its location practically on the beach. Three floor-to-ceiling glass walls give you unfettered views of the promenade, sea wall, and the unique beauty that is the grey-blue water as it stretches out and away until it touches the blue-grey sky at the horizon. The inside of the café is a mixture of tables and chairs, sofas and tables, and easy chairs and tables, all cleverly arranged so they are easily accessible from the stainless-steel serving counter. Beyond that there are a couple of doorways, I'm assuming they lead to the kitchen and the back office. The best thing about this café, though, is how close it is to the flat. I can make it in under seven minutes if I walk especially fast. It's the perfect place to meet clients. When I walked in I spied a cosy sofa and chairs arrangement on the far side of the counter that would be sheltered and private enough for us to talk, but also comfortable enough to allow them to relax. I'm either going to have to be here from opening time when I have meetings so I can bagsy that space, or I'll have to see who I can charm into setting it aside for me. First though, coffee.

The barista turns from playing with the coffee machine and makes his way slowly to the counter. He's almost languid as he walks, unrushed and carefree – either he's the owner or he's a very laidback employee. At 7 a.m., I suspect he's the former because no employee that laidback would even consider getting here at this time. It's early spring, at this time the world is drenched in the orange-grey half-light of this side of the planet still turning to face the Sun. 'Sorry, we're not open yet,' the barista says.

'Oh. Well, the "open" sign is showing and the door's open, so I just assumed . . .'

He listens intently, carefully, to what I say. When I finish, he rests his elbows on the counter, rests his face in his hands. Frowns then sighs. 'I used to open this early, believe it or not, but no one ever came. It seemed to me those who were up this early and were walking to work, needed to get nearer to Brighton before they got a coffee. Probably because they'd had one already at home and by this point of the journey another was too soon. On a weekend sometimes I open up early, catch the clubbers on their way home. Especially Pride weekend – I have a lot of customers that morning. But mostly, I open at eight and it works.'

'Right. So I'm not going to get a coffee from you?'

'Not before eight, sorry.'

'OK.' I don't move. 'I'm not going to get a coffee even though I've stood and listened to you talk for far longer than a person who doesn't know you should have to?' I say.

He grins. Naturally he has flawless teeth because he is disturbingly, almost unrealistically, handsome. He seems to have been drawn and constructed from the blueprint for the perfect man, rather than birthed like the rest of the human population: the shape of his eyes, the size of his nose, the curve of his mouth, are all precisely proportioned, his dark brown skin is smooth and touchable, and his hair is shaved at the sides and at the back, short and neat on top.

'I suppose I could make an exception just this once,' he says. 'It'll teach me to remember to lock the door.'

'Thank you.' I unhook my bag from over my shoulder and place it on the black vinyl padded stool beside me. It's not often my cheekiness pays off. I hop up on to the stool next to my bag.

'Don't get comfortable,' he says. 'It's a coffee to go.'

'I know, but there's nothing wrong with sitting while I wait.'

He moves to the far side of his machine, places coffee beans into it. There's a brief grinding sound before he removes the small metal basket, the shape and size of a small tea sieve. He taps down the top with what looks like a metal stamp. In all the times I've been to cafés to buy coffee, I've never watched someone make it before. There's always been a queue, a rush, something better to look at. Watching him work is fascinating. When he fits the solid metal sieve thing into the front of the machine, he grabs a paper cup and stands it beneath the curved metal spout where he inserted the sieve.

'Where are you coming from with that cute little accent?' he asks over his shoulder. While he speaks he pushes a button and the black liquid of my coffee swirls down the curved spout into my cup.

'"Little" accent?' I reply.

He bobs down in front of his fridge, removes milk and glugs some into a metal jug. He moves to the other end of the machine and places the jug over the spout that I know is the milk frother. It hisses a little as he heats and froths the milk.

'Sorry, where are you coming from with that cute accent of yours?' he corrects.

'Nowhere,' I reply. In my head, in my heart, that is where I am from: nowhere. 'I'm from nowhere.'

'Everyone's from somewhere,' he says.

'*Not me*,' I reply silently.

'I can't place your accent. Usually I'm quite good with them, since I speak to so many people on a regular basis. But yours, it's a mystery.'

'I was born in Brighton and lived out near Lewes until I was about three, so that's where most of my accent comes from, I guess. We then moved to a place called Otley just outside Leeds where I lived most of my life, I went to university in Liverpool, and recently I moved to Leeds proper, which has all probably influenced my voice. Add to that the fact my dad was Scottish, and my mum, even though she's from Leeds, sounds like she grew up in Buckingham Palace, and you get an accent like mine.' *Add to that the fact that I've never felt I've belonged anywhere and you get a girl from nowhere. You get me.*

The milk is frothed and hot, so he moves back to my cardboard cup and pours it in then spoons on the white foam. 'Wouldn't you say that was more "everywhere" than nowhere?' the coffee guy says.

'Depends on how you look at it, I suppose,' I reply.

'Most things do – depend on how you look at them, I mean,' he says. The white, moulded plastic lid with the cut-out oblong drinking hole is fitted on to the cup with a dull pop.

'Thank you for the coffee,' I say to him. We stand at the door, his hand resting on the metal handle. I don't want to leave. I'd like to sit here, experience the world through the picture windows, and to carry on chatting to this person.

'It's a cappuccino,' he states. 'I know you asked for a coffee, but you look like you're going to have a cappuccino kind of day.' He makes no move to open the door. Maybe he doesn't want me to leave either. Maybe I've fascinated him enough for him to let me stay a while longer.

'I'm not sure what a cappuccino type of day is, but I'm looking forward to finding out.'

His gaze drifts casually to my left hand, the one not holding the cup. 'That's an impressive number of rings,' he says.

I am a walking advert for my work: I always have on at least my butterfly pendant, a necklace which holds a couple of rings, earrings, and at least one ring on every finger. Each ring shows off a different technique I have tested out, gives clients something solid and real to examine. My hands feel naked, vulnerable and incomplete without my rings; my neck feels bare and unfinished without my necklaces.

'Thank you,' I say to him.

'Any of them…' he stops, embarrassment suddenly crawling across his features like an army of ants out looking for cake crumbs. 'Erm…any of them, real?'

That wasn't what you were going to ask, I think. *I'm surprised you were going to ask the other thing, but that wasn't what you were going to ask.* 'If you mean are any of them made from precious metals, then they all are.'

'Right, right. Of course.' His hand jerks open the door. 'I'll see you then?'

'I might drop by again.'

'Well, you do that. What's your name, out of interest?'

'I told you, I'm That Girl From Nowhere.'

'Cool. I'm Tyler. No way near as exotic as yours, but I thought I'd tell you. In case you wanted to know.'

'Bye, Tyler,' I reply.

'Bye, TGFN,' he says.

7

Abi

To: Jonas Zebila
From: Abi Zebila
Subject: Just a quickie
Tuesday, 2 June 2015

Jonas,

Gran is coming home today. Mummy actually told me that she'd rather Gran went to somewhere people could take better care of her but Daddy wouldn't hear of it.

Mummy seems so sad, so burdened. She loves looking after Lily-Rose, she told me that, but everything else seems too much for her at the moment.

The other day I was in the loft looking for my old dolls' house that Ivor has been promising to bring down for Lily-Rose for months. In one of the boxes I found Mummy's drawings, paintings and sketches, like the ones she made on the boxes we used to sleep in as babies. She's so talented. She could teach art or even sell some of her stuff. Over the years she's drawn and sketched and painted a lot of butterflies. They're breathtaking. No two butterflies are the same, but the patterns on the wings are so perfectly symmetrical, you'd think they were done on a computer. I sat there going through them and completely forgot the time.

When I'd finished going through the artwork, I felt almost bereft that it was over. I couldn't help wondering why she stopped drawing and painting except for the stuff on our boxes.

Is that what's going to happen to me? Am I going to become so consumed by being a mother and wife that I end up giving up my passions? That's what scares me about being with Declan properly. The idea that I'll lose myself; I'll simply become an extension of him and Lily-Rose, and I'll disappear.

When I was cleaning up the dolls' house with Mummy and Lily-Rose, I asked Mummy why she never decorated any of our boxes with butterflies since she'd practised them so many times. She looked alarmed and said, 'What do you mean?'

'I saw your artwork in the loft. That was why I was so long. I liked the butterfly drawings the most. I was wondering why you didn't decorate any of our boxes with butterflies. And actually, why did you stop drawing?'

'I only decorate the baby boxes, you know that,' she said.

'What about not putting any butterflies on one of our boxes?'

She just stared at me like I was talking a different language until Lily-Rose said, 'Can I see the butterflies?'

Mummy frowned at me and gave me this *Now look what you've done* look, and said, 'There is nothing to see.' And that was the end of that. She got up from the floor in the living room where we were doing the cleaning and went off to start dinner. If I had a talent like that I'd be talking about it all the time, not pretending I didn't know what my own daughter was talking about. What's the betting if I go back up to the loft tonight those pictures will have disappeared?

What do you think? Was I being insensitive? Maybe she had a miscarriage and the butterfly box would have been for the baby she'd lost. Oh, I feel awful now. Maybe that's it. Why she feels so distant sometimes. It would make sense. I know I'd feel worried about everything if I went through that. Add that to how Gran treats her sometimes and I'm not surprised she doesn't share much with me. Sorry, I'm being insensitive to you now.

I'm not sure if you want to talk about what happened, but how are you and Meredith after everything? I'm guessing because I haven't heard anything to the contrary that nothing's changed? I've been keeping an eye online on what you've been up to. Congratulations on your award. I'm really proud of you.

I miss you. Remember how it used to be me and you against Ivor? That man always took himself far too seriously even when he was, like, twelve. At least you knew how to have a laugh. I wish...I miss you. I know I said that already but it needs repeating. As many times as I can until you reply. I miss you. I miss you. I miss you.

Love,
Abi
xxxxx

P.S. Mrs L says hello. Again!

8

Smitty

Mum is in her pink silk dressing gown, sitting on the sofa, staring into space when I return to the flat. The TV is off and the room is now bright from the rising sun.

I was heading for the shop and my workshop, but for some reason my feet had turned towards home instead when I left the café, Beached Heads. I thought it was because I was bunking off work, but actually, I must have known on some level that this would be a bad day for Mum. It's been almost three weeks without a serious setback, so today she is obviously due one.

Usually a healthy-ish pink, Mum's face is pale, each line more pronounced than usual. Her blue eyes are glassy and unfocused. Grief. Grief has made her fragile, delicate and friable; sorrow has carved itself deep into every part of her.

'Oh, Mum,' I whisper. Along with my bag I place my half-drunk coffee on the TV shelf in the living room, then go to her. She doesn't move. I put my arms around her and gently tug her towards me. We're not the huggy type, Mum and I, but she needs this.

'I'm not meant to be without him,' she says.

It's been too short a time for her not to feel like this, and too long a time we've already spent without him.

'I think feeling like that is normal,' I say. Anything else I say will sound trite and rubbish and as if I'm telling her how she should grieve. My mother's grief is a world away from mine. He was my dad, he was her whole world. Even before he became ill Mum didn't seem to function very well without him. If he was away for whatever reason she would find it difficult to concentrate, she'd be up and down several times a night, would stare into space as if counting down the minutes until he returned.

I found it hard every day, knowing I wouldn't see him again, wouldn't be with him again – Mum must have found it impossible. Despite everything, I couldn't have left her in Leeds on her own. She would have fallen apart.

'Clemency, I'm so glad I have you. Please don't leave me. You must promise me you won't do that to me. You won't leave me.'

When Mum says things like this, however infrequently, they are said to last a lifetime, to burn in my head like a beacon in case I forget who she is and what she means to me. When Mum begs in her own quiet way, she is begging me not to do that thing I could do that would replace her. When Mum pleads and asks me not to leave her, and it probably is once in a blue moon, she is imploring me not to look for my biological parents. She doesn't want me to find the woman who gave birth to me. To her, it's not about me needing to find people who look like me, those who could hold the pieces that complete the puzzle of the quirks of my personality or adding another branch to my family tree that could help me to stop feeling like I'm from nowhere and could be from somewhere. To her, it's a source of unknown terror and anxiety.

Mum doesn't have Dad any more so the thought of me finding another mother, maybe half-siblings and maybe even finding another father, is frightening to her. Her fears have been heightened, cranked up to a level nearing hysteria now Dad isn't here to reassure her she wouldn't be replaced. He was good at that, at calming her fears and encouraging her to accept any decisions I made.

Even then, *even then*, it's always been an unspoken agreement that I wouldn't do it while she was alive. Me moving to Brighton, where I was born, must have pushed the panic button in her mind. She must have been convinced that I was about to renege on our deal. Her fears are mingled, like dye in water, with her grief and uncertainty about the future.

I look over at the cup sitting beside my green, many-pocketed bag. I'm not enjoying this very much if it's a cappuccino kind of day. Shame really, as Tyler the coffee man's cappuccino is very good.

I bring myself back to my mother and to what she wants me to do. 'I promise, Mum,' I state. Well, what else am I going to say to the woman who gave me everything, especially now that I have no one else but her.

With Seth, April 2015, Leeds

'I'm so sorry about your dad,' Seth said.

He'd been saying this repeatedly. I guessed it was his way of trying to make himself believe it – if he kept saying it, it might, in one of the repetitions, become a fact in his mind. Seth and Dad were similar kinds of people: laidback, fiercely protective, generous with their time and affection.

We moved through the darkness in our flat, both heading for the bedroom to strip off our funeral clothes, get into something else, anything else but these black garments.

I'd offered to stay with Mum, of course, but after the wake, she wanted to be alone. We stayed to clean up, loitering and tidying as much as possible because we were both reluctant to go home. When I left I knew that would be it. I would be admitting my time there with Dad had come to an end and I couldn't bear for that to be true right then.

Instead of taking my clothes off, I collapsed on to the bed, flat on my back, a starfish out of water, staring up at the ceiling. It reminded me of the picture of Seth from when we'd first moved in here. He'd starfished on the bed and I had taken a snap of him. Then we'd lain together on the bed and Seth had held the camera up to take a photo of us together: two loved-up starfish in their new home.

Seth sat on the edge of the bed and kicked off his shoes, which we'd never normally wear in the house, let alone into the bedroom. I felt the motion of him loosening his tie, releasing his top button. 'Shall I make a coffee?' he asked. 'Or do you want something stronger? I think there's some port left.'

'No, stay here a minute.' Maybe longer. Maybe for ever. Maybe if we stayed where we were for ever, nothing would change. Everything had to change now Dad was...now we'd reached this stage. Maybe if we stayed here, though, maybe if I didn't let Seth out of my sight, nothing else would have to change.

He stretched his long body beside me, stroked his fingers down my face, tucked my hair behind my ear. We hadn't been together properly for the last four months. We'd spoken, had kissed briefly in the times I'd come back home, but not this. I touched his face, resting my hand on his cheek, and he came towards me. Our lips met and we both closed our eyes, connecting ourselves together. I pushed his jacket over his shoulders. I was aware of the thick silk of his tie as I tugged at it until it was undone. The small, matte-black buttons of his shirt came apart easily until he was bare-chested, the paleness of his skin visible in the half-light of the room. He pushed my ankle-length dress up, over my thighs, around my waist, to my chest until he gently tugged it over my head and discarded it beside the bed. My fingers went to his trousers, slipped the shiny, black tongue of his slim belt though its loop, out of its buckle until it was free, then I moved on to his button, pushing down the top of his trousers. His fingers unhooked the small metal clasps of my bra, slipped it off, before they moved on to removing my knickers, plain and black, as you'd expect for a funeral.

A gasp, a deep cry escaped from my throat as he entered me. A new sensation; in all the time of being with him, I'd never felt such a perfect mingling of agony and pleasure as he pushed himself into my body.

'I've missed you,' he murmured beside my ear. 'It feels so good to be inside you again.'

'I've missed you so much,' I whispered back. I dug my fingers into him, urging him to go deeper, to completely fill me up. He responded, pushing harder, slower but harder. The pleasure came from being together again, having each other back, reminding ourselves of what we shared. The pain came from knowing why we'd been apart for so long. The orgasms – loud, urgent, ecstatically raw – came from that blending of desolation and joyful reunion.

Seth lay on his front, his head in profile on the pillow while his fingers played with my hair, coiling curls around his fingers. I lay on my back, staring at the ceiling again.

'We could have made a baby,' he eventually said.

He'd put words to the panic that was amassing inside. We could have. No contraception, not even withdrawal. I'd felt when he was about to, but I hadn't wanted him to, I'd clung on to him, keeping him with me until it was too late to change the outcome. **Have unprotected sex… and end up paying for it for the rest of your life**, started to flash in my head.

'That'd be pretty amazing, though, wouldn't it?' he said. 'I know we put those plans on hold these last few months but it'd be incredible if we did it now.'

A baby. Me. I loved children. Playing with them was never a chore. Sienna, my cousin Nancy's daughter, had once stayed with us for three months while Nancy was off finding herself, and I'd loved that. I had loved taking care of Sienna's every need, waking up with her in our flat, going to sleep with her in our flat, being with her.

But…But…A *baby*. *Me?* How would I know how to care for it? Would I really want to keep it? And even after all the discussions, it still scared me that I knew nothing of the potential anomalies in my DNA; disorders unknown to me because I couldn't just ask my mother or father about any medical conditions that might run in the bloodline, in the family.

A *baby*? *Me?* What about the father, too? How could I trust him to stick around when my biological father hadn't and had made it necessary for my biological mother to give me away or 'place me for adoption', as I was meant to say and think.

In all the dreams and fantasises I had about how I came to be adopted, the ones I could never tell anyone, I knew this one was the truest. This was the one that would fit most comfortably with reality. My mother, who was probably young, told my father she was pregnant and he in turn rejected her. Probably called her names, and questioned who else she'd been with. Then he went incommunicado because he wanted nothing to do with her or the child she was carrying. She tried to get him to change his mind, but then she found out he was seeing someone else – had been all along – and she knew it was hopeless. And when she told her parents they were so disappointed, they didn't have the money or the means to bring up another child. The shame would have killed them, too. She had nowhere to turn, so she did the best she could. She found a box and she decorated it in butterflies, the most beautiful creatures in nature, and she made it comfortable for me to sleep in. And she cried and cried when she had to hand me over, but she made sure I got the box because it was something no one else had. It was all she could afford to give me, but it was something completely unique and completely invaluable. Like the jewellery I made for people – it may have been inspired by other pieces but everything I made for others was made with that person in mind. That person was one of a kind, so was the jewellery I made for them.

No one else had a butterfly box like mine. I used it to store all my precious photographs, and even though it had been bashed about over time because of the many moves I'd been through, the times I hadn't been as careful as I should have been with it, I still had that box and I still treasured it.

I couldn't have a baby if I couldn't trust its father. I turned to Seth, carefully considered him. I hadn't grown used to his features over the years, I was always surprised by how attractive he was to me every time I looked at him. I had spent years looking at him, but until that New Year's Eve when we'd first had sex, I hadn't seen him. When I finally 'saw' him that night, I could never be used to those features again. Each time seeing him gave me a tiny thrill in the bottom of my heart.

'Seth…' I began. I had planned to wait, leave it for a bit until I did this, but now I'd been reckless and stupid, now I'd given in to the flashing neon sign in my brain about unprotected sex with a virtual stranger, I had to do this now. I had to ask him. The very fact I had to ask set us back twenty-odd years and made him a virtual stranger again. And the fact that I knew what he was going to say, how he was going to answer, meant not only was he going to stay a stranger, but also that I would have to go through with my plan. I wanted to be wrong. Desperately. But I knew what the answer was going to be.

'Seth, do you have something you need to tell me?'

His sudden flash of panic that I might know was almost physical as it scattered through him like the fallen beads from a snapped necklace. He caught himself, though, reasoned that I couldn't possibly know, and gathered up those panic-broken beads, strung them back together. Calm and composed, he replied, 'No, not that I know of.'

I shut my eyes. *Wrong answer.* The reply I was expecting, but had been hoping I wouldn't get. I had prayed, actually prayed, to a God I only partially believed in, that Seth wouldn't do this to me or to us. 'Seth, *please*. I need you to be completely honest with me, no matter what it is, just tell me. *Please*, forget about what's happened with my dad, and the fact we haven't seen each other properly in weeks, please, you can tell me anything. *Anything.*'

'No, Smitty, there's nothing.'

Disappointment drifted through me like a cold, creeping gust of wind. He wasn't the person I thought he was. It's the big moments that test you, push you, encourage you to be better in every way that you can. It's the small, intimate, seemingly insignificant moments where the choice you make alters who you are at a fundamental level.

'I can't be with you any more, Seth,' I told him. I could ignore it, pretend, bury it deep so I could forget. Or I could do what needed to be done so I could sleep at night. 'We have to split up.'

Part 2

9

Smitty

'One coffee for the lady with the notebook and camera.' Tyler, the barista from Beached Heads, my favourite coffee shop in the whole of Brighton, places the coffee cup – the one decorated with yellow and white daisies that I love most – in front of me without so much as a rattle of the cup on its matching saucer. I've been in here a lot, have managed to grab the more private sofa at the back like I planned, and have basically been able to drink my body weight in coffee every working day without ever having to make it. Win-win-win.

'Thank you,' I reply. I have to keep my eyes on the coffee cup and not raise them anywhere in his direction because I've developed the most embarrassing crush on him. After my late-teenage Dylan crush I didn't think I could be like this about someone – no matter how good-looking he was. I thought age, experience, plus a long-term relationship, had acted like weedkiller on that particular type of emotion. However, that weed was clearly lying dormant, waiting for the right combination of circumstance and person to fertilise it and make it shoot up. Tyler, the apron-wearing, sous-chef-hat-donning owner of Beached Heads, is my new crush.

With horror I realise he has pulled out the chair opposite me and is sitting himself down. When it isn't seven in the morning, the place is usually busy, alive with the hum and thrum of people who have stopped off for a drink and a stare at the sea. 'I've got to ask, what is it that you do exactly?' he asks me.

'Exactly?'

'Or even vaguely,' he says. 'You've been coming in here for nearly two weeks now, meeting different people, taking photos of their jewellery, of them, making notes. What is it that you do?'

'Isn't it obvious?'

'If it was, I wouldn't be asking. Also, I need to get confirmation before I decide whether or not I'm going to turf you out for conducting business on my premises.'

'I'm a jewellery maker.'

'Right. Right.' He nods slowly. 'How come you don't actually make jewellery, then? Why are you always hanging around my place?'

I look up at him. He's sitting back in the circular, leather armchair, his arms folded across his chest and his head on one side. He waits for my answer with an affected puzzled look. I have to smile. I just have to. 'I like it here,' I say.

'More than you like making enough money to pay your mortgage?'

'I don't have a mortgage. I have a flat I rent with my mother. And a shop that I haven't quite got around to opening yet. My, erm, landlord is not going to be happy with me, but in between meeting clients here and making the pieces they commission, the shop has taken a bit of a back seat.'

'What's your name, Nowhere Girl?'

'Clemency Smittson. My friends call me Smitty.'

'Do you want me to help you set up your shop?'

'Why would you do that?'

'Because I want to.'

'Fair enough. I'd love you to help, but I'm not going to let you.'

'Pray tell why not?'

'Because the real reason why I haven't done it is I'm not ready to. With most things, if I don't do them even when I should, it's because I'm not ready to or it's because I really don't want to. I can't see how it's going to look up here yet.' I tap my right temple with my right index finger. 'Until I can see it, there's no point in trying to make it a reality.'

'I do that,' he says. Another grin. This one would quicken even the most uninterested person's heart. 'I'm not sure I approve of you taking advantage of my good nature by using my shop because you can't be bothered to fix up yours.'

'Erm, excuse me, but how much coffee do I buy? I'm pretty sure I'm keeping your business afloat.'

'Ahhhh, so much delusion in one so young.' Tyler grins as he says this.

We could be friends, I realise. *This man could be my friend and I would be able to put down a root, ground myself to this place where I have washed up. Start to fill up my wall again.*

'Can I take a photo of you?' I ask him before I think about it.

'Are you going to make me some jewellery?' he asks.

'Would you wear it?'

'Probably not,' he replies. 'No offence, but I'm not the jewellery sort.'

'None taken.' My fingers reach for my instant camera, raise it to my face. 'Can I take a photo anyway?'

He grins again. 'If you must.'

A reminder ricochets so painfully through me, I have to pause, my finger resting on the white plastic button unable to move. Lots of people say that, not just Seth.

I push the button, take a picture of my new friend.

With Tyler at Beached Heads, May 2015, Brighton/Hove
I'll write on the bottom later. I'll put it on my wall with four blobs of Blu-Tack and it'll be another patch on the wall; another moment to ground me in the now and here.

With Seth, May 2015, Leeds
'Smitty? Clem?' he called as he entered our flat, almost at a run. Obviously he'd seen Lottie parked outside and thought I had changed my mind about everything. 'Are you home?' Excitement at the thought of me being back and the hope of what that might mean danced all over his face, and flowed through his voice. In his

hands he held the shiny black dome of his motorbike helmet. He carefully slid it on to the hall table then unzipped his jacket. 'Are you ...'

My face obviously told him that I wasn't back. I wasn't home. I hadn't changed my mind.

'What are you doing here?' he asked, a little more sober, a tad less giddy.

I pointed at the boxes, unable to tell him what else I'd actually been doing. 'Finishing off my packing.'

'Please come home. Talk to me. We can sort this out.'

'No, Seth, it's over. I've told you that. How many more times? It's over.' I grabbed my jacket from where I'd dumped it on the cubic mountain of my boxes in the corridor and slipped it on, hoping it would cover what I'd hastily shoved in my back pocket before running out of the bathroom to hide the other pieces of evidence.

'Don't I deserve better than this?' he asked loudly.

I said nothing, but instead moved to leave.

He stepped into my path. 'How does this even work anywhere except in your mind? We make love for the first time after weeks and weeks apart, then you tell me it's over and you're moving to Brighton as soon as possible. Then you spend the night on the sofa, go to stay with your mother the next day and refuse to talk to me. How is that any way to treat someone? Anyone? Let alone someone you love?'

If you'd told the truth, if you'd just admitted it, this wouldn't be happening, I thought. 'Look, I'll call or text next time,' I said. 'Arrange a proper time to come and finish this off so we don't have to see each other. I'm sorry, I shouldn't have come here without warning you. I thought you were at work all day today. Do you want me to leave my key?'

He glared at me. Angry, confused, hurt. All mirror images of what I had felt since I found out about him and *her.*

'Stop it, Smitty! Talk to me.'

Talking was our thing. We rarely argued, would simply get short and snippy with each other, and when that lost its appeal, we'd make up without actually making up. I wasn't sure we knew how to argue properly, how to shout and scream and slam doors. Mum and Dad had never done it and I'd never seen the appeal of all that noise to get your point across. But then, neither of us had ever really done anything that needed shouting about, until recently. I could yell at him for what he'd done, and I could see how angry he was, how bewildered and hurt by my refusal to talk to him – so angry he could probably shout, too. But it was all too much right now. If he'd only answered in the right way. We would have been in a difficult, fraught place but we'd be there together, working through it with each other. But the lying on top of what he'd done? That was what had ended this. I could not get over betrayal *and* lying. Not right now.

'We had a chance to talk and you said there was nothing to tell,' I reminded him.

And there it was again: the flash of panic that I might know, the rationalisation that it'd be impossible for me to know. 'If you've got something to say, just say it and stop playing games,' he said. The rage was bubbling out of him into every word.

'Do you want me to leave the key?' I asked. We had nothing more to say to each other and I didn't want to be in the flat any longer, especially not with what I had secreted away in my back pocket moments before he entered the flat.

He glared at me again. And again I saw the almost perfect reflection of what I felt. 'Keep the key. Don't keep the key. Makes no difference either way to me,' he eventually said. He shrugged. 'What I want doesn't matter to you, does it?'

Seth's body brushed against mine when he headed towards the kitchen at the end of the corridor. He couldn't stand to look at me, nor to watch me leave.

He stood at the kitchen window, though, his hand against the glass, watching as I left the building and then got into Lottie. He didn't move while I started her up and pulled away from the kerb. I suspected he stood still and expectant for a long time after I'd turned the corner out of sight, probably hoping I'd change my mind and come back to him.

At the first litterbin I saw, I pulled Lottie over, fished the plastic white stick I had weed on earlier out of my back pocket and threw it in the bin without looking at the result. I didn't need to, not really. I knew what it would say.

'I'd like you to tell me a story about you. Not the jewellery, but you,' I say to the woman beside me.

'Me?' she replies.

'Yes.'

Like the photos I take, I collect other people's stories like a magpie collects shiny things. Sometimes I wonder whether I would need to collect so many stories if I knew where I came from. Then I would wonder if I'd be able to do my job, make and relove jewellery, if I didn't spend time trying to unwrap the layers of who my clients were, to find the right use and look for their forgotten, unused, discarded pieces of jewellery. If I didn't sometimes feel like that forgotten item at the back of a bedside cabinet, would I try so hard to make other things special and lovable?

'I'm not interesting enough to tell you a story,' Melissa, the woman in front of me, says. She's about my age, maybe a little younger. She's well dressed in a suit jacket, smart jeans and white T-shirt, and able to meet me in Beached Heads at 3 p.m. Her fingers are bare of rings of any description and she has ordered a double espresso without even thinking what she'd like. From that I've guessed that she doesn't have children and works flexible hours in a fairly well-paid job. I've also guessed she's not married, engaged or in a long-term relationship. The double espresso makes her my kind of person.

'Yes, you are,' I say. 'I'm sorry to contradict you, but I know you are. Everyone is. And it's the people who say they're not interesting who generally are the most interesting.'

'OK. Erm...' She raises her gaze up to the ceiling while she thinks. 'Well, one of the things about me that people do think is interesting is that I was adopted.'

'So was I,' I say.

Her brown eyes, cautious and guarded before, are now alight with curiosity, wondering if she's found a kindred spirit. 'Really? What age were you adopted at?'

'Birth. What about you?'

'I was about one.'

Melissa relaxes a little now, she's more comfortable with me. We have a point of contact, something that links us, unlike other people she meets. I remember once looking up the statistics on how many people were adopted each year in the UK, because I wanted to find out how many people out there were like me, and there were enough. Enough for me to know that I'd meet someone one day who'd understand what it was like to live with people who weren't linked to you by blood, and DNA, and shared genetic history. It was comforting to know how many others there were out there, but beyond that momentary consolation, I didn't *feel* better. It wasn't as if any of the other people like me would be able to heal the fractured pieces of who I was.

'Is this jewellery something from your birth family?' I ask. On the royal blue velvet cloth laid out on the table in front of us is a large oval gold locket, the type people used to keep a lock of hair in, with a long, thick-linked chain. It's a lovely piece – the simple locket case has a few swirly lines that radiate up from the bottom of the pendant.

'Yes. My birth mother left it to be given to me on my eighteenth birthday. It's all a bit Little Orphan Annie, but there you go.' She shrugs her bony shoulders, trying to make light of what is actually difficult for her. 'My parents handed it over and I've had it sitting in a drawer for years. When I saw your advert I thought I'd find out if there is something I can do with it.' She points to the platinum locket that rests just below the base of her throat. 'As you can see, I already have a locket that I wear all the time.'

'Are you in reunion with your birth parents?' That's the language of adoption I've picked up from reading the internet. 'Reunion' instead of 'contact'; 'birth parents' not simply 'parents'. Knowing if she is or isn't will all feed into what this piece becomes, how I reshape and redesign it.

Locks of her wavy brown hair fall forwards as she hides her face to pick up her duck-egg blue espresso cup and put it to her lips. After the sip, her fingers reach out, push at the chain of the locket on the blue velvet background. She makes odd shapes of the gold links with each prod and poke. I hear what she is saying, without words, loud and clear: that it is none of my business.

I have to get her back. I had her and now she's pulling away from me again. If she continues to withdraw, there will soon be a gulf too wide for us to breach. I want to relove this piece. It's important to her, this woman who seems to be just like me.

'My, erm, birth mother left me a cardboard box that I used to sleep in.'

'Really?' Melissa raises her head, checking whether I am making it up. With that look she's back, engaged with me again.

'Apparently it's a Finnish tradition dating back to nineteen forty-nine or something. The Finish government gives new parents a box full of baby things that they'll need and the box doubles as a crib. I'm not an expert, but I don't think my birth mother was from Finland even though she gave me to the social worker in the box and said I was to sleep in it for as long as I would fit in it.'

'Do you still have it?'

'Yes.' All the butterflies on the box are hand-drawn and hand-coloured. The largest is on the bottom – its wingspan covers the entire surface, and the wings are mirror images of each other. Each colour is perfectly twinned; each intricate vein etched in black and reflected on the other wing. It must have taken her hours to do each wing, let alone the rest of them, each a different size, every one a unique, beautiful winged creature that looked fragile and lifelike. Sometimes I wonder why she chose butterflies, often I wonder why she spent so much time making something so beautiful and unique for someone she didn't want around, most of the time I don't think about it at all – it's easier that way. Over the years my obsession with butterflies has waxed and waned, depending a lot on how I feel about my birth mother at any given moment on any given day. It's the reminder of my box that makes Mum dislike butterflies.

She doesn't like to remember that I came to her in it instead of out of her body.

'Do you mind if I see some of your photos?' I ask Melissa. 'The ones on your phone will do. It'll give me a better idea, visually, of what your life is like and what the finished piece needs to fit in with. No worries if not.'

Unbothered by my request she hands over her mobile with the pictures screen up. I flick through them, watch her life unfold before my eyes. She has a sister, two parents. Her sister is younger, has two children. Her parents are both white-haired but were both probably once dark. Melissa isn't, she is quite fair-skinned and light-haired, but if you didn't know, you'd never know. She looks enough like them to pass for a blood relative, to be one of them. Unexpectedly and quite violently, a lump of envy forms in my throat. What would it have been like to have grown up with someone who looked even a little like me?

With Mum, March 1982, Otley

'Mum, why don't I look like you?'

Mum looked scared. I was four years old but I could tell she was a bit worried and scared. 'You do, Clemency,' she said. She picked up her big bag and took out her sewing. She didn't look at me at all.

'I don't, Mum. I've got brown skin and you've got peach skin. I've got black hair and you've got yellow hair.'

'That doesn't matter. I still love you. No matter what you look like, I still love you.'

'But Nancy looks like her mum. Why don't I look like you?' I didn't understand why she wouldn't tell me. She'd looked so worried and now she looked sad.

'It doesn't matter,' she said again. 'Nancy...It doesn't matter. All that matters is that I love you, no matter what you look like.'

'OK,' I said. 'OK, Mum.' I patted her hand because I didn't want her to cry and her eyes were all wet. It made her sad that I didn't look like her, and I knew, even though she said it didn't, it mattered lots and lots.

'Can I ask you something about being adopted, seeing as you're a stranger and I never have to see you again if I don't want to?' Melissa says. She speaks in a rush, obviously desperate to get the words out before she changes her mind.

I have given her back her phone, I have pulled myself together. It honestly didn't matter that I didn't look like my parents; that wherever we went when I was growing up, and even now, I stood out from the crowd as different, as other. Mostly it didn't matter. 'Sure,' I reply. I'm going to lie. It's easier to do that than to become 'The Adopted Person' whose experiences someone uses as gospel for every discussion they ever have going forwards about adoption.

'Did you sleep around a lot?' she asks.

I stop laying out the square, white-framed Polaroids of my previous work and designs on the table to look up at her.

'I used to,' she continues in her flustered rush. 'I've met a few other people who were adopted and I've wanted to ask them if they did it, too, but I never got up the courage. I was really promiscuous at one point and my therapist – yes, I do that, too – suggested it might be because of stuff I'd internalised about what women who gave up their children were thought to be like back then. Nowadays it doesn't matter, but I suppose people must have thought badly of women who got pregnant and then had to give up their children for adoption. She said it was possible that I'd been acting that out as a way of connecting with my birth mother. I don't know if that's right or not, but I was curious if you were ever like that? Or if it was just me? I hope I didn't offend you.'

'No, you didn't offend me.' My mother was madly in love with my father, I'm sure of that. In every version of my birth story I have thought up over the years, I know she was in love with my father and didn't sleep around. I think she was just unlucky – they probably got caught out the first time they did it. And he panicked. 'No, it wasn't just you,' I say to Melissa. So much for lying. 'I did it too.'

'Really?' She closes her brown eyes and her face becomes a tapestry of sheer relief. She's not alone. I'm not blood, but I do belong to the same group as her, the same family. I was adopted and I used to do the same thing as her. 'I seriously thought there was something wrong with me. That I was the only one.'

'I suppose I did, too. For me, it was about being wanted. If someone wanted me, even if it was just for sex, then it felt good.'

'Yes! I was like everyone else because someone wanted me. Even if it was just wanting my body for sex. So many people take being wanted for granted.'

'I know. But I'm not sure it's only down to having been adopted. I mean, there must be loads of people out there who sleep around just because someone wants them.'

'Maybe so, but it's nice to talk to someone who understands.'

'It is. It really is.'

10

Abi

To: Jonas Zebila
From: Abi Zebila
Subject: AQOTWF
Monday, 8 June 2015

J,

I don't want to be emailing you only if there's a problem so I'm just letting you know that All is Quiet On The Western Front. There's a woman I know whose mum texts her that when she's babysitting to let my friend know all is well and the baby is asleep.

All is well and the Zebilas are – mostly – asleep. No unusual dramas of any kind.

Gran seems to have stabilised quite a lot since the hospital stay (which of course gives credence to what Mummy has been trying to say about her being in a home where she can get specialist care). Mummy has disappeared the artwork as I thought she might.

Declan is gearing up to one of his monthly meltdowns about us living together again and being a proper family. I can feel it coming. Mummy and Daddy are still pretending that Lily-Rose was the Immaculate Conception and that Declan doesn't exist. Even when we go to spend the weekend with him at his flat, they never ask where we've been or what we got up to. He can't see why I won't move in with him full-time, but you know, every time I think about it, I remember the look on your face when you told Mummy and Daddy what the things Gran had said and done had resulted in, and that if they wouldn't stick up for you and Meredith against Gran, then you weren't hanging around any longer.

Is Declan worth giving up my family for? He was such a dick when I told him I was pregnant. We were both nineteen and both meant to be doing the university thing after we'd finished school together, but I couldn't believe how badly he behaved. I know, I know, it lasted all of three days before he was begging me to give him another chance, but it still makes me cautious about committing totally to him. That's why I've never properly lived with him – we've both kept our own places until now when I'm living here. He could do it again.

I suppose my only way forward is to move to Montenegro with you. Ha-ha, you'd love that, wouldn't you?

What did you think of the pictures? Do you want some more? Do you want me to get Mrs Lehtinen to send you some of those Jim bars? Or maybe I should pass on your email address to her. I may just do that if you don't reply!!!

Talk to me, big brother, please.
Abi
xxxxxx

11

Smitty

'Tell me a story about you,' I say to her. 'Not the jewellery, but you.'

'My darling, if I told you a story about me, I would be here all day. I mean, of course, you would be here all day. I am here all day anyway.' Her voice has the slightest husk of an accent, one I do not recognise. She speaks with a slight hesitancy, the caution of someone who sometimes has to translate words in her head before they leave her mouth. 'Tell me about you.'

'There's really nothing to tell. I'm here to help you, anyway.' We're sitting in the large community room in the retirement village where she lives. It's bright from the stark overhead lighting, and airy from the glass floor-to-ceiling windows that overlook the large courtyard. Several blue easy chairs are placed around small, low coffee tables. Apart from the lack of a counter and leather seating, it could be Beached Heads.

On the table in front of us is a light-wood box with a hinged lid that is carved with different types of musical notes. Inside, she has a collection of gold and silver items, brooches, pieces with precious gems that look like real sapphires and emeralds. Pearls, too. Mrs Lehtinen, a widow who has lived at the home for a few months, is the third person I am seeing here today and she has by far the most extensive collection of jewellery. The others had modest assortments of jewellery and talking to them, seeing the condition of their hands, I knew I would make their pieces into elasticated bracelets or simply necklaces so they could wear their collections with no catches to negotiate, no clasps to undo.

Apparently one of the staff saw my advert in the local magazine and asked the residents if they'd be interested in having me look at their jewellery. Six were interested. Mrs Lehtinen is one of those people who seems to exist in a soft-focus glow: her hair is white with a candyflossy haze, her skin is the colour and consistency of a peach, her eyes are a gentle blue. I don't recognise where in the world her name might come from, just like I can't place her accent.

'You look like one of the girls who works here,' Mrs Lehtinen says. 'Abi is her name. You look so much like her.'

'Do I?' I say. I always look like people apparently. During my second year of college, I had people coming up to me constantly telling me they'd started a conversation with me in the library, the canteen, the bar, the car park, only to find they were talking to another girl. 'She's your absolute double,' they'd say. When I finally met her, we discovered the only similarity between us was that we were both brown-skinned, and even then, not the same shade of brown. Other than that, we were different heights, weights and had completely different features. But apparently none of the people around us could see that. We'd both raised our eyebrows at each other, nodded sagely, and had to stop ourselves from laughing out loud. 'You look nothing like me,' we both said at the same time.

'You are her double,' Mrs Lehtinen says.

'I hear that all the time,' I say diplomatically. 'I think I must look like a lot of people.'

Mrs Lehtinen smiles at me. 'You think I'm a silly old woman, don't you?'

'No, I don't.' I really don't. 'Do you want to show me some of your jewellery? Tell me about the different pieces if you don't want to tell me a story about you.'

'I collect jewellery like I collect ailments,' she says. 'I am never really sure where any of them come from or when I am going to get rid of them.'

I grin at her. I see she is one of those people who needs to be dealt with differently. She won't tell me her story until I've told her something about me.

I remove the butterfly pendant from around my neck. I hold it out to her. I notice Mrs Lehtinen's hands as she relieves me of the necklace. The rest of her – right down to her powder blue twinset – may be soft-focusy but she has lived. Her wrinkled, weathered and *used* hands tell me so. Her mind must be a treasury of stories, as varied and interesting as her chest of treasures in front of us.

She's surprised, as most people are, by the lightness of my pendant. It looks heavy, solid, its strong, thick lines create an expectation of heft, but it has very little weight because it is hollow.

'This used to be a pair of earrings,' I explain. 'I got the earrings when I went on holiday. You know how, when you're on holiday, something you buy looks amazing and you love it, then you get it home and the shine comes off it and you realise that the thing that was the most amazing thing in the world is now hellish? That was these earrings. They were incredibly uncomfortable. The shape, though, like teardrops, reminded me of the closed wings of a butterfly. I like butterflies, always have done, so I thought I could remake the earrings into something I could wear. It is not very good, because I was just starting to make jewellery.' I run my fingers along the solid lines where the wings meet. You can still see the rivulets of the solder, something I would painstakingly file smooth if I was making the piece now. 'I cut into this part of the earring, then I had to file both edges into curves to make them fit. Then I had to solder them together.'

It sounds so simple, that I just did it, but the pain I went through: I had sobbed as the solder ran into the wrong places because I hadn't painted enough of the yellow-green liquid flux into the right areas; I had cried again at the moment when I had finally got the solder to stay and it snapped off because I was too vigorous with the filing. 'I used a large silver jump-ring and soldered it on to the wings to make it into a head. See?' I moved my finger over the curved antennae on each side of the butterfly's head. 'The small antennae were made by melting and soldering on the little links you put through your ears.' As I speak, she turns the pendant over and over in her hands. 'I wear it all time now so it's gone from a pair of earrings that sat in a drawer mostly forgotten to something I love to wear. I want to do that with some of your jewellery.'

'It is so simple but *kaunis*.' Mrs Lehtinen's hands turn over the pendant and her eyes, upon which she has now placed the glasses she wears around her neck on a gold chain, continue to scrutinise it. 'What is the word? Beautiful. But not as ordinary as beautiful. No, no, I don't mean beautiful. In Finnish the word is *henkeäsalpaava*.'

'*Henkeäsalpaava*,' I repeat as close to what she said as I can. I nod while I say it, acting as though I understand completely what she is getting at. She's Finnish. *Does she have children?* I wonder. *Grandchildren? Did they sleep in baby boxes, too? Did she decorate them or were they as plain as they were when they were given to mothers by the government?*

'I haven't met many Finnish people in my life,' I say.

'I am surprised at that, there are many of us around. Even here, in Brighton.'

She's not really giving me her full attention, she seems obsessed by the pendant. It isn't that perfect. I love it, but I can see all its flaws, all the ways I would have made it differently now I am more experienced at what I do. Back then I was trying too hard to make things perfect and didn't always manage it. In 2015, having done this for years, I still aim for perfection, but I don't panic because anything that goes wrong, I know I can usually fix. Or at least make it look like the problem was intentional.

'Do you like butterflies?' I ask her.

'It is not that,' Mrs Lehtinen replies. 'I am always fascinated by them because I remember a long time ago I knew of a baby who had a *perhonen* box.' She traces her fingers over the wing curves of my butterfly pendant.

'A what?' I ask, scared to repeat the word in case it comes out wrong and I end up swearing at her.

'A butterfly box,' she says. 'A box covered in *perhonen*. In Finland, when a baby is born, the government gives the mother a box full of everything they need – clothes and nappies and the like. And the box has a mattress too so the baby can sleep in it.'

I know this. The tingling that has taken over my body tells me that I know this. The sudden shortness of my breath tells me that I know this. I nod at her.

'I told the young girl of the family I used to live next door to about it when she was expecting. Many years ago. I told her and she made one. She decorated it with *perhonen*. Beautiful butterflies. She used such *henkeäsalpaava* colours. She had a baby girl.'

When I was eight Dad took me on a rollercoaster for the first time. We were on our annual trip to Blackpool and I was giddy with the excitement of finally doing something grown-up and adventurous with my dad. We sat next to each other and he held my hand. Right at the top of the rollercoaster, just before the car began its descent, I felt weightless; as light as air, as though I weighed nothing. As if I was nothing. I was suspended above the Earth and in those seconds I felt like I was flying. I was a butterfly, as light as anything.

I feel like that now. I am suspended above the Earth, weightless, light as air.

'Does she still have the butterfly box, the little girl?' My voice is working even though I am as light as air, as weightless as a butterfly.

'I do not know. The baby... They... She went to live somewhere else. They said they sent her back to their country in Africa to grow up with family because the girl was too young to look after her properly. But I do not think that was the case. The girl's guardian, she was my friend and she was so proud. She did not like scandal. We were never to speak of what happened, nor the baby. I suspect...' Mrs Lehtinen stops turning my pendant over in her hand and places it carefully on the table beside her open jewellery box. 'But what do I know? I am just a silly old woman.'

She is just a silly old woman and I am still as light as air. My body tingles and my lungs do not work properly, but I am as light as air.

'You're not a silly old woman,' I say. *Ask her. Ask her what happened to the girl who had the baby. Where she is now. Ask her.*

Mrs Lehtinen's eyes are suddenly, surprisingly, on me. She is as far away from a silly old woman as it is possible to get. 'The girl, Abi, the one you look like, she is also the daughter of the woman who made the butterfly box. She had a box, too.'

I stare at her. *Does she know? Has she guessed who I am? Who I might be?* I do this, though. I'm constantly looking at people and wondering if we're related, if they could be a half-sibling or a parent. I've never had a relative who looks like me, who acts like me, who's interested in the same things as me. I'm always searching. This is probably an extension of that: I have come across a coincidence and I am using it as a passive way to search for more information on who I am and where I have come from. I didn't go looking for this, it came to me.

Of course it's a coincidence, that's what most things are in life. We believe in Fate, we believe in kismet, we believe in pre-determined happenings, when really, it's all down to coincidence. There must be hundreds of children out there who slept in butterfly boxes when they were born. Hundreds, if not thousands. I mean, what are the chances of me actually sitting down opposite the neighbour of the woman who gave birth to me? Slim to none, I'd say. And what are the chances of the other child of the woman who gave birth to me working here, too? Not even slim, just non-existent. I am seeing things that are not there.

'OK, Mrs Lehtinen, are there any pieces of jewellery that you'd like to wear again and I can help you with?' I am back. I know this is all nonsense, my brain searching for familiarity – *family* – in the world of strangers I have grown up in, when I know who my family are. Here I am, back on solid ground. I am no longer floating, hovering above reality. I am back to doing what I am here to do.

My hand reaches for my butterfly pendant. It is trembling. *Stop shaking*, I tell my hand. *Stop shaking, you're showing me up*. Mrs Lehtinen is watching me but my hand won't stop shaking. I enclose my butterfly pendant in my hand, hide the tremors. I hook the thick chain over my neck and flip open my toolbox, take out my camera. Mrs Lehtinen stares at my yellow and black tool box – years ago I decorated it with butterfly stickers.

That was at the time when I was particularly obsessed with butterflies. Back then, I would have the same recurring dream that I was in a park full of butterflies. I would be surrounded by hundreds and hundreds of them, all different, all beautiful, but I wouldn't notice any of the creatures around me because I was frantically, desperately searching for my baby. I had lost my baby in that park and I needed to get him back. It was obvious what that was about. I use my foot to slide my butterfly-covered toolbox under the table, out of Mrs Lehtinen's line of sight.

'Shall I photograph some pieces and photograph you and then go away to think of some ideas?' I say.

'Why don't you go and talk to Abi? She is down the corridor in the office. She is the deputy manager. She is a lovely girl. Always so helpful to everyone, but especially to me because I know her grandmother. I'm sure she'll tell you all you need to know about the baby boxes.'

'I'm more interested in your jewellery and how I can make it work for you, to be honest,' I say to the woman in front of me. 'And I have other people to see as well. There are two more after you. So I…erm…don't really have time to do that.'

'You will come back to see me?' she asks.

'Erm…yes, if you want me to. But do you think you will want any of your jewellery remade?'

'I'm sure I will. Take your photographs, and come back to see me with your ideas.'

I'm shaking too much to lay out the jewellery properly. I take a few of the pieces out, but mostly I photograph them in situ in the box. With my hand still tremoring, I snap her picture, the flash causing me to jump a little each time I take a shot.

I know it's a coincidence because that's what happens to people like me.

73

'Dad, why don't I look like you and Mum?'

'Ah, Clemmy, that's a good question.' Dad's large hands picked me up and sat me on his lap. From the glass-fronted sideboard beside his chair, he plucked the picture of us from when we went to Blackpool for the day. Dad had to ask somebody he didn't even know to take a picture of us all. 'The thing of it is, everybody is different. We all look different in our own ways. See, here, your mum and I, we look different. She's got blonde hair – it mostly came out of a bottle but I didn't tell you that – and I've got dark hair. And you've got black hair. We're none of us the same.'

'But why is my skin different to yours? You and Mum have the same skin.'

'We don't, actually, Clemmy, but I know what you mean.' Dad stopped talking and stared at the photo for a long time. I was scared he would do what Mum did and look like he was going to cry. 'The thing of it is, Clemmy, I was meant to tell you this with your mum here. She'll be raging at me for not waiting for her, but I'll tell you anyway. You know how a baby grows in their mum's tummy?' I knew that. I was four but I knew that. I still didn't know how the baby got out of the mum's tummy and into the baby pram, but I thought I would ask Dad that another time. 'You didn't grow in your mum's tummy.'

I was frightened suddenly: why didn't I grow in Mum's tummy like everyone else? 'Why not, Dad?'

'Mum can't grow babies in her tummy, nobody knows why. You grew in another lady's tummy but she couldn't look after you. And the lady who was a social worker said that we could look after you if we wanted, and we could be your mum and dad. We really wanted to. When we first saw you in that butterfly box we knew that we really wanted to be your mum and dad.

'You have the same skin as the lady whose tummy you grew in, but we have the same smile, me and you, and you laugh at the same things your mum does. And we all like to throw stones in the sea. We don't look the same but no one does, not really. We have more things that make us the same than things that make us different.' His finger, which was big and fat like a sausage, pointed to the picture again. 'You see how we've all got the same type of ears? Round, not pointy. And my curly hair is a little bit like yours. Your mother's would be curly a bit like yours if she didn't put those damn rollers in every night. And here, look at our hands: square at the end of our fingers. We're the same and we're different. And being different is just as good as being the same.'

I didn't understand why the mum who grew me in her tummy couldn't look after me, and I didn't understand what he meant about there were more things the same than different. But I did understand that he couldn't say we had the same nose because we didn't. And not the same mouth. And not the same eyes. And definitely, definitely not the same skin colour. His was peach, mine was brown. Dad thought that was good. It made Mum nearly cry, but Dad thought it was good. I didn't understand why they didn't both think it was good or they didn't both want to cry. Maybe that was another different thing that was good.

I gave Dad a hug. I thought he needed one.

12

Smitty

There are moments in your life you can't plan for.

They happen, hit you, render you incapable. I am in the middle of a moment where nothing I do will stop it from happening. Every second that passes is another step closer to that moment.

In my mind, in the sequence of freeze-frame moments that I see the world in sometimes, I am heading back to Lottie. I have my butterfly-covered toolbox of tricks in one hand, my green, many-pocketed bag is slung across my body, and in my other hand I have my car keys. I am walking away from this place and I am going to my van for a sit down and a think. I am not doing this. I am not standing outside a door that has a brass plate emblazoned 'OFFICE', contemplating knocking.

Only a silly, deluded person would do something like that. I am not a silly, deluded person. Much.

I've probably violated all sorts of security protocols and I'm almost certainly being watched on a camera right now as I stand here, hand raised to knock.

This is an ordinary corridor in an ordinary and strange building. This probably shouldn't happen in an ordinary corridor. On television, when this happens, the people involved meet in places of significance or a café or a park. Wherever it is, there is usually some kind of sentimental memory attached. Also, probably most importantly, they have prepared themselves, they have thought about what they're going to say. They don't take the word of an old woman they've never met before and decide to do this.

I am being ridiculous. It's understandable, but ridiculous nonetheless. The promise I remade my mother four weeks ago comes to mind, rising up like a phoenix from the depths of the flames of what I am doing. I promised her I wouldn't do anything like this while there was even the slimmest of chances that my biological family would take me away from her. The promise phoenix beats its wings at me and I know I can't do this. I can't do this to my mother. She's too fragile to be able to handle this. Whatever this is.

Imagine, too, Smitty, what you would actually have to say: 'Excuse me, I think you may be my sister. I'm the child your parents gave away before you were born. Yes, that's right, you call for security and call for a psychiatric assessment, too, because that's exactly what I would do in your position.'

Before anyone can see me, I snatch up my toolbox and get the hell out of there.

With Dad, February 2015, Otley

Dad was weak some days, so thin and fragile, his skin translucent with a blue-green-black network of veins beneath the surface, and his body so obviously wracked with pain. Other days it all seemed like some awful mistake, that the doctors were all wrong and he was on the mend. He had little appetite, little thirst, and every time I tried to get him to take something in, he would refuse, or 'Later, *quine*, later' me.

'Have you ever thought of finding your first parents?' Dad asked me. Today was one of those in between days, where he seemed to hover almost comfortably between waning and might improve. He had probably been waiting for one of those days to ask me that, although I wasn't sure how he managed to fix it to land on a day, like today, where Mum would be out for a long period of time.

'No. I don't generally think about them, Dad.'

His face made a smile, one that I'd become so accustomed to over the years, and I struggled again to believe what was

77

happening, what I'd one day have to live without. I had pictures of Dad, so many pictures, but none were good enough, none captured the perfect symmetry of his smile, the way his top lip would move upwards a fraction more, the way the smile would connect with his blue eyes. 'Smitty, I'm not your mother. You don't have to pretend with me.'

They were so together, Mum and Dad. The kind of couple who never seemed to argue for long, who were openly devoted to each other and really would only be parted by death. Yet, they dealt with the whole 'adopted daughter' issue so differently. Mum never wanted it mentioned, like she could pretend away the fact I was not biologically theirs, and Dad, he was like this: always willing to talk about it.

'I do think about it sometimes, but not all the time. Or even often. Or very much at all. It's not as if they've made great moves to find me.'

'Would you want that? To be tracked down like they do on those television shows?'

'No! I can't think of anything worse. I can't explain how I feel, Dad,' I admitted.

It's always there – you don't grow up like I did and simply forget how different you are from your family and most people around you – but it's simply that the sense of difference sometimes recedes to the back of my mind and I'm not bothered about finding them. And, sometimes, my curiosity bubbles over, like a pot that has simmered for too long and the gentle blue flame is edged up and up until it is orange and fierce.

'I should want to find them, and I do,' I said to Dad. 'I also think about what it would do to my life, having to get to know people who I should want to know. I worry about what it would do to you and Mum to think I'm looking elsewhere when I have you at home. I also think about them and how they've probably got lives that are sorted, and the last thing they need is to have me turning up wanting in on that. If it was as simple as searching and being a fly on the wall of their homes so I could see what they were like but only engage when I want to, I'd do that.'

'I hate this disease, Smitty. It's robbed me of the time I should have spent telling you...' His eyes were heavy, his frailty acute and overtly torturous. 'I should have encouraged you earlier to find them. To know where you come from...I didn't do right by you.'

'Please don't say that, Dad. You've done *everything* right by me. All my life you've always been there. I can't stand to think that you feel you did me wrong. I don't want to find them at the moment. I may change my mind in the future, I may not, but right now I'm happy as I am.' Even though I hate being untethered, feeling as though I don't belong anywhere, I couldn't be that unhappy if I wasn't actively trying to change that.

'When you were little, you used to say to me that you were from Scotland, like me.'

'I don't remember that.'

'You would tell me all the time, "I'm from Scotland, just like you".'

'That does sound like something I'd say.'

'*Quine*, I would burst with pride knowing that you felt that way.'

Inside Lottie, my balance returns. Calmness descends. My heart stops turning over itself in my chest, my lungs remember how to slowly draw in oxygen and carefully expel carbon dioxide.

What I was about to do...That isn't like me. I have never been that impulsive. I plan, I think things through, I visualise and prepare. I'm not sure which would have been worse: her being my half-sister or her not. Either way, I would have had to tell a complete stranger that her mother has been lying to her for most of her life. This would have been based on nothing more than the word of another complete stranger, who spent most of her time thinking and speaking in Finnish.

'Stupid, stupid, stupid, stupid,' I tell myself. I hang on to the steering wheel, bending forwards. My stomach is not settling, it isn't as easily soothed and fobbed off as my heart and my lungs. My stomach believes Mrs Lehtinen. My gut is telling me that she is right. I am the little girl who slept in the butterfly box, whose mother went on to give birth to another girl sometime later. 'Stupid, stupid, stupid.'

Even if it is true, there is nothing I can do about it. Simply thinking about it causes the phoenix, fiery and burning, of that promise I made my mother to beat its wings at me, the heat flashing through me. I can't do it to her. I can't break her heart when she's only at the beginning of the journey of the grief of losing my dad.

Tap, tap, tap against Lottie's window. So quiet and hesitant it takes a few moments for the sound to properly register.

Tap, tap, tap again. More certain, more sure this time. I do not need company right now. If there is one thing I do not need it is to speak to someone. What I need right now is to be left alone, to have a breakdown on my own before I go home and pretend to my mother that I haven't inadvertently broken my promise and I haven't almost ruined the life of some poor woman who happened to work in the same nursing home as a potential client.

Tap, tap, tap. Again. This person should have got the message that I'm not up for talking. Although, to be fair to them, they may think I'm dead or something and want to be sure.

The bones in my neck click as I raise my head and turn in the direction of the tapping.

I've never imagined being electrocuted before, but this feels like it. It feels like all the volts that used to pass through the power station where Dad once worked have been sent through me at the same time. Even through the grimy, salt-splattered window, the person is clear to me. My gaze does not move from the window while my fingers grope around for the window handle. With the grey plastic grip in my fingers, I slowly slide it open. The person in front of me is immediately crystal clear and I am looking into a mirror.

It's a mirror that can take away the years, hide your wrinkles, change your hairstyle, give you spots and blemishes in different places, but it's a mirror all the same. I am looking into my own face as it probably looked ten years ago.

'Are you OK?' she asks. 'Mrs Lehtinen said you seemed upset and would I mind coming to check on you before you left.' She sounds nothing like me, of course. She's from here and I'm from nowhere. She pauses, stares at me like she's only just seeing what I'm seeing.

'I'm guessing she meant you as you're the only person in this car park.' This is said distractedly – the mirror is starting to work for her, too. She's looking into it and she has more wrinkles around the eyes, more blemishes on her cheeks, her face is filled out a little more, her hair isn't sleek and straight to her shoulders, but curly and shorter. But the eyes are the same in this mirror, the nose is the same shape, the lips are the same size, the forehead has the same curve. 'I only do these things for her because she's an old family friend.'

I don't speak. My mouth does not know what to say. My brain knows what it should say but that would be ludicrous. She would probably freak out if I told her.

'Sorry,' she says after her eyes have repeatedly examined every part of my face, each time finding more and more similarities: the imperfection in the slope of my left eyebrow, the slight indentation at the tip of my nose, the way my right ear is a tiny bit more curved at the top. 'Sorry for staring, but why do you look exactly like me?'

'*I don't look like you,*' I want to say. 'You *actually look like* me *because I was here first.*'

My shoulders shrug at her first of all. Then my mouth decides it needs to speak. It needs to do something because staring and shrugging aren't the way to resolve this.

'I look like you because I think I'm your sister,' I say. And it takes all my strength not to burst out laughing because it's the most ridiculous, unbelievable thing I've ever said in my life.

13

Smitty

When we breathe it's almost synchronised, only a fraction of a second keeps us apart. A lifetime and a fraction of a second's breathing time separate us in these quiet, uncertain minutes. I want to say something. Something pithy and clever, something that'll cement me in her mind as someone she'd like to be connected to. My mind isn't working like that: its fingers keep reaching, grabbing at words, phrases, sounds, even, to piece together and say, but those things keep slipping away, out of reach, unobtainable.

We are sitting in the flower garden as it's time for afternoon tea and most of the residents who are able will be having tea and cakes down in the rec room where I was with Mrs Lehtinen.

'This can't be happening, right?' Abi says. 'Cos if you ever met my parents, my mum, you'd know that this couldn't ever be happening.'

'I'm guessing your mum never mentioned me. Not to you or her husband.'

'Husband? My dad, you mean. My mum's been with my dad since she was seventeen. She came to Brighton to start university, and stayed with my dad's parents cos they knew her parents back in Nihanara, you know, the country in Africa?'

I nod, I've heard of it. If I'd had any idea that was where my DNA came from I might have paid more attention in my geography classes.

'They fell in love after a few months of knowing each other, and just before my dad finished his first law degree they got married.'

She recites the story as though she has heard it several hundred times. I used to be the same. I'd ask Mum and Dad about how they met, when they got married, over and over again. I used to pore over their pictures, looking at their clothes, their faces, the faces of the people around them. I wanted to know everything about their love and their life before me.

'My mum and dad did everything so right, they always do everything so right, that's why this can't be happening. Cos my mum? Sex before marriage? In the same house as my grandmother? Giving a child up for adoption? No way. NO. WAY.' She shakes her head. 'They still say a prayer before dinner. Even now. There is no way.'

All right, I think, *no need to rub it in. I am their dirty little secret. Their.* It sounds like Abi's father is my father too. We are full blood sisters. They stayed together and got married. Had another child about ten years later. Forgot the child in the butterfly box ever existed because she didn't fit into their cosy new life. I wonder why they left it so long? Maybe they kept trying and trying and it never happened. It might even have occurred to them after months and months of no joy that maybe they should have stuck with the one they had first.

'*I think I need to leave.*'

'What did you say?' Abi asks.

My hands fall away from my face, trembling as I swivel slowly to look at her again. It's uncanny – our features are arranged so similarly, I could be looking at a picture of myself from at least ten years ago.

Ten years ago...

Ten years ago Seth asked me if we could talk about having a baby. I'd stared at him for a long time, horrified at the suggestion. Yes, obviously we were together for ever as far as I was concerned, but a baby was the last thing on my mind.

'Have I said the wrong thing?' he asked.

'I, erm, Seth, babies...I...' I shook my head. 'I don't think I can.'

'Not ever?'

I started to breathe deeply, I was about to start hyperventilating, panicking. 'I can't...I don't know anything about where I come from, what sort of stuff is in my biology. What it would do to a child I have. I hate going to the doctors anyway because there are all these things they ask you and I can't ever answer them because I was adopted and my mum won't let me find my other parents, not even to ask about my genes, so I'll never know. It'll be worse with being pregnant, having a baby, that's all about what can be passed on. And I won't know. I'll never know—'

'Hey, hey, hey,' Seth said and grabbed me into a hug to quell my panic. 'Let's talk about it another time. Or not. We'll see how things go. It was a stupid suggestion.'

'No, it's not. We can talk about it another time, OK? Just not now.'

Ten years later, him mentioning that we might have made a baby was the start of the last conversation we had as a couple. Ten years ago there was so much going on, and I still looked as young and naïve as Abi.

'I said, I think I need to leave,' I reply.

'Oh. Right.'

'This isn't...I'm not coping very well with this and I need to leave.'

'Why don't you come meet my parents? Maybe they'll be able to explain all of this. You might be my long-lost cousin instead of, you know...Which would be mad, but kinda cool, too.'

'Did you used to sleep in a cardboard box?' I ask.

Abi frowns at me, her eyes darting up and down over me, checking me out again. 'Yeah, why? Wait, how'd you know?'

'I slept in one, too. It's an old— '

'Finnish tradition,' she finishes. Her scrutiny intensifies.

'Did she decorate it in butterflies? Your mum? I assume it was your mum who decorated it, and not your dad.'

'No, I had hummingbirds. My eldest brother had eagles. My other brother had doves. Yes, Mummy drew them.'

Brothers? *Brothers.* I have a sister. I have brothers. They didn't wait ten years to try again.

'I really need to go now.' My bag clatters to the ground when I stand and I immediately throw myself to my knees, gathering up my belongings, shoving them away because I feel exposed enough, I don't need her to see anything else about me, to have something potentially negative to relay to her parents.

'I seriously think you should come meet my parents,' she says while I replace my bag's contents and search thoroughly for anything I may have missed.

'No.' I shake my head. 'No, thank you.' Am I simply turning down an invitation to tea or the chance to meet my biological parents, the people who gave me the blood that flows through my veins? 'I need to go.'

'But—'

'No offence, but over the years I've imagined meeting the people who could potentially be my biological family and it was nothing like this. If you don't mind, I'm going to leave now. I need to go home, sit down, start to get my head around it.'

'What do I tell my mum and dad?'

My shake of the head looks more dismissive than I feel inside, and the up and down flap of my arms seems far more exasperated than I feel. 'I don't know,' I tell her, earnestly. 'They're your parents.'

14

Smitty

My body is tingling all over. My body is numb. Both sensations are there and I'm not sure how I'm driving.

That automatic part of you that takes over when necessary must have kicked in. I half expected Abi to come running out of the building, trying to flag me down, stop me, talk to me. I've watched too many movies, I think. If I was her, I'd be turning myself inside out pretending that it was all a coincidence. That the woman who fled was a fantasist. Anything else passing through my brain would be admitting that there's a possibility that my parents are liars. All parents are liars, of course. They tell you lies all time for your own good – 'If you pull your face like that and the wind changes it'll stay that way', 'The ice cream van plays music when it's run out of ice cream', 'You were a good baby who never cried' – but they're not fundamental lies. All parents are liars, but they pray you never find out the truth about the lies of omission that are etched into the fabric of their personalities, indelible stain-like reminders that before they were parents they were human beings and made human mistakes. Some of those mistakes are stupid and pointless, like a tattoo of the name of the first person you ever loved; others are huge and life-altering – like surrendering your child for adoption.

I've done a bad thing to Abi. She will be turning herself inside out trying to pretend that her parents aren't human enough to make such huge mistakes. She will have to go home and face them.

Red. The traffic light is red and I stare at it. Red for stop. Red for blood. Red for danger. Maybe I should go back. I can't let her do that alone. She's done nothing wrong. If I go back, though, go with her to her house, I'll have to face them. I'll have to speak to those people. The first thing I'll do is blurt out, 'Why?' and they'll say... They'll say... What I always knew and this has confirmed: that it was me. It can't have been about my mother being all alone. It can't have been any of the reasons I've conjured up and worked out and come to decide were the truth over the years. If they are together, if they had more children, if they're still living in the same house they did all those years ago, there must have been something wrong with me.

An orchestra of car horns penetrates my thoughts. Green. Green for go. Green for move. Green for pastures new. Green for emeralds, popular in engagement rings. My foot pushes down on the pedal, and nothing happens. Green for go. I push hard, the pedal is to the floor, and nothing. Green. GO!

The orchestra is loud, insistent, angry. The heat inside my head will melt me. I want to take off all my clothes so I can feel the air on my skin and it can cool me down. Other pedal. I need to push the other pedal to go. My foot moves, slams down too hard on the right pedal, Lottie leaps forward, jerking me with her. At least we're moving now, at least all that stuff is behind me and I'm moving forwards.

The further away it is behind me, the easier it'll be to forget. To pretend when I get home. The orchestra fades away, the echo of a memory of a stupid mistake I made at some traffic lights. The soundtrack I have now is nothingness. Silence. This is the silence of the lonely ones, of people like me – we who do not know how to talk, or to share, or to open up our truths to the people around us, for fear of how it will be used against us.

Mum is in. The television is telling her something about ruins in Turin. I'm sure she'll be avidly watching that and doing her Sudoku with her glasses perched on the end of her nose, and tea cooling in the white and yellow mug she favours most.

I'm not shaking. I am, but if I tell myself enough times that I'm not, it will become a reality.

'Clemency, is that you?' Mum's voice calls. Today is a good day. The tentacles of pain and grief are not wrapped so tightly around her heart, its poison isn't tainting her as potently. I know this by the volume of the television, blaring out enough to be heard throughout the flat; I can feel this by the calmness in her voice. If I was going to tell her – ever – today would be the day to do it.

'No, Mum, it's the milkman,' I reply. I stand outside my bedroom, the wide corridor suddenly narrow and claustrophobic, not big enough for the secret I've hidden away in my heart and mind. The large honey-coloured wooden blocks of the parquet floor swim in front of me, their pattern suddenly a nauseating kaleidoscope of half-focused images and formations.

'Clemency! Do you have to?' Mum calls. 'Can't you just for once say, "Yes, Mum, it's me"? Do you have to be sarcastic every time?'

'Yeah, but— Yes, Mum, it's me,' I say.

'That's better,' she replies. There's no doubt a smile on her face, fuelled by the affection she now has for me because I didn't argue with her for once, nor try to explain that saying things like that were just part of who I am. Instead, I simply did as I was told. Anyone other than my mother would be suspicious of why someone had suddenly changed a habit of a lifetime. But Mum doesn't know because she always thinks if she tells me off enough, I will do as I'm told. If I were in Mum's position, though, I'd guess without a doubt that I was being cheated on.

That's what I'm doing. I'm cheating on my mother. Even though I didn't mean to, and it really did 'just happen', I'm still cheating. Betraying her. Making her biggest nightmare part of my reality.

'Would you like a cup of tea?' Mum asks.

I want to tell her. I want to throw myself on to the sofa beside her, rest my head on her shoulder and explain what happened. Then I want to explain about the cavernous hole that has unexpectedly, terrifyingly opened up inside me simply because of who I met today. The hole is always there, of course, and mostly I ignore it. Usually

I replace the area where it is with the idea that I don't belong anywhere and that I don't need anything else to explain why I feel the way I do. Rarely, very rarely, I obliquely acknowledge the hole and feel for a little while that there is a part of me missing.

There is a part of me missing. I feel that now. It is huge and gaping and potentially unfillable. I want Mum to be able to listen to all that and understand without worrying about what it will mean for her.

I want my mum. My real mum, I mean. The mum who'll be able to listen to all that and understand and put her arms around me and tell me it will all be OK. I want my real mum, except I don't know who that is.

'Clemency! Do you want a cup of tea?' Mum repeats.

'No, thanks. I'm going to get on with some work.'

'Don't work for too long,' she calls back. 'You know how involved you get.'

'Yes, Mum,' I say. It's her of course; she's my real mum. How could I, for even a moment, have ever thought otherwise? *She's* my real mum. And I've cheated on her.

15

Abi

To: Jonas Zebila
From: Abi Zebila
Subject: NEWS!!!!!
Thursday, 11 June 2015

Are you sitting down?

I hope so. If you're not and you're reading this on your phone, SIT DOWN. You are not going to believe what I'm about to tell you.

We have a sister. Apart from me, you have another, real-life, full-blooded sister. It's too complicated to explain all of it right now, but it was her that Mummy drew the butterflies for. This woman said when she was a baby, she slept in a box decorated with butterflies by her mother, who she never met because she was adopted as a baby.

All the while I'm talking to her, I'm thinking, this is mad, she's not my sister, how can she be when Mummy and Daddy have been together since the beginning of time and have only done it three times to have us? And if she was really our sister then they would have...BEFORE marriage, and you know how much of a crime that is around here.

When I told her to come back to the house to meet Mummy and Daddy she got up and ran away. But butterflies. It all makes sense now.

All right, so by now I'm properly spooked. There's some woman out there with my face and a sleep box like mine, so I leave work as early as I can. I come home, Mummy's in the kitchen, Gran's asleep in her room, Daddy's still out and Ivor is on the computer in the living room with Lily so it's safe to talk. I'm actually pretty impressed with myself that I didn't think twice about going into the kitchen and shutting the door and fronting up to Mummy about it.

'Abi, when you have washed your hands, wash the rice for me and put it on,' Mummy said.

I went across the room and stood right next to her. 'Mummy, do I have a sister that you had adopted?' I said.

Yeah, all right, it's not the most subtle or diplomatic thing to say but I had to get it out quick before I lost my nerve.

She was crushing big fat juicy plum tomatoes in her black mortar and pestle (you know the one Daddy brought her back from Nihanara the last time he went over there) and she just stopped. Only for about two seconds, then she started up again.

'What foolishness are you talking now, Abi?' she said. 'Please, wash your hands and then put some rice on. Make sure you put enough on for today and tomorrow.'

'I just met her,' I said. 'She looks exactly like me and she says she slept in a box covered in butterflies. I brought her home to meet you.' Yeah, I know that last bit was mean but you know what Mummy and Daddy are like – they won't admit to anything unless you have proof. As it turns out that was the worst thing I could have said because it shook Mummy up so much she knocked the black bowl off the worktop and it smashed on the floor and the tomato juice went everywhere.

Mummy looked really, really scared and said, 'She's here? You brought her here?'

I knew it was true then and I knew it was bad because she didn't even notice about the bowl. I sort of shook my head, really nervous, and said that I'd wanted to but she ran away. 'Is it true?' I asked.

She still looked scared but she nodded. 'You must not tell your father that you have seen her, nor your grandmother.'

'Do they know about her?' I asked. And she got angry! She's the one lying all these years and now she was angry when she was caught out and I asked what I thought was a perfectly valid question.

'Of course they know about her. Who do you think her father is? And you must not tell Ivor. None of them are to know until I'm ready to tell

91

them, do you understand me?' I didn't say anything because what sort of a person would agree to something like that? 'Do you understand me?' she said again, more sternly, so obviously I'm the sort of person who would agree to that because I did. I sort of nodded and said yes, and I didn't cross my fingers or toes. But she didn't say I wasn't to tell you, so I am.

Can you actually believe it? A sister. A SISTER. And I can't tell anyone. Except you. I think Mummy wants to meet her, to see for herself, but after the way she ran away today, I don't think that's going to happen.

So there you have it. Big news. I'm typing this from Declan's. I couldn't trust myself not to shout something at the dinner table so I packed a bag for Lily and me and we're going to stay here for a few days. Declan's over the moon, Lily's less than thrilled because I forgot her homework and I refuse to go back for it.

I don't know how I feel about all this. I could scream at Mummy and Daddy, I really could. But on the other hand I know what good it would do me. I so want to see her again. A sister. I've always wanted a sister. (No offence.) I really hope there's a way I can get her to talk to me.

Lots of love
Abi
xxxx

16

Smitty

Mum is sitting at the kitchen table; she has a copy of *Friday Ads* spread open in front of her, a cup of tea in her hand. At this time of day the kitchen is a suntrap, light streaming in through the windows like water down a waterfall. Mum seems to be bathed in a golden glow because she is at the epicentre of the waterfall of light. She is dressed, hair done, make-up applied, ready for whatever the next few hours hold.

I struggled out of bed this morning after a sleepless night of replaying and reliving yesterday. It's been a night of confusion and self-reproach and fear of what to do next. No matter which line of thought I followed, which path my fantasies led me, which way I tried to reason myself out of the mess, there really is only one thing to do next.

What I should do next is this: tell Mum.

Today is a good day and if I tell her now, it won't set her too far back. In this light-drenched kitchen I should tell her and she can help me decide what to do next.

My fear, a visceral terror of her reaction, wouldn't allow me to think of what to actually say, but it shouldn't be too hard. 'Mum, I met my biological sister yesterday' would work. 'Mum, I know this will upset you, but yesterday I met my sister' that would be enough, too. 'Mum, I need you to listen to me for a minute without saying anything. What I'm about to say will be unbelievable and really quite cool if you think about it but I've found my birth family.' 'Mum, I have a sister! I know! Isn't that incredible!'

I clear my throat, which emanates from me as a small, choking sound. I'll simply start talking. Whatever it is that comes out of my mouth, I will state it clearly and firmly, and I brace myself to face her response full on.

'I'm going to buy myself a bicycle,' my mother announces when she sees me.

'Who with the what now?' I reply. That, I was not expecting.

'There are bicycle lanes all over Brighton, all down the seafront, I'm going to take advantage of them. I'm going to buy a bicycle.'

'To ride?'

'Yes, of course, to ride.'

'You?'

Mum loudly settles her cup on the table and fixes me with a stern glare, her mouth a tight circle of indignation and irritation. 'Yes, me.' *Do you have some sort of problem with that?* she adds silently.

'Really?' I say. Everything I was meant to tell her has been wisped away on this random revelation.

'Yes, really,' she says crossly.

'Really, really?'

'You are just like your father.' Her voice is brittle. 'You have no faith in me whatsoever. You think I'm not capable of doing anything beyond cooking and sewing and cleaning. I will have you know that when I was a young girl I had a bicycle and I used to go everywhere on it. I went to work at the factory on it and used to go out with my friends.' Mum's huff continues: 'If you must know, I met your father while I was out riding in the countryside with my friends.'

'Sorry. I was just a bit shocked, that's all. Get a bike. It'll be fun. Great idea.' *I won't spend all my time worrying about you out there on the roads, wondering what havoc you'll cause,* I think. *I'm sure there won't be police at my door at least once a week telling me that you've been banged up in jail because you've taken some poor unsuspecting motorist to task for daring to come near you. I'm certain that this plan of yours is going to work out* brilliantly *for all concerned.*

'It will be,' she says. She may as well cross her arms over her chest and stick out her tongue in a giant, defiant fit of pique.

'*I have a sister, Mum!*' I'd love to shout that at her. It'd wipe that sulk clean off her face. A bike. A freaking bike! 'Right, well, I'm off to work. You enjoy looking for your bike.'

'I will.'

'Don't forget to get a helmet.'

'I won't.'

This was not how today was meant to start. I haven't even had a drink and I'm being forced out of the house by another of those 'moments with Mum' I'm expert at walking into. Each time I get to the end of such a 'moment' I look back and find that it was usually precipitated by me not knowing when to keep my mouth shut, and Mum not knowing how not to be herself. *A bike!* How was I meant to not comment at all when this woman – with her criticism of every other driver on the road, whose constant shouts at me to slow down and 'mind that car' made a five-hour journey to Brighton feel like I'd taken a wrong turn and was headed instead to Hades – decides she's going to join those people out there?

I should have told her about Abi, though. This isn't the sort of thing I should keep from her. I need someone to help me with what comes next. What do I want to come next, though? I left without getting Abi's full name, without giving her my number or my full name. I suppose she could find me if she wanted to, and I could find her if I wanted to.

Do I want to, though?

Do I want to get in touch with her? Do I want to see her again? I ask myself that question again and again with every one of the eighty-seven steps I take on my way out of the building.

Of course I do, I conclude as I open the door. *Of course I don't*, I decide as the door shuts behind me and I am out in the open air. *Of course I do and of course I don't.* I have no idea which answer is the best one.

*

Tyler's café is buzzing – energetic and alive with customers. It's just past eight and everyone seems to have got the memo that told them to come here for breakfast and a chat.

'What would Madame From Nowhere like to try today?' Tyler asks. I hop myself up on to my favourite stool, place my bag on the seat beside me. 'I have some wonderful smoky coffee beans that would make an interesting double-shot espresso. A nice Chilean blend – fair trade, of course – that would make a delightful mocha, and a truly unique Mexican mix that would make an out-of-this-world cappuccino—'

'No cappuccino!' I say this much louder than necessary. A few people turn to look at me and Tyler's eyebrows come together in confusion. 'I do not want a cappuccino type of day today,' I state calmly.

'I've got a jar of instant I save for emergencies, if you want?'

'That'll do nicely, thank you.'

He uses my favourite bucket teacup with the lemon-yellow and white daisies on a pink saucer, to make me a flat white. I knew he was teasing about the jar of instant. 'Do I detect something troubling in the usual Tour de Force that is Smitty's world?' he asks. I draw the coffee towards myself across the counter and my fingers reach for the sugar pot. Four shots of it later, I begin to stir, creating the gravelly sound of undissolved sugar against porcelain. He watches me overdose my drink with the sugar and eventually states, 'Ah, I detect a huge disturbance in the tour de force.'

'I thought it was only bartenders in American movies who talked to their customers about their problems.'

'And me.' He leans on the counter, brings his head down to my height. 'Didn't I tell you I trained in America? True, true. I was a bartender in a cocktail bar. I am well qualified to listen to problems.'

'I'm kind of stuck,' I say without really thinking about it. 'There's something I half want to do that will hurt someone else if I do it. But I don't think I can *not* do it, partly because I've already set the wheels in motion. I didn't actually mean to set the wheels in motion, it sort of happened. And now I'm stuck between doing it and not doing it and not knowing if I'll realistically not be able to do it. But if I do it, then where does that leave the person I'll potentially hurt?' The surface of my coffee is smooth and unbroken. Under the surface, a dozen, maybe a hundred dozen, tiny chemical reactions are taking place as the sugar dissolves.

'Sounds tricky.'

'Tricky isn't the half of it.'

'How would you solve it if it was a work problem?'

'I wouldn't have this problem if it was a work problem.'

'Just say it was. Say you had a jewellery piece that you wanted to create that you technically couldn't do without destroying half of your office? Studio? Workshop?'

'Workshop.'

'You can't create it without destroying part of your workshop in the process, but you know how great it would look in the end, how it'll push the boundaries of jewellery making and will have people talking about it until the end of time. What would you do?'

'I don't know.' I sigh and stare into the depths of my coffee, hoping to capture a glimpse of one of those chemical reactions. 'I'd maybe think of a way of protecting my workshop but still make the piece? It's not the same, though, people and things. My workshop can always be rebuilt – even if it's not rebuilt in the same place. This person who'll get hurt, I can't ever undo that hurt. I don't like hurting people. Especially not this one.'

'If they're that important to you, aren't you important enough to them that they'd be all right with whatever it is you want to do? Isn't that the nature of caring about someone?'

'In theory, yes. In reality, not so much.'

'Now, see, I don't think that's true. I think when you love someone you try to understand and be supportive of the things they really want to do.'

'So if you were married and your wife really wanted to run off with your next-door neighbour, you'd try to be supportive of that, would you? Or would you be incredibly hurt and unable to get over it?'

Tyler's frown ploughs deep lines into the perfection that is his face. 'Who told you about that?'

I draw back. 'Oh, no. Did that happen to you? God, I'm sorry. I didn't think. It was just an example I plucked out of thin air.'

His face creases up. 'No, it didn't happen to me. Just messing with you. I don't know, it's not an easy answer, but it doesn't sound like your dilemma will have you running off with someone unsuitable. It sounds like it's something important to you. And as simplistic as it sounds, people who care about you want you to be happy, even if it is sometimes at their expense.' Tyler stands upright.

That sounds so true and noble, how we'd all love the world to work, but does it really? Do we all at some point have to submit ourselves to pain because it will make someone we care about happy?

A digital buzz emanates from my bag and its sound, although technically 'silent', cuts through the good-natured hum of conversation in the place. Tyler grins at me like we're old friends, and disappears back into the kitchen area.

The number is a mobile and I don't recognise it. I know who it is when I slide my finger across the screen to answer the call – it *could* be a new client, it *could* be Seth calling from a new phone, it *could* be anyone in the world. It's obvious who it's going to be, though. It's what I would be doing if I was in their situation.

I inhale. Pause. Say, 'Hello, Clem speaking,' with as much confidence as I can.

'Hi,' she says. 'It's Abimbola…Abi. From yesterday?'

'Yes. Hello.'

'I talked to my mum last night,' she says. When I say nothing, Abi continues, 'She really wants to meet you.'

Without ceremony or much thought, I take the phone away from my ear, hit the flashing red 'call end' button, and quietly, calmly, I then turn off my phone.

17

Abi

To: Jonas Zebila
From: Abi Zebila
Subject: Damn!
Sunday, 21 June 2015

Really, Jonas, really?! I tell you we have a secret sister and I get nothing from you? Nothing at all? Not even the slightest bit of curiosity?! Do you think I made her up or something?.

Well, I didn't. I found her number and called and she hung up on me. She actually hung up on me. I'm still smarting about that three days later. Especially since her phone seems to be permanently off now.

Mummy's keen on seeing her, too, even though she'd never admit it. She spends all her time staring into space, as if she's back reliving that time of her life. I can't even begin to imagine Mummy doing it. Any of it. The sex before marriage, the handing over a baby in a butterfly box. I'd love to ask her about it, but I know she won't talk. She'll just clam up and pretend it's all a mistake.

I tried to show her Clemency's website and she just sat looking at it like the computer wasn't there. I can't even begin to understand what's going through her head right now. Or Clemency's. I just realised, I didn't tell you her name – that's it: Clemency.

Since she hung up on me I've been trying to find out as much as I can about her, but do you know how many photos there are of our sister on the internet? Pretty much none. Do you know how easy it is to find out information about her? Really bloody hard. She's got an unusual name so you'd think it'd be easy to find out about her, but no. *Nada*. It's like she doesn't really exist. But I know she does because Mrs L clearly knew who she was, which is why she sent me to talk to her, and there's the website. And I met her.

Jonas, I really need someone to tell me what to do right now. I can't tell anyone else about this. Where would I even begin telling Declan? He thinks we stayed there the other night because I've fallen out with Mummy, which I have in the most quiet way possible. I am so confused.

Abi

xxxxx

Part 3

18

Smitty

Mum has her bike. Technically it's a tricycle, which makes me less worried about her wobbling into traffic on two wheels. It's a much more substantial vehicle and she has a greater surface area on the road, which can only be a good thing.

Whenever it was wet outside and Seth would speed off to Wakefield for work on his motorcycle, I would worry because he was so vulnerable and had less space on the highways than cars did. All it would take would be one slip on a patch of water or oil, or the misjudgement of a corner, and that would be it. He'd be gone. I'd have lost him and I could have prevented it if I'd stopped him from riding his damn bike.

My fears are similar about Mum, except I fear for those who dare to cut her up, too. I was dragged along to a bike shop out in Littlehampton and was expected to make approving noises and comments, which I duly did.

Guilt about not telling her about Abi unfurled its silky red ribbony threads and bound my questioning tongue so tight I barely spoke during the whole trip – I simply nodded and smiled approvingly. Even when she chose a black helmet with biker girl flames along the sides, and big brand-name trainers almost blindingly white, which she insisted on buying specifically for cycling, I smiled and nodded and showed my full support. Guilt also allowed me to watch her try on pair after pair of shiny Spandex cycling shorts until she came to the conclusion all on her own that khaki Bermuda shorts were more her thing.

It's too impossible a thing to tell her about Abi. Every time I try, my mouth will not form the words. I know, eventually, Mum will be fine, she will understand that I did not go looking for this and I did not want it to happen. It's the initial reaction I don't want to deal with. The way her face will become a blank of incomprehension. How she'll sit back in her seat or will sit down heavily. The way her eyes will cloud over as she tries to formulate the first of many questions to find out if it was truly an accident or if I had betrayed her after all she'd done for me. How I'll have to keep reminding her that I love her and I haven't been in touch with them since.

I feel guilty too about not answering any of Abi's calls or texts. That is also an impossible thing to do. I want to speak to her so much it's almost physically painful, but to do that I have to speak to Mum first. Or I have to set in motion a life where I lie to my mother. I left Seth for lying and I do not want to become a person who does it and then justifies it as necessary. I want to talk to Abi, reply to her, but instead I screen all calls from numbers I don't know and I only call back the people who are clients or potential clients.

In this café-bar courtyard area of a boutique wine hotel in Brighton, I'm waiting for a new client and thinking about Mum out there on the mean streets of East Sussex on her bike. I've spoken to this new client a couple of times on the phone and he needs me to make an engagement ring for his girlfriend. He wants to propose at the end of the month and was hoping I would be able to make the ring quickly. 'I can't rush it,' I told him, 'it won't turn out right if I rush it.'

'No, no, I don't want you to rush, it's just it's our anniversary then, and I want to propose.'

Why leave it so late? I asked in my head. I thought of Seth, of course. How he persuaded me against my better judgement to have an engagement party two years ago. I was very proud of myself that when the inevitable happened and we had to cancel it while actually standing in the hall, dressed up and ready to party, I didn't say to him 'I told you so'. And Seth was good, too, in that he popped all the one hundred and fifty balloons and ate as much of the buffet as he could before we had to bin it.

'I'll see what I can do,' I promised the client when I dislodged the memory of how that night went from my mind. I told the client, Declan, to meet me with photos of his girlfriend wearing her favourite items of jewellery, to bring any ideas about the design and a list of her favourite things that could potentially be incorporated into the finished article. From talking to him it turned out that he didn't want a stone set, which would make it easier, but he did want an elaborate design. I'd wanted to meet at Beached Heads, of course, but this guy could only meet me in his lunch break from work without arousing suspicion from his other half, so I'm here.

A few steps away you have the main road along Brighton seafront with its attendant noise and busyness, beyond that the aqua-green railings that are punctuated by entrances to steep stone steps that take you down to the promenade and then to the beach. Yet, this courtyard feels secluded, quiet, like you could be in a large villa on a private island. There are huge parasols sheltering each table, which from above must look like a giant patchwork quilt with the seams made of daylight. I'm drinking coffee in an ordinary cup. Whenever I take a sip, I experience what feels suspiciously like a pang of missing Tyler. Obviously I fancy him, I won't pretend to myself I don't, but *missing* him? That's beyond ridiculous when I still have Seth texting me every other day and I don't know Tyler well enough to miss him. Or maybe I'm missing Seth and, because I don't want to, I've transferred those feelings to Tyler. That sounds far more likely.

I lazily flick through my photo album of Polaroids of my work. In the back of my head I am still looking for inspiration for reworking Melissa's locket from her birth mother into something new and wearable. I keep coming back to making the locket body into a watch and using lengths of the chain to make the strap. I can't make clockwork, though, and if I got someone else to do it, the price of the piece would be astronomical. But time seems so appropriate for Melissa: she had that locket waiting for her for such a long time.

'You're going to hate me, I know, but I had to do it.'

My fingers holding the corner of a page and about to turn it over, stop working. My heart feels like it has been fired out of a cannon and is now rattling against my chest, trying to find an exit point from my body. I carefully, slowly, raise my head to her.

'Look, I know it's not good what I've done.' Abi pulls out a chair and sits down opposite me. 'But hear me out, please?' She rushes on whether I intend to hear her out or not: 'You dropped a huge bomb-shell on me. It's not easy to just walk away from that. I only wanted to talk to you.'

I lower the corner of the page in my hand, sit back to regard her. She has wonderfully shiny hair. It's sleek and hangs just below her shoulders. She has perfectly applied make-up – she obviously learnt long ago which shades of blacks and browns emphasise the shape and size of her eyes, which tints of foundation give her a flawless complexion, which hues of lip-gloss endow her lips with that glossy sheen. She's wearing a well-cut, expensive-looking suit jacket over a burgundy, ankle-length dress.

We're dressed the same. Except my outfit has probably cost a third of what hers has. My burgundy dress was from a shop I found in the Markets in Leeds five years ago, my jacket was found in a second-hand shop in Wakefield and was taken in to fit only after much pressure on Mum three years ago.

'Aren't you going to say anything?' she asks.

I shake my head. If I don't say anything, I can truthfully say to Mum later, 'And I haven't spoken to them since.' There is no way I can avoid telling Mum any longer.

'Why won't you talk to me? Aren't you completely freaked out? Cos I am. My whole life has been this huge, colossal cover up. If you met my mum and dad, your mum and dad, you'd know they were never the kind to do this sort of thing. I've always thought that they only did "it" three times, you know, what with them having three kids. But they . . . Before marriage and everything. And they just gave the baby away and got on with it.'

'*That's me you're talking about in that matter-of-fact tone,*' I want to say to her.

'I keep thinking we're supposed to be hugging and crying and stuff because of those TV shows.'

Reluctantly I smile at her because I know what she means. This feels a little under-emotional and inappropriate. We're supposed to have exchanged letters, phone calls and arranged to meet on neutral ground. We're supposed to have prepared ourselves for this moment once we knew the other existed. The meeting is meant to be a moment of great apprehension followed by great joy. Real life isn't like it is on the telly, why do I find that so surprising?

'Are you seriously not going to say anything?'

'Who was the guy with the engagement ring?' I ask.

'My child's father. He wants us to get married. If I'd let him, he'd have actually come today to get you to make an engagement ring. But I'm not marrying him.'

'How old's your child?' I ask. '*How old's my niece or nephew?*' I should have asked.

'I'm not telling you until you tell me why you've been avoiding me.'

'It's too hard to think about.' I can feel tears filling up my eyes, ready to fall. I shake my head to will them away. 'It's too scary.'

'Aren't you even curious? Not even a little bit?'

'Yes. But it's all been sprung on me by, I don't know, Fate I suppose. I didn't mean to meet you. It was never meant to be like this.'

'It's the same for us, too.' Us. She's including my parents and my brothers in that. I wonder who else knows about this when my own mum doesn't.

'I was also avoiding you because I haven't told my mum. She—'

Confusion dances on Abi's face for a second. 'Oh, you mean your adoptive mum.'

'I *mean* my *mum*,' I reply. My tone is as sharp as the saw I use for piercing and in response Abi draws back a little. I won't have her do that, I won't have her dismiss or downgrade my parents – she has her mum and I have mine. 'I haven't told her I met you,' I say carefully. If I expect her to choose her words wisely, then I should do the same. 'Mum lives with me. We've only just moved down here and my dad died recently. I don't know what the thought of all this will do to her. It's not as simple as being curious. If I'd gone looking for this I could have prepared myself and her a bit more. I didn't, so I'm having to get my head around it in pieces and chunks. I need to steel myself to do the next thing. I would have called you back eventually.' *At least I hope I would.* 'But not until I'd told my mum and not until I was sure I was ready to deal with another chunk of this.'

Remorse, pure and potent, crawls across Abi's face as she looks down at her hands and my fluttering heart begins its frenetic dance of escape again.

'What have you done?' I ask.

Abi's right leg begins a slight but anxious jiggle. 'I, erm...'

'What have you done?' A terrified type of nausea creeps up my throat.

'She couldn't wait. She wa—'

'Oh, God, no.' I need to leave. I need to get out of my chair and run as fast as I can away from here. In case of a fire, you're told to exit the building as quickly and safely as possible; to leave everything where it is and run – do not, under any circumstances go searching for your belongings. I need to run, I need to not sit here and allow my belongings, the people I belonged to, to come for me. I need to run but I can't move. 'Please, no.'

'She only wants to see you,' Abi pleads.

Abi turns to the glass wall that separates the courtyard from the inside of the hotel's café and beckons to the person beyond. I didn't even notice someone sitting there, I hadn't felt the weight of someone observing me, scrutinising every inch of me while I spoke to my sister.

Run. Get out of this seat and RUN! Inside my head that is what I'm screaming. I cannot move. She's going to walk out of there and right up to this table and she is going to speak to me. And I am going to...I don't know what I'm going to do.

She looks nothing like my mum. My mum has peach skin and grey-streaked brown hair that she's finally stopped dyeing, and she wears Bermuda shorts to ride her tricycle.

This woman looks nothing like my mum. She looks almost exactly what I would expect to look like in seventeen years' time, but not like my mum. I think I want to get up and hug her. I think I want to scream at her, 'WHY?' I think I want to walk away and never, ever look back.

'Hello,' she says. A simple and honest greeting. All the best conversations start with hello. I do not know what to say so I say nothing.

In her hands she holds a small cream box, on the outside of which she has drawn and coloured butterflies. She places the box in front of me. 'This is yours,' she says as if she doesn't mind I haven't said anything in response to her 'hello'. 'I made it to keep my pictures of you.' She sits in the seat that Abi has vacated and she smiles at me like I'm a baby. 'Talei. That's what I called you. Of course you won't remember that. It means precious one.'

I think I want to cry. I want to break down and cry until there's nothing left inside me. A teardrop escapes from my eye and lands on top of the miniature version of the butterfly box I keep my precious photos in.

I stare at the woman opposite me.

She continues to smile at me as if she knows me, as if she's always known me. As if I am all her dreams come true.

I can feel a pressure building up in my head that will cause me to explode. Gently, because I don't want to disturb it, I push the box off my photo album, it really is nothing to do with me.

I am on my feet now. The woman smiles a bit deeper, but there's sadness now and desperation. She doesn't want me to leave. How can I stay here, though?

'Talei,' she says.

'*Stop calling me that!*' I shout inside. '*That isn't my name!*'

'Clemency,' she says then, as if she has heard my silent screams. 'Please, just stay for a while?'

I shake my head. *No, no, I can't.*

'Please?' She says it so quietly, so kindly, I know I should change my mind.

No, no.

She picks up the box, holds it out to me. 'Take this at least. It's yours. I made it and kept it for you.' My teardrop, perfectly preserved, sits on top of the butterfly, distorting in that tiny section the look and shape of its lilac and pink wing, causing a small patch of black veins to bulge.

I don't want to take anything from her, but are there photos inside? Of me? Of her? Of the other people who are my family? My trembling hand rubs at my face, tries to dry the tears then reaches, still shaking violently, for the box.

'I wish you wouldn't leave,' she says.

I wonder if that's what I thought about her, the last time I saw her. I'm curious if in my small baby world, governed solely and wholly by the instinct to stay alive and knowing who was meant to do that for me, I looked at her with my blurred newborn eyes as she walked away and thought, *I wish you wouldn't leave.* I wonder how long I cried for her, wishing she would come back for me, would take me in her arms, would fill my senses and world with that smell of mummy that all newborns are meant to know instantly. Did it occur to her as she walked away, went off into her new, childless life, that I would be craving that? I doubt she thought that thirty-seven years later she'd be saying the same to me.

I fumble in my jacket pocket, the nylon lining too cold and slippery to provide any comfort until I come across the emergency tenner. It always sits there, a neatly folded escape route if I need to pay quickly without rooting through my bag for my purse or the unsheathed change languishing at the bottom. I slide the brown note under my cup to stop it blowing away.

'We'll see you soon,' she says. She smiles, although there are probably as many tears in her eyes as there are in her voice.

'Yes, we'll see you soon,' Abi adds.

I wonder if either of them realises how much of a threat that sounds. How dangerous it is to someone like me who has been tricked and then trapped into this situation.

I nod. I find it hard to be rude and unfriendly to people, even at some of the worst times of my life. This is, it has to be said, one of the worst times of all. But I still can't come right out and say no.

19

Smitty

Seth. I need him.

Around the corner, on the busy main road, I stand in the archway entrance to the Ship Hotel, hidden from the street, and from the two people I've fled from, and with a shaking hand take my mobile from my pocket.

He'll understand. He always understands. He'll know what I should do now. I call his number. He answers halfway through the second ring, I imagine he looked down, saw my name, snatched up the phone and hit the answer button.

'Smitty?' It's only my name, but his voice, that I've been hearing for twenty years, soothes its way through my sensibilities. My body unclenches, my chest, which I hadn't noticed was tight and almost immobile, is now freer, air is entering and exiting my lungs properly. Suddenly I'm able to breathe at the sound of him. I need him.

'I—I...I—I...'

'Smitty? Is that you?'

What am I doing? I don't get to call him. He's not for that any more. We're not together, he's not that person.

'Clem, are you OK?'

'I'm sorry, I'm sorry. I shouldn't have called you. I'm sorry. Bye. I'm sorry.'

With still-shaking hands I cut off the call. I shouldn't have rung him, it was instinctive, what I've been doing for more than ten years. Even before that, if I had a problem, Seth – not Dylan – would be the first person I called. In a moment like this, calling him was the obvious, natural thing to do. I have to break that habit, learn to cope on my own.

A white and aqua-green taxi pulls up outside the hotel. Its passengers spill out, laughing, joking, collecting suitcases from the open boot as if the world hasn't been turned on its axis. When Dad died, that was the most hurtfully confusing thing of all: everyone carried on with their lives as if something huge hadn't happened. Half of my world had been devastated and everyone acted if nothing had happened at all.

The taxi driver talks the whole way back to my flat. I must have answered because he kept talking, asking me questions, and there were no long awkward pauses that told me I was meant to be replying.

I am still shaking, trembling violently, as I open the door. When the door clicks shut behind me and I turn the corner into the main part of the corridor, the enormity of what happened descends again and I can't breathe. I try to draw air into my chest. Nothing happens. I can't breathe, my chest is on fire, my heart is like a speeding train without wheels that races and races on the spot.

'Clemency!' Mum calls from the living room. 'Is that you?'

My photo album, my bag, the coin change from the cab ride, my purse I didn't put away, my heavy bunch of keys, and that box create a huge sound when I drop them so I can push my hands against my chest, try to force air into my body.

Nothing happens, no air enters my lungs. I've had a panic attack before. It was like this. I couldn't see. Couldn't stop myself from shaking. Couldn't breathe.

'Clemency?' Mum calls.

Breathe. Breathe. Breathe. I need to breathe.

I hear Mum put her puzzle aside, take off her glasses, get up from her seat. Or maybe I am imagining hearing all that since my breathing is vociferous, gasping, and my heart is thundering in my ears.

'Clemency.' Mum is horrified when she arrives in the corridor. At the mess from all the things I dropped, probably at the state of me.

She comes to me, circles me with her arms. When I was ten I came home in tears at the things some of the boys at school said to me. The names they called me, what they said about where I came from, but mainly from the way that my cousin Nancy shrugged and said, 'Well, it's true.' Mum had put her arms around me. 'I'm going down to that school tomorrow – if their parents don't skelp their hides, I will,' Dad shouted. That was one of the few times I'd seen him so angry.

'Hush, now, Don,' Mum said. In her arms, so close to her, I could smell the sweetness of her make-up and the bleach that she'd used to clean the kitchen. 'That's not important right now. The only thing that's important is our Clemency.' She stroked her hand over my hair. 'You'll be OK, Sweetheart. You'll be OK.'

'What's happened, love?' Mum says to me twenty-seven years later. She is filled with concern, over-brimming with worry.

I can't speak, nor breathe, nor stop my heart from the pain it's causing me by hammering so fast. She draws me closer and because I am taller than her I have to stoop to rest my head on her shoulder, to let her comfort me. I can smell the lavender and rose citrusy tang of her perfume, the vanilla and cocoa scent of her conditioner.

'Is it Seth? Has he done something?' she asks. 'Said something?'

I shake my head.

'You need to tell me what's happened, love, if I'm going to make it better.' That's what mums do, isn't it? They make it better, even if you're really old, your mother puts her arms around you and makes it better. She doesn't turn up out of the blue and try to give you gifts she's made and call you by a different name.

Mum's hand strokes down my back, soothing me. Considering she doesn't do this very often, she's very adept at it, seems to know where to press her hand so I feel better, my body relaxes, I start to be able to breathe. Maybe it's because we're all the same. Maybe, no matter who we are, a touch in the right place, a caring, loving hug will cure whatever ails us. Maybe I should have hugged that woman. Maybe I would have felt something for her if I'd let her put her arms around me and do what my mum is doing to me now. It might have changed everything if I'd given her a chance.

'Come on, love, I don't like to see you so upset,' Mum says. 'You're not one to cry unless something is terribly, terribly wrong.'

She's right. I carefully pull myself together, upright, out of her hold until I can stand up by myself. Inhaling, exhaling, is a blessed relief – my entire body rejoices in this simple action. I rub at my eyes until they are dry, then furiously dry my hands on the folds of my dress.

'What's happened, love?' Mum asks. I like that her accent, her real, natural one, comes out when she talks sometimes. It takes away the parts of her that I tend to fight with and lets me see the one who knows how to hug me and tells me I'm her whole world.

'I just…' I need to tell her. It's going to hurt her, my mum with the Yorkshire accent who hugged away my worries. I have to tell her. I can't not. 'I just met my— I just met the woman who gave birth to me.' It wasn't that hard to say after all. It was really quite simple and easy. Like breathing – until you can't do it properly. I did it properly, I know I did, because Mum doesn't look all that shocked.

In fact, her face develops a smile and after a few seconds to let the news sink in, she says, 'Well, that's wonderful news. There's no need to be upset, it's absolutely wonderful news.' She reaches out and takes my hand, and I know then that she's seen the small butterfly box that lies on its side with a few black and white photos of a baby spilled out on the parquet. She saw the box and worked out what had happened. 'Come and sit down and tell me all about it. It really is the most wonderful news.'

20

Smitty

Mum doesn't truly think it's wonderful news. I can tell by the way she's trying *really hard* to smile. From the fear spinning in her eyes, I can tell she thinks it's terrible news but she doesn't want me to have another panic attack. She's also doing what I did whenever she asked if the other children were still picking on me at school – she's pretending everything's fine, like I did with her, to spare my feelings.

'Now, tell me what happened,' she asks gently. She holds my hand and I know her eyes are pretending that I'm not wearing this jacket, which she hates so much even though she did take it in for me. 'Did it not go as you expected?'

'I didn't plan it, Mum!' I'm screeching. Screeching like the deranged person I feel I am right now.

'Sorry, sorry,' Mum says. She soothes me with her tone, with a few strokes on my hand. 'Tell me what happened.'

'You have to promise you'll listen to me without interrupting and you won't get cross or think I'm lying. You have to promise.' I sound like I'm fourteen.

'I promise.'

'Which part?'

'Pardon?'

'Which part do you promise about?'

Mum stares at me blankly. Actually, I sound like I'm five.

'Which part do you promise about, Mum?' I insist, still in five-year-old mode.

'All of it?' she replies.

I sigh, relieved. If she does get upset I can remind her of the promise she just made.

'Will you tell me what happened now then, love?' Mum asks. She's showing remarkable restraint in the face of my completely irrational behaviour.

'About two weeks ago I went to a nursing home and I met this old woman who was a neighbour of . . . of those people.'

'Which people?'

'You said you wouldn't interrupt.'

'I know, love, but I'm not completely understanding you.'

'She was Finnish, this woman. It was her that they . . . those people . . . got the idea for the butterfly box from.' Mum nods, now she understands. 'And she said that the daughter of those people works there.'

'Daught— Sorry.' Mum purses her lips to stop herself talking again.

'I went to talk to her then I changed my mind but she came out to the car park and I spoke to her. We had a chat and I found out that she has two brothers and her parents have been together for nearly forty years. So her parents are both my— ' I'm finding it hard to say the word in relation to them and me. 'I came home and I wanted to tell you but I couldn't, so I didn't. She kept ringing me but I didn't reply. So she tricked me. Got someone to pretend to want to talk to me about an engagement ring, you know, the man I was telling you about who wanted one done really quickly? Then suddenly she's there and then *she's* there.'

I look at Mum, expecting her to speak. She doesn't. Her lips are still pursed, as though waiting to be sewn together.

'*Her*,' I say.

'Your birth mother?' Mum says when she realises I need her to talk now.

I nod. 'Yes. My birth mother.' I can say it now that Mum has said it first. She's broken the taboo so I can too.

'I bet you were a bit surprised.'

A bit surprised? A BIT surprised? A BIT SURPRISED?! 'Yes. It was too much for me, I had to get out of there.'

'You must have been in all sorts of turmoil. I bet she was, too.'

I glare at my mother. I don't mean to, but it sounds like she is putting herself in *her* shoes.

'Don't look at me like that, Clemency. It will have been a very difficult thing for her to do, to come and meet you like that. She won't have known what your reaction would be, and imagine seeing for the first time someone you haven't seen since you gave birth to them. Imagine how terrifying it would be. She must have been in bits anticipating it.'

At least she got to anticipate it, not like me, who had it sprung on them, I think in reply. 'I suppose you're right,' I say.

'I'm sure she's thought about you all these years and I'm sure she was just bursting with the things she's wanted to say to you after all this time. Did you speak to her at all?'

I shake my head. 'She gave me the box with the photos that's in the corridor, but we didn't really speak.'

'Would you like to see her again?' Mum asks.

'Would you mind if I did?' I reply.

I'm carefully watching my mother: I see the edges of her smile touch her eyes, but don't take over them. I see the strain from having to smile, the clenched tightness of the hand that is not stroking my back. 'It's not about me, love, it's about what you want,' she says eventually. So eventually that inside I think: *I knew it! I knew you didn't think it was wonderful news.*

Mum doesn't want me to get hysterical again, which is why she is playing along for now. She's probably hoping this whole experience will have put me off, will stop me from even contemplating getting in touch with them again.

'I don't know what I want to do,' I say. As much as it's the truth, I need my mother to be honest with me. She needs to tell me what she really thinks. Over the years there's been one abiding message that she has sent me: do not go looking for your other family. Do not do anything that will upset what we have. Dad wouldn't have minded, but with Mum, it was obvious it would have been to her a huge rejection of who she was and what she had done for me. Why she was now pretending not to mind could only have been down to her not wanting me to become hysterical again.

'OK, love,' Mum says quietly. 'I understand.'

21

Abi

To: Jonas Zebila
From: Abi Zebila
Subject: Total disaster!!!!!
Wednesday, 24 June 2015

Well, that went well, NOT!

I set up a meeting with Clemency using Declan as bait through her job and she completely freaked out and ran away when she saw Mummy.

I actually felt sorry for Mummy. When I told her I'd arranged a meeting, she looked so happy and terrified at the same time. She didn't say much on the way there, and when she sat in front of Clemency for the first time the look on her face reminded me of how I felt the first time I saw Lily when I gave birth to her. I was completely freaked out. I loved her, don't get me wrong, and I thought my heart was going to explode because I had such a fierce need to hold her, but I was also really shocked. I kept blinking at her, wondering if she was real and if she had really come out of my body and if she was really something to do with me. Mummy was looking at Clemency just like that.

Mummy was devastated when Clemency left and I was gutted, too.

This is all so messy and horrible when they always show you on the telly people just getting hugged and being happy. This is all so big and out of hand, I wish, wish, wish I'd never done as Mrs Lehtinen asked and gone to check on Clemency. Then I'd never have known and none of us would be feeling this bad.

I'd never know, though, what hypocrites Mummy and Daddy are. There, I said it. You've always said they were, but I wouldn't accept it because they're Mummy and Daddy and we're supposed to do what they say and believe them about *everything*.

On the way home Mummy didn't talk much at all. She stared out of the taxi window, then as we pulled up outside she said, 'I have to tell your father.' She said it like he was going to blame her or something.

'What about Gran?' I said, because sometimes I don't know when to leave well enough alone, do I?

Mummy breathed out slowly and angrily. 'Yes, her too.'

I can hear voices downstairs – they're quite loud but not loud enough for me to be able to make out what they're saying so I'm guessing Mummy's told Daddy and Gran. I wonder how they'll take it? Thankfully, Lily is staying over at Declan's so she won't witness any shouting.

What do you think I should do now? Do you think I should leave Clemency alone or get back in touch? What if I ask her to do a DNA test with me so we can see if we are related? Because it could still all be a huge coincidence. And if it is, that means she can go back to her life and Mummy and Daddy will realise they need to be honest with us in future if they want to avoid things like this happening.

What if she's not the only one? I keep thinking about that possibility. What if there are more children they had adopted who are going to turn up one day?

I think a DNA test is probably the best way forward and then we'll all know where we stand.

Love,
Abi
xx

22

Smitty

'Would you mind if I did see my birth relatives again?'

It's two days later. Mum is about to go for a ride on her tricycle and I am going to work via Beached Heads. In the past two days we haven't talked about it. Mum left me to look at the baby photos on my own and I didn't. I simply put the box on top of the other butterfly box at the bottom of the wardrobe, looked at the composition, realised that it looked like the big box had given birth to the smaller box so had to move the smaller one to my bottom drawer where I keep my hats, gloves and scarves, which I'm obviously not going to be going through any time soon.

Mum, who had hoisted herself up on to her bike, steps down again and turns towards me but doesn't rotate enough to look at me fully – instead she stares mostly at the sea. It's rough out there this morning; the waves seem wrathful, their anger appearing as a white, frothy rage upon the tops of the grey surf. I wonder if that's what Mum is feeling inside about this.

'Why do you ask?' she replies, quietly.

'Because I want to know how you honestly feel.'

'How I honestly feel,' she murmurs. A long pause then: 'Yes, I would mind.'

Oh. I thought she might try to sugar-coat it, talk around it, gauge if I'm thinking of doing it.

'Why?' I ask.

We've never talked about this openly, it's all been carefully, wilfully, left unsaid.

The pads of Mum's hands are covered by fingerless cycling gloves and she raises her fingers to unclip her Hell's Angels-inspired helmet and take it off. She ruffles her hand through her hair and continues to contemplate the sea. The first line of 'Somewhere Beyond the Sea' plays through my mind as I watch her.

'Because I'm scared you're going to get hurt again if you do this. What if they reject you? How will that make you feel?' She hooks her helmet on to the padded leather seat of her tricycle, traces the outline of one of the flames.

'I don't know. I haven't thought it through. I just know— '

'I have. I *have* thought it through and I know you wouldn't be able to withstand such disappointment and hurt.'

'Mum, I've withstood worse.'

'Like what?' she demands.

'Like what?!' I'm amazed she has to ask. 'Like losing Dad. Like my— my relationship with Seth coming to an end.'

'They're not like being rejected by your mother.'

'But she's not my mother, is she? You are. At the moment I barely know her.'

'At the moment.' Mum seizes on this so immediately I wonder if she has been waiting for me to say something like that. 'When you do get to know her, you'll start to think of her as your mother.'

And you think that will mean I'll love her more than I do you, I think. Mum acts like my love for her is fragile, transient and transferable; as though I'll never have room in my heart for two people with the tag 'mother'. As though it is a forgone conclusion I'll reject her in favour of the person who was there first – even though I have barely met the woman.

'How do you know that?' I ask.

'I just know. A mother knows these things.'

'So if you had a biological child you'd have loved them more than me?'

'Don't be ridiculous.'

'How is that ridiculous, Mum? You're saying that if I get to know someone I'm biologically related to they'll replace you, so why is it ridiculous for me to say the same about you having a biological child?'

'It's not the same,' she snaps. Defensive, angry, my mum snatches up her helmet, plonks it heavily down on her head. Fumbles crossly at her chinstrap. 'You know very well that it's not the same.'

'I really don't,' I reply. Out loud. For once it's something I don't keep in.

'Yes, you do,' she hisses at me. She mounts her bike, indignation on her features, and without another word or look in my direction, she cycles across the small car park in which we stand and heads to the cycle path that snakes around the building and towards Portslade, the opposite direction to the one I'm heading in.

'I really, really don't,' I say to her retreating form. She doesn't indicate as she turns the tight corner around our building and rides off at speed.

'So much for it being wonderful news,' I mutter.

Tyler's coffee is going to have to be nothing short of spectacular to see me through this day.

23

Smitty

'I've had a few ideas about what to do with your pendant but the one I keep coming back to is a watch because of the connection with time.'

'Oh, right,' Melissa says. She sits on the other stool in my work-shop and her attention doesn't rest anywhere for long – she looks like a meerkat, constantly looking around, trying to take it all in. My workshop is neat and tidy. In general, I am not neat and tidy, my life is full of chaos and piles of paper and several dozen jobs I meant to finish. But wherever I work has to be immaculate, tidy, precisely organised. I have hung all my larger tools on the walls, there are designated pots for the files, the daylight lamp sits in the left-hand corner of my bench, in the right-hand corner is the soldering area.

'It's so cool in here,' Melissa says suddenly. She spins herself on the stool. 'I'd love to have a place like this to work in, instead of just an office.'

'I'm really lucky, I know.'

'It's not so much luck, you have worked for this, haven't you?'

'Yes.'

'So, not luck as much as good fortune from hard work.'

'I suppose you're right. About this watch idea...?'

'I don't really wear watches.'

I open up my sketchbook, already ashamed about how bad my sketches are. 'Have a look at the idea I had,' I say. 'Excuse my sketches. The locket would become the watch, it'd be protected from knocks by the locket lid, and the strap would be made from linking the chain together in small sections, like this.'

Melissa stops fidgeting and visually exploring and gazes down at the lines I've made with a soft, 2B pencil. Her face, sceptical when she first looked, changes. 'Actually, that looks kind of . . . nice. Classical, but still funky. If people even say "funky" any more.' She turns her head to the side, examines the photo of the pendant pinned to the corner of the page and the drawing more carefully. 'I really like it. So what's the problem?'

'Why would you think there was a problem?' I ask.

'Because you could have emailed me those sketches.'

'Well, the only sticking point is I'm not a watchmaker, I'd have to outsource that and it would be a bit pricey. I don't want to get quotes until I know you at least like the general idea.'

'I do like the general idea, yes.'

'Excellent, I'll get some quotes and we'll decide how to proceed from there.'

'Great.' She picks up my set-square that lives in one of the pots beside the soldering station. 'What do you use this for?'

'Drawing straight lines, mainly. It's useful for checking I've cut a line straight if I cut a piece out of sheet metal, too. Also, I check edges where two ends of a ring meet because they need to be perfectly straight otherwise soldering is a nightmare. Well, nightmare is a bit of an over-exaggeration, but you get what I mean.'

Melissa nods thoughtfully. 'I've been wanting to call you,' she says like a wayward churchgoer finally returning to the confession booth.

'I've wanted to call you. In fact, I did call you. You're right, I could have done this by email or phone. I wanted to see you, though.'

'I'm glad it's not only me. And I'm glad you did call. I know I went a bit funny when you asked if I'd met my bio mother, but I don't often get to talk about it all to someone who's been there.'

'Have you met her?'

'Yes.'

'Not good?'

'I don't know what good is. We kind of get on, but she can be a bit full-on. I get it, I get that she's been storing up all this love and emotion and she's desperate for us to have some sort of relationship, but.... I've got parents. But then I feel guilty thinking like that because she's only doing her best. And she didn't want to give me up. It's so hard sometimes. Hence the therapy.'

'How did your parents take your deciding to search for your birth mother?'

'They were supportive, up to a point. I didn't realise until I was eighteen why they made such a huge thing of giving me a locket on my sixteenth birthday – and reminding me to wear it until it was something I put on automatically. I then can't start wearing the other one, can I? Which kind of taints the locket I wear and makes me feel a bit odd about my parents, and it spurred me on to contacting you about making this locket wearable.'

'That's not fair of them.'

'They always said that they didn't mind me searching, encouraged it even, but then when I actually did it, they started to get a bit funny. Really down on mothers who give up their children. Kept reminding me that I might find out something I didn't like – that I could be a child of rape or incest or something hideous like that. It was true, but God, I didn't need to hear it from them of all people. I think some of it was genuine concern, but there was a lot of jealousy too.'

'Tell me about it.'

'Are yours being funny?'

'It's only me and my mum now and it's a different situation but she won't admit she's jealous, too.'

'What are you going to do?'

'I don't know.' That's the kicker. I don't know what to do. I want to meet my birth family again, properly, but then I don't. What if, like Melissa's parents said, I find out something I don't like? It's not as if I can simply not search for them, they're in my life. Finding out things I don't like will come from getting to know them. Something I can avoid.

'Have you applied for your adoption papers?' she asks.

'Oh, no, it's too late for that. Way, way too late.'

I explain to her the bare bones of the situation and she listens with her eyes wide and her mouth open. At the end of it, she is silent for a while. So am I. Listening to myself tell this tale to someone else who hasn't been there makes it sound horrific. Horrific as in the emotional devastation those tiny, fragmented meetings have caused. It might have been better if it was planned. If everyone had a chance to think, to pause before each meeting, maybe I would not have this much panic rushing through me.

That is it. Panic. *Thank you, Melissa*, I think. *Talking to you has let me understand that I'm in a state of panic, even when I am not having a panic attack. You can't think properly when you're in a state of panic.*

'You could still apply for your adoption papers,' Melissa says. 'It might stop anyone from rewriting history if you do meet them again. Some of the stuff in my adoption papers... It reminds me when my birth mother gets all misty-eyed about how she was wronged and I was "stolen" from her that at various points she could have made another decision. It wouldn't have been easy by any stretch of the imagination, but still there was another path she could have taken that she didn't. Some of it, of course, was from the social worker who seemed to be really judgemental, but some of it... Written by her, so there's no doubt. I have to remind myself she was young and in an impossible situation but, you know, blah, blah...' Melissa smiles. 'I don't say that to her, of course. I never say anything like that to anyone – no one wants to hear it. That's why I wanted to call you – I got the impression you might understand.'

I nod. She's got me thinking now: I should apply for my adoption papers. See if I can find out what was going on at that time, what was being said, possibly what they were thinking when they packed me up in that butterfly box and sent me to live with someone else.

'What's this?' Melissa asks. She holds what looks like a mini chimney-cleaning brush with gold and black bristles on a thin metal rod.

'It's a polishing brush.' I point to the others that sit in their stand. 'Each one gives you a different type of finish – that one is for a satin finish, this one will give you a bit more texture. There's also traditional sandpaper of different gradients that I use to smooth down edges. Plus those files. For me, the finish of a piece is everything – it's an important part of making jewellery.'

'Will you teach me?' Melissa asks. When she says it she seems surprised herself.

'Teach you?'

'To make jewellery. Will you teach me how to do it?'

'I'm not sure I could.'

'All right, how about you make a ring or something and I come and watch you?'

'If you want. But I'm sure you'll find it pretty dull. I don't because I love what I do, but you might.'

'I really, really won't. Tell me what all these tools are for and then another time I'll come back and watch you work.'

'Yeah, if you want.'

Melissa beams at me. 'And if you want me to be with you when you get your adoption papers, I'd be more than happy to do that.'

'Thank you, thank you so much.'

'All right.' She brushes off that moment of intimacy with a brisk tone. 'Tell me what this is?' She has picked up the saw that hangs on the hook at the edge of my desk, the thin but sharp filament-type blade only secured in the clamp at one end to make it less dangerous.

'Come on now, Melissa, you don't know what that is? And you can't even guess?'

'Hey, you! I wouldn't take the Mick out of someone brandishing a dangerous weapon. I could saw bits of you off.'

I relieve her of my implement. 'We call it piercing not sawing.'

'Oh, right. What's that?'

Piece by piece I take her through the equipment in my workshop, all the while the thought of applying for my adoption papers grows and grows in my mind.

Part 4

24

Smitty

Clem, I'm not sure what's happened,
or why you couldn't speak, but if you need me
I'm always here. Aš tave myliu. I've always loved you.
I miss you. S x

I've read that message over a hundred times – every day I call it up
and stare at it and allow the beads of hope to string themselves
together until a long and seemingly endless chain of possibility has
been spun around my heart. Maybe I should give him another
chance. Maybe we can work it out. It's these messages that make me
think about giving him another chance. The desperate, angry,
demanding, 'talk to me' ones strengthen my resolve, but these ones
that remind me that I'm loved by him, how much I love him... they're
the ones that make me want to try again.

There's a picture in the original butterfly box that lives at the
bottom of my wardrobe of Seth and me on our first foreign holiday
together, where he learnt that phrase – to write it and to speak it. It
was one of those trips that nothing remarkable happened on, but it
was so special because we were together and for as long as I could
remember that was enough. Being together, talking, messing about,
planning his next move at work, were more than enough for us.

I sat in the window seat of our room in the very expensive hotel that we stayed in, staring out over the square. It was March, but there was so much sun. The air was soaked with it and I sat wearing Seth's large Aran jumper and a pair of knickers. I had my camera in my hand and was trying to capture the light, snatch it from the world outside and store it in the photo that would come out of the camera. None of the angles seemed to fit properly, none of them would show how beautiful the light was, the city was. None of them ensnared that brilliant red-orange of the terracotta-coloured bricks of the square, none of them showed the perfect lines of the sandstone town hall building. Through the camera lens, everything seemed flat and ordinary and bland, instead of vibrant and lively and *alive*.

'Come back to bed,' Seth called. He was face down in the soft, white sheets, covered by the thick duvet.

'Not until I've taken the perfect photo of the way the sun hits the town, what it does to it.'

'Coming back to bed is far more fun. Come here and I'll prove it to you.'

'You've got nothing over there that interests me, buddy.'

'Not even a huge lump of amber that I bought when your back was turned yesterday?'

'Show me, show me, where is it?' I dashed to the bed, climbed on and bounced up and down. 'Show me, show me.'

Seth rolled over and grabbed me, tugging me down on to the bed beside him. 'That was too easy.'

'Lying about materials for my work.' I laughed. 'Are there no depths to which you will not stoop?'

'Apparently not. Although I did buy you some amber yesterday so I'm not technically lying, but rumours of its size may well have been greatly exaggerated. The man who sold it to me said it was a superior quality so it cost a bit more.'

'Right,' I said. I handed Seth the camera as he had a longer arm than me, the distance at which he held it would make a better picture.

'Click' went the camera, and it snapped us as we mostly were at that time: dishevelled, together. Seth placed the camera on the bedside table. 'You don't sound like you believe me. He was a good bloke was Irmantas,' he said.

'I'm sure he was.'

Seth shook his head in despair. 'Can I get my jumper back?'

'No, I'm wearing it.'

'I'm cold.'

'Well, get back under the covers then.'

'I can't. I need to go do something and I need my jumper. The others are all the way across the room.'

'What, you mean our room that is the size of a postage stamp?'

'I'm cold,' he insisted.

'Oh, for the love of—' I replied. I struggled out of the jumper and threw it at him. It landed over his head, draped down on to his face. He removed it and underneath the large woollen folds he had a huge grin. I realised a moment before he threw the jumper across the room out of reach that I'd been scammed for the second time in less than a minute.

'You make it so easy!' He laughed, his face filled with the mirth and kindness I'd noticed in him the first time we met. He was older, his face more lined than back then, but his smile, his innate pleasure at the life he had, was still there – it ran through him like the barely formed words in rock. Dylan, who dipped in and out of my life at the best of times, had all but dropped me when I got together with Seth. This was his prediction come true and, Dylan claimed, he couldn't stand to watch us be loved up when we were both still too young to be that settled. Dylan spoke as though me falling out of love with him and in love with Seth way before New Year's Eve 2003 was somehow done to spite Dylan.

Still laughing, Seth's eyes greedily ran over my naked body, surveying it as if he wanted to secure mental images of each line and curve to pore over at another date. He hooked his fingers into the top of my knickers. 'You're still wearing far too many clothes for my liking,' he said. The laughter had gone, replaced by a deep throaty lust. He threw my knickers in the same direction as the jumper then immediately pushed apart my legs. His fingers dipped into me and I inhaled sharply. 'Do you like that?' he asked.

'Oh, yes,' I gasped.

He pressed my legs open wider, lowered his head, pushed his tongue—

'Clemency!' My mother's voice snaps me out of remembering and forces me to stand upright from my slouch over the shopping trolley. My face feels hot with guilt and shame, as though she knew what I'd been thinking about when she barked my name. She marches down the aisle with a huge bottle of cream soda – nightmares of Christmases and New Years past – in each hand.

She glares at me, at the phone in my hand. 'Is that another message from that man?' she asks sternly. *That man* being Seth, of course. Anyone would think that I had run into him a few times and he wouldn't leave me alone. Or that I'd revealed to her how badly he treated me. But I hadn't because he hadn't. We had to split up because he lied to me and that was extremely shocking to me. Because he'd never been like that, had always been open, honest, trustworthy, the horror of finding out that he was capable of betraying me was far too much for me to stick around. Mum, though . . . She'd never liked him. She'd never liked any of my boyfriends but she tolerated the others because they never managed to take me away from her. Which Seth did and I don't think she ever forgave him for that.

'Yes, it's a message from Seth,' I say.

She seems so certain that people can take me away from her: Seth, my birth family. Mum acts like I am fickle with my affections, that anyone who looks in my direction will replace her. Which is ludicrous. I've come to a decision, though, and I need to tell her.

I push the trolley down the aisle after her and we turn left, heading for the front of the store into the tinned goods aisle. Mum has a list in her hand and marks off each item with a small, neat flick of her wrist as she leaves a tick. Mum has gone eco-friendly since she got her trike: for the weekly shop she rides to the supermarket, we shop together, and I drive all the bags home while she, safe in her ecological saintliness, cycles home. I almost, *almost* fell into the trap of explaining to her that getting me to drive was still adding to our carbon emissions, but caught myself just in time. There are some battles not even worth considering, let alone fighting.

'Mum, I think I'm going to ring Abi, my, erm, my sister. I think I want to see them.' I say this barely above a mumble because I know she'll hear. She's only hard of hearing when it suits her.

She takes the news as well as can be expected: she stops in front of the tins of soup, and treats them to the long, silent glare and rigid expression I should have been receiving.

'I think I want to meet them. All of them.' I feel sorry for the soup, the look she is giving it could boil it in its tin. I decide to buy the soup and hide it in my bedroom because it's taken the visual equivalent of a bullet for me today, so the least I can do is buy it and not eat it. I continue hesitantly: 'Even if it's just once, I'd like to find out what they're like. Maybe get some questions answered.'

'I understand,' she says, monotone.

Really? You might want to tell your face that because it's saying to the soup and me that you don't understand at all, I think. Instead I say: 'Thank you. For understanding.' I almost thanked her for letting me do it but I caught myself. I am thirty-seven, I don't need her permission. Her blessing would be good; her blessing would silence – or at least quieten – the guilt demons that have been plaguing me, but I do not need her permission to do this.

'When you go to meet them all, I'll come with you,' she says. She smiles then, treats the soup to a beatific grin before she turns it on me. Now she has decided how she can make herself a part of this, can control it to a certain extent, her whole demeanour has unclenched and she radiates the relaxed, swaggery aura of a person who has expertly restrained a wild stallion that had dared to bolt.

Dad. The ache of missing him echoes through every part of me. He would have understood, he would have told her not to get involved. He would have stuck up for me and stopped her. If she still insisted, he would have told me to do it in secret and tell her after the fact. If Dad were here, no way would this be happening according to Mum's rules.

This isn't fair. She knows it too. I open my mouth to tell her, to explain that this is something I need to do on my own, for me. I shouldn't have to consider her feelings in a situation that will already be fraught and emotionally difficult.

'Fine,' I say.

'Good.' She grins at me, beams at the soup. I take the tins of mulligatawny off the shelves and drop them carefully into the trolley.

'Excellent idea, Clemency,' Mum says. 'We'll have soup for lunch. That was your father's favourite. Let's go and get a crusty loaf as well.'

'I'm so sorry, soup,' I whisper.

'Oh, and if that man keeps sending you messages, you should think about calling the police,' Mum adds, on a roll now. 'He needs to understand you want nothing more to do with him.'

I think I'm going to shout at her. Right here, in this supermarket, I think I am going to start screaming at her. First Seth, then my birth family, and now this poor unsuspecting tin of soup. I know I'm being ridiculous about the soup, but sometimes I feel pushed to the edge of sanity by her.

I want to scream at her that if she hadn't pretty much let my cousin Nancy get her own way about pretty much everything, I would still be with Seth. I would not have moved down here, I would not have met Abi and I would not be about to eat a tin of soup whose sole crime was to take a glare bullet for me.

'Right,' I say instead. Because I am a coward. And Seth should have known better.

With me, March 2015, Leeds

I wanted my bed. Having been sent home by Dad and Mum to go see Seth, get some proper sleep, give them some space (although they didn't say that), what I wanted more than anything was my bed. 'I'm not going anywhere, Smitty,' Dad had reassured to get me to leave. 'I promise you, I'm not going anywhere.'

Seth wasn't in, although it was one of his days to work at home, but I'd noticed by the sheets and blankets folded neatly on the arm of the sofa that he'd been sleeping in the living room. He did that whenever I wasn't there because he hated being in our bed without me. I was going to make it up to him, that was the plan. I needed to be with Dad and Mum at that time, but afterwards I would refocus my attention on Seth. But not right then. Right then, I wanted to sleep for a little while and pretend that my world wasn't crumbling around me. That my dad wasn't about to leave me.

My fingers pulled back the duvet and a scent – delicate and fleeting – rose up to greet me. It was so momentary, like a trick of light, that it was gone before I properly noticed. I continued to pull back the duvet, certain it was nothing, until I saw what was obviously a long, brown thread, visible against the white sheet. It wasn't thread, of course, it was a long, straight brown hair. As if the shock of the moment had temporarily wiped my memory, my hand went to my head to check that the hair in the bed didn't belong to me. Mine was, of course, black, short, tightly curly. Seth had shaved his light brown hair to a grade two again, it wasn't his.

I dropped the duvet back into place. Someone else had been there, that was obvious. I knew he wouldn't, though. Seth wouldn't. Seth would have just had someone over to stay. That was why he was sleeping on the sofa. He hadn't mentioned the person who was brunette, most likely female, was staying during any of our nightly talks because he didn't want to upset me. Although why one of our friends staying would upset me was a mystery. Unless it wasn't a friend. A non-friend with straight, long brown hair.

Shaky, unsteady on my feet, my stomach a tumbling barrel of nausea, I sat on the floor beside the bed. This wasn't the time to deal with this. Maybe in a month or so, when...I didn't want to think about that either. There wasn't much I could deal with and this was one of those moments. On the wall of photographs that I was facing, my eyes were drawn to the 'With Seth, finally!! January 2004' picture.

My gaze then moved over to the photo of my family from last Christmas I had tacked on to the wall. On the left-hand side of Seth stood my cousin Nancy. She had her arms looped around her daughter Sienna's shoulders as she grinned at the camera, but she was also, very noticeably, leaning on Seth. She was very clearly making her physical presence felt. She only needed him to be weak one time, he only needed to let his guard down for a moment, and we would be here: I would be finding a long brown hair in my bed.

This was not the day to deal with it, though. This was not anywhere near the right time to have to deal with it.

25

Abi

To: Jonas Zebila
From: Abi Zebila
Subject: Update
Friday, 26 June 2015

Dear Jonas

I think it's safe to say that this is a different place now. I thought things were about to get a whole lot worse when Daddy and Gran found out and I wasn't sure how Ivor would take it, but I don't know, it's like someone has thrown all the windows open and a cleansing wind has blown through here and the heavy weight that was hanging over us – this secret our parents have had all these years – has been swept away.

It's not one big love-in by any stretch of the imagination, but it feels like a more honest house. Ivor took the news pretty badly. When Mummy and Daddy told him, he looked so *injured* first of all. Like they'd betrayed him by having a child older than him or something. He sat and stared at them for the longest time.

'Is there anything you want to ask?' Mummy asked. And he just got up and walked out. Reminded me a bit of Clemency, to be honest. Since then, he's not talked about it, changes the subject if someone tries to bring it up. It seems he really does feel this was done to spite him.

Now the secret is out, Gran, who seems more stable, just glares at Mummy a lot but doesn't say anything. I hate to think of her doing this, but it seems like Gran has been using this big secret as a way to control

Mummy all these years. Mummy still does everything for her, but it now seems to be on an equal footing. It's hard to explain because it's never been a blatant control thing, we all know what Gran is like, but now it's not there any more it's plain to see that it was there originally, if you see what I mean?

I can't tell what's going on with Daddy. He seems a bit shell-shocked but also a little relieved, almost. Maybe he hasn't liked lying all these years and he's pleased the truth is finally out. Him and Mummy haven't rowed about it since the other night, not within my hearing anyway. They've stopped talking altogether, it seems. I mean, not in a nasty way, they seem to just stare at each other a lot and not find the right words. I think neither of them wants to be the one who starts that conversation about what they did all those years ago.

After Ivor walked out, I went over and hugged Mummy and she put her arms around me and held me so close. I don't even remember the last time we did that. I also told Lily-Rose. I don't think it's fair that the adults know something so big and she doesn't. Despite Mummy and Daddy's rubbish example of being parents, I'm not going to do that. I want to be as honest as possible with my kids. I told her I had a sister that I had only just met and she said, 'Does that mean she's my sister?'

'No, she's your aunt, you're her niece.'

'Will she come to our house for her tea?' she asked.

'I hope so,' I said. That was as honest as I could be. I've decided to leave it up to Clemency to get in touch and that decision is like a mild form of torture. I want so much to see her again. Just like I want you to get in touch.

You know what, though? Even if Clemency doesn't get in touch, I got to hug Mummy for the longest time so, for that alone, I'll be eternally grateful to Clemency.

Get in touch, please. Even if it's a three-word email to tell me you're alive, that would be enough.

I love you.
Abi
xxxx

26

Smitty

There's a plain white envelope labelled

Clemency Smittson

between us on the wall we're sitting on.

It's been between us, weighted down by a large pebble, on this wall that bisects the promenade and beach in Worthing for more than half an hour, since we collected it. Neither of us wants to be the one to pick it up. Both of us have been attempting conversation but it dries up almost straight away because we know the envelope has to be opened.

Abi is dressed for work because that's where she was this morning. She went into work as normal, then I met her a little walk away so that I could drive us here to Worthing, somewhere no one we know is likely to see us. We were here two days ago – another sneaky half-day holiday for Abi. She suggested in one of her earlier texts that we get a DNA test so we both know where we stand and I thought that was a good idea.

'Do you want me to do your hair for you?' Abi asks me. I knew from the way she kept picking at her nails and sucking in her cheeks and nodding slowly to herself that she'd been psyching herself up to saying something, but I didn't realise it would be this.

She's being kind, I know. Judging from the look of her and the look of her mother, she's probably thinking any further meetings will be smoother, will have them more accepting of me, if I sort out my hair.

I get that, a lot. My hair is a mass of shiny, midnight-black squiggly lines, fat ringlets, wavy curls and tight frizz that hangs down to my cheeks. It's not that bad, I don't think, it's a part of who I am, but for other people, the white ones who say if they were black they'd have an Afro, and the ones who spend hundreds of pounds a month on getting their hair perfect and can't understand why I don't comb it or straighten it, my hair must mock them because the only category it fits into is 'Liked by Clemency Smittson'.

With Dad, September 1985, Chapeltown (Leeds)

'Excuse me, I need your help.' Dad's voice was so loud and different amongst the chatter of these women. They were so pretty and glamorous and had dark skin just like me. Dad was the odd one out for once. Usually it was me who was the odd one out, but here everyone looked like me and no one looked like Dad. Or sounded like him.

'You all right, love?' one of the ladies asked. She was probably the prettiest, she had big, big hair, all shiny and black. I liked her eyelashes best. They were super, super long – when she blinked they touched her cheeks and I could see the gold fairy dust on her eyelids.

'Aye, I need your help with my daughter's hair,' Dad said.

All the women stopped talking and laughing and chatting and reading their magazines, to look at me. The only sounds in there were the droning blowing of the big dryers and the reggae music playing on the radio. I stepped closer to Dad, held his hand a bit tighter. I didn't like everyone looking at me. People were always looking at me because I was the odd one out and I didn't like it. At all.

'Is this your daughter, love?' the lady with the fairy-dust eyelids asked. She put down the hairdryer in her hand but kept hold of the hairbrush with black bristles that looked like a microphone as she came towards me. She was as tall as my dad because she had gold shoes with high, high heels.

'Aye, yes. Say hello, Clemency,' Dad said.

'Clemency, that's a right pretty name.' The woman was crouching down, she smelled of bubblegum.

'Can you help me? I need to learn how to plait her hair. Without making her cry. She cries if I try to do anything to it.'

The lady stood up again. 'Where's your wife, love?'

'It's a long story,' Dad said. Mum wouldn't have liked him bringing me here. It was like the time I asked her why I didn't look like her and it nearly made her cry – Dad bringing me here would make her cry. 'Suffice to say, it's me that has to learn to do this. Can you help me? I'll pay.'

'No, it's OK, love. You'll have to wait, but I'll teach you what I can between customers. If you want, you can come back next week with a proper appointment and I'll teach you how to wash her hair properly.'

'That would be good,' Dad said. 'Wouldn't it, Clemency?'

I nodded.

'We'll be back next week,' Dad said when we were about to go home.

'She's a lovely girl,' the pretty lady said. 'So good.'

'She is that,' he said. 'Are you sure I can't give you any money for your time?'

'No, it's nice to see a father taking care of his daughter. I hope your wife appreciates it.'

'We both appreciate each other,' Dad said. 'You get no prizes for bringing up your children properly – and so you shouldn't.'

Mum never said a word about my hair, not ever, not once. She used to cry sometimes when she tried to comb my hair and I would cry because it hurt so much. She would look at my hair on a Saturday afternoon when Dad took me out to get us out from under her feet, and I would come back with a new hairstyle and smelling of the dark green Dax the woman taught Dad to slick on the partings between the plaits. She would say nothing on Mondays and Thursdays when Dad would sit on the sofa and I would sit on the pancake-flat green velvet cushion on the floor in front of him while Dad greased (that's what the woman called it) my hair and redid the plaits. Mum never mentioned my hair at all when Dad started to do it – like a lot of things, she just pretended it wasn't happening.

'No, you're all right,' I say to Abi about whether I'd like her to help me with my hair. I suppose I should be offended, but I'm not. It really doesn't bother me what other people think about my hair nowadays.

'I didn't mean to upset you. I just thought if you wanted some tips...'

'I'm not at all offended. It's sweet of you to ask, but I like my hair like this.'

'*Really?*' She's openly horrified.

'Yes. You could sound a little bit more disgusted by the idea I might like the way I look, though. I won't be at all upset.'

'Sorry,' she says. 'Sorry, sorry. Mouth running away from brain, there.'

'No worries,' I say with a laugh.

'Have you ever had your hair straightened?' Abi asks. When I raise an eyebrow at her, she lifts her hands in surrender. 'Just asking, out of curiosity. Not pushing it as a lifestyle or hairstyle option.'

'No. My dad wouldn't let me for years. He even had a stand-up row with a hairdresser once who wanted to put relaxer on my hair.'

'Why? Not that my mum or dad ever let me get a relaxer. It wasn't till I went to America to stay with my aunt that I got one. Daddy was so mad.'

I have an aunt in America. Interesting.

'The hairdresser was teaching Dad how to look after my hair from about the age of eight, and when I was thirteen she said she was going to put a relaxer on it and Dad said no, I was too young. The hairdresser didn't think so and they had a huge row about it. Right there in the shop in front of everyone.'

'Seriously?'

'They were like two prize fighters going toe to toe. She kept saying that it would be easier to care for my hair and Dad kept saying he didn't want easy if it meant putting strong chemicals on my head. And she was saying how lots of girls my age had it done. And he was saying he didn't want me looking like everyone else if it meant doing that and I'd be able to decide for myself when I was eighteen. You have never seen the likes of it. Everyone just sat there with their mouths open.'

'Your dad sounds really cool.'

'He is. He was. Still is, I suppose. All those things he did in the past that made him cool happened, so he is cool. He seemed to "get" me, if you know what I mean? Even from an early age if I asked him a question he'd answer it. Age appropriate as they say, but he didn't like to keep secrets and stuff from me. Drove Mum up the wall – she's one of those "don't talk about it and it's not happening" types.'

'Yeah, my mum's like that,' Abi says.

I smile to myself, training my eyes on the envelope.

'I meant our mum, our mother,' Abi says. 'Oh, I don't know what the hell I'm supposed to say.' She stares at the envelope, too. 'Do you want to open that thing and then we can decide what to do next.'

'Bossy, aren't you, for a younger sibling?' I say.

'If you don't boss, you don't get heard.'

'OK. But I'm not opening it.' I didn't need to open the envelope because, just like I didn't need to look at the pregnancy test result I threw away in Leeds, I knew what they were going to say.

Abi's face creases with incomprehension. 'What?' she asks.

'I have no need to. I know what the results are but I'm guessing your family are needing some extra reassurance, which is why you suggested the test.'

'No, that's not why I suggested it. I did it . . . Never mind. I'll open it then.'

We have similar fingers, square at the end rather than tapered. Dad had the same shaped fingers, too. My dad, that is, not her father, *our* father. I can understand why she was frustrated before, it's hard to keep track; to know what to say without causing offence. But I've been thinking of it as Mr Zebila fathered me, Mr Smittson 'dadded' me. Mrs Zebila is my mother, Mrs Smittson is my mum. I wonder what they'd think if I said that to them? If any of them would take offence at how they've been categorised.

The sound of the envelope being ripped open is magnified, incredibly loud above the sound of the people and the surf and the doom that is about to befall us rolling in the distance.

The sound of reading is quite loud, too. I can almost hear her eyes moving back and forth over the lines on the page. And then she gasps.

I turn to look at her. 'What?' I ask.

'Oh no, oh no, oh no!' she says dramatically. Her eyes are wide, the lines of her face are taut with shock and horror.

'What's the matter?' I ask again.

'I can't tell you. I don't think you're going to want to hear it,' she says gravely.

'Just tell me. I don't care what it is, just tell me.'

She shakes her head. 'It says...' her voice peters out. She sighs, then swallows hard. 'It says something horrible. It says I've got a big sister who keeps running away, who makes jewellery for a living and is probably going to have a serious sense of humour failure in about two minutes.'

I blink at her a few times. 'Really?' I say. Maybe I wasn't as sure of the results as I thought I was.

'Yes. You and me, baby, we're sisters. And there ain't nothing you can do about it!'

'And, hey! You cheeky cow, what were you saying about the results being something horrible and me running away?'

She waves her right forefinger at me. 'Sense of humour failure!' she sing-songs at me.

I grin at her. Then needle her in the side with my forefinger. She yelps, dodges away from me and laughs. She seems so happy that I am her sister. Watching her laugh, unbridled joy gushing out of her, I realise that the emotion branching through me like a fast-growing tree is happiness, too. I am lucky. I have a sister. And it is the woman next to me. Laughing like nothing bad could ever happen now that we've found each other.

Part 5

27

Smitty

Their house is absolutely massive – you could probably fit about five of Mum and Dad's house in here. Without moving my head, I glance sideways at Mum. She is staring at the orange-brick house with double-glazed sash windows and black-and-white tiled path, and probably wishing she hadn't come now. Or rather, that I hadn't come, which is what necessitated her pitching up with me.

It's odd seeing it finally, the house where I could have grown up. Abi says they've lived here since her parents got together and she's moved back in during the last few years. It is grand and imperious, all of Mum's nightmares come true. She had tried to insist that we meet somewhere in Brighton, at a café or restaurant, but I had to gently tell her:

a) 'This meeting isn't about where you would feel most comfortable, but where I would feel most at home.' (Absolute wrong choice of word that raised a high red colour in her cheeks and elicited the bullet glare.)

b) 'I wanted to meet all of them in one go to get it out of the way and Abi's grandmother is housebound so she rarely leaves the house.'

Mum had continued to insist on 'neutral ground' so we were all on 'an equal footing' until I said, 'Fine, if that's what you want you can simply not come and we'll go for a "neutral ground" meeting at another date.' After that, meeting at their house was acceptable after all.

We stand outside the house, fifteen minutes early, having already walked three times round the large oblong-shaped block as we were very early. I didn't want traffic or, more importantly – Mum's sudden need to do 'stuff' (like dust behind the radiators in all the rooms and de-junk the hair-clogged shower) right before it was time to leave, to make us late. She was nervous in Lottie, now she is creeping closer to a full-on anxiety breakdown.

It would have been better if this house, their home, was a hovel or even the same size as the one we lived in for most of our lives. When we lived down in Lewes our house was large – not as large as this, judging from the pictures I've seen – but it was nice and in a well-to-do area. I'm not sure Mum ever got over the fact we had to move up to Otley because Dad lost his job in the recession of the early eighties and we had to live in a small, two-bed cottage. I loved the cottage, it was my home, but I sometimes saw the way Mum looked with envious eyes at her brother Colin's house, and knew it hurt her that we had been so 'reduced'.

I place my hand on her shoulder and she almost leaps out of her skin. 'It'll be fine, Mum,' I reassure. I'm not used to seeing her so nervous and unsure of herself. She's always been so confident and self-possessed. 'I'm sure they'll be nothing but grateful towards you.'

She nods.

'You don't have to do this, you know,' I say. It's partly to comfort her, it's also to allow myself the chance to hear that out loud. If I hear it spoken, which makes it sound possible and true, maybe I'll believe I don't have to do this. Maybe I can change my mind and walk away and not open myself up to the chance of another rejection of who I am.

'Do you think you'll ever want to trace your biological parents?' Seth asked.

'I don't think so.'

'What, not at all?'

'All right, I admit, sometimes when Nancy's over and she's joking around with Mum and Dad, I do feel like I don't fit into the picture of the three of them together. Like they're the family and I'm the one watching from the outside. It's only sometimes, but at those times I do wonder what it'd be like to be surrounded by people who I look like.'

'Being surrounded by people who you look like can be overrated,' he replied.

'Yes, but at least you've had the chance to find that out for yourself. I have to take your word for it. It's not an issue if you don't get on with your parents. I'm not allowed that. If I dare say anything about the way Mum is sometimes... I get put in my place pretty quick.'

'Put in your place by who? Have they met her? Do they know she can be a bit... *much* sometimes?'

My body bristled with loyalty and protectiveness. No one, not even Seth, was allowed to pick up on my mother's 'quirks'. I loved her and she drove me crazy, but I bore the brunt of it so I got to comment.

'Don't get upset, I'm not saying she's a terrible person, and God knows she hates me with a passion, I've just seen the effect she has on you. I'm asking who puts you in your place if you mention how... *much* your mum can be?'

'It's hard to describe, but over the years, if I've ever broken ranks and had a moan, I'm almost always met with an attitude that I should be grateful I wasn't left to rot in a children's home or that I wasn't aborted, that Mum rescued me.'

'People say that? They actually say that?'

'All the time. When you're adopted you're kind of fair game. There's a story that plays in people's heads: either your adoptive parents are saints or you were stolen from your birth parents. There's never any middle ground. And either way, you have to be grateful and understanding of both sets of parents' feelings.'

Seth gathered me to him, kissed my neck and held me as close as he could. 'I hate every single person who has ever made you feel like that. If I ever hear someone say something like that to you, they'll be surprised by what I say in reply.'

'It's not your battle, Seth.'

'Course it is. We're a team, Smitty. We're a family. And families look after each other and stick up for each other.'

'I suppose they do,' I replied.

'And if you want to search for your birth parents, I'll support you and do whatever I can to help you find them, and if you don't want to find them, I support you in that, too. Whatever it is, you know I'll always be by your side.'

I liked the way he said 'always'. I knew he meant it.

I've rung the doorbell.

I wasn't sure if I should do that or if I should knock. Decisions about doorbells or knocks on wooden, stained-glass-panelled doors shouldn't be so fraught, I know that, but I wanted to make a good first impression. Or second impression in the case of *her*. And fourth impression in Abi's case. (I haven't told Mum I've seen Abi because she told me she would come when I was meeting *all* of them so there was no need. Obviously that argument would stand up in a court of law; in the Court of Mum I'd be toast.)

The royal blue door flies open and Abi is standing there. Her other brother lives in Montenegro, apparently, so can't be here today, but our eldest brother will be present. So will her grandmother and her parents.

The air around her froths and foams with the desperation you feel when you're about to meet the family of the person you love for the first time. I remember the sheer terror I felt when I brought Seth to properly meet my parents – my stomach was in knots and I had to keep getting up to wash my hands they were so slick with anxious perspiration. He'd passed (just). He'd been similarly nervous when I met his folks and I'd passed with flying colours. I hope it's like that for me today. I hope I pass. I hope they like me.

'Hi,' Abi says. She grins at me. We've spoken, briefly, every day since we had it in writing that we are sisters. She has been so nervous about arranging this, and on top of what I feel, I truly hope it goes well for her, too.

'Hi,' I reply.

Her gaze goes to Mum. I told her I was bringing my mother, and she probably assumed I was doing so for moral support – not because Mum is so anxious about the thought of me 'defecting' to another family that she has become like the KGB during the Cold War era – always on the look out for any signs of changing loyalties.

'This is my mum, Heather Smittson,' I say. 'Mum, this is Abimbola, Abi, who I've told you about.'

Abi's face, twenty-four and unblemished and unlined, is moment-arily surprised. It never occurred to her in all that time when I said 'Mum' that she would be white.

'Hello, Abi, pleased to meet you,' Mum says.

'Oh,' Abi says, shaking herself out of her surprise. 'Hello. Great to meet you.'

She's looking at me now, her gaze is inquisitive, wondering, I suspect, what it was like to grow up with non-black parents, what my experiences of the world were, how it felt to be me. One of the doors off the wide, carpeted corridor opens and a little girl of about five appears. She leans her head out first, staring at us from the other end of the corridor. She takes in the sight of us standing in front of the open door. Whispers drift out of the room, but she ignores them, and the rest of her appears. She is dressed for church – well, how Mum used to dress me for church: knee-length pink dress with a lace, round-neck collar, white socks pulled up to the knees, black patent shoes, pink ribbon bows at the tops and bottoms of her plaits.

She approaches us along the corridor, hesitant but only slightly so. I would never have had the confidence to do this at her age, I would have stayed in the room with the rest of my family, waited until I was told what to do, what to say, how to act. When she arrives at our end of the corridor, she presses herself against Abi's leg in the way I've only ever seen children do with their parents. I have another niece. I call Sienna, my cousin Nancy's daughter, my niece instead of my second cousin because that's how she feels, but here is another one. Another niece who, quite strikingly, judging by the way Mum is staring at her with a mixture of shock and recognition, looks exactly like I did at that age.

'*Lily*,' Abi hisses. 'I told you to wait with Grandma and Grandpa.'

'Are you my new auntie?' Lily asks me.

'Yes,' I reply before I have thought about how that will make Mum feel.

The little girl nods thoughtfully, considering this. 'Who are you?' she asks Mum.

'That's my mum,' I reply.

Lily nods again. 'OK,' she says. 'Hello.'

'Hello,' Mum replies.

'Everyone's waiting in the living room,' she adds. 'We're not allowed to talk. We all have to sit there waiting for you. Even Uncle Ivor and he always talks. He talks and talks and talks and talks. I think he likes to hear his own voice.'

Abi seizes her daughter's shoulders, massages them gently as if she might find a mute button if she presses in the right place. 'This is Lily-Rose, my daughter,' she says. Abi slips so easily from being twenty-four, young and naïve, to being twenty-four-year-old, long-suffering mother and highly mature.

'Nice to meet you, Lily-Rose,' my mother says before I can say anything.

'Are you going to meet Grandma and Grandpa now?' she asks.

I need to get out of here. I need to be away from here and in my bed with the covers pulled up over my head. I need to be in Leeds, in my bed with the covers pulled up over my head, waiting for Seth to come home from work and tell me that all of this has been some twisted dream from that plate of dodgy scallops I ate when we went out for our anniversary the other night. I need to not be here.

'Yes,' I reply. 'Yes, I am.'

'That's good. They're nice,' she says.

With my small butterfly box, yesterday, Hove
Light poured into my bedroom. I had the windows partially open and the outside noises filled the room with the chaos of life passing by the flat and the relentless forever of the sea. With that noise as an accompaniment, I didn't feel so lonely while I did this, even though I needed to do it alone. If things were different, if I was still with Seth, he'd be waiting outside, ready to come in and be with me the moment I told him I needed him.

There were three photographs in total. All black and white. I am wrapped in a blanket, swaddled and unable to move, in the first one. The top of my head is covered with a crotcheted or knitted bonnet, my face is staring up at the camera, unfocused and unsuspecting. On the back, my date of birth is noted, along with: 2.42 p.m. The time of my birth, I guessed. I hate my birthdays. I love other people's birthdays, I lavish such attention upon them and plan so much, but mine...I, thankfully, didn't have many friends so there was no need to worry about being annually forced into holding birthday parties and events nor having surprise parties sprung on me.

I closed my eyes, allowed images from earlier birthdays to develop in the darkroom of my mind. For most of my childhood it was the same: I would sit like a statue in front of a delicious-looking cake, candles burning, while Mum and Dad, and quite often my cousin Nancy and her parents, would sing a song that was meant to celebrate my time on Earth. Every time I would make a wish and blow out the candles. I would make the same wish every year: to never have to do this again, to never have to mark another one of my birthdays like this again. Who would want to celebrate one of the worst days of someone else's life?

For her, the woman who gave birth to me, it wasn't a culmination of nine months of excitement and apprehension and planning – it was the end of the wait to be rid of me. It was the day when she could get on with the rest of her life having finally shed the millstone that was growing inside of her. How could I celebrate that, knowing this was when the burden of my existence began?

I hated birthdays, every single one of them. I hated having to pretend that it was a time of celebration and joy and welcoming me to the world, when it was simply the day I arrived before I was shunted off to be someone else's problem.

I opened my eyes to look at the next picture. It was of me, not as squashed, my eyes more open, obviously a couple of weeks older. I was in the butterfly box, dressed in white, one arm is reaching out towards the person taking the photo, the other is resting on the side of my face, as if I am thinking very hard. The date on the back confirms what I thought, it is me two weeks later.

In the third photo I am about a month old. The only part of me showing is my face. My eyes are wide and focused, staring at the camera, waiting, it looks like, for something to happen, something to be said. Two weeks later (I know it was two weeks later because that's another day my parents always marked by taking me out for ice cream and pop) I began my life in the Smittson house. I gained a new name, I gained two parents who wanted me.

As well as the date, it also said: '*Always in my heart, Precious One*'.

The box was a little large for only three photos. I wondered if she took any more. If she kept any more, or these were the only three she had. The ones she kept all these years. Our handwriting was very similar: clear and plain, no elaborate swirls or embellishments, we want to get our points across in a quick, no-nonsense fashion. I stared at the handwriting for longer than I did at the photos. My real connection to her, a real reminder that beyond looks, there was something else we had in common.

The sea began to pour into my brain, the world was loud and magnified, too much of everything filled my senses. I dropped the photos back into their too large box and I stretched out on the floor – there was too much going on around and inside me to move, to get on to the bed, to sleep.

I closed my eyes. At that moment I wanted to make a butterfly using silver wire. I had tried in the past. I fashioned the wings with my fingers instead of pliers, and they had both been that perfect squashed-heart shape, almost perfectly symmetrical. But they'd been fragile, even though I'd used five-millimetre wire; they'd been too fragile for me to add the glittery bead for the head or the wrapped wire shape for the body. It should have worked, I should have been able to make a butterfly, but all I was left with were two wings – flawlessly shaped, infinitely too delicate to be of any use to anyone.

I'm like that, I decided as I lay on the beige carpet of my bedroom. I was too delicate, incomplete and unconnected to be of any use to anyone, least of all the woman who gave birth to me.

I have no idea what is going to happen next. They are all in this room in this house that should look like a museum, should look cold and unloved because it is so large and it looks from the outside that the inhabitants could afford staff to do the hard stuff. But inside it's similar to the type of home I grew up in: carpets that are worn in patches, coats and jackets hooked over the banister, shoes placed haphazardly on the shoe rack. A helmet resting on the platform of Lily's green and blue scooter.

This corridor is clean, the floor vacuumed, the skirting boards and paintwork dusted, but it's also comfortably, ordinarily messy. These are normal people. Normal people who I am related to.

My breath goes in and out at a normal rate. Everything here is normal.

The lounge is bright, two comfortable, beige leather sofas are the centrepieces to the room. One faces the large, ornate fireplace, the other sits to its side, both of them crammed with cushions of various shapes, sizes and colours. There's a vivid red carpet, there are photos lined up neatly on the mantelpiece, each in gold frames. There is a chandelier, swollen with crystal teardrops, hanging above us. The large window has gold curtains with a red vine pattern.

I want to note the quirks of décor so that if I never come back, I'll still have memories of the place where I could have grown up. And I need to take in these details to avoid looking at the people in front of the fireplace.

Mum is two steps behind me, and Abi, who was behind Mum, navigates around us and, holding Lily's hand, moves past the sofa to join the rest of her family who are lined up like Russian dolls in front of the fireplace.

'Welcome home,' the man who stands at the centre of the people in the room says. My father. Not my dad, my father, the man who donated half of my genetic code. 'It's good to see you at last.'

With that, my mother, the woman who donated the other half of my genetic code, bursts into tears. Abi is not far behind her, and then, shockingly, my father turns his back to me, rests his hand on the mantelpiece and begins, it seems from the shuddering of his shoulders, to cry too. Abi's grandmother sits in a wheelchair beside Abi's brother, staring at me, her face wet with tears. Abi's brother is barely controlled and I know he wants to break down, too. Only Lily looks more confused than moved. I dare not turn to look at Mum in case she's at it too.

I wasn't expecting this, I wasn't braced for crying people; I wasn't prepared to not cry myself. I'm not crying, am I?

I touch my face and my fingers are dry when I look at them. No, I'm not crying. Is that normal? Am I normal? Why am I not crying? Why? Because this really is no crying matter.

28

Smitty

'If you ever say that about my daughter again, I will put you six feet under!'

I'd never heard Dad's voice like that: so loud and so cross. When he laughed, my dad made a big noise. People used to look at him and start laughing, too. And when he was happy he used to talk really, really, really fast like no one could ever catch him cos his voice was like Roadrunner. And, sometimes, when he was cross with me he would talk loudly and send me to my room. But he never, not ever, shouted like this.

I didn't know what Uncle Colin had said to make him shout, but it felt like the windows were shaking when Dad yelled. We'd gone to Uncle Colin and Auntie Marcia's house for our Sunday dinner and we were all eating and Mum was saying how lovely the roast was and Auntie Marcia was telling Nancy to eat her vegetables like I was. Then Uncle Colin said something really, really quiet and that was when Dad slammed his fist on the table and everything rattled and everyone stopped talking and eating and I couldn't get to breathe properly.

'Girls, outside, now!' Dad said. 'Now!'

Mum put her hand on Dad's arm and that didn't do anything apart from make him look at me and Nancy and repeat, 'Now!'

Auntie Marcia got up and came over to Nancy who was really

scared, her eyes big and wide, and Mum looked at me and nodded quickly, like I should go as well. I got up and realised I was shaking and my eyes were wide like Nancy's. And then we were sitting outside on the back step, and I could hear lots of loud adult voices and then Dad shouted, 'If you ever say that about my daughter again, I will put you six feet under!'

What did he say about me? I wanted to ask Nancy. *What did he say that would make Dad so angry?*

I couldn't ask Nancy, she had her knees right up to her chest and she had her head on her knees and she had her arms around her legs and she was rocking back and forwards like a Weeble.

What did he say about me? I wanted to ask Mum and Dad. But they were inside and the shouting had stopped. No one was talking inside the house and Nancy wasn't talking to me outside the house. *What did he say about me?* I kept asking myself. *What did he say?*

'Come on, *quine*, we're going,' Dad said to me, and he bent his big, strong body and scooped me up. Dad didn't carry me much any more, I was too much of a big girl, but this time, he picked me and held me close. When I hugged him goodnight, he always felt like this, like the strongest man in the whole wide world.

I looked to the door, waiting for Mum to come out. 'Heather!' Dad shouted. 'You come now, or you don't come at all.'

Mum walked slowly out of the house, very slowly, like she didn't want to leave. Like she was actually thinking about 'not coming at all'. I was scared. That scared inside I sometimes felt when I heard the monsters moving in my room at night. When I saw funny shapes on the walls. But this was worse. Much worse. I didn't know what was happening or what Uncle Colin had said. Or what it was about me that made people say not very nice things all the time. Uncle Colin said not very nice things all the time, so did Nancy. Auntie Marcia said things sometimes. But this was the first time Dad had got so cross. Mum usually said they didn't mean it how it sounded and not to tell Dad because he wouldn't understand. She was right. Dad didn't understand that they didn't mean it, that's why he got so cross. He didn't understand.

'He didn't mean it, Dad,' I whispered, to maybe make him under-stand. 'They never mean it.'

Dad looked at me and he seemed a bit surprised. Then he looked at Mum. 'We have things to discuss,' Dad said to Mum. 'At length.'

But he didn't mean it, I wanted to say again. I didn't, though. I had a feeling that Dad wouldn't listen.

It's calmed down, thankfully. Almost as quickly as it started people stopped themselves from sobbing, pulled themselves together and we all, *all,* pretended that it hadn't happened.

Now everyone is sitting, chatting, and I am no longer the centre of attention. I've never liked being the centre of attention because I spent so much time as the odd one out, it's nice to be unnoticed. I am sitting on the sofa with a mother on either side of me. They sit close to me, like they want to hold my hand. Mum has her bag on her lap but she's poised, prepared to snatch up my hand if the woman on the other side of me goes anywhere near my other hand.

My other mother has her hands folded neatly on her lap. I don't know her as well as I know Mum, but she isn't relaxed, she seems set to grab me if the woman on the other side of me makes any sort of physical contact.

They are both silent for long periods then start to talk at the same time, stop to allow the other to speak and then lapse into silence again. Abi is chatting to her father in front of the mantelpiece, her grandmother sits beside them in her easy chair and seems to occa-sionally join in their conversation, but mostly she just sits still and stares at me. Lily and her uncle, my brother, are putting together the pieces of a brightly coloured giant floor puzzle of the world in the area under the window where all the toys are contained in two giant red tubs. After the crying, I had introduced Mum to them. Wary and confused, they all shook hands and said how pleased they were to finally meet, none of them relaxing their body language.

My brother is called Ivor, my father is called Julius, my mother is called Kibibi and my grandmother is called Soloné. There is food, placed on the sideboards and the side tables, tea has been made, everyone has seemed to have loosened up. To each other, probably to themselves, they are pretending that they are absolutely fine with what is happening, who has come into their perfectly ordered world. However, bubbles of awkwardness circulate the room, popping at different moments: I look up and see Ivor watching me when he should be pushing puzzle pieces into place with Lily; I notice Abi pointing to what could be invisible rings on her fingers as she talks to her dad, obviously explaining to him that the ones I wear are probably made by me; I am being smothered by the anxiousness that radiates from the two women on either side of me. All the while, Abi 's grandmother continues her motionless, silent vigil over me and my arrival in her home.

With Dad & Mum, March 1983, Otley

'We're not going back there, Heather.'

'He's my brother, Don, you can't stop me from seeing my brother.'

'You can see them any time you like, Heather. But you're not taking wee Clem over there. Not any more.'

'She and Nancy are like sisters, you can't separate them.'

'Aye, you're right. But Nancy can come here if they want to play together. My Clem isn't going over there for them to look down on. He actually said we had no idea where she came from so we didn't know what she might turn out like.'

'He didn't mean it.'

'Aye, that's what Clem said, too. She's heard all that before and you don't think there's anything wrong with it. You make her stay with these people when they say disgusting things to her and around her. The fact you can't see anything wrong with that, Heather, makes me very sad. She's our daughter. You don't let anyone speak to her like that. Especially not so-called family.'

'He's my big brother. He helped us out when we needed him.'

'He lent us a bit of money when I lost my job and we paid him back every single penny and you think that gives him the right to talk about a child like that? Any child would be bad, but our own child? I don't know how you can stand to look at yourself in the mirror.'

'He doesn't mean it. They don't mean it.'

'Come on now, *quine*, there's no need to cry. It's not so bad. Come on, don't cry. You know I can't stand it when you cry.'

'I'm doing the best I can for everyone.'

'I know, *quine*, I know. But we can't put Clem through that again. We're meant to protect her, not let other people hurt her, no matter who they are.'

'How long have you lived in this beautiful house, Kibibi?' Mum asks. She is finally able to speak without her sentence being accidentally interrupted by my other mother.

'Many, many years. I was born in London, but my parents decided to go home when I was sixteen.' I chance a look at her, properly. Her face is thinner than mine, she has longer eyelashes than me, her nose is the same shape as mine but smaller, her smile is like mine, though. We share the same smile. Although the same shade, her skin is smoother than mine, less blemishes, probably because more care and thought have gone into looking after herself over the years. She's wearing a two-piece skirt suit with short cap sleeves. Every one of the hairs of her head has been perfectly straightened and she wears it in a shoulder-length bob. She and Abi are pure style. 'My parents wanted me to continue to study in England, because I had been accepted to start university a year early, so I came here to live with Julius's parents because our families had been friends in the Duyalt Province in Nihanara.' She pauses, wondering if we either of us know where it is, I'd guess. 'Julius's parents had this house from when he was about ten years old. They rented it first of all, then his parents bought it.'

'That is a lot of history,' Mum says. She sounds patronising. I'm not sure if she realises it, but she is talking down to my other mother. 'What did you study at university?' Mum asks.

'I was going to be studying international business law . . . but I did not start.' Because of me. Because she got pregnant and had me.

For some reason, silence descends upon the whole room at that point, so everyone hears what she said and all the adults know what the unuttered part of that conversation means and it freezes their tongues, causes more of those awkwardness bubbles to explode all over us. I am the centre of attention again and my body becomes an inferno of regret and shame and guilt.

'Come,' Abi's grandmother suddenly orders. She speaks slowly, haltingly. 'Come here, child,' she adds. Without hesitation I stand and go to her. I have to crouch down because she clearly isn't able to get up.

'My eyes are not so good,' she says. 'I didn't see you when you were born. I want to see you now.' She examines me and I examine her. Did she mind not seeing me when I was born? Was she desperate to, but decided to not get involved because giving me up was for the best?

Abi's grandmother, *my* grandmother, seems to linger on every line of my face, every blemish, every facial nuance that might link me to her. She doesn't like my hair, I can tell by the way her gaze pauses at my mass of untamed curls and then moves on with a sliver of disdain in her eyes.

'You are truly a Zebila,' she says, still faltering in her speech. She has found enough similarities between her son, who I have not looked at properly yet, and me to say that. 'Welcome home, child... Welcome home... I can only thank God that... Mrs Smittson brought you back to us safe... I knew God would look after you... all these years, and in His infinite... wisdom He has decided... now is the time to bring you home... Thank you, Mrs Smittson, thank you.'

She probably doesn't mean to, she probably doesn't even realise she is doing it, but she has made it sound as if I have been in suspended animation, my parents, Heather and Don Smittson, standing like silent guards outside my suspension chamber, waiting to find the Zebilas so my life can begin.

'Mama,' my first mother says, 'Ta— Clemency is probably tired, this has probably been very overwhelming for her. Maybe let her come and sit for a little while longer.' She wants me back beside her on the sofa. She doesn't want anyone, not even a relative, taking me away from her.

'This is my grandchild. She has been returned . . . to me after many, many . . . long years,' my grandmother admonishes even though her words are still slow. 'I will speak to her for as long as I want.'

'Would you like to see some photographs of Clemency growing up?' Mum doesn't seem at all put out by how she was just dismissed as nothing more than a caretaker. She is on her feet and from her bag she has pulled out a photo album I did not see her stow away in there. It is white, covered with a plastic case, and between the plastic and the cover there is a picture of me. I am about eight years old wearing a blue hat with a pompom on top, a brown coat with a white fuzzy fur ring around the hood. I have green woollen mittens on my hands, and socks pulled up to my knees. I am grinning at the camera with all my teeth on show and my chin tipped forwards. I don't remember that photograph being taken, I don't remember being that girl in the photo, but I am happy. I remember being happiest when it was Mum, Dad and me.

My first mother, birth mother, biological mother, whatever I need to call her, gasps. She wants to see the photos, she wants to pore over them and possibly reimagine the life she could have had with me around. Everyone in the room looks at her, waits for her response to Mum's question.

In the space that follows her gasp, my grandmother states: 'I would like to look.' Mum was asking my first mother, everyone knows that. No one says this though, no one dares. Everyone simply pretends they don't notice the tension that stretches like a giant rubber band between my other mother and my grandmother. My grandmother has commandeered this moment, something offered by one mother to another mother, and made it her own.

'How about we all look together?' Mum says brightly.

'No, that's fine, you all look.' My mother is on her feet, picks up two of the plates, still laden with food. 'Tal— Clemency, would you mind helping me to clear some of these plates?'

This is her two fingers to what my grandmother has done: she gets the photos, my other mother gets the real thing.

The room continues to be shrouded with quiet and stillness until, plates in hand, we exit, closing the door behind us.

With Nancy, June 1987, Otley

'Why did you do that?' I asked Nancy.

She shrugged her shoulders and didn't look at me. We were sitting in her bedroom and I still had tears on my cheeks from being shouted at.

'But it's not fair, Nancy. You knocked over the pot of ashes, why did you tell them I did it?'

Nancy screwed up her pink mouth and looked at me like she hated me. She did that sometimes. Sometimes she would link her arm through mine and tell me I was the bestest friend she'd ever had, but sometimes it was like this – she got me into trouble and she looked at me like I was her very worst enemy ever, ever.

'Why, Nancy?' I asked her again.

She shrugged again. 'Cos you never get in trouble. It's always me. And it'd have been worse if they thought I did it. But you can't do anything wrong, not ever.'

'But I didn't do it.'

'Yeah, well, they think you did. All the time Auntie Heather says how well behaved you are and how you're such a good girl, and everyone's always looking at you and saying how nice your hair is and how darling you look. They're always telling you how special you are because you were chosen. They don't think you're that special now, do they? I bet they wish they'd never chosen you at all.'

Uncle Colin had walked into the sitting room that we weren't really allowed to go in, but Nancy said we should, and saw us in front of the pot of grandma's ashes, when all the grey-black dust inside was all over the floor and you couldn't see the gold, swirly pattern of the carpet. He had growled, 'Why you—' And then shouted for Mum.

When he said, 'Who did this?' I didn't say anything because I thought Nancy was going to tell how she had stood on her tiptoes to try to get her picture down and had knocked the black pot on to the floor.

'Clemency did it,' Nancy said. 'I told her not to come in here but she did it.'

I looked at Mum, then looked at Uncle Colin. And then Uncle Colin shouted at me. Told me I was evil, and naughty, and I would go to hell because I hadn't confessed. He said he was glad I wasn't a real part of his family and he was ashamed that Mum had brought up such a terrible child. He shouted and shouted and didn't stop until I was crying and shaking. Mum didn't give me a hug, she just looked sad and unhappy and like she believed Nancy that I did it.

Mum didn't even say anything when they sent me to Nancy's room then sent her there because she shouldn't have followed me into the sitting room. I couldn't even tell Dad about this because we weren't supposed to go to Uncle Colin's house any more after what he said about me when I was little.

'That wasn't fair,' I said to Nancy.

She shrugged again because she didn't care.

'One day, my real mum and dad are going to come for me and I'm going to tell them about this and they'll make you tell the truth.'

Instead of looking scared or worried or upset, Nancy sat up on her bed and smiled at me. She smiled at me like the cat in the *Alice in Wonderland* stories – big and wide and a bit scary. 'I'm going to tell Auntie Heather you said your real mum and dad are going to come for you. You're going to be in trouble. You're going to be in trouble!'

Mum sometimes got upset if people said she wasn't my real mum, she'd be even more upset if I had said it too.

I sat on the floor of Nancy's bedroom, wrapped my arms around my stomach and started to cry again. It actually hurt, a real physical pain was inside my stomach, one I'd never felt before. If Nancy told Mum what I said she would be so upset, Mum would cry and that would be my fault. I would have made my mum cry. I wished I could take back what I said. I wished I could go back in time and knock over the pot of Grandma's ashes instead of Nancy, then everyone would be cross with me for the right reasons and I would never have said something that would break my mum's heart.

'Sit with me for a moment,' my other mother says once we are in the kitchen and have placed the dishes we cleared on the side. The kitchen is another homely space with a comfortable-looking sofa and a large dining table they must have all sat around to eat – I can imagine the noise in here, three children, two parents, grandparents. Them all talking, laughing, sharing, nicking food from each other's plates, spilling drinks, completing homework. It was like that in our home, too. Just quieter. 'Sit, sit,' she says indicating with an open hand to a space at the dining table.

My heart is like a weight inside my chest: too heavy to beat but desperate to escape. We sit at one corner of the table, she is at its head, me on her left.

'I'm sorry for the way I turned up the other day,' my mother says. 'I should have thought through what I was doing to you.'

'It's fine.'

'Abimbola says you make jewellery,' she says. 'Did you make those rings you are wearing?'

I look down at them: the thick silver one, the copper and silver twisted ones, the copper and silver texturised one, the plain silver one, the linked yellow gold ones, the pleated platinum ones. Those are the ones I made first, my practice rings. The others came later, were made with just as much love and attention but in less time, with more experience with every measurement, cut, heat up, cool down, pickle, shape, file, solder, polish and finish. 'Yes. I remake old jewellery and make new stuff, too.'

She reaches out and cautiously takes my left hand to get a better look at the rings. 'I am envious,' she says. 'I have always wanted to be able to do something like jewellery or sculpting or even simple moulding. When I see something in my head it is so clear, so vivid, but when I attempt to make it, it does not quite turn out how I expected.' She laughs. She laughs how I laugh, with her head thrown slightly to one side, her cheeks plumped up and her eyes slightly closed. 'To say the least.'

'That's what drawing and painting are like for me. I think I'm so artistic because in my head the image is so brilliant and perfect. My hands, however, never seem to be able to do that on the page. Luckily it seems to work with jewellery. You can draw, though, so that's something.'

'You can make jewellery, which is like sculpture, is it not? You are artistic. Simply not drawing artistic. I am not physically artistic.' But we are both artistic, she seems to be saying, we have another connection.

'I suppose that's true,' I say. I wish she would laugh again. She reminds me most of the connection between us when she laughs.

'You were... you were happy?' she asks.

I can't be honest with her, not if I don't want to hurt the feelings of this intimate stranger. She is staring at her hands and at my hands. Yes, I was happy. And I was miserable, too. I was happy, I was miserable, I wanted an escape route, I never wanted to leave home. I laughed so much my body hurt, I cried so hard my eyes ached. I had a mostly normal childhood. 'I was OK,' I confirm. 'I was fine. The Smittsons are good people.'

'I did not want to give you away,' she says quietly. She continues to study my hands, her hands, to focus on not looking at the rest of me.

'Then why?' I ask. *Why, why, why?* And: *How could you?* And: *What was wrong with me?* And: *Why didn't you come back for me?* And: *Have you thought about me all these years?* And: *Why, why, why?*

'I was seventeen. I had no family around me. The Zebilas were worried about what people would say about the unmarried daughter of a friend who lived in their house suddenly being with child. They thought people would believe your grandfather was responsible. He would never have done such a thing but they worried what people would say.

'Your father... he was still completing his studies and could not financially support us. I battled with myself for many weeks. Mrs Stoner, the foster carer, a nice English lady, let me come and see you almost every day. I was not supposed to, the social worker said, but

Mrs Stoner let me. I would hold you, sing to you, feed you... you were so small. She would let me bath you sometimes.'

More whys from what she reveals, not less: *Why didn't he give up his studies to support us? Why didn't his parents with their big house and money want to help? Why didn't anyone think to organise a secret wedding so you could keep me as husband and wife? Why could you hold me and sing to me and bath me and still walk away? Why didn't you look for me?*

'The social worker told me I would forget. She said I should get on with my life, look forwards not back and I would forget. She said you would go to two people who would know how to look after you as only adults can. I couldn't do that properly, she said. I was too young.'

Why did you believe her? Why didn't you believe that I was your baby and I would need you, not anyone else?

'I never forgot. How could I? I have thought about you every day.'

Why didn't you tell your other children about me? Why didn't you let my grandmother see me – she might have changed her mind about me then? Why?

The answer was obvious, of course: Why? Because she was seventeen. At seventeen I had slept with about ten different people, trying to make connections with others wherever I could because sometimes the endless abyss of aloneness and being 'different' would threaten to swallow me whole. At seventeen I still thought my 'real' parents would swoop in and take me away from all the bad things that had meandered through my life like the slow-moving but persistent flow of a river. I remember studying for A levels, listening to Take That and complaining about Dad not letting me straighten my hair while all the white girls around me – including my cousin Nancy – were still slathering on chemicals to curl their hair to look like mine.

If I was in her situation at seventeen – and I so nearly was – I would have kept the baby. It would have broken my parents' hearts but I would have done it, I would have kept me. I have to remember, though, that I was seventeen in 1995. I was not a teenager in 1978, single, living with a family who obviously didn't want me around, without a job, without a friend nearby except the man who got me into this situation and who obviously didn't want anything to do with my child. I know all this but, rhubarb, rhubarb, rhubarb. The knowing and understanding doesn't change the hurting. The hurting is like a furnace inside me sometimes that is fuelled by never feeling good enough, or worthy enough, or lovable enough, to be anyone's first choice. Except for Mum and Dad, except for Seth. They are the only people I've met over my lifetime who have chosen me first every time. If I look at what I've done, how I've twisted myself into so many difficult shapes to be able to be who someone else wants me to be, I realise that not even I am my own first choice.

'You look so much like Abimbola,' she says with a smile. I like her laugh, I don't like this smile. This smile is the type you use when you are cooing over a baby: maternal, loving, sentimental. It freaks me out. I'm not a baby, but that is clearly who she is seeing. Either Baby Talei or Abi but not me, Clemency the adult.

'She looks like me,' I tease. 'I was here first, remember?'

'Ah, yes, I'm sorry. She looks so much like you.' She grins. Then seriousness descends, covers her body and makes it stiff, forces her hands to stop moving. 'You were really all right?' she asks again, just to be sure.

I nod. I was mostly all right. Weren't most people?

29

Smitty

With Dad, August 2014, Otley

'When are you and Seth going to be having children?' Dad asked.

'The twelfth of never, probably,' I replied offhandedly.

'Is it you or him?' Dad asked.

When I did not reply, simply carried on with my search through the on-screen TV guide for something to watch that we'd both like, Dad said, shrewdly, 'You, is it, *quine*?'

'Yes,' I mumbled.

'Can I ask you why, or will you change the subject?'

'Can you honestly see me with a baby, Dad?'

'Yes. You would be a perfect *mither*. If Nancy can do it, and I've never had much faith in her abilities, why do you think you can't?'

I shrugged.

'You don't need to know the past to have a future, *quine*. You simply have to have faith that you will do your best.'

'It's not the past I don't know, Dad, though, is it? Please don't be upset by this, but it's the things going on with my body that I don't know about that could do something to my baby because I don't know anything about where I came from. There could be all sorts of things inherited in my personality that could make me a terrible parent. I don't know enough about myself to know who I really am.'

'Ach, *quine*, does anyone? You are thirty-six, you must have some idea of who you are, what you like, what you don't like. Nobody knows who they are all the time. We surprise ourselves constantly. We scare ourselves even by being capable of doing things we did not know we could do.' He rested back in his chair, weak suddenly. I was draining him with this talk, I had to stop it.

'Let's change the subject, eh?' I said.

'No. I need to say this. You are my *bairn*, Clemency Smittson. My Smitty. You were also someone else's daughter first of all. But ultimately you are who you are. You may talk like someone else, you may look like someone else, you may think you have the same values and beliefs as someone else, but you are you. Any child you have will be the same. They will be who they are, despite you.'

The pictures seem to have loosened everyone up properly. When my mother and I return to the living room they're chatting and laughing. They are all giggling and chortling at Lily who is doing rather accurate impressions of me from the pictures.

Lily is currently pretending to be me when we came down south to go to the stately home and giant maze at Hampton Court. I know the picture well, it was up in Mum and Dad's living room until the move. I think it might be in Mum's room now. I'm about nine and I'm standing in the middle of the maze. I have one hand against the green maze wall, my other hand on my hip, and I'm grinning at Mum who was taking the photo. I have on navy blue jeans with a white stripe down the side and a red, short-sleeve top. Dad had done my hair especially for the occasion in two pigtails, wound round and round like Princess Leia from *Stars Wars* because she was my favourite, and after years of trying, he'd finally managed to make it work.

Lily puts her right hand on the fireplace and her left hand against her hip and dramatically juts that hip out. She purses her lips in an exaggerated pout instead of a smile.

'You're a cheeker,' I say to her as I laugh.

'These photographs are brilliant!' Abi says. 'There are so many of them and, my goodness, did you love to pose!'

'They are cool,' Ivor says. This is the first time he's spoken and his voice is deep, not as deep as his father's, but rich and soothing, tinged with an East Sussex burr.

I glance at him. He stares at me in response. Since I arrived he has been watching me, probably wondering if I'm 'real'. If I'm his 'real' sister, if I am a 'real' Zebila by blood, if my intentions are 'real' or if I am there to trick his family out of money. He's wondering what the 'real' reason is I am here. People have been wondering if I'm real all my life, why should he be any different?

'Child,' my grandmother says. All of us in the room except Mum look up. She is looking at me, talking to me. 'Help me to my room.'

Ivor moves forward, arms out, ready to help her up, as does Abi. 'I asked the— I asked Clemency,' she says to stop them. 'My room is down the corridor,' she says. 'Help me.'

It must be fun living in this house with two people vying for control all the time: my mother had ten minutes alone with me in the kitchen, now my grandmother needs to get her share, too. They're probably like this the majority of the time, having refined the subtleties of the game over years and years of living together. I love my parents, I adore Seth's parents, but the *thought* of living with them for pretty much all of my adult life would drive me more than slightly insane, let alone doing it.

My grandmother rests heavily on my arm, and her weight causes me to miss a step. We move slowly and carefully across the room, every piece of furniture an obstacle, every slightly unlevel piece of carpet a hazard. 'See you later, Gran,' Ivor says.

'See you later, Gran,' Abi and Lily echo. Will I be expected to do that? Call her 'Gran' when I leave her. Because that will not be happening. I still haven't properly labelled her that in the privacy of my own mind, it'll take even longer for whatever that label is to come out of my mouth.

Her room is the other living room in the house. She obviously can't manage stairs, and after she has pointed me in the right direction, I edge along at her pace until we reach a white, six-panelled door. I'm expecting, I think, a room that is dark, dingy, that smells of inaction and age and confinement. I'm expecting flock wallpaper, heavy, closed drapes. Instead, the white, opaque blinds are open, and like the lounge the room is filled with light. The window is also open, and a breeze has been through the room, clearing away any hint of fustiness.

There is a large bed at the far end and along its side are metal rails like the ones you'd find in a hospital, obviously to stop her falling out. On the pillow is a leather-bound book, the words *Holy Bible* embossed in gold on the cover. Pushed up against the wall beside the bed is a large chest of drawers which is topped with dozens of square white boxes, and even more small amber medicine bottles, most with their white, printed labels facing out. There are two large, comfortable-looking easy chairs in the room, positioned near the window; between them is a bookcase filled with books with cracked spines.

'There,' she says. My grandmother points to the chair beside the window and nearest the bed. She lands heavily in her seat, rests back and stares at me again. She has been doing that a lot. My father hasn't looked at me since he welcomed me 'home' and all she has done is look at me. I thought, at first, it was her seeking out any similarities, but it's more than that. Maybe it's that 'real' thing. Or maybe it isn't. But there is definitely *some*thing.

'Sit, sit,' she says.

Cautiously I lower myself into the other seat. Something has changed: in the atmosphere of the room, in the dynamics between us. Maybe it's because we're alone, but I am suddenly on edge, nervous, unsure.

'God has brought you back to me,' she says. 'He is wise and He is good. Just when I need Him, He has answered by bringing you back to me. You are ... You are going to help me. I need you to help me,' she says. 'I was not sure what I wanted to do was the right thing until I saw that God has sent you back to me.'

I wish she would stop saying that. I believe in God in many ways, but the way she says it, uses it, makes me defensive. It makes me question whether I truly have a faith or if it is something I have because Mum and Dad took me to church every week. I like to keep my religion to myself, to say prayers when I need and want to, to take comfort in knowing that sometimes I can feel connected to something bigger than myself that is 'out there'. Maybe God, maybe The Universe, maybe simply the sky that covers us all. Whatever it is I believe, I don't force it on to others and I like it better, I like people better, when they don't do it to me. Everyone can believe what they like, all the more so when they don't push it on to me.

I press my lips together to stop myself speaking. To stop myself from saying that I'd rather she left Him out of it if she could.

She begins to shake, and shame blossoms in my chest. I'm being too hard on her. I take my comfort in a divine being when I need to, maybe she is the same. When you are ill, too, like she obviously is, you may need to take that comfort more constantly. I shouldn't judge her for that.

'You will help me, won't you?' she asks.

'If I can,' I reply. I wonder what she thinks someone she has just met will be able to help her do when she has a whole family down the hall in the living room who are at her beck and call. 'What is it you want help with?'

This woman, my grandmother, who has only really been in my life for the past hour, fixes me with a gaze that is determined and a little frightening, woven through with strands of defiance. Maybe I was mistaken; maybe those outside this room aren't as devoted and loving as I thought. Whatever it is that she wants to do is clearly something they're unlikely to agree to. She says nothing for a time, and the longer she stares at me with her brown eyes, the colour dimmed by age, the more a feeling of dread meanders outwards from the pit of my stomach. I should not be sitting here having this conversation with this woman. I should have brought her back here and left her to it. The longer I sit here, the longer things are going to go wrong for me.

Eventually, so eventually I thought she was planning on remaining silent, she speaks. Cautiously, haltingly, she says: 'My time has come. I am too old...too sick...too tired to carry on in this world.' She pauses but her eyes continue to drill into me. 'My time has come. I want...I want to leave this Earth. I need you to help me.'

There's a ringing in my ears, in my head, and I know it's because I'm imagining things, hallucinating, probably dreaming. And the ringing is my alarm clock trying to get me to wake up from this dream that has slid quietly and unknowingly into a nightmare. I need to wake up. I do not want to be speaking to someone who has asked me to...

'Did you just ask me to help you to die?' I ask. I'm not asleep. The ringing in my ears isn't an alarm clock, it's the sound of sheer disbelief as it moves through my body.

'Yes.'

I wrinkle my face at her. This must be some kind of test. A test for what I don't know, but it must be. Or some kind of joke, which is unfunny and has no punchline that would ever make it funny. Any minute now she's going to laugh, she's going to tell me not to take everything so seriously and that it was all just a joke. Not funny. But then, the things that some people find hilarious – hideous, meanspirited, unpleasant stuff – have never appealed to me. 'I think I'd better go,' I say to her. I stand up. The longer I sit here and no 'Only joking!' is forthcoming, the more sick I feel.

'You will help me,' she says. This is not a question, a request from a virtual stranger, it is a prediction. She seems to know something I don't.

'I don't think so,' I say. I'm not used to being so direct and firm with someone older than me, it goes against the respect for elders that I've had instilled in me since I was tiny. This isn't an ordinary situation, though. This needs to be knocked on the head right away.

'You will, Clemency...This is the reason...why you met Abimbola...as you did...My family was not complete without you...Now it is. And it is...because you were brought back to help me.' Her certainty, her conviction about what is going to happen, what I'm going to do, is enough to shake me. Not simply upset me, but make me question whether that is why all of this has happened

179

in the way it has happened. Maybe this is what I'm meant to do. Maybe I am meant to help this woman die.

'No,' I say to her sternly. I'm saying it to myself as well, of course. Because it's the most ridiculous idea that I would have been brought back into their lives for this. 'No. I am not going to do it. So please stop asking. I'm going to go now. It was nice to meet you but now I'm going to go. Goodbye.'

'I will see you again,' she says. Another prediction wrapped up like a present in the folds of an unsubtle threat. 'I will see you again. You will help me.'

30

Abi

To: Jonas Zebila
From: Abi Zebila
Subject: Update
Thursday 2 July 2015

Jonas, my brother,
They've just left – Clemency and her mother have been for a visit and it went well. I didn't want to say anything until it'd actually happened – I half expected her to cancel at the last second, but she didn't. Like I say, I think it went well.

She sent me a message almost straight away saying:

'Thank you for arranging today.
I feel so lucky to have you in my life. Clemency x'

So that's something? She didn't run away, although when everyone started crying I wouldn't have blamed her. Yes, dear brother, you read that right, everyone started crying. Proper, full-on sobbing – even Daddy, even *Ivor*. It was a mess. If I was her, standing there watching a bunch of virtual strangers crying because I'd walked into a room, I would have run for it. Ironic, huh, that the one time I'd have expected her to hit the road, she stood there and took it.

She brought her adoptive mother with her. Clemency calls her 'Mum'. She's white, by the way. So was her adoptive father. It never occurred to me that either of them would be, let alone both of them. Her mum, I suppose I need to call her, is so nice, she brought a photo album. It was so strange, seeing all those pictures of Clemency growing up and looking exactly like me. She seemed happy in the photos – she was always smiling.

Gran asked Clem (I don't think she'll mind if I call her that) to help her to her room. She was gone for ages, and when Clem came back she definitely had the look of someone who'd been Gran'd. I don't know what Gran said or did, but Clemency had that expression on her face that everyone has after spending time with Gran. I hope Gran didn't put her off.

Everyone's being really quiet now, it's only Lily-Rose who's talking at all and she wants to keep going through the photos. Mummy is clearing up and looking off into the distance like she's reliving her life again or something, and Daddy has looked through the photos several times with Lily-Rose. Ivor's gone out to wherever Ivor goes. He seems embarrassed that he cried, too, and also, I don't know, angry isn't the right word. He seems put out, maybe scared about what Clemency will mean for him and his position in the family. I really can't think what else it would be.

Brother, it's at times like this that I miss you. You were noticeably absent today. You would have loved Clemency, she would have loved you. Aren't you just tempted to break the silence to find out about her? Not even a little?

Love you. Miss you.
Your sister,
Abi
xxxxxxx

31

Smitty

I watched Mum try to control herself. She did a great job: she managed to control her face, her tears, her voice, but she couldn't control her hands from shaking.

Their living room felt so small, so hot, so claustrophobic. I looked down at my hands and they were trembling. I was shaking, too.

'It'll be fine, *quine*, I promise you,' Dad said. 'I'm fine. I'll be fine. We caught it early. We'll all be fine.'

I nodded at Dad. He didn't lie to me. Mum had no problem with it, she always did what she thought was best even if it meant twisting the facts to suit the reality she wanted to paint. But Dad? He never did that. Even if it was something he knew, I didn't want to hear he would find the words to tell me the truth. He was telling me the truth right at that moment, but I also knew at any given moment that truth could become a lie.

Mum and I arrived home in the silence that we travelled back in. We barely acknowledged each other when we retreated to our separate rooms. There was nothing much to say, nothing we could dissect together because our experiences of the past few hours were so different, so disparate, I don't think we'll ever find any common ground over this.

Once I have closed the door behind me, I throw down my bag and head straight for the wardrobe nearest the window and remove the large butterfly box. Unceremoniously, I put the lid to one side then ferret through the box, crammed with the photos of my life, and remove all the pictures I have of Dad. I lay them on the chest of drawers which sits beside the wall where my photo wall is slowly taking shape. The photos I have just liberated from the box, which still have blobs of Blu-Tack on the back, need to go on the wall. I'm putting Dad back where he belongs, back where I can see him. I work feverishly but carefully, the need to have him visible again makes my fingers move at speed.

I can't believe what that woman asked, I keep thinking as I reinstate Dad. *How dare she? How DARE SHE!*

My dad would have done anything to be here, he would have given anything to have stayed with us, with his family. I would have given anything to have him back, to spare him what he went through. The thought of anyone not feeling like that about life stirs up a tornado-like rage inside me. To have *that person* think I would be interested in being a part of anything that would shorten a life, something so precious, makes me so angry I can barely think without wanting to break something.

I should tell my other mother. I should tell my father. I should tell Abi. I should tell someone who will be able to stop her, talk sense into her. Let her know that she has options other than that. *They* know her, and even if they don't get on with her all the time, none of them would want her to feel like that, to do that.

Dad is slowly returning to my wall. As I put him back up, I am seeing him as he was. Frowning at the train timetable when we were off on a day trip to Birmingham. Wearing my mortarboard at graduation. Dancing with Mum at the party after Sienna's christening. Drinking a pint of Guinness at the Guinness factory in Dublin when we went there for his fiftieth birthday. Wearing his red and white Christmas jumper and yellow cracker hat. With his head in his car trying to fix it with no idea what he is doing. Sitting on the beds in my various rooms in my shared houses during my college years and always wearing the same frown because he can't believe how much I am paying for a tiny room. Standing outside our old house in Lewes, holding my two-year-old hand, pointing at Mum who is taking the picture.

There are so many, so many that need to be put up. Each time I pick one up, the memory it holds diffuses into my fingertips, blooms through my blood, until I am remembering all those times.

The last photo I reach for I had not looked at properly when I took it out of the butterfly box until my fingers were almost upon it: *Dad with Seth, February 2013, Engagement Party Time!*

Even though the party never happened, I didn't add a sad face or mention of its cancellation to this picture because it is such a perfect image. Dad, in his navy blue suit, has his arm around Seth while Seth in his tight, navy blue suit that complemented my silver dress, has his arm around Dad. The pair of them could not look happier, more prepared for a night of *birling* (a big night of drinking) and celebrating. I did not want to taint the image by adding any sadness, any of the misery that came next. Should I put up this photo? I'm not sure it has a place among all these other images when I am trying to move on from Seth.

If I touch it, too, I'll only properly remember. I'll only be reminded how much I miss them both. I can do something about how keenly I feel the loss of one of those people, the absence of the other is beyond my control.

And that woman, *that woman* wanted me to help her end her life. I grab the photo, any memory no matter how tainted is better than the thought of what *that woman* wants me to do.

With Seth, Dad & Mum, February 2013, Leeds

Seth unhooked his arm from Dad's shoulder after having a picture taken with him, and wandered across the hall to me. I stood in the centre of the large space, spinning and looking in every direction, desperate to take in every last inch of the place. Seth had made it perfect.

The thirty or so tables that ringed the dance floor where I stood were draped with white paper tablecloths, printed all over with a design Seth had come up with that linked the 'S' of his name with the 'C' of my mine into a pretty monogram. The tables were scattered with silver and gold champagne flute-shaped confetti and each table had an empty wine bucket waiting for the ice cubes and accompanying Prosecco bottle.

The room was awash with silver and gold balloons with the same 'SC' design emblazoned on them, and the disco lights swung this way and that, to make the place dance with pretty, multi-coloured lights. In the corner, Seth had set up his mixing table and I had practically got down on my knees to beg him not to play hard-core rap all night (no one needed to see either set of parents attempting to dance to that) and to let a couple of his friends have a go so we could spend a bit of time together.

In the large entrance area outside the hall, Dad was now helping Jorge and Max, a couple of Seth's mates from work, to set up the bar. Mum was making a huge fuss about not very much and I didn't even mind. Dylan was meant to be coming but I knew he wouldn't because he still, *still* felt we were rubbing his face in the fact we'd got together.

'You like?' Seth asked. He took my hand and twirled me around. The soft, satiny folds of my silver, knee-length dress flared out while he spun me. Bubbles of happiness fizzed and popped in my veins, I was giddy in a way I hadn't been before. I'd been dubious about this, but he'd persuaded me into it because we weren't going to get married for a while and he wanted to make a public declaration about our love for each other. I'd agreed because I loved Seth and I wanted everyone to be in no doubt how I felt about this man who twirled me, whose fingers mine easily slotted between, whose body I constantly missed like a physical ache deep inside, who was the first person I went to when anything happened.

We had different tastes in music, different ideas about what made a good read, we often fell out over stupid things, I worried all the time when he went out on his motorbike especially in the rain, he often got annoyed that all my jewellery-making tools and equipment were all over the flat instead of tidied away in one of the five yellow toolboxes he had bought me, but we were intertwined. Like the initials he had linked together on the tablecloths, balloons and napkins, we were interlinked and I couldn't remember a time when I hadn't been with him. I had made my engagement ring from that piece of amber he had bought in Lithuania and everyone was going to see it tonight.

'I LOVE!' I said to my fiancé. 'I love, love, love.'

In one move he tugged me into his arms. He was clean-shaven, his hair clipped short, and he smouldered with such deliciousness I wanted to lick him like he was a lollipop.

'I love, love, *love* that dress you're wearing,' he murmured into my ear. His hand ran salaciously over my bum. 'I can't wait to have you in it.' He drew me even closer to him. 'And I can't wait to take it off you and have you all over again.'

'Clemency!' Like an expert surgeon's knife, my mother's voice cut cleanly and precisely through Barry White's 'My First, My Last, My Everything' and the fug of lust we'd slipped into. Seth and I shot apart, as we always did when my mother had that voice on her.

'Yes, Mum?' I asked.

'Where are the extra—'

Mum was cut short by the doors to the hall being thrown dramatically back. In came Dad, heavily supporting a dishevelled, limping Nancy.

I couldn't move, stood and watched as Dad helped her in. With a look to me, Seth went to help Dad place Nancy in a chair.

Her black mascara, something I'd *never* seen her wear before tonight, streaked down towards her cheeks like desperate fingers reaching out for help. Her usually flawless skin was blotchy, her neck was flushed a vivid red-pink colour.

'Oh, Nancy, love, what's happened?' Mum rushed over to her, crouched down beside her chair. 'Are you all right?'

Between gasping, sobbing breaths she told them what had happened: she had been on her way over, having got Sienna settled early with Uncle Colin and Auntie Marcia (who were babysitting instead of attending), so she could help. On her way she must have taken a wrong turn or something because suddenly she was lost and then she noticed she was being followed and *then* they stole her handbag and watch and thankfully that was all they wanted but she'd twisted her ankle trying to run away in case that wasn't all they wanted. But she was worried because they seemed to be hanging around, looking for people to mug. Maybe they knew there was a party going on and thought they'd pick off the guests who were alone.

She was telling this to her assembled audience of Mum and Dad, Jorge and Max, because I knew from the second I saw her it was all fake; a ridiculous fabrication from a woman who was too jealous to let me have even this moment to myself.

'*They're always telling you how special you are because you were chosen. They don't think you're that special now, do they? I bet they're wishing they never chose you at all,*' Nancy had said to me when we were nine and she had blamed me for something she had done. Over twenty-four years later she was trying again to stop me being special as she always did.

'Thank goodness you got away,' Mum gushed. 'Thank goodness you're all right.'

She's definitely all right now, I thought.

'I think I'd better call the police,' I said. Her reply would confirm my suspicions, or would show me to be a spiteful cow who couldn't even cut my cousin some slack after a terrifying experience.

Nancy sat up a little straighter in her seat and vigorously shook her head. 'No, no, don't worry about it. I'm sure they're long gone.'

'But you said you thought they were hanging around,' I said.

'Well, maybe, but since I got away, they probably won't hang around in case I tell anyone.'

It was all a lie. Of course it was. Dad peered at me for a long few seconds before his gaze moved on to Seth, then returned to watching me. I wasn't sure if he knew or simply suspected, but he hadn't taken her at face value, hadn't automatically believed her like Mum had. Like Jorge and Max had because they had no clue what she was like.

Seth and I locked eyes. We knew what would be expected of us, we were both well versed in the protocol of Nancy. I didn't even give a hint of the 'I told you so' I would have been justified in firing at him. But we couldn't. Not over such a blatant lie. No one believed it, surely?

'I think we should cancel the party,' Mum said in the silence when neither Seth nor I said it. 'We can't have anyone else put in danger for a party. It's a good thing it's early enough to do that.'

'But everything's set up,' Dad said. 'We'll just send a message to people to be careful, to travel in pairs, and if they can't do that, we'll come out and meet them.'

'Clemency will never forgive herself if something happens to someone on the way here, Don,' Mum replied. She was talking for me, telling other people what I felt. Dad looked at me, then at Seth.

'You'll be all right, won't you, Nancy?' Dad asked her.

Nancy gave a brave, silent sob and swallowed hard. 'I–I think so,' she said to Dad, while turning her beseeching eyes on Mum. 'I–I'll be all right.'

'No!' Mum said firmly, and hugged Nancy closer. 'No, we can't have anyone else ending up in this state just for a party. You understand, don't you, Clemency?'

I stared at Mum, unable to reply.

'I'd better start calling and texting people to let them know the party is off.' Seth's voice was a frustrated monotone. He said it to save me from answering Mum. That was why I loved him: he always had my back, as they said in the movies.

'I think that would be for the best,' Mum agreed.

'Yeah,' Seth stated flatly. 'For the best.' Anyone else would think the timing was suspiciously perfect to give us enough time to cancel the party before most people had set off, but not Mum. Dad was watching me again, probably understanding how terrible I felt, but he didn't say anything else. He'd tried, but when it came to Nancy, no one could tell Mum anything.

I put the photo down. I can't put it up. I pick it up again. I have to put it up. It's not about me and Seth, it's about Dad. It's about this photo being taken right before it all started going wrong. Right before Mum and Dad sat me down and told me again. Except there was no firmness, no certainty when he stated how fine he was going to be. It was simply the act of telling me what was happening next in his life. This was one of the best photos I had of him before the changes started.

With Dad, July 2014, Otley

We started measuring our time together in the stages of his not being able to do things. He was fine, so fine for so long I'd allowed myself to forget. We were all, I think, lulled into that suspended animation of nothing changing, so that translated into the equivalent of everything being fine.

Until the tests that showed something had altered. And then the moments when the first steps on that path to the other end began. Tentative, slow and fearful but necessary and inevitable. My heart beat as though it was coated and smothered in a thick, viscous treacle that made it agony to exist, knowing what Dad was about to go through. I didn't truly know, of course, I could only guess and imagine and hope that it was not as awful as I thought it would be.

Then our calendar changed, our clocks changed. It stopped being about seasons and months and the countdown to Christmas, it was replaced by the times of the required daily dosage of medication; it was slowly but definitively about when he stopped being able to do things. First it was not being able to make it to the doctor's surgery for his appointments.

'You know, *quine*, I'll never see the outside of this house again,' he said to me while Mum showed the doctor out after his first home visit. I stared at Dad, mute with the horror of what he'd just told me. It was going to happen, soon. I would have to be without him, soon. He smiled at me, his tiredness and what was happening to him not able to dim the essence of who he was. My dad. One of my best friends, but first and foremost my dad.

I don't know if he told Mum the same thing, but the next change was when it became clear that he couldn't manage the stairs so

Mum and I moved the chest of drawers out into the landing and replaced it with his favourite chair from downstairs. He gave me the same smile as he settled into his chair with his paper, glasses perched on his nose. '*I'll never see the downstairs of this house again,* quine,' he said with that smile. And, ah, I smiled back because I understood him, and, ah, the agony from my chest coated and smothered in treacle, made every breath hard and laboured. I semi-moved in to give Mum a hand, I went part-time at work, tried to take on as little private work as I could and resolved to make it up to Seth as soon as I could.

When it wasn't as long between not being able to leave the house and not being able to go downstairs and him having to have a catheter installed, I knew it was time to move in properly.

With Dad, April 2015, Otley

Mum and I would take it in turns, sit by his bed and read. He slept a lot, and when he wasn't asleep he would try to talk to us. But he couldn't. It was hard, the pain would make him mute sometimes, and he would try to hide it. His face, so noble and strong, would be grey with the agony, each line drawn taut as the pain ripped slowly through him. And when there wasn't pain, there were the hallucinations, seeing what wasn't there, having conversations with people long since gone. He kept seeing his grandmother, asking her when she would take him to the beach, wondering why she didn't reply. Crying and shouting when she wouldn't reply.

I wanted to hold his hand and keep holding it as long as I could. He'd always been there during my beginning and middle; he'd held my hand so many times during the hard bits, he'd made those difficult times easier, bearable, and I wanted to be with him for every last minute. I wanted to help him at his end. I could never think about it, though, even when he told me. It was something I didn't contemplate – him not being around was unthinkable. Then, when it was probable, likely, I still clung to the idea that there would be a cure. Something would happen that would change everything and he'd be around to hold the baby Seth and I had agreed to have, to come with me to see the films no one else would even entertain watching, to call for a quick chat.

My phone, on the floor by my feet, buzzed for the tenth time that day and I stooped to switch it off.

'Who is it that keeps ringing you, *quine?*' Dad asked me. I'd been sitting beside his bed reading while he slept and his voice, croaky and sore, made me jump a little. He was bleary-eyed from sleep, his face a network of sleep-dampened agonies.

'Ahh, just this woman from Doncaster who wants me to make some wedding rings for her. You'd think I was the only ring maker in the world.'

'Not the only ring maker in the world, just the best.' His voice, like sandpaper drawn over gravel, sounded so painful to make. I wanted him to stop talking so he wouldn't be in agony just from speaking to me, but I wanted him to speak to me. The more he spoke to me, the easier I found it to not believe what was coming.

'You would say that, wouldn't you?' I told Dad.

'Smitty, sweetheart...' He kept pausing between words, drawing breath to make the sound that was his voice. 'You need to... get back to work... go and see this woman... make her rings.'

'I don't want to, Dad.'

'Don't stop living... because of me... please, go...'

'Do I have to?' I used to say that to him all the time when I was growing up.

His face managed to find a smile. 'No, you don't... have to... But I'd like... you to. It... would make me... happy... to see you... living.'

'That's emotional blackmail, isn't it, Dad?'

'Yes... I'll use... anything.'

'OK, I'll go ring her and arrange to meet her later in the month.'

'Sooner... rather than... later.'

'OK, Dad. I'll go see her as soon as she's free.'

'Good girl... Good girl.'

With Dad, May 2015, Otley
'Clemency, my little Smitty,' Dad said. He was sitting up as he

spoke. He hadn't sat up in what seemed so long, but now he had plump white pillows supporting his lower back, and he was upright. Shades of pink tinged his cheeks, and the lines of his features that had been stretched taut like piano strings with pain had slackened. He seemed calmer, more relaxed, the agony – acute and unrelenting – seemed to have receded because the right balance of opiates and other medication pumped through his veins. 'I wanted to say how much I love you and how proud I am of you.' He could even talk a bit easier. 'You are everything I could have ever wanted in a daughter. I ... am the luckiest man alive ... I am so honoured to have been your father.'

'You're still my dad, Dad,' I replied.

His smile was that of someone who knew something I didn't. Fear blew through me like an unexpected northerly wind. He knew it would be soon. 'Shall I cancel this woman?' I asked. 'Stay here instead?' I had arranged for the woman from Doncaster who wanted the rings to come to Otley town centre – that was the furthest I was prepared to be away from him – and was just about to nip out to see her.

'Ach, no, *quine*. I'm just being a silly, sentimental old man. I want to ... say things when I feel up to it. I am so proud of you and who you turned out to be.'

'I'm the lucky one. You're a brilliant dad. I'm going to rush back from this appointment so I can read you the paper. If you ask Mum to wait for me, I'll do it. Is that a deal?'

'Deal.' He smiled again. He received my careful hug and even more gentle kiss without reciprocating because he didn't have the strength.

At the door, I looked back at him and he eased his hand up, the translucent palm, a network of blue, green and grey veins, held high as he said goodbye.

By the time I returned, he was gone. He went peacefully in his sleep with Mum sitting beside him, holding his hand. The nurse who had come to check his meds arrived a few minutes later. *'Why didn't he wait for me?'* I wanted to ask Mum. *'After all of this time, why didn't he wait for me so I could hold his hand, too?'*

'*Because he was still being my dad right up until the end,*' was the answer, of course. He knew it would have been too much for me to be there. Dad knew that although I wanted to be there, it would have destroyed me if I had been. My whole life, right down to his last breath, Dad protected me.

I am pushing my luck. I had to get out of the flat, away from the sadness and the remembering. I had called Melissa, but her phone went straight to answer machine. I'd almost called Seth, had gone to type in his number when a 'Smitty, I deserve to have you talk to me at least' type text from him popped up on my phone and I knew I couldn't. It wouldn't be fair on him to just get in touch when I needed support, and to be honest, his text made me think he had a nerve considering what he'd done. So, I decided instead to push my luck by going to Beached Heads and seeing if I could persuade Tyler to let me in even after closing time, make me a coffee, talk to me until I started to feel better.

Outside his café, which is indeed closed with the outside tables brought in and stacked neatly between the counter and the window, I stand at the door and peer in. I can see him behind the counter. He is using a white cloth to clean his machine, but he is unhurried, the movement more like pottering than essential work to be carried out before he can speed off home to his life away from here. I'm like that sometimes, especially nowadays when I know all that is waiting for me is an evening spent sitting next to Mum, trying not to rise to everything that comes out of her mouth that I take issue with. Cleaning up at work, moving boxes around the shop while I pretend I'm going to sort it out soon, is always preferable to that.

I move to knock, then decide to literally push my luck – with the metal handle in my hand, I push at the door. Someone is smiling down on me because it opens. It'll be so much harder for him to turn me away now that I'm inside.

'One coffee, please?' I say from my favourite place at the counter.

'We're closed!' he says without turning around.

'But the door was open even though the closed sign was showing,' I state.

He pivots slowly on the spot until he is facing me. I grin at him in what I hope is a winning way. 'Ah, you.' He says it deadpan but his expression betrays a soupçon of joy to see me.

'Yes, me. Isn't this the most excellent part of your day so far?'

His perfect left eyebrow hitches itself up briefly before he frowns at the door, puzzled. 'I could have sworn I locked that. I learnt my lesson after last time.'

'You don't mind, do you?' I ask.

'Would you mind if I came barging into your workplace and demanded you make me a ring after hours?' he asks.

'No,' I say. 'I genuinely wouldn't.' I clear my throat, add as casually as possible, 'Anyway, I don't only want a coffee. I was hoping you'd be able to teach me how to make it on your machine there.'

'What? No way! Only fully insured people behind this counter, baby.'

I'm not sure how serious he is right now, but I need something to take my mind off today. It's not fair to burden him with that responsibility, but I am desperate. If he doesn't help me, I will be forced to ring Seth and I can't do that. Not to him, not to me.

'I'll level with you,' I say, maintaining eye contact. 'I've had a really odd day. So many strange things have happened, so many painful things have been revisited, and I just want one of your coffees and to have some fun. If I have to settle for a coffee, that'll do. Some fun would be ... probably more than you're willing to give and more than I deserve but I thought I'd ask anyway.'

He stares at me for long minutes. It's probably a few seconds, but standing exposed as I am in front of him it feels like minutes. 'You have to do everything I say,' he states.

My grin is almost one hundred per cent relief, but I restrain myself from clapping my hands in delight.

'One deviation from my instructions and you're outta here. No second chances when it comes to using professional, potentially dangerous equipment.'

'It's a coffee machine, Tyler, how dangerous can it be?' I scoff.

195

'Oh, suddenly the expert, are we?' he says.

'No, no, sorry, sorry,' I say.

'Go on, get round there, and don't touch anything until I come back with your apron.'

'I get an apron?' I say gleefully.

'Yes, you get an apron.'

'This just gets better and better!' I can't stop myself from jumping up and down.

'Enough of that! There is no messing about while we do this,' he says before he disappears behind the left-hand door. The second he is out of sight I jump up and down again, only managing to stop when he reappears, carrying a blue apron with *Beached Heads* embroidered on to the front in gold thread.

'Come here,' he says. Standing in front of me on the other side of the counter, he hooks the apron over my head, carefully uses the loops to tie it once at the back of my waist, then slowly moves the ends to the front and ties them into a small bow. I watch his hands work and when his fingers rest on the bow for a few seconds, I raise my eyes to find him staring intently at me. 'Ready?' he asks.

I nod.

He smiles and I can't decipher what it means, if it means anything.

'Just so we're clear, Smitty,' he says. 'Me teaching you to do this does not mean the next time you come in here you get to help yourself.' He steps back, gives me space to move in front of the machine, wiping away the moment that had been brewing between us.

'Of course not,' I say.

'I mean it, Smitty. I catch you behind this counter and you're permanently barred.'

'OK, OK, if it means that much to you, I won't start to help myself.'

'Good.'

'Tyler,' I say quietly.

He pauses mid-reach for the coffee beans that sit on the shelf to the right of the machine. 'Yeah?'

'Thank you.'

'What for?'

I grin at him. I hope my gratitude shows in the strength of my smile, the sadness that probably still haunts my eyes. 'I think you know.'

He nods. 'You're welcome,' he replies.

Part 6

32

Smitty

I didn't think I'd be back here so soon. Or ever, actually. She had put me off, the fear that she would do that to me again had been enough to make me send Abi 'hello' texts but leave it there, and it was sufficient to make me decide to never come back to this house ever again.

Yet, here I am, about to knock on the door. I haven't told Mum I'm coming here. I couldn't do that without feeling as though I am betraying her. And nor could I allow her to come along to this. Meeting my grandmother by birth to discuss this is something I have to do alone.

She was very clear about what time I needed to be here: two-forty-five exactly. I am guessing that this is when she will be alone in the house. Everyone out at work, my other mother probably collecting Lily-Rose from school. We probably have half an hour to talk before people return. She must be very confident about her skills of persuasion if she thinks that's all it'll take.

For the past four days, every day, several times a day, I have had the same message on my mobile and the phone at the workshop: 'I must talk to you, Clemency. Remember what your name means. We are family. Remember what that means. Please answer your phone.' I didn't even notice that there was a phone in her room but she kept ringing, leaving the same pleading message that is designed to get me to talk to her.

Every day I would stare at my phone after I had listened to the messages from this woman who I am related to by blood and blood alone. Yes, it's thicker than water, but what does that actually mean? Does blood being viscous and thick instead of runny and thin like water mean she can ask me to do whatever she wants and I will not question, will not refuse, I will just do?

I knew one thing without a doubt, she would keep calling until I responded. Better to just meet her, listen to her and then tell her I couldn't do it.

I lower my hand to my side. How did I end up here? About to talk to someone about doing the unthinkable? Before I can raise my hand again, the door is opened. The woman standing in the doorway wears a beige, belted raincoat and has a large black doctor's bag on the floor by her feet while her handbag is hooked over the crook of her arm. She is slender, her long brown hair tied back into a loose bun. Under her coat she wears a navy blue nurse's uniform with the white stripe around the collar. She's a district nurse out on a home visit. Dad had them towards the end, their visits and numbers increased in frequency the closer it got to that final day.

'Hello!' she says. Her smile is wide and bright, friendly and welcoming. I wonder if this is a requirement of being a district nurse – an ability to instantly put people who are going through difficult times at ease. Dad's three nurses were so kind and calming that not even Mum could keep up the high stress levels she was operating on for long. 'Are you the visitor that Soloné has been waiting on?'

'I guess so,' I say.

'She's been beside herself. I don't think I've ever seen her so excited. You must mean a lot to her.'

I offer her a smile in response. If she had any idea who I really was, who my grandmother wanted me to become...

'Can I go through?' I ask.

'Yes. But she's just had some of her medication so you won't be able to stay for too long before she's tired and needs to sleep.'

'Thank you,' I tell her.

'Hello?' I call out when the district nurse, whose name I forgot to ask, has shut the door behind her. 'It's me, Clemency.'

I stand in the hallway, reminded again how lived-in and family-filled their house is, and wait for a reply, an invitation to come into this world that I could have been a part of. A large clock ticks somewhere near, I didn't notice it last time I was here. Wood creaks, the air is unstill, the house seems to shift and move, trying to accommodate the way it is almost empty.

'Hello?' I call again.

I count the ticks: thirty. Thirty until I hear: 'Come, Clemency, come.'

I move to the room I helped my grandmother to, where the door is open. She is practically propped up in the chair by the window. When I came last time I didn't realise how much of an effort she had made to look normal. She reclines in the chair by the window. She is wearing a white nightdress covered in small yellow flowers, and a blue dressing gown, but she seems incredibly frail despite her solid weight. She trembles, too. It is not pronounced or overt, but it is noticeable. Her hair is a wiry white and black, her skin sagging against her features. She looks fragile. The woman I spoke to the other day did not seem fragile.

'You are welcome, Clemency. Please, sit. Sit.'

I hesitate, of course I do. If I go into her room I am allowing myself to become a part of this, I am saying: 'Yes, I might do this thing.' Eventually, though, I sit as I have been asked to do.

'My apologies for not being able to greet you properly at the door.'

'That's fine.'

'Are you keeping well?'

I nod. It depends what she means by well. I was well before I met her and the rest of my family, I am well now that I have met them. I was also troubled before I met them and I am troubled now. I am not unwell though. That is what she means and that is what I nod at.

'How are you?' I ask.

Her face finds a smile that is rueful and amused, it seems she is laughing at me. I suppose it is a stupid question to ask of someone who has brought me here to talk about how to end her life. I don't know how I'm supposed to act, though.

'We do not have much time,' she tells me. 'I must ask you again what I cannot ask anyone else to do. You must help me to die.'

I stare at my grandmother by blood and wait for her to say something else. What she has said is nowhere near enough to get me to agree to do this thing. She stares at me in return, her expression makes it obvious that she won't be saying anything else. She has uttered 'You must help me to die' and that is enough as far as she is concerned.

Does she think that I am so grateful, so happy to be in reunion with my birth family, that I'll do whatever she tells me to do?

'Why must I?' I ask. 'I hardly know you. Why would I?'

'That is the reason I asked you. That is why it has to be you. When Kibibi told me she had found you, I knew that God had answered my prayers. When I met you, I knew it was true. Only you can do this. No one else would do it.'

It seems this woman is saying that all that time she spent watching me the other day told her one thing: I am a killer. 'What are you saying? I try to avoid hurting anyone and anything – I've been vegetarian so many times over the years because I can't stand the thought of what meat really is. Why would you say that to me when you don't know me?'

'I am sorry, Clemency, I forget myself. I am only thinking of myself. I would like so much to get to know you but I do not have much time.'

'Why do you want to ... Why?' She doesn't look *that* ill, despite the trembling and the pallor of her skin. She doesn't look like Dad did near the end.

'I am sick, I am old, I am tired.' She says it simply, concisely, and then stops talking.

'What are you sick with?' I ask.

'Talking is difficult,' she says. 'To talk without slurring is very difficult.' She pauses. 'I have a heart condition. It was managed. It *is* managed. Then the diabetes is out of control. It was managed. For many years it was controlled.' She stops again. 'But my heart, the angina. I had an attack and they tell me the diabetes has caused it.' Pause. 'Then my heart, my diabetes. And then I am told the way my arm does not swing when I walk, the seizures, the facial...' another pause '... the facial movements. I have Parkinson's.' Pause. 'I am not going to get better. I will be on drugs for the rest of my life.' Pause. I notice, now she has mentioned it, the tic on the right side of her face. It is only occasional, but it is pronounced. 'I have so many drugs. So many needs. Over time it will be worse.'

I try to remember what Dad said about it. When he had to tell me that it had spread, that the chemo was no longer working. Did he tell me how he felt, or did I guess? I did not want to press him if he did not want to articulate it so I don't think he did tell me. I simply assumed he would feel how I would feel. Although I obviously didn't know how I would feel since it was happening to him and not to me.

'I am no longer in control of my body, of my face, of my life.' She pauses. 'My husband is gone. My children are scattered. My grandchildren who are near have their own lives.' Pause. 'I am not needed. I am a burden.' Pause.

'You are not a burden,' I say. 'No human being is a burden. Never say that.'

'You are the right person to do this.' Pause. 'You value people.'

'Most decent humans value people. And if you know I value people, then how could you ask this thing of me?'

'How I am today is the best I will feel for the rest of my life.'

'That doesn't mean you should end your life.'

'If I am not a burden now, I will soon become one.'

'Please...'

'At some point, very soon, I will not be able to do anything for myself.' Pause. 'I will need help with everything. I do not want to burden others with that.'

This was what it was like with Dad, of course. But I did not mind. Mum did not mind. He seemed to mind, he did not like not being able to help himself, take care of himself. That he needed help to do the most basic things from washing his face to going to the toilet. From the little I know of people, and the even smaller amount of info I have about this woman, that level of dependency would be awful. Loss of dignity, people call it.

I stare at the woman facing this loss of dignity, and sadness overcomes me. Her pride, her need to not lose face in front of other people, even the people who cared for her, made her want to give up on life. She would rather be away from other people than be 'weak' in front of them.

'You do not understand,' she states.

'To be honest, no, I don't, not completely. Part of me understands, of course, and I'm sort of impressed that you seem so determined to do this. On the other hand, no, I don't understand. Your family would be heartbroken without you.'

She laughs quietly, the tic on her face suddenly moving rapidly before settling again. 'You are my family, too, Clemency.' A pause. More laughter. 'Did you forget that?'

'But not like the others,' I say.

'My dear, you do not want to be like the others.'

The look that had passed between my other mother and my grandmother comes to mind, the mutual dislike, the overt signs of a power struggle. What would that be like? How would I feel being looked after, having my intimate needs taken care of, by someone I didn't like. A coldness slips through me and settles in my stomach at the thought of having to ask my cousin Nancy to fetch me a bedpan or even remember when to bring me my medication. Seeing that look on her face, experiencing the weight of her disgust and dislike, making myself vulnerable to her so I can simply survive. I wasn't sure what the source of the animosity was between my birth grandmother and birth mother but it would not be a sustainable situation: looking after someone you hated, being cared for by someone who resented you.

'My biggest worry.' Pause. 'Is another atta[...]
renders me.' Pause. 'Helpless.' Pause. 'Locked in. N[...]

That sounds a bit like my terror of being buried a[...]
and failing to claw my way out of a coffin, knowing I'm [...]
under a ton of dirt. I know my terror, which borders on a pho[...]
is mostly irrational, hers isn't. Because, not only is the confined
space her own body, it is also a perfectly rational worry with what
is slowly and insidiously happening to her health. Involuntarily, I
shudder at the idea of mentally trying to claw my way out of my
own body, knowing I'd never be able to. Knowing the only way
out is...

'Thing is, how am I supposed to do it?' I say to her. I can
understand a bit better where she is coming from, but that doesn't
mean I can do what she wants. There are a million trillion miles of
road between understanding why she might want this and actually
doing it. 'I mean, do you expect me to put a pillow over your face or
something?' I freeze for a moment at the thought of it. 'I wouldn't
be able to do that. Or anything like that. It's simply not in me.'

'When you tell me you will help.' Pause. 'I will tell you what to
do.'

'So you will do it? I only have to help you?' That may not be so
bad if I don't have to actually do it.

She raises her hands from her lap and the tremors, which do not
seem so pronounced in her body, are shockingly violent in her
hands. She lowers them again. 'I cannot.'

I would have to do it. I would have to kill her. I know I'm supposed to call it 'helping her to die', aiding her in 'fulfilling her final
wish', 'being merciful'. In truth, though, I would be killing her.
Ending her life. It would be what she wanted, but it would not alter
the facts of what I had done. And I would still be arrested if the
police found out what I had done. I would still be ostracised by the
family I have only just found if they discovered what I had done.

My birth grandmother, a woman I have met for a total of about
three hours, would like to make a killer of me with herself as my
first victim.

she moves suddenly forwards, a violent jerk that causes my heart to lurch. I move towards her, immediately desperate to help. I could look after her, I think. I could look after her and then she might not want to do this. 'No,' she says firmly.

She struggles and pushes against the arms of the chair until she is upright. I stand too, ready to catch her if she should fall. Ready if she needs me. This sort of thing I can do, this sort of help I have no problem with.

She moves forward, reaching her hands out towards the high dresser with five drawers beside her bed, even though it is at least three strides' distance from where she is. I do not attempt to help her again, I simply wait for her to move, poised to help. She stumbles, but manages to shuffle and jerk forwards, aiming for her bed, I guess. It would be easier if I helped, but I can see the lines of defiance and pride that are set in her face.

As she reaches the dresser she stumbles again, more severely this time and her fingers, groping blindly for the bevelled edge of the dresser, slip away and she falls forwards, her body hitting the dresser, dislodging most of the neatly lined up medication. I catch her before she stumbles backwards and falls to the ground. She is unexpectedly heavy, a veritable dead weight in my arms, and I stumble, too, but manage to keep my balance.

'Let me go!' she orders.

I resist the urge to do as I'm told and instead, with my arms hooked under her arms, I move her to the bed and allow her to place her hands on it then lower herself into a seated position.

'I did not need your help,' she barks at me.

I bet you're a treat to look after, I think.

'You must leave,' she says. 'I will call you.'

Lucky me, I think. I hide my face by dropping to my knees, gathering up the containers littering the floor by her bed like I am gathering pebbles on the beach to use as inspiration for my jewellery. 'Right, fine,' I say. The names of the drugs run idly through my head as I line them up as neatly as I can. There is no way I can begin to know if they were in order of consumption, and if they were, which is the right order to stack them, so I don't even try.

Besides, I have been dismissed. It's probably best to leave as soon as possible. 'You think.' Pause. 'Promise me.' Pause. 'You will think.'

'I will,' I say. 'But I don't know you. This is something you can't ask a virtual stranger to do.'

'We do not have much time...my illnesses make it difficult... but would you like to get to know me?'

More than anything, I think. I didn't realise how needy I could be until this moment. 'Even if I did, that doesn't mean I'd be able to do this thing.'

'I know, Clemency, I know...But come back to see me...for a short time, we can talk...And you can tell me about yourself...about your life.'

'You want to know about me?'

'Of course.'

I shrug. 'OK.'

'And you must promise to at least think about my request.'

'I...I...I promise. To think about it. Nothing more.'

'I do not need any more than for you to think.'

'OK, I will think.'

The woman in front of me eases herself backwards, seemingly stronger than she was a second ago. A fleeting thought dances across my mind: *Was she putting on that show to get me to do what she wants?*

Of course she wasn't. Who would do that sort of thing?

'Goodbye then,' I say. I am standing at the door.

'Goodbye,' she says. 'I look forward to seeing you again.'

I leave the house with the memory of her smile, something that seemed painful for her to do, and a deep sense of unease that not only am I keeping things from Mum, I'm going to be keeping my meetings with my grandmother secret, and she is expecting me to do it. Whatever I say, whatever I promise to think about, whatever I know deep down inside that I can't do, she is expecting me to become her killer.

33

Smitty

'Can I see your jewellery?' I ask her.

We don't have much time together, only the thirty or so minutes between the district nurse leaving and my other mother returning with Lily-Rose from school. My grandmother told me that my other mother often took Lily to the library on the way home or sometimes to run around in the park, but the thought of her catching us together was a risk I didn't want to take. My other mother still hadn't called me to arrange another meeting and I didn't want to impose myself upon her. It was nice to be with someone, like my grandmother, who made it clear she *wanted* to be with me. I wasn't stupid, though – I knew what motivated her interest in me, but that didn't matter because even if it was for snatches of time, it would be nice to get to know a little bit about her.

'Of course, of course.' She moves to indicate the chest of drawers where her medication is stored, but the shaking in her hand is so pronounced and severe she stares at it as though it is not connected to her body, like she has never seen it before. The horror seems to dawn on her anew that this is her body, her arm she has lost control of, and then grief unfolds carefully and precisely on her features as she seems to mourn what this means for her body and her life. I avert my eyes – I do not want her to know that I have noticed her distress at what is happening to her. It is private, not something I should be a part of, no matter what she has asked me to do.

'The bottom drawer,' she says quietly, her upset like a thin paint wash that covers her words – there but not immediately obvious. Still there though, still an indicator of what she is truly feeling.

The district nurse had given me a huge smile on her way out, nodded as though she approved of my visit – and I could see why when I entered the bedroom – my grandmother had seemed pleased to see me, lighter and freer somehow. Relieved, too, I'd imagine.

As I lower myself to the bottom drawer, without intending to, I pause to look at the medication on top of the cabinet: some of the tablets and capsules are distorted behind the colour and curve of the glass and look like the little jars I keep beads in. I know what ails her, but what are all these tablets actually for? How do they alleviate the pain she is in? *Do* they alleviate the pain she is in? If they do, there would be no reason for her to be contemplating what she is, surely?

From the bottom drawer I remove a heavy, large, shallow, lidded box that is a pale beige, the thickness of the butterfly box I once slept in, but not decorated like that one. 'This?' I ask. I hold it up and she nods slowly. Her tremors seem worse today, her face tired and agonised at the same time. I should not stay here too long, but I need to get to know her if I am going to think seriously about what she asked me to do.

'Yes,' she says.

I place the box on the floor by the bed so she can see it, and sit cross-legged in front of it. For some reason, the idea of taking photos of this stuff seems unsavoury as though I am planning to kill her for it. I want to see it, though, because jewellery is how I get to know people.

'You are a true Zebila,' she says suddenly. Although her tremors are more pronounced and have destabilised her mood, she seems able to talk more clearly and fluently today. Maybe that is how it works, with the conditions she has – some days your body, beyond the basic necessities for survival, will concentrate on being able to do one thing.

'What do you mean?' I ask. *Has Abi shown her the DNA test results?* The idea of that panics me, makes me think that after everything they still didn't believe I was one of them.

'When Abimbola said you made jewellery, my heart soared. We are from a gold family. Your grandfather's great-great-grandfather was one of the first Nihanarans to own a gold mine. The Europeans tried to trick him out of it and then with later generations they tried to steal it from our family, but it never worked. It has been passed down through our family until now. My eldest son, Douglas, he is in Nihanara, he runs the family business.' She rests back on her mountain of pillows. 'You are the first one to work with the family metal.'

I don't make much gold jewellery from scratch because it is expensive and not worth having unless it is pure, but I do relove a fair amount of it since once someone has a piece made from gold they're often loath to part with it.

'That is something that makes you special in this family,' my grandmother says. Considering she didn't even see me after I was born, she is laying it on a bit thick – but I don't mind. It's a way of getting to know her; finding out what she is really like. What she is really like is that she over-eggs the pudding because she thinks it will get me to do what she wants. Which shows how little she knows about me.

I open the box and inside there is a universe of wonder. It's almost as though someone has created my fantasy world inside this box. That was why it was so heavy, there is so much inside, and it is disorganised and meshed together, and like something from my very best dreams. I'm not sure where to begin – I have to unravel pieces from each other, which adds to the excitement building inside me. Having to do this starts the reloving process: I can see what different shapes the item can be twisted into, shaped and made. How it can look next to different materials, jewels and other stones and precious items.

The first piece I reach for is a thick link bracelet, heavy because each link is solid, eighteen-carat yellow gold. It'd be impossible to wear for any length of time – male or female – without developing wrist ache. I run my fingers over the flattened top and bottom of the bracelet. They are smooth and cool to my initial touch, leavened to allow them to rest flat against the wrist. 'Is this yours?' I ask.

'Yes. Julius's father gave it to me when we were courting in Nihanara. He did not realise that it was a man's bracelet.' My grand-mother chortles, quietly, the most she can manage, I guess, and the laughter she is able to produce livens her face. It tells me she must have been so in love with my grandfather, the way she laughs at the thought of him. 'He had no idea. It was far too heavy, too thick.' If I was to relove this item, I would take it apart, break it down to its tiny component links and then remake several items to suit the owner. I usually start with the person, but in this case, it would need to be broken down and rebuilt.

'Tell me a story about you. Something that no one else knows,' I say to her. 'Not about the jewellery, anything about you.'

She seems to go away to another place while she thinks about this. Her body tremors, her face twitches violently on her right cheekbone, but her eyes are still and steady as she contemplates what it is she does not mind me knowing that no one else knows. 'Your grandfather, he was called Ivor, too, he was not the first man to win my heart,' she confesses. 'There was another boy who . . . he was from another family in the same city. We had grown up together. I met him at school. The three of us, we were friends but it was clear to me as we moved through our years who I was to marry.'

A shiver of recognition shimmers through me – it sounds like the situation I was in with Dylan and Seth. My grandfather was her Seth – not the first to win her heart, but the one she realised she loved and wanted to be with forever. I stop myself there, prevent myself from remembering where that eventually led.

'Didn't the other boy love you enough?' I asked. Or was it like with Dylan and me – did she finally stop loving him when she realised how uninterested he was in anything except keeping her dangling on a line for when he needed an ego boost or an unchaste Christmas kiss.

My grandmother frowns at me as though I am being ridiculous at the very idea that someone wouldn't love her enough. 'Not at all. They were both in love with me.' It must be nice to have that certainty of how other people feel about you.

'If you loved him, he loved you, and he was the man you were meant to marry, then why didn't you?'

'He was not the man who I was meant to marry. Ivor was.' I must look confused. 'Ivor Zebila was from a decent family. They had status and wealth.'

'The other boy didn't?'

'He was nice, he had some wealth, but he was not a Zebila. Everyone knew of the Zebilas. They were respected and coveted.'

'That was important to you?' Status, wealth, power. Everything done for show.

'When you grow up with very little, you learn what is important and necessary to have in life. Their parents could both afford the school, my parents had to work long and hard to make enough money to send me, the eldest of their six daughters, to school. I knew what was important, what I had to do for my family.'

So not like Seth, Dylan and me at all, really. I know nothing of what it must have been like to be in love with someone but to do your duty and marry someone else because it will mean your family is taken care of, your sisters will be able to go to school and your parents will not have to work so hard.

It still rankles, though, that she would choose money, wealth and status over love. She is doing a very good job of removing any images I might have had in my head of her being a fluffy grandmother, ill and sickly, who is coming to the end of a life lived with and filled by love. She is showing me she will do whatever it takes to get what she wants.

'Did you love my grandfather?'

'Of course. I grew to love him over the years, very much. He chose me because he knew I would make a good wife, I would improve the standing of their family by giving him strong children. You asked me to tell you something that no one knew and that was it. Are you disappointed?'

'No, no, just surprised at how candid you are.'

'I see.'

I look down at the bracelet again. I would struggle to remake this piece even if I had broken it down. It would need to be completely melted to start again. Or maybe...I pick it up again. If I were to reshape one of the links into a circle, I could make it into a flower pendant. Solder the different links on to the circle. Or maybe the links laid out in a seemingly random pattern, linked into an asymmetric chainmail design, that would sit across the chest. It would be heavy but, like the other design, showy, large, unmissable. This is what she would like – the outward appearance of wealth. I move the links, see how they look next to each other.

'Would you like to take that?' Mrs Zebila asks.

'Pardon?' I realise what she is talking about. 'No, no. Thank you, but no. I'm curious. I love looking at jewellery, it's one of my favourite things to do. Which is why this collecton is simply amazing to me.' Carefully, I lay the bracelet back in the box.

'I insist you have it.'

'No, I have no use for it. I don't keep things I don't need or don't fit into my life.'

Silence passes between us because I'm not sure what either of us are meant to say to my unintentional reminder of who I am. Instead of speaking, I place the lid back on the box. 'I think I'd better go.'

'You will come back tomorrow?' she asks eagerly.

'Do you want me to?'

'Yes, of course. Clemency, it is such a pleasure to see you.'

I know she wants something, but it's nice to hear. 'I'll come back tomorrow then.'

34

Abi

To: Jonas Zebila
From: Abi Zebila
Subject: Is it me?
Thursday, 16 July 2015

Dear J,

So here we are. Two weeks later and *nada*. I've had daily texts from her saying hello and asking how we are, but nothing more. No asking to meet up or to talk on the phone, nothing.

Clearly she's keeping us at arm's length. Declan – yes, I finally told him everything – reckons it's to do with Gran. But he would say that, seeing as he's terrified of her. We're all on a knife-edge in the house, except Lily-Rose who asks to see the photos again and again because she's fascinated by having so many photos of this woman who is her aunt, once being as small as her. She's not that close to Declan's sisters, mainly because Declan won't spend that much time with them. Not sure why, but you know what? My family's F'd up enough, he's not forthcoming on sharing that with me.

I hear Mummy and Daddy talking sometimes in the middle of the night, and, you know, they can't seem to get over this barrier between them and say what they really feel. I mean, if I had the child I hadn't seen in nearly forty years walk into my life, I'd be talking with the only other person who'd understand how I felt. They can't seem to do that. They're a lot nicer to each other nowadays, and there's far less of an atmosphere, but they don't talk.

Declan and I talk all the time even when we're not living together. He's actually been really supportive during all this, and I wish I didn't have that fear of being with him all the time. If I start to rely on him, will he let me down again? I know it was years ago, but I'm sort of waiting for him to do it again.

Maybe that's what Mummy and Daddy are thinking. That if they talk, they have to go over what happened, and why they did it, and what it means about them. Because I can't imagine what's going through their heads.

Ivor is on another planet. I don't know what his f-ing problem is, but he's been saying stuff about Clemency being a con artist. He never says it in front of Mummy and Daddy, but if it's just me and him, he'll make some comment about how we're such a trusting family and how she could be from anywhere. I've told him to tell that to Mummy and Daddy if he truly believes that – funnily enough, he won't.

I wonder if Declan is right and this is all down to Gran – Clemency did look like she'd seen a ghost when she came out of Gran's room. Maybe Gran told her to back off? But she wouldn't do that, would she? Look who I'm asking!!! Gran cried with the rest of us, though, so I'm not sure why she'd warn Clemency off.

Thing is, Gran's not always rational these days. That's a realisation I'm coming to accept. She isn't making sense a lot of the time, she forgets things, she becomes incredibly angry if you point out something contra-dictory. On top of the other stuff wrong with her, I'm not surprised Mummy wants to get her proper, specialist care from people who can tend to her needs around the clock, give her meds at the right times in the right doses. Also, sometimes it's a struggle to get her to take the meds. She doesn't want to, doesn't like the side effects, wants to skip some in case they're what's making her ill.

I've said to Daddy that I'd get her a nice room at our place, I could work out a good deal, I'd see her almost every day, there are nurses who are trained to deal with people who aren't handling their long-term ill-nesses very well. When I mentioned it at dinner, after Lily-Rose was in bed, Daddy got really angry. 'That's not how we deal with problems in this family,' he said. We were all sitting there and he raised his voice.

'We find a way to take care of family members, we don't move them out and abandon them at the first sign of trouble.'

None of us said anything and even Ivor looked uncomfortable. It took Daddy a couple of minutes to realise what he'd said in the light of all the recent revelations and he seemed very embarrassed and ashamed. Maybe that's what the problem is, why he and Mummy can't talk – they're ashamed of what they did. Not that I think they'd ever admit it to anyone – not even each other. Kind of ended the discussion about what next for Gran, though.

Why doesn't Clemency call? Things got so much better at home after she arrived, and now we're all in this limbo of waiting for her to get in touch again. I miss her. I miss you.

Lots of love,
Abi
xxxx

35

Smitty

Her jewellery box is like nothing I've ever been through. I thought Mrs Lehtinen's was incredible but my grandmother's is out of this world. I want to run my fingers through it, feel the different textures dribble through my fingers. I have been to see her on ten of the past fourteen days. Sometimes she has had to struggle to the door, because it is not a day when she is visited by the district nurse, and I have sensed her mortification at being helped back to bed.

My guilt at not being in touch properly with Abi grows every day, but my visits are not just so I can get to know my grandmother, but also for Abi and the rest of her family, too. It might not be much, spending time with my grandmother to get to know her, seeing if I can stop her thinking about what she wants to do, but if I get this right they'll never even know what she was planning. And they will have their grandmother, mother, mother-in-law – whatever role she plays in their life – around for as long as possible. I know she thinks I have been doing this to steel myself to be able to do it, but in reality I want her to see that life is worth living. I am being selfish, yes, but like I wanted Dad around as long as possible (and he wanted to stay as long as possible), I want my grandmother around as long as possible, too.

I have looked through her jewellery – every piece is real – and she has told stories related to every item. The multi-strand pearl choker and matching bracelet that she wore to meet the President of Nihanara at the Nihanara High Commission in London when my grandfather, Ivor, was still alive: 'I wore traditional Nihanara dress in a royal blue silk. Ivor had it made for me.'

The gold and emerald necklace – each of the twelve emeralds the size of a penny – that she was given by her husband after she had her first son, Douglas: 'He was so proud I had given him a son that he spent far too much money on that necklace. I had nowhere to wear it, of course.' Then there were the large, twenty pence-sized diamond earrings that she wore to my birth father's graduation from law school: 'It was one of the proudest days of my life.' The lily-shaped brooch studded with rubies and sapphires that she had worn to my brother Ivor's graduation from university: 'Another of the proudest days of my life.'

I had brought some dividers from my workshop and put them in the jewellery box – on the days she could barely speak, I would go through it all, untangling what I could and organising them into categories and colours. On the days she couldn't speak, I would simply go through the jewellery and make up stories about the items I found – the white gold tennis bracelet, the plaited white gold and yellow gold necklace, the diamond-studded cuff (which seemed quite radical for someone as conservative as her) – as I might have done if I'd had access to the box as a child. The days she could speak, she would try to give me whichever piece of jewellery I had been looking at and I would always have to say no.

On the eleventh day, when I did not want to pore through her jewellery any more, listening to the stories that came with each piece, I sat and looked at her. She seemed better, stronger. Maybe this is what she needs: someone to look after her, spend time with her, rather than simply feeding her, medicating her, ensuring her basic needs are met. I could be that person. Or I could try. I could fit in these visits around my work, which would bond us and would allow her to think that maybe carrying on for a little longer may not be so bad. They are only snatches of time that I have spent with her, but with her jewellery and her stories, I feel like I have got to know her a little better, I can see her as my grandmother rather than simply the woman who gave birth to the man who impregnated my birth mother. I have a sense of what she is like, but that doesn't bother me. Maybe if I did spend more time with her, if I did listen to her worries, she might come to realise that carrying on for a little longer need not be so bad. I am being arrogant, I suppose, arrogant and selfish, but I have developed a kind of grudging admiration for who she is, how uncompromising she has been throughout her life. I like her in the way I would possibly like my cousin Nancy if Nancy hadn't spent what felt like her every waking moment trying to destroy me. My grandmother may not be likeable or to everyone's taste, but I have found myself enjoying the time I have spent with her these past couple of weeks. It's been at the expense of seeing Abi, who I would love to spend time with, but this has been necessary and far more urgent.

'I am not scared of dying,' my grandmother says to me, as though we are in the middle of a conversation.

I nod at her, I feel she has more to say. Today is a day when she can speak with long gaps to gather herself. And I think she can sense that today is the day where we have reached a crossroads with this arrangement. It's been miraculous that it has lasted this long without us being caught out, and it can't continue.

'You asked me to tell you something about myself that no one knows,' she continues. 'I am not scared of dying. I am scared of merely existing.'

'But haven't you felt better this past little while? You seem better.'

'I am existing. Not living. I am counting down time until the end.'

'But if you got involved in more things, found stuff that you enjoyed doing, you might not feel like that,' I say.

She lifts her arms, reminds me of the quaking in her hands – the way she is not in control of herself. The way that even if she does find something she enjoys it would have to be suitable for her needs.

'Clemency, I am not scared of dying. I am scared of being locked into this body, unable to escape, unable to tell anyone to let me go.'

That horrific image of being in trapped inside myself – unable to move, to speak, to let anyone know how much I still understand and feel – sends chilling vibrations through me and reminds me again of that terror of mine of being trapped and having to claw my way out of anywhere, but to have my prison be my own body...I shudder again.

'You could leave a living will, a do not resuscitate order? Tell people now that's what you want.' Doing that would be better than what she is asking of me. I am not a person who is impressed by money and position, like my grandmother is, we have very little common ground, but she is still a part of my family I have only recently found. I do not want to have to live with the memory of her death when I have only had a glimpse of her life.

'Yes, I could,' she says sadly, disappointed that I've even suggested this when it feels like a suitable middle ground.

'Why isn't that a good option?' I ask.

'My illnesses, they have taken over my body, I am at their mercy...I can be sure of nothing but the knowledge that when this disease is good and ready it will take me...I do not want to leave this to chance...I do not want to linger...I want the chance to choose. My one last decision that my illnesses cannot take away from me.'

I know what she is saying because these past few days I have learnt she has a need to be back in control, in even the smallest way possible. But it still feels so wrong, wanting me to do this. 'Why didn't you see me when I was born?' I ask. This still niggles at me. She wants me to do something so huge for her, but she did not want to see me when I first came into existence. And, in some ways, it feels like she only wants to see me now because she wants something from me – if she did not need me, I would not exist for her.

She stares at me, gathering herself to produce a chunk of speech that is coherent and fluent, not halted and slurred. 'I was a proud woman. I wanted to see you, my first grandchild, but...I was scared of what people would say. I was worried about what our family would look like. An unmarried young girl is suddenly with child months after moving into my home. I thought people would believe that my husband, not Julius, was responsible. Most of all, I did not see you because Julius...he was not ready for the responsibility. He was too young.'

222

He shouldn't have had sex then, crosses rather uncharitably through my mind. When I started having sex at fifteen, I wasn't ready to be a parent. I probably would have done it if it was necessary but I wouldn't have been ready for it.

'Did he want to keep me?' I ask her.

She manages to pull her twitching face into a smile. 'You do not want to know the answer to that question,' she replies.

'I do, I really do.'

'Clemency. . . . I do not know you well. I wish I did not have this clock above my head that will stop me from getting to know you. I would like the time to know you, so I could explain the answer to that question. But even if my body lives on, locked in or not, my mind will not allow me to know you more than this. This is the most well I will ever feel again. This is the most I will ever get to know you. I will never know you enough to explain.'

That causes tears to spring into my eyes and my stomach swirl with a fluttering of ice butterflies. No matter how much time I spend with her, this is the most she will ever get to know me.

'I am grateful I have lived long enough to meet you. I wish I had not been so proud. I wish I had more time.'

'I don't know what to say,' I confess when I have gathered myself together.

'Say you will think about what I have asked of you,' she says. 'I am not scared of dying, remember that. I am scared of merely existing. Say you promise you will think about what I have asked of you.'

I sigh deeply, take a deep breath to replace the air my sigh has stolen. This time, I know when I say it, I will mean it – I will be doing nothing but thinking about it. 'I promise,' I state.

36

Smitty

In my nightmares, things happen to me and I am powerless to stop them. I can usually see what is about to happen, how things are going to turn out, but I can't change the outcome. I am usually too shocked or too frightened to fight back or even to speak.

This is one of my nightmare moments. Except I am wide awake.

I have wandered back from my workshop, my head full of how to negotiate a lower price for the latest quote for Melissa's locket to become a watch because it is astronomical. Even if I didn't charge her for my work it would be too much. I have also had another call from Mrs Lehtinen, wanting me to come back and show her some design ideas. I'm sure she just wants an update on whether I am the girl in the butterfly box. I have five wedding rings to make as well as a twenty-first birthday pendant to design for the world's most picky mother. As I walked home – no Tyler in Beached Heads, I noticed – I dreamed of a sit down, followed by a long hot shower.

I was tired, but I was enjoying the haze of work, the fug that I have been constantly carrying with me, because it stopped me thinking about the other stuff. A distance away from home, I clocked the outlines of a woman and a young girl on the bench nearest my block of flats. The woman wasn't simply sitting on the bench, she was reclining on it with her shorts-exposed legs stretched out in front of her. Sunglasses adorned her face, and the wind teased her hair while she intently read from the mobile in her left hand. Her right hand she used to brush her hair out of her face, twirling the ends of random locks around her fingers. The girl, her head surrounded by blonde ringlets, was dancing and singing around the bench, putting on a show for the uninterested woman she is performing for.

I was in a haze, my head in the clouds, and it took a moment for me to get here, to this moment. This moment where I register that I am in a nightmare situation because the person on the bench is the monster from almost every single bad dream I have ever had.

This moment, when I realise what is unfolding in front of me, is like that other moment in a nightmare where I try to stop running, but my feet slip and slide and I can't stop because I'm in motion, my body is propelling me forwards, closer and closer towards the monster. But the fear and horror I feel makes me reek, and the monster catches my scent, stops what it is doing and looks up, away from its mobile, in my direction. I can't stop, I have nowhere to run to, because the monster has seen me, and it takes its sunglasses off, lowers its mobile and smiles at me before it trills, 'Hi!'

She is shrill when she longs to be husky, sexy, the stuff of men's wet dreams. 'We just happened to be in the area.'

'Auntie Smitty!' Sienna squeals. She hurtles across the distance, squealing my name as she runs. 'Auntie Smitty! Auntie Smitty! Auntie Smitty!'

At speed she collides with my legs and I almost topple backwards but manage to keep upright. She wraps her arms around me like she is a koala and I am the trunk of a tree. Slowly, I lower myself to her height and wrap my arms around her. 'You must have grown about eight foot,' I say to her, but I can't take my eyes off the reclining monster that is smiling on the bench.

My cousin Nancy has a really successful website. Everyone seems to love it. It's called Guide To Femininity and it's all about how to be feminine in the face of a world where, apparently, we women have forgotten how. She actually makes a living from it now because for the last six months or so, since there's been a change in content and focus, her blog has received some critically acclaimed attention and people have been falling over themselves to advertise on it and sponsor it and have her give advice in their publications. There's even been talk of a book deal, which will take her profile to the next level, although that's not materialised yet because she's still at the stage of considering her options.

Nancy is not my 'real' cousin. We're not connected by flesh and blood. She's my mother's brother's daughter. And she's brunette. And white. And nothing at all like me. We grew up together, saw each other almost every day because we went to the same school and stuff, but we're not 'real' cousins. She tells that to anyone she meets. I never say things like that because, to me, it's not relevant, but to Nancy it's probably the most important thing there is about our connection. We are not 'real' cousins.

With Nancy, April 1986, Otley

'Why aren't I your "real" cousin?' I asked her. I was genuinely confused. What wasn't real about me? My dad said the stuff on telly wasn't real, that monsters that live under your bed weren't real, that a lot of the storybooks I liked didn't have 'real' stories but I was real, I thought. I could touch myself, I could see myself in the mirror, I ate real food and I drank real drinks, and I slept in a real bed and wore real clothes. Why wasn't I real to Nancy?

'You're just not. That's what Dad says. You're not my real cousin. He said Auntie Heather could pretend all she likes but you're not a real member of the family. It's just the way it is.'

'I am real, I am,' I said.

'No, you're not. You really, really are not.'

Sienna is holding up my hand so she can use me as the axis for her pirouettes. Last time I saw her she was trying to perfect this move. She is effortlessly expert now: with a slight bounce she is up on to the rubber toe of her pink DMs, the flat of her other foot rests on her inner knee, her arm is up, clinging on to my hand, and spin, spin, spin. She's a red-blue-blonde blur as she spins herself three times without pause. 'Mum says we're going to stay with you for a long time,' she informs me as she spins. 'I might even go to school here.' Spin. 'That's right, isn't it, Mum?'

226

'*Nancy,*' my cousin hisses to correct her. Nancy's daughter is meant to call her 'Nancy' instead of 'Mum' because any woman who has a child needs to reclaim her femininity by retaining her given name at all times. This means even having your offspring call you by your name to prevent you from being seen as 'just' a mother. If I had a child, which I don't so maybe what I think isn't relevant, I would want them to call me 'Mum' no matter what it did to my femininity because they're the only person/people in the whole world who could call me that. I'd savour that as the rare and precious gem it was . . . but maybe that's just childless me. 'And no, that's not what I said,' Nancy says to her daughter.

She revolves to face me, switches on the beseeching eyes and winning smile, forgetting it is me she is talking to, not Mum. 'I said that we'd come to see her Auntie Clem and if she had space we'd ask if we could stay for a little while because we can't really afford a holiday this year.'

Sienna stops her spinning, cocks her head to one side, gives her mother a Paddington Hard Stare that would put to shame not only Mr Wallace the sweaty-palmed estate agent but also the bear after which the look is named. 'You did say that,' Sienna tells her. 'You really did.' She turns to me, the PHS gone. 'Do you have space?'

'Erm, I'm not sure,' I say. An outright no to this child is never possible.

'Where's Grandma Heather?' Sienna asks. She has no issues with blood connections and being real – everyone is related to her if they talk to her long enough. 'We rang the doorbell and Grandma Heather didn't answer. Mum said we had to leave so early this morning and get Grandma Heather to let us in while you were at work so we'd be sitting drinking tea waiting for you to come back from work.'

'I'm sure I didn't say it like that.'

Her daughter gives her the side-eye. 'Yes, you did, Mum.'

'Nancy. Call me Nancy.' Sienna never does call her Nancy because, I suspect, she thinks it's stupid.

'You said it'd be harder for Auntie Smitty to get us out if we had our feet under the table by the time she saw us.'

'I think you misunderstood.' Nancy grins at me, pushes her sunglasses on to the top of her head, checks her phone and then reholsters it in the back pocket of her shorts like it's a gun. I think Nancy would cease to exist if she was ever parted from her phone, and all the stuff – the internet, social media, her website/blog – that is wrapped up inside the phone like a swaddled baby in a manger. 'She's so funny. You must remember how funny she is.'

I keep my attention on Sienna. 'My mum is probably out on her bike.'

'Grandma Heather has a bike. True, true?' Sienna asks.

'More of a trike. But yes, true, true. She goes out most days on it. She's got a little basket on the front for her packed lunch and she goes off exploring.'

'You are not serious!' Nancy exclaims. 'I just can't imagine your mum doing that.'

My gaze returns to my cousin for a moment, before it moves on to the sea behind her. I can't let them stay. Much as I'd love to spend time with Sienna, I can't even let them into my flat. If they cross the threshold they will not leave again. Nancy will do what she always does and convince Mum that they deserve to be living there, and that Nancy is entitled to my bedroom while I am relegated to the box room with the single bed and worst views in the flat. If I let them into my flat I will have let Nancy get away with what she's done. Again. Not just this last time but all the times over all the years.

'Auntie Smitty,' Sienna says, tugging on my jacket.

'Yes?'

She uses her hand to indicate she wants me to come closer to her. Obligingly, I bend to her height. 'I need the toilet,' she whispers into my ear. 'Right. Now.'

I straighten up. Nancy gives me a small shrug of helplessness.

Well, that's that then.

With Nancy, July 2009, Karina's Jewels, Leeds
The shop was empty and I was running a cloth over the glass cases for something to do in the lull. Business had been slow lately and I'd

been waiting for Karina to give me the go ahead to make some new pieces. She was still considering my proposals because she wasn't convinced they made good business sense. They did. I was only planning on doing more of what had been selling but she was still vacillating.

It was a blessed relief to have the bell ting as someone entered the shop. The relief lasted less than ten seconds. Nancy, wearing hot pants, vest top and jewelled flip-flops, walked in and grinned at me. Nowadays, if I saw her away from family occasions it was because she had to deliver some bad news.

'Hi,' she said shyly.

'Hi,' I replied.

'I have some news,' she said. She bit her lower lip nervously, lowered her eyes and took a several deep breaths. 'I'm just going to tell you, if that's OK?'

I nodded and braced myself, waited to hear what it was.

'I'm pregnant,' she said. She patted her stomach. 'Three months but I'm not really showing yet. Probably because of how super-fit my body is.'

'That's amazing news!' I squealed. I went forwards, hugged her. I hadn't hugged Nancy in years, I would rather hug a giant sewer rat normally (I have a rat phobia), but this was different. This was the sort of news you were always happy about if they were happy. 'Congratulations!'

'Thanks, Clem,' she said. She stood back. 'I wanted to tell you myself because I wasn't sure how upset you'd be.'

'Upset? Why would I be upset?'

She lowered her eyes, stared at the ground for a few seconds. It was the perfect amount of time for her to know she'd destabilised and worried me, and the right amount of time for me to plant my feet firmly on the ground so I wouldn't fall over at whatever revelation was coming next.

'The father...You have to understand that he wanted to tell you himself, but I said I'd do it.' *I wanted to see your face, to experience your pain,* Clem added silently. I braced myself to hear Seth's name. To discover that he had succumbed. 'It's Dylan.'

'Dylan? Dylan,' I repeated. '*My* Dylan?'

She nodded.

I took a step back. My Dylan had got her pregnant. He would never take that next step with me, he would never cross that friendship barrier and do more than kiss me to wind up Seth, but he'd knocked *her* up. My feelings for him had evaporated long before I fell for Seth, but this was still a blow. 'But...when...' My voice failed me. It couldn't be true. I kept all such people away from Nancy because she always made a play for them, always tried to get one over on me. Seth was the absolute love of my life. *Now.* But I had to admit a small patch of my heart, an area so small it was barely there at all, lived forever as that eighteen-year-old girl who fell in proper love for the first time ever with Dylan.

'Remember Seth's party a few years back?' Nancy had the reaction she wanted with that revelation, she could discard that faked humbleness and revel in twisting the knife. My pain was like oxygen to her sometimes. I never knew why. 'I know I gate-crashed, but we got talking. I went over to Sheffield to see him and one thing led to another.'

Seth's party was back in 2003. 'Six years ago? You've been sleeping with him for six years?' *And he never mentioned it? Not possible.*

She nodded. 'Well, it fizzled out for a bit. I ran into him a few months ago and we discovered that we still had feelings for each other so, you know, one thing led to another again. We didn't want to hurt you so thought we'd keep it a secret.'

She had slept with Dylan only a handful of times at the most. I knew how Nancy twisted things; she wasn't outright lying because she knew I could check with Dylan and he would tell me the truth if questioned. What she was saying was this: she'd gone to see him and they'd fucked once. To have travelled all that way she must have really liked him but of course, Dylan being Dylan, he wasn't interested so she gathered up her dignity, as tattered as it was, and walked away. Six years later she crosses paths with him again, they hook up again. This time she's sure it'll work out differently, that over time his heart would have grown fonder for her, because her heart has certainly grown fonder for him, and being older, she thinks that maybe he'll be ready to settle down with her. But it doesn't work out like that. So the next couple of times they hook up, she plans to find a way to tie him to her. She probably thought a pregnancy scare would be enough to bond them, to maybe get him to consider how life wouldn't be so terrible if they were forever linked. But obviously that didn't work out and the scare became a reality. And he obviously hadn't reacted positively, because if he had, or if they'd been truly dating, she would have told me with him standing beside her. This, *this* was just a brief, not-even-long-enough-to-become-sordid fling. And he had done that. Knowing who she was, he had done that.

'That's even more brilliant news,' I said. I wrenched a smile across my face, staple-gunned it into place and yanked my arms up, moved my body forwards to give her another hug. 'My cousin and one of my best friends having a baby together. That's the best of both worlds for me. Thank you so much, Nancy. I can't wait to tell Seth, he'll be over the moon, too.'

'You don't mind?' she asked, confused and uncertain. She was wondering why I wasn't breaking down, where my pain and upset and hurt had vanished to.

'Why would I mind? I was a bit shocked at first but this is amazing news. Shall we go out and celebrate later?' I asked her. 'Obviously, soft drinks for you, but I'll drink enough for the both of us.' I could ask her for a drink because never in a million years would she go for one if she thought I was happy about this.

'Yeah, yeah,' she said. 'I'll call you about it.'

Once she left, I kept myself together for another half an hour to make sure she had truly gone. Then I flipped on the 'back in five minutes' sign, locked the doors and went into the back, fell to my knees and sobbed my heart out. My sobs were an outpouring of the pain of Dylan wanting her when he had never truly wanted me. After all those years of making me think he could possibly fall for me, after flirting mercilessly with me at Seth's party, he had slept with *her* straight afterwards. Her of all people. It was such a deep betrayal by someone I still thought of as my friend.

I spent far too long in the back crying. I had to do it there, alone, because no one else would understand, especially not Seth. He'd think I was still in love with Dylan when I wasn't, when I had stopped feeling like that about Dylan ages before Seth and I got together. At the end of it, what I was crying about wasn't even the fact that Dylan had slept with Nancy. It was the fact that after all these years, Nancy had managed to find another way to prove that I wasn't real.

My cousin Nancy wanders from room to room in my flat, taking in the décor, noting which rooms you can see the sea from, which rooms have carpets and which have floorboards. She's like a homebuyer, mentally rearranging the furniture, seeing how she'll make it hers once she takes over the place. That's a given now, of course. Sienna is in the long, wide corridor, hopping on to alternate parquet blocks with alternate feet, exclaiming 'Tah-dah!' each time she lands successfully on one foot.

'I like your house, Auntie Smitty,' she tells me every fourth block.

'It's lovely, isn't it?' Nancy states. She has returned to stand outside the main bedroom, my bedroom, mobile in hand ready to snap a photo. That'll be up on her blog, Twitter, Instagram and Facebook soon – tagged as where she's staying for the summer with a view to staying permanently. She'll probably then do a selfie by the window to get the sea view in shot, so everyone who follows her and has friended her can see what she's looking at while she types up her latest missive from the world of femininity.

The thumb on her right hand, topped with a perfectly manicured dusky pink nail, hovers over the camera-shaped button on her mobile. She moves the phone carefully, trying to capture the right light.

'Clemency! Are you home?' Mum calls from the front door.

'Yes, Mum,' I say back. Nancy doesn't take her photo. Instead, she turns towards my mother's voice, her face is radiant with joy because Mum's here. And Mum is someone who'll speak to her at last. In all the time Nancy has been here, outside and inside the flat, it's been unsettling for her that I still haven't spoken to her. Because, well, why the hell should I?

'We're here too!' Sienna sings. She runs back down the corridor, turns the corner to where the coats are hung and where my mother is entering the flat.

'Sienna? Oh my Lord! What are you doing here?'

'We came for a holiday! Mum said if we like it we're going to stay and I can go to school here.'

'I didn't say that!' Nancy says. She goes to the source of the voices, lifts her arms to receive and give a welcoming hug to my mother before she disappears around the corner.

'What a wonderful surprise!' Mum says.

'You made it sound so amazing in your letters and postcards we had to come see for ourselves,' Nancy tells Mum. Her words are muffled, I presume from when she hugs my mother. 'It certainly is wonderful.' These words are punctuated by kisses.

'Clemency!' Mum calls. 'Isn't this a marvellous surprise?'

'It's certainly a surprise,' I state quietly.

'Well, of course you must stay. Mustn't they, Clemency? It'll be so lovely having the two of you around for a while.' Mum is offering room in my home to my monster. I don't know why that's such a surprise to me after all these years, but it is. 'Clemency! It'll be lovely having them around for a while, won't it?'

'I'm going for a shower,' I say loudly. And without waiting for a reply, I go into the bathroom, shut and lock the door.

With me, April 2015, Otley

Hi Clem. How's it all going?
We haven't had a catch-up in so long.
What's new with you?
Listen, if you're trying for a baby, let me know.
I've spoken to lots of fertility experts for the blog,
so I can give you lots of tips.
Talk soon. N x
P.S. Don't forget the folic acid!!!!

Her hair in my bed, the latest posts on her blog, this text sent out of the blue. It still wasn't the right time to deal with this, I was too exhausted, too tapped out by what was coming with Dad, but I had to make plans. I had to talk to Seth, but first of all, I had to have a Plan B because I couldn't sleepwalk into Nancy ruining another part of my life.

They're like three generations of a family. When I finally emerge from the bathroom, I stand unnoticed at the doorway watching this family tableau. The daughter reclines on the sofa with a glass of wine in a red goblet, the mother sits in the armchair, her glasses perched on her nose as she goes through her latest Sudoku puzzle, the grand-daughter lies on the floor eating a bowl of sweetcorn, tuna and pasta with her fingers while glued to CBeebies. I'm the outsider in this place, there is no space for me here.

This was what it'd been like at the Zebilas, my other family's house, except they had four generations and there'd been a lot more crying. I looked like them, I had the same blood, but I was an outsider, someone who had to be welcomed in and even then, didn't quite fit.

What I am looking at now, just as I was looking at with the Zebilas, is a family. And I don't really fit into either one. Like the outsider I am, I retreat, return to my room before anyone can raise the issue of Nancy taking over my room because it has a desk and I already have a space in my workshop to work. That's what will happen. That's what's always happened. When it comes to Nancy – not so much Sienna but Nancy – Mum often thinks being in my thirties is just like it was when I was eight and I gave Nancy my doll because she cried so hard that my one had prettier, nicer clothes than hers. And Mum believes that being in my thirties is like it was when I was twelve and I let Nancy 'borrow' my brand new raincoat because hers had a rip in it even though I knew I'd never get it back. And Mum is certain being in my thirties is just like when I was sixteen and I had to give Nancy my revision notes because she hadn't had time to do them, what with all the dates she'd been on. Mum thinks it's just like being thirty-two, calling one of my best friends to congratulate him on knocking up my cousin and having him tell me that it was all a mistake and he wished he'd used contraception, no matter what she'd said about being on the Pill. And when I wouldn't let him get away with that because he was just as responsible as she was, him saying that he wished he could get out of it, or failing that, if she was going through with the pregnancy, that she'd have 'it' adopted or something, so he didn't have to be involved. (To my silence on the phone at that, he stammered, 'Oh, Smitty, I didn't mean— I just— I'm sorry, mate, that was out of order. But you know what I mean.' I knew what he meant, yes, and I was so relieved at that moment I wasn't still in love with him.)

I retreat to my bedroom before the scenario that has played out in my life so many times starts to unfold here, too. I'm also sure to lock the door. It makes me feel safer from the monster outside.

37

Abi

To: Jonas Zebila
From: Abi Zebila
Subject: Sod this for a game of soldiers
Monday, 20 July 2015

Nothing new here, really: Clemency is still freezing me out despite the bullshit 'how are you' text every day. Mummy and Daddy are still not talking about anything beyond everyday surface stuff. Ivor has, thankfully, stopped his insane theories since I roared at him that we'd done a DNA test and he could see the results if he wanted. I've never shouted at him like that before, but he caught me at a particularly hormonal moment.

Lily-Rose continues to be the light of my life. I'm attaching a scan of the picture she drew of you and Meredith the other day. She just suddenly drew it without any prompting from me. I think knowing about Clemency has reminded her of you and Meredith. I'm not sure about your hair being so big, but I can see a likeness, can't you? Oh, wait, you won't be replying so you can't tell me if you see a resemblance or not. Yes, you're pissing me off as well.

All this is not helped by how bad Gran is right now. She seemed to rally for a couple of weeks, she seemed to have a new purpose, but now she's sliding again. It's so distressing, especially as there's no one who understands. She's alienated everyone and even now, she can turn on you so suddenly, be so vicious, everyone is just cautious around her and

I can't explain how scared I am about the thought of her not being here any more.

Declan has had his monthly meltdown, asking why we won't get married. I couldn't even be bothered to reply. I'm feeling low, J, really low.

Abi

xxxxx

38

Smitty

Mum has insisted I bring her to Beached Heads. Since we met my other family I am her new special project. She has been carving out time for us to spend together, and she wants to know about my life.

She lurks outside my room, probably listening to my phone calls, she comes into whichever room I am in in the house to see what I'm up to and so we can spend some time together. With Nancy and Sienna here, I'm amazed she is bothering so much with me. But they're hers, I suppose, already permanently bonded by blood. I am now an unknown quantity. Which is nonsense because Mum does know me. Every time she successfully guilt-trips me proves she knows me, every time I bite back at one of her ridiculous statements proves she knows me, every day that I am on this Earth and she is too proves she knows me. She's my 'Mum' but it seems she's the only person who needs convincing of that.

Mum, though, doesn't feel like my 'Mum', the entity who I love more than most people on Earth, and is on a mission to reassert herself. Part of that involves invading my space here at Beached Heads.

Tyler is working. He moves easily behind the counter, smiling, humming quietly, generally infusing the place with the kind of joy you don't often find in places where you spend money. My crush on him is slowly becoming out of control. Ever since he taught me to make coffee, gave me a place to forget who I am for a little bit, I have managed to become as giddy and fizzy as a teenager around him. Instead of being imbued with the feelings for another that a thirty-seven-year-old would have, emotions that can be analysed and categorised, written about and discussed, whenever I step in the glass doors of this café on the beach, all my other worries fall away and I am plunged into a vat of raw, unfathomable, delightful nonsenseness. I am too old to be feeling this and that's wonderful.

Mum and I sit in one of the sofas by the window. 'This is a lovely place, Clemency. I can see why you like it here.'

'Hmmmm…' I reply. Tyler wipes the spout of the milk steamer and frother with his ubiquitous white cloth and it's suddenly, irrationally, the most erotic thing I've seen in weeks.

'Welcome, welcome, faces old and new,' Tyler says. He stands in front of our table like a tall sentinel – ready and waiting to do our bidding.

'Interesting choice of words there, Tyler. Care to elaborate which one of us is which?'

He claps his hands quietly together then hangs his head with his hands still clasped. 'And there we have it, my foot firmly in my mouth with no chance of getting it out without causing too much damage.' He rotates rapidly and marches away, back behind his counter. A few seconds later, he returns. With a flourish, he says, 'Hello, Clemency. Or would you prefer I call you Smitty today?'

'Either is fine with me.'

His apron is well-starched, navy blue with an elaborate BH embroidered on the front in gold thread, like the one he put on me when we made coffee. 'Well, it is lovely to see you again.' He turns his attentions to Mum. 'Hello, it's fantastic to meet you, too.'

I have to introduce them and I'm going to have to suffer the silence, the stare, the sudden need Mum will develop to root through her bag for something important while the awkward moment passes. This is why I keep my worlds apart. When you separate pieces of yourself like the sections in a cutlery drawer, things don't bleed and merge into each other, things don't need complicated explanations.

'Tyler, this is my mother, Heather. Mum, this is Tyler, he owns Beached Heads and makes the best coffee ever.'

'You're too kind,' Tyler says, and extends his hand to my mother. 'Pleased to meet you, Mrs Smittson.' Mum will like that: introduced by her first name but he instantly defers to the formal and altogether more respectful way of addressing her.

Mum takes his hand. 'How do you do?' she says. I've never heard her say that, ever. She sounds like she's the Queen meeting a lowly subject.

'Do you share your daughter's obsession with coffee, or are you more of a tea drinker?' Tyler asks. He hasn't missed a beat, hasn't thrown one questioning or incredulous look our way. 'If I may be so bold as to suggest my special, loose-leaf tea blend? If you don't like it I'll happily serve you any other beverage *and* a piece of cake free of charge. Not that I was going to charge you for the drink anyway. Your daughter holds some influence round these parts.'

I almost giggle. *Giggle!* I am an out-of-control teenager. 'That's very kind of you,' I say when Mum does not speak. 'Do you want the tea, Mum? Or a normal cuppa?'

'I do not know where you have conjured up the idea that I drink "cuppas",' Mum says. 'However, yes, the blend sounds promising. I will indeed sample a drop.'

'*Hello, Mum, Queen Elizabeth called – she wants her accent back,*' I say to her in my head.

'Excellent choice,' Tyler says. He grins at me. 'And you, Clemency?'

'A double mocha, easy on the cream, heavy on the cocoa.'

'Another excellent choice.'

Mum doesn't speak until he is safely behind his counter. Her gaze constantly strays in his direction, checking, I think, whether he is close enough to hear her when she leans towards me, lowers her voice and says, 'Is he always that forward?' Her ultra-posh accent has gone. 'It's most inappropriate.'

'Yes, he's always like that. And, as you can see by how popular this place is, it generally works. People keep coming back for the friendly, personal service.'

'I'm sure the café's location has a lot to do with that,' she replies.

'Wild horses and no amount of sea views would keep me coming back to a place if the person in charge was rude and dismissive.'

'I agree, it's all fakery to drum up business. I can't abide false people.'

'I didn't say that, Mum. I said he was always like that.'

'And you went on to say that it was a way for him to drum up trade.'

'I didn't.'

'You did. You said he was like that to keep people coming back.'

'I didn't mean it like that.'

'But that is what you said.'

I have forgotten my golden rule: there is no point arguing with my mother. Even if she is wrong and I am right, there really is no point arguing with my mother. And just in case I've forgotten the first part of the rule it is this: there is NO POINT arguing with my mother.

'*What. And. Ever,*' I say to Mum in my head.

'Pardon me?' Mum says, her face stern and shocked at the same time.

There is a chance – a rather large chance – that I said that out loud.

'Is that what you're learning now? How to speak to me like that?' *Is that what your new family is teaching you?* She adds silently.

'No,' I say remorsefully. 'I'm sorry. You were deliberately misunderstanding and then misinterpreting what I was saying, though.'

'That is not my idea of an apology, Clemency Smittson.'

'I'm sorry, Mum. I shouldn't have spoken to you like that.'

'Thank you for your apology,' she says with good grace. It's easy to show such grace when you're technically in the wrong and you've managed to get someone to apologise to you TWICE in under thirty seconds. If that happened to me, I'd have all the grace in the world, I'm sure. I wonder why Mum thinks she isn't my mother when our relationship is full of moments like this. These are the moments you only share with your truly beloved ones.

'One pot of my special blend, and one double mocha, easy on the milk, heavy on the cocoa.' He's used my favourite daisy cup and for Mum he has selected a lilac cup that matches the scarf she has draped around her neck. With me, in jewellery making, the perfect finish is everything; with Tyler and his café service, the detail is everything. I'm embarrassed at myself for how desperate I am to find any sort of connection between us no matter how tenuous. It's all kinds of pathetic. And fun.

'Thank you, Tyler. I'm sure it will be delightful,' says my mother, the Queen.

I decide to ignore her and concentrate, instead, on my crush on the man walking away from me.

I have been expecting Mum to ask me if I have heard from the Zebilas, and if we have a time to see them again. When she asks, I will tell her everything, but she hasn't asked because I suspect she thinks she knows everything since she has gone back to doing what she did whenever I lived at home: listening in on my phone calls by lurking around my door. (Whenever I catch her at it she does a good job of looking as if she was innocently passing.) I leave this moment between us silent, give her the opportunity to ask and be answered. I will be relieved that I can talk about who I have seen and why. The moment passes, undisturbed and unruffled.

'Mum, did you and Dad ever talk about how he felt towards the end?' I ask, as a roundabout way of starting the conversation I probably should have with her.

'I'm not sure what you mean,' she replies.

'I mean, did he worry about being a burden on us? You, mainly, obviously?'

Mum's eyes glaze over; she gazes into the recent past, suddenly lost and floating in the sea of yesterday. 'Yes,' she says quietly. 'It was his biggest worry. Which upset me more than a lot of the other things that happened. He shouldn't have worried about that. It wasn't important.'

'But to him it was, I suppose?' I say.

'Yes. I loved him. For better or worse.'

'Did he ever feel it was too much and want it to end?'

'Did he tell you that?' Anger simmers beneath her words, in the way her face sits. 'Did he say something about that to you?'

'No,' I reply. This wound has clearly not healed for Mum and I have unintentionally busted it open.

'Don't lie to me, Clemency. He asked you, too, didn't he?'

'No, Mum, I am not lying. The only thing he ever asked of me was to go to see that woman from Doncaster about her wedding jewellery. I didn't want to go but he asked me to so I did.'

Mum's eyes rake over me, scrutinising me for any hint that I am keeping things from her. 'You're sure?'

'What is this? He didn't... Why, what did he ask you?'

'Only the most selfish thing a person could ask of another,' she practically snarls. She's never like that about Dad, not ever. Then she catches herself, realises who she's talking to. She leans forward, grabs her teacup and sips at it.

'Did Dad ask you to help him die?' I ask Mum.

She sips her tea, ignores me. She is not going to discuss this with me, and me asking isn't going to do any good. She is resolute, her face set and determined, then she changes her mind. She swivels in her seat until she is fully facing me. 'Yes, he did. He asked me because he was in so much pain. He was in a type of agony I hope never to experience and he wanted it to be over. He'd had enough and I didn't blame him. It was too much in that moment, but as soon as he asked he took it back. It was only at that moment. He knew how selfish it was.'

'He didn't ask me,' I reassure Mum. 'Like you say, it was a selfish thing to ask and Dad would never do that to me.'

'Why are you asking?'

'I'm missing him. Thinking about him. I didn't want him to think we ever thought that about him. That he was a burden. Because he wasn't.'

Mum places her cup back on its saucer, it rattles enough for her to need to steady it with her other hand. 'I think it is time for me to go home. Nancy and Sienna will be back from exploring now. Are you coming?' she asks. She doesn't acknowledge what I have said, doesn't even seem to notice that I have spoken. This is too much for her today. I didn't realise it, but today is probably not a good day and she has been hiding that with her snippy attitude.

I shake my head. 'I'm going to finish my coffee and then go on to work. I have some stuff to do before Monday.'

She looks across the busy room at Tyler and then back at me. 'Fine,' she says. 'I'll see you at home later.'

'Bye, Mum,' I say.

She nods at Tyler, a brief acknowledgement that he has served her well, and then leaves without looking back.

With Mum, May 2015, Otley

Mum had that face on her. Most of the time she looked like a normal woman with her blonde-brown, grey-streaked hair wound back into a bun, and soft features, and pink lips. Right now, though, she had that face on her.

'It's one song, Mum,' I told her. 'One song. He wanted it played.'

We were both wearing black, had done for the last week or so. It wasn't intentional for me, simply what my hand went to whenever I opened the wardrobe or drawer. I felt like covering myself in black, it was comforting and gentle, the sombreness from inside me creeping outside. I closed my eyes and I saw Dad. If there was a lull in the day, a moment when I could be still, I would think I could sense him nearby. Mum was never still, calm, inert. She was always on her feet, cleaning, cooking, sorting. She wrote letters. She made arrangements. She had planned the funeral all by herself. She had done everything, organised everything, except for this one song.

'No,' she said. 'It's not right. Not decent.'

'Mum, it's what Dad wanted. He wrote it in his last letter. He told you about it more than once.'

'He wasn't himself towards...At that point he didn't know what he was saying.'

'He's always said it. So many times. Even before he was ill. In fact, he said it right from when he first heard it with me.'

'It's not decent.'

'You've said that, Mum, and saying the same thing over and over isn't going to change the fact that it was what he wanted. You can have all of your other hymns and readings, but this is what Dad wanted. You have to honour that.'

Back to that face.

You can have that face all you want, but it's still happening, I thought.

'There's no way the priest will allow it,' Mum said.

'We'll see,' I replied.

With everyone, May 2015, Otley

We had readings that brought tears and hymns that spread comfort. And as the chosen four rose to their feet, took their places to carry him out, the opening chords of the song he'd wanted since 1987 rose up from the speakers placed around the church.

The priest had been no trouble – he wouldn't deny a deceased man's request.

I watched the people around me react: frowns of confusion and recognition, wondering if they were really hearing this tune filling the church. Seth, who stood at the front of Dad's coffin, hitched an eyebrow at me. He couldn't believe I'd managed it, that I'd got Mum to let me play Dad's song.

When Dad took me to see *Dirty Dancing* because I had no friends to go with, he said he wanted that song played at his funeral. 'The words are so true. You and your mother, this is what life is about. Promise me, *quine*, you'll play it at my funeral.'

'Promise,' I said without a second thought. Because I was nine, and that day was never going to come. I never thought I'd have to convince Mum to let me play 'I've Had the Time of My Life' by Bill Medley at Dad's funeral because Dad was a big man with a huge laugh and he was never going to have a funeral, so I could promise him anything he wanted.

Tyler leaves it at least ten minutes after my mother has gone before he comes near my table. 'Now that I've met your mother,' he says, 'I think it's fair to ask you what I've been wondering since you first walked into my café.'

'What's that then?'

'I've been trying to work it out by very subtle means, and now I'm just going to ask you outright: are you seeing anyone?'

As if on cue, as if he knows that something has made me think of him, Seth's text tone sounds in my pocket. It'll be one of those texts where he simply asks how my day has been, how I'm feeling, reminding me he loves me. And it'll make me question the wisdom of what I've done, whether I should have stayed with someone who lied to me more than once. Not even a lie of omission, an outright lie. He's backed off recently, no asking me to talk to him, just asking how I am. An easy way to get me to think about him even if I won't return his calls or texts.

'No,' I say to Tyler. *Because I am not. No matter what his texts say, no matter how much I want to be, I am not with Seth any longer. We are over. We have to be over.* 'I'm not. I'm flattered that you're interested, though.'

'I'm flattered that you're flattered. Does that mean if I ask you out sometime you're likely to say "yes"?'

'It does.'

'Good to know,' he says. He wanders off to the counter with his checked tea towel slung over his shoulder and my mother's empty teacup and saucer in his hand.

Seconds later he returns without the tea towel, apron and sous-chef hat he wears. ' "Sometime" didn't involve an apron, tea towel or hat,' he says. Another grin. 'Have you ever been roller-skating along the promenade?' he asks.

I shake my head. I always wanted roller skates. Lots of the girls in my school had them. Hillary Senton had pink ones with pink wheels and she brought them in one time and all of us wanted to touch them, to have a go. But she wouldn't even let us stand too close to them. I wanted pink ones like hers, but even if they weren't pink I would have loved to have a pair, to be like the other girls. But we couldn't afford them, Mum and Dad said. We could hardly ever afford things that other children had. I don't remember feeling resentful about it, more sad. I used to stare at the ceiling at night dreaming that when I grew up I'd have a lot of money and I'd be able to buy whatever I wanted. Funny how as an adult that never translated into buying roller skates, a pink bike or the latest, most up-to-date *Girl's World*.

'Would you like to come roller-skating with me along the promenade? I can make us a bite to eat here after the café has closed and then we can head out on the skates. See how far we get.'

I am being asked out by the man I have a crush on. I am being remarkably calm about that. 'Sounds good. When?'

'This coming week I've got events here every night so the café's going to be open later than usual. But next week, I'm all yours. Potentially.' He scrunches up his face, closes his eyes in a grimace. One eye cracks open a fraction. 'That sounded so wrong. Did you understand what I meant in the broader sense?'

I nod.

'So, next week?'

Two buzzes and a bleep sound in my pocket, a reminder that my life isn't uncomplicated. Not that I'd forgotten. About Seth. About my biological family. Nor about what my grandmother has asked me to do. Having something else to think about, to look forward to, feels like a chance to be an uncomplicated person for a few hours. I've forgotten what it's actually like, to not have anything to worry about.

'Next week, definitely.'

39

Smitty

'What are your plans for today?' my cousin Nancy asks me when I come into the kitchen. She and Sienna have been up for an hour or so, I heard them and I'd been itching to go in and join them, but I couldn't face this part of that scenario – speaking to Nancy. They've been here six days and I have managed to avoid speaking to her as much as possible. Unless she asks me a direct question in front of Sienna or Mum, I don't reply, I don't acknowledge her. I've spent a lot of time at work to avoid speaking to her. If I told Mum what Nancy had done it would upset her (not the Seth part, Mum would blame that on Seth, anyway) but it would devastate me if Mum did what she always did and tried to find a way to excuse Nancy for this latest treachery.

'I'm working,' I say. I only reply because Sienna is sitting beside her mother, trying to stack cornflakes on top of each other as they float in her cereal bowl of milk.

'Oh. You work too hard, you know that?' Nancy says. 'You're too young to be this stressed about work. You need to take care of yourself.' I wish she would come right out and say whatever it is that she wants because I find the faux-friendliness unpalatable.

She has her hair piled up on top of her head, tendrils of it tumbling around her face. She wears shorts and vest-top to sleep in. It's been unfortunate for her that she didn't manage to convince Mum to convince me to let her have the big room. She tried, but I'd avoided being around long enough for Mum to ask. And I locked my room during the day so Nancy wasn't tempted to move in while I was out. I don't move from my current place near the kitchen door because Nancy is going to say something else. I was supposed to reply to what she said but as it wasn't a direct question, I didn't bother.

'Would you mind taking Sienna today?' she asks. 'You'd like a day with your auntie Clem, wouldn't you?'

'Yeah!' Sienna says.

'I just need a little "me" time to catch up on some work, return a few calls, you know?' Nancy asks. 'You don't mind, do you?' The way she says that, the intonation of the question, makes it sound like I am Sienna's other parent and I've been slacking off in my duties.

More than anything I wish that Nancy would admit that she struggles with being a lone parent, that it's hard work and she resents Dylan for not being involved. (Seth is always on Dylan's case about not being part of Sienna's life. Dylan's stock reply is: 'Being involved with her means being involved with Nancy, and that is not an option.' And Seth always says, 'Yeah, tell that to your daughter when she grows up realising you're the feckless fool that you are.') I wish Nancy would be honest with herself, with the world in general. There are so many people who would be comforted to know that even she, Super Feminine Woman, finds it hard to be everything all the time to her daughter. That would be far too honest, though. Far too risky. She might be seen as normal, she might not be seen as perfect. Instead, she puts posts up on the internet giving tips on being feminine *and* a mother while she can barely get dressed at weekends, she pretends she has important work to do to guilt-trip people into babysitting for her, and she shows up with a two-year-old Sienna at mine and Seth's flat and leaves Sienna to get something from the shop and doesn't return for three months, claiming that she needed time to find herself.

I would respect Nancy a whole lot more if she had just come out and asked me to look after Sienna today. It's not as if I would say no. I never do when it comes to Sienna.

'You fancy a day with me?' I ask Sienna.

'Uh-huh,' she replies. 'Mum said we'd go to the pier today but I don't think she wants to any more. Do you want to go to the pier with me?'

'I think we can do much better than that,' I tell her. 'Why don't we go and look for some more shells and unusual pebbles so I can make more jewellery?'

'Yeah!' She wriggles off her seat until she is under the table and scoots across the floor on her hands and knees. She dashes out of the door, ready to wake Mum up so she can help her get dressed.

'Thanks, Clem. This is really helpful. I need to get on top of work. There's so much piling up and—'

I have to leave the room while Nancy is still talking. I can't engage with her, I just can't.

Sienna rarely walks anywhere if she can dance instead. She twirls and skips and stops to do complicated sideways steps. The promenade is perfect for her, she has the freedom and space to do all these things and we are in no particular hurry. The sun climbs higher in the sky as we move towards Brighton and more and more people pour on to the seafront. We left Nancy to catch up on work, which actually consisted of her and Mum sitting at the kitchen table, poring over Nancy's phone, plotting out the way to Bluewater so they can spend the day shopping together.

I'm not sure if it's Abi or Lily who sees us first, but it's Lily who runs towards me, waving and smiling. 'Hello!' she calls to me. 'Hello!'

'Hello, hello!' I reply.

'Who are you?' Sienna asks. Her excitement at seeing someone her height is unbridled.

'I'm Lily. What's your name?'

'Sienna. I'm five. How old are you?'

'I'm five, too!'

'Hi,' I say to Abi.

'Hello,' she says frostily. I don't blame her. I'm not sure I would be able to bring myself to speak to me if I were her.

'My aunt makes jewellery from shells,' Sienna says. 'She made me this.' She reaches inside her top, removes her necklace with its quick-release catch at the back so it will not strangle her if it gets caught. The necklace is made from a shell I found on the promenade. Three nights ago there had been high winds that had whipped up the sea enough to scatter pebbles and shells up on the promenade. On my way to work the next morning I'd found the small, smooth conch-shaped shell, with a patch of brown like a tan across its back, and a sprinkle of freckles along its smooth underside. Its freckles reminded me of the ones that came up on Sienna's nose when she spent too long in the sun, and the patch of brown reminded me of the colour of Lily's eyes when she had been doing impressions of me. I'd picked it up, deciding to make something for both of them. I made two moulds from the shell, filled them with silver clay, allowed them to dry, then fired them. I polished them both, then strung them on to soft leather strings with quick-release catches. The original shell, I returned to the beach after taking a photo. 'We're going to look for some stuff to make jewellery,' Sienna says.

Lily reaches out, and with the gentleness of someone older, touches the necklace. The clay had captured every line and ridge, every smooth curve.

'I've got the picture of the shell she made it from on my nana's wall. I have to share a room with my nana,' Sienna explains. 'Do you want to come and get some shells and she can make you a necklace, too?'

'Do you think your aunt will make me one?'

Sienna tips her head right back, the curls of her blonde hair cascading down her back as she does so. Her eyes are the colour of wet earth, the exact same colour as Dylan's. 'Will you, Auntie Smitty?' she asks.

'Of course,' I reply.

'Is that your aunt?' Lily asks Sienna.

'Yes,' Sienna says proudly.

'But that's my auntie Clemmy,' Lily replies. She tips her head back to stare at her mother. Her mass of long, glossy black plaits tumbles down her back as she does so. 'That's what you said, isn't it, Mummy? This is Auntie Clemmy.'

'Yes,' says her mother, my sister. 'This is your aunt.'

'My Auntie Smitty's name is Clemency. Are you my aunt and Lily's aunt?' Sienna asks me.

'Yes, I am,' I reply.

'How come?'

'Because Lily's mum is my sister and your mum is my cousin.'

'Does that mean we're sisters or cousins?' Lily asks.

'Sisters!' Sienna says excitedly.

'Not really,' Abi intercedes quickly.

'Cousins!' Lily exclaims.

'Erm...' Abi begins. She is about to shatter their illusions. She wants to be accurate, to state that Sienna is really my second cousin, that these two aren't really connected at all. Those many, many times Nancy gleefully reminded me I wasn't real somersault through my mind.

'Do you want to be cousins?' I say before Abi can speak.

'Yes!' they both reply without hesitation, the very thought of it seems to be the best thing to have happened to them both since Christmas ended.

'They can be cousins if they want to be, can't they?' I ask Abi.

'If they must,' she mumbles, clearly not happy. It's understandable, this need for accuracy is what you'd expect from someone who has always had siblings, who has never had to justify their connection to another person.

'Yay!' they both cry and spontaneously hug each other, two friends who have only just met, now bonded together for life as family.

'Come on, let's find some shells.' Sienna grabs Lily's hand and the pair of them dash off towards the stone steps that lead down to the beach. They both wear shorts and T-shirts, and have matching lime green Crocs.

'We're supposed to be going swimming at the King Alfred!' Abi calls, but they ignore her.

The steep drop from the pebble-filled upper beach doesn't daunt them – they both run towards it, giggling as they hold hands, laughing while the ridge gives way under their weight, pushes them down further towards the lower part of the beach. When the pebbles and shells and fragments of shells stop moving beneath them, they leap forwards and run towards the sea, their loud, vocal happiness rising up like a trail we're meant to follow.

'Lily, stay out of the sea!' Abi calls, and speeds up. I speed up too, and we go through the same routine, waiting for the shifting ground to stop moving beneath our feet before we head towards them.

They're crouched by the water's edge, shallow, seaweed-streaked pools of not quite escaped sea sitting in the soaked sand around their feet as they search for the perfect shell. Their voices tumble and spill over each other in their excitement, and yet, in the commotion of speech and discovery they understand each other, they hear what the other is saying.

'When I was about five, my mother took a load of photos of me and Sienna's mother on Blackpool beach and we looked exactly like those two,' I say to Abi.

Nancy hadn't understood then that I wasn't real, that I wasn't her proper cousin. We were friends and we liked each other, a lot. We were pinky-promise best friends forever then. There were other pictures, ones taken on later trips to Blackpool, and they all looked the same, but they never felt the same. I hope Lily and Sienna are friends forever. That they refuse to believe anyone who tries to tell them that they're not real cousins, that they hang on to this feeling of having someone who they've fallen for in the way children do for other children.

'Are you seriously going to pretend that this is all normal and you've been in touch with me?' Abi says, affronted.

'Sorry, I'm sorry. I should have been in touch.'

'Yeah, you should. Why weren't you? I mean, I thought it was all right that meeting. We were all a little overwhelmed but it's not fair for you to duck out and send me bullshit "How are you?" texts.'

'I freaked out,' I say honestly. Aside from trying to convince my grandmother to change her mind about me helping her to die, I had freaked out because a lot of realisations were dawning on me like the rise of the Sun on a winter morning – slow to appear but

253

powerful every time it is glimpsed. 'It was all too much for me. Everyone was crying and I wasn't. And I'm only now coming to terms with the fact that my parents got married. I wasn't put up for adoption because my mum was very young and on her own or had been slung out by her family – she had this family and a big house and they still didn't want me. She was in love with my father, he was in love with her, they went on to get married and have more children. So the bottom line is, they didn't want me. I'm sorry I cut you out. But I think about you and Lily all the time.' I reach into my bag, remove the small pink velvet bag that holds Lily's necklace. I press it into Abi's hand. 'I made this for her, it's the same as Sienna's.'

Abi frowns down at the trinket bag. 'You've been walking around with this in your bag?'

'I made it three days ago. I kept it in my bag because I constantly told myself that I would drive over and drop it off at your work or through your front door or something.' I inhale deeply. 'I'm a coward. It's really that simple.'

Abi says nothing as she continues to examine the bag in her hand, but she's chewing the inside of her mouth, her eyes are in another place, she's very obviously thinking over what I said.

'My parents didn't take that many photos,' she says. 'There were a few, but... It's weird, saying that, actually, because I seem to remember there being lots of cameras and lots of negatives around, but we hardly ever had any pictures out. But me? I've got about six thousand photos on my phone of Lily.'

'Six *thousand*?' I am a prolific photo taker but not even I have that many photos of one subject.

'You'd think there was no other thing to take a photo of in the whole world, wouldn't you? I can't help it. When she was first born I had this idea to take a photo of her every day so I could see how she changed over time. Who knew I'd end up with a baby that I could barely put down – even when she was asleep. Some days I wouldn't be able to go for anything like a proper wee until eight o'clock at night. I lived in my dressing gown those first few weeks.'

'Mum, Mum, what about this?' Lily is holding out a long, flat shell, its curved back ridged with shades of pearlescent grey. She flips it over in her palm and its underside is a smooth, shiny pearl colour. Flecks of wet sand cover it, but I can do something with that. Lily has a good eye.

'I don't know, ask your aunt,' Abi says.

Lily moves her hand towards me. 'I think it's beautiful,' I tell her. 'I'll definitely be able to do something with that.' Pewter silver for the top, white gold for the underside. White gold paste is hard to come by, though, so I may have to gold-plate it. Which is pricey. 'Shall I keep it safe for you until I can make your necklace?' I ask her.

She grins without showing her teeth and her plaits dance when she nods. She watches me as I unbutton the thigh pocket on my trousers and slip the shell inside.

'Sienna! Sienna!' she calls as she skips back to her new-found cousin. 'I've got one. I've got one.'

'Didn't your parents help?' I say to Abi. 'I'd have thought they'd be all over their first grandchild.'

Abi snorts dismissively, her eyes darken as she's suddenly transported back six years. 'Yeah, we've all moved on from me being nineteen, pregnant and unmarried. They were so over-the-top angry about it that I had to move out. I ended up living on my own in a tiny flat in the middle of nowhere because my parents didn't want to know unless I agreed to tell them who the father was and to marry him. After six months or so of watching me struggle and accepting that I wasn't telling them the father's name, and even if I did I wouldn't be getting married, they let me move back home.' The resentment at how they were swirls in her eyes. 'My gran was the worst for it. She kept on blaming my mother for not bringing me up properly, like Daddy hadn't been there when I was growing up.

'My brother, Jonas, he tried to help, so did Declan, Lily's dad. But he was young, too, and his parents were freaking out. And Jonas was going through his own shite. It was really hard. Jonas couldn't believe it that I moved back in with them after all that they'd done and said.

I moved out when Lily was nearly two then came back again about a year ago when Gran got bad. Like I say, we've all moved on from those early dark days.' She makes a small, disgusted 'ha' sound under her breath.

'Is that why you haven't told them you're pregnant?'

Abi's eyes seem to triple in size – the horror of what I've said descends upon her features and she turns on me. Her hand clamps around my arm, her fingers dig into the space between the muscle and bone of my bicep. 'How do you know? Is it obvious? Who else have you told?'

I shrug her off. I rub at where she grabbed me to ease the pain she's caused. 'You look a bit off colour, but you seem to be glowing, too. I just guessed. I haven't told anyone. Why would I? It's your business.'

'If you've guessed it's only a matter of time before Mummy does. I can't go through all that again. Last time she guessed and asked me outright. I couldn't lie. She looked at me like something disgusting she'd stepped in, and Daddy overheard and went through the roof. I wanted to tell her this time so I'd be in control. But if it's obvious to you then it'll be obvious to her.'

'Don't you think they'll react a bit differently this time?' I suggest gently. 'Not only are you older and self-supporting, there's a reason why you can remind them that everyone makes mistakes. Assuming it was a mistake.'

'It wasn't a mistake,' she says. 'We planned it. I love Declan – Lily and this one's father. He's just...'

'Married?'

'No! No way! He's a bit flaky and a "bit some time".'

'I don't get you.'

'He's one of those men who you know are good for some time but long-term it probably won't work out. He wanted to get married last time and he wants to get married this time, we go stay with him almost every other weekend and we were talking about living together before Lily and I moved back in with my parents, but he's... I'm... Nothing lasts when it comes to love, love.'

Seth. The hazel-green swirl of his eyes comes to mind. The lazy smile he fires me before he puts on his helmet. His strong fingers that sneak between mine like a whispered secret as he takes my hand when he's nervous.

'Have you tried to make it last?'

'No, suppose not.'

'How do you know then?' I ask.

'I don't need to run into the sea fully clothed to know I'm going to get wet jeans, I just know it.'

'True.' But love isn't like running into the sea fully clothed. With the sea and a fully clothed dash into its depths, there are no surprises. With love, there is sometimes a surprise around every corner, a chance to grow and learn and find the ways you are perfect just as you are. I'm not going to say that to her. What do I know? I'm living three hundred miles away from the love of my life and about to go on a date with a man I have a teenage crush on. What do I really know about love? Instead I say to her: 'Abi, if they start to have a go, you've got the perfect comeback.'

'What's that?'

I suppose I should be pleased that she's forgotten who I am, what I am to her. I raise my forefinger and turn it towards my face, a pointer as to her perfect new comeback.

'Oh, God, yes. I almost forgot.'

Almost.

The girls won't stop hugging. They keep promising they'll see each other again soon, and that they can have a sleepover and that they can do drawing together and look for more shells on the beach and ride their scooters up and down the beach and read books together at the library and climb in the park and have another sleepover and a tea party.

'Are you going to disappear again now?' Abi asks.

'No. No, I won't. I'm going to come with you to tell your parents about your pregnancy, if you want me to.'

'You'll come with me?'

I nod. 'Of course.'

'*Really?* Why?'

'Because you're my sister. That's what sisters do, isn't it?'

Abi smiles, and nods.

'Right, so that's what I'll do.'

40

Smitty

She bottled it. We had it all planned: Abi would take Lily to a friend's house and I would wait for her, we'd come back together and do a whole 'look who I saw near Lily's friend's house and who I invited back for a cup of tea' scene as a background, and then we'd sit down around the kitchen table and Abi would do it. Or I would do it. But one of us would do it and Abi could stop pretending she had food poisoning from the works canteen and get on with being happy to be having another baby.

I should have known from the way she was hyperventilating the whole drive back, and then how she took about five goes to actually put the key in the door and then another full thirty seconds to turn it, that she was a flight risk.

'Hello!' she called out, her voice wavery and paper-thin. 'I have a visitor,' she added when she received no reply from her mother or grandmother.

As soon as her curious mother appeared from the kitchen, Abi decided to flee. 'Saw Clemency. Asked her for tea. Need to go to work. Emergency. Bye.' And that was it – she literally fled the house. I'm sure she actually ran down the path, too, shutting the gate behind her like an obstacle that would slow down anyone who decided to drag her back and force her to unburden her mind.

My other mother blinks a few times at me. She looks as though all her numbers have come up on the Lottery. It's the reaction I need, one that lessens the anxiety about not telling Mum about this meeting. 'Would you like a drink?' she asks.

'A coffee would be brilliant,' I say. I am speaking quietly because suddenly I'm shy with just the two of us. We spoke the other time, but everyone was on high alert and there was so much pressure. Today we have none of that.

We take our seats at the kitchen table, the same ones we had last time I was here. 'The photographs Mrs Smittson gave to us were wonderful. Your father and I have looked through them several times.'

'I'm surprised he looked at them. He didn't seem that interested in me the last time I was here,' I say. I hope that doesn't sound too bitter or accusatory, just the statement of fact it is.

'He is interested. This has simply been difficult for him. None of us are sure of the best thing to do. In those situations, those who are most unsure of themselves often do nothing. He is interested. Of course he is.'

I nod. 'Do you have some photos of you from when you were younger that I can see?' I ask. 'I'm curious about what you looked like back then.'

She shakes her head, the strands of her shoulder-length bob move like black silk threads. 'I don't like to be the focus of any attention. I have very few photographs of myself. They are in the loft, I think. I will bring them out the next time I see you.'

'That'd be great,' I reply.

'Do you like your grandmother?' my other mother asks out of the blue.

What sort of a loaded question is that? Is there actually a right answer? 'She's all right, I suppose,' I state.

'You have a secret, I can sense it, Tal— Clemency. If I asked you what it was, would you tell me?'

'I've spent more time with Abi than I have with her but you don't want to know what Abi has been telling me.'

'*Don't trust that woman.*' The words are almost hissed at me and I have to pull myself back in my seat. A thick, poisonous venom is laced through every rivulet of those words and they shock me. Is that how irrational and unbalanced I sound when I talk about Nancy? And why is she suddenly talking about this? Aren't we supposed to be bonding, not setting up a slagging session about someone else?

'I am sorry, I am sorry.' My other mother's face is anxious now, her hand movements fretful. She's worried that she has pushed me away, alienated me by showing in that moment the truth of her feelings, the fact she has the ability to feel such emotions at all.

If I think about what she did in having me placed for adoption, I still struggle. I expect her to be frozen, stuck at that moment where she was forced to make a momentous choice and unable to move on from that. It's not fair to think she would be suspended in time, but part of me, the part who has been 'other' all her life because of the choice my birth mother made, expects it as the least she can do and feel. Guilt always stitches its haircloth inside my chest when I have these thoughts about my other mother because I am being unfair. I shouldn't want anyone to feel how I do sometimes: trapped at a point in time. My point in time where I am trapped is that moment when I realised I wasn't with the parents who gave me my DNA. From then onwards I always, *always* felt that I was from nowhere and was unwanted by everyone. My other mother's ability to marry my father and have more children proves she has had some semblance of a normal existence.

'Why don't you like her?' I ask my other mother.

'It is not as simple as not liking her,' my other mother states. 'When I first came to this house, she treated me like one of her daughters. She was so kind and loving towards me. But when she discovered that her son was interested in me, that he was the one who was the father of my child, she became a person I did not recognise.

'She did not approve of her son being interested in me. He had a big career ahead of him and it did not involve a wife and a child before he had graduated from law school. I was not good enough in her eyes and she did not want me or anyone connected to me to become part of her family. I do not think she would ever have approved of me because I was not from the right family stock: my parents did not have the wealth of the Zebilas and I had not been chosen by her. The first son, according to your grandmother, has to conquer business, the second son has to marry well.'

She is hinting that it was my grandmother who forced my adoption. 'Couldn't you have got married anyway, despite her protests?' I ask.

'This was 1978, Clemency.' That is the first time she has said my name without pausing, without having to get the 'Talei' bit out of the way first. 'We did what was requested and expected by our parents.'

My other mother's brown eyes look over me carefully. Is she wondering if I am the type of daughter who would do as my parents told me?

'People talk about the seventies and eighties like the freedoms you all enjoy in this day and age were automatically given when the decades changed. It was not like that. We were not in the fifties and sixties, no, but we grew up with parents from those years. Your grandmother did not want me here, and I could not have gone to Nihanara to my parents with a child born out of wedlock. The shame would have killed them.'

Shame. It is a label, tagged into my skin, into the arrangement of my DNA. Shame is what I am, what I represent. This is a reminder of why I hate my birthdays – each one is a marker of who I am. That in the time before I was born there was no excitement, there was only shame, fear, confusion, worry. My very existence, according to my mother, the only person whose authority I have to go on, meant that I could possibly have killed someone with shame by simply being born.

'When I went to the hospital to have you, I was put on the ward that was for girls who were not married. I met a lot of English and Irish girls there and only one of us was going to be leaving with her baby. The rest of us, we had the parents who had grown up in the fifties and sixties, who only knew that a child born out of wedlock was wrong. And it is wrong.'

'Wrong'. I can add that to the list of words that tag who I am. 'Shame', 'Wrong', 'Not real'. If I was a wall, those would be the things that graffiti artists would spraypaint on me.

'We loved our babies but we were told we could not keep them. And we did as we were told.' My mother stares down at her hands. 'I fought her as long as I could. But in the end, I could not fight them both. Your father made me accept that it would be better for you to have two parents who would have money and who would be able to give you the life I couldn't.'

'You think it was all her and not him?' I say. It's difficult enough knowing what to call them all outside the confines of my head, but when we're having this type of conversation it's impossible to give them titles that are associated in my head with family, connectedness and love.

'Your father had, like me, been brought up to do as he was told. He would not have wanted to go against his parents.'

'Even if it meant keeping his child?'

'His mother always gets her way. That is why you must not trust her. If she is trying to create a relationship with you it is because she wants something. Which is why I'd like you to tell me what you talked about.'

I could take this demand, couched in quiet, unassuming, friendly terms, as a good sign: she is treating me how Mum treats me – like a daughter who will do as she is told. But I can't help thinking: *Who do you think you are? My mother, or something?*

The obedience Mum gets from me is given because she raised me. It's mostly annoying and unhealthy but it is what it is because she is the person I love, who helped me to grow up. Someone can't march in and make such personal, intimate demands on me when they weren't there. Maybe through no fault of her own, maybe through choices she made, maybe through fear and youth, maybe through a combination of all those things, but still, she doesn't get to make demands on me.

I can't say this. I can never say this. Because she might turn her back on me. She may never want to see me again. And, indignant as I am, I couldn't handle that. I feel something for her. When I look at her I ache for the person I think she was back then – trapped into this decision that she felt she had to make. And I ache in a desperate, almost manic manner to find a way over this breach between us. I want her to be my mother. There is a space for her in my life: one space is filled by Mum; the other is still occupied by Dad. But there is another space next to them where she would fit, she could be the other type of parent I need sometimes. I have a 'Mum', I need this woman to be my mother. I had a 'Dad', I would love Julius to be my father. But Julius isn't here, and my other mother is, and I want her, more than anything, to be my mother.

I say: 'She was telling me about her illness. She doesn't want anyone to know how unwell she feels.' This is as close to the truth as I can get without betraying my grandmother and lying to my other mother.

'She wants you to feel sorry for her,' my other mother dismisses. 'She has been ill for years. She doesn't want to look after herself properly. She much prefers to have others running around at her beck and call. She had servants back in Nihanara and being unwell has given her the chance to have that in her life again.'

Whoa! I draw back again. 'That's a bit unfair,' I say. 'She has some serious, life-limiting if not life-threatening conditions.' *She has the perfectly rational fear of becoming trapped inside her own body.*

My other mother's face changes, as though she is about to start crying. She looks emotionally dishevelled suddenly. 'This is what has happened to me,' she says, the tears seep into her voice. 'I am capable of dismissing another person's suffering because I dislike her so much.' She closes her eyes. 'I sometimes feel like I am a teenager again.' Is she admitting that she does feel stuck in that moment she made that choice all those years ago? 'I sometimes feel like no one will ever understand me or realise what it is like to be in an impossible situation.' She opens her eyes to find me watching her with my heart paused, my breath caught, as I wait for her to be honest again. 'Then I remember I am being silly. I am an adult and I made the right choice at that time.'

'Yes, I suppose you did,' I say to her statement. It stings. At every point, rubbed raw by the fact of being adopted and finding out that she went on to have more children with the same man, it stings to know this. It also suggests that she would make the same choice again. In which case, why not simply admit it? *Why not say that you didn't want to give me up for adoption, but the alternative to not doing so was a price you weren't prepared to pay?* I think. *Why can't you admit that you were young and frightened, and had just given birth, so when you were offered the respectability of marriage, and a child in wedlock – which happened less than two years later – in return for signing the adoption papers, you took it?* It might not be palatable for her to hear herself say that, but it's the truth. And it's better for me to hear that so I know that it honestly wasn't me. 'I suppose your mother-in-law thinks that, too, seeing as it's what you say she ultimately wanted.'

My other mother is horrified by how she sounds, what is coming across from everything she is saying and not saying. 'I did not mean it like that. I would not make the same choice if I was in that position again.' She looks at me like I'm an adult, like Clemency. 'Please believe me when I say I made the right choice at that time for all the wrong reasons. I would make a different choice if I was in that position again. I know that now. What I am trying to say is that your grandmother was an adult with more experience of the world and more opportunities than I. She was like a second mother to me but when I displeased her she showed me how little she thought of me.'

'Did she scream at you when you told her?' I ask.

'I didn't have the opportunity to tell her. She asked me had I missed my time of the month and when I said yes, she knew.'

'That must have been hard.'

My other mother gives me the type of smile I give Mum when she is minimising something Nancy has done. '"Hard" is not the word I would use.'

'What did my...your...what did *he* say to her about your condition?'

'She called a meeting to shame me in front of the family, to tell them all what a dirty girl I was and how I had disgraced them and myself. When she asked me the boy's name I...I thought your father was going to tell them. To claim me. But he did not.' The expression on her face shows the hurt she must have felt then, still feels now. 'He was too scared. She discovered it in her own way, in her own time.'

'What did she say? Did she take it back once she found out it was her son?'

'One thing you must know about the Zebilas – once their mind is made up, it is almost impossible to change it. Your grandmother decided that I was a dirty girl who had led her son astray – nothing has changed her mind about that in all these years.'

'But you did end up married to him,' I state.

'Yes, I did. Because it was what your grandmother wanted.'

'I don't understand, sorry.'

'Your father proposed to me and said once we were married and he had finished law school we would find a way to get you back. In the meantime, I had to let you go to people who could take care of you. Your grandmother...' My other mother stares at her hands, at the unassuming gold band on the fourth finger of her left hand. She is wearing the family metal. 'Your grandmother made it clear that he was right to offer me that. It was the right thing to do. And she would have to ask my father for my hand in marriage. To do that, she would have to tell them about what I had done.'

The shame would have killed them.

'I see...' I say. I do as well. What she is saying is: when you do what my grandmother wants she is fine, but when you deviate from her plan for you, she makes your life a misery.

'I don't think you do, Clemency. It was the right choice because it was ultimately right for you, but I made that choice out of fear for myself mainly. I should have put you first. I may have made the same decision at the time, but I did not realise back then that you must always, *always* put your children first, no matter what you are offered. And your grandmother, she wielded absolute power over me from that moment on. This is the first time since I signed those papers that I have felt free.'

My grandmother isn't all that bad, I try to remind myself. I actually quite like her. But if what my other mother is hinting at is true then I have no real idea who my grandmother really is, nor what she is capable of. But then, do any of us know what we're capable of when our lives are threatened with change?

'I need to go now,' I say to my other mother. 'I have work to do.' *And I don't emotionally know what to do with all that you have confessed.*

'Will I see you again soon?' she asks.

Considering the conversation, I'm so surprised she has asked that I have to stop moving and replay the question in my mind and think about it before I answer. 'Is that what you really want?'

She wants to see me, but unlike my grandmother there doesn't seem to be anything obvious she wants from me except maybe to spend time with me. This whole time with her has been so confusing, muddled, full of confessions and regrets and certainties about the right thing being done, and I don't know how to feel about my other mother right now.

'I would like that very much,' she says.

I nod. 'OK, then, I'll come back and see you again soon.'

She grins at me as I stand.

'I'll just go and say goodbye to— ' I point towards my grand-mother's room.

My birth mother replaces her grin with a tight-lipped smile and offers me a sharp nod. She's probably hurt that I have heard what she has said but I am still choosing to engage with the woman who possibly pressurised her to give me up for adoption. I have to see her, though. I can't explain to my other mother why, that I've started to bond with my grandmother, that I've been trying to stop her ending her life early, that I have promised to think about helping her to die. That there is all this stuff going on which means I couldn't cut out my grandmother even if I tried.

My grandmother doesn't answer when I knock on her door the first time. The last time I came here it took her a while to reply when I called out from the corridor. But even as I wait, the sound of the clock counting out time, I know she is not going to answer. The other side of the door seems too silent, too still. Each tick of the clock seems to resonate into the bedroom, and return a hollow sound.

I hear my heart in my chest. It echoes, too, into the room behind the door. Each beat takes longer to sound out, and when it does, it seems to be magnified. My knuckles rap loudly this time. The knock ricochets around the corridor and is loud enough to bring my other mother to the door of the kitchen.

'What is the problem?' she asks.

'There's no answer.'

Her eyes flick to the clock. 'It's not time for her sleep. She will need her medication soon.'

She is down the hall in a few strides, she knocks on the door but doesn't wait for a reply before opening it. I wait on the threshold, not sure how much a part of this I will be.

'Clemency,' my mother says loudly but calmly. 'Call an ambulance.'

It begins then, the nightmare that she said she didn't want to happen. My grandmother wanted to look Death in the eye while she went, she didn't want Death to sneak in and take her slowly and painfully, leaving her powerless and afraid. Or to take her in even more minuscule increments, by making her a prisoner in her own body. That nightmare is being set in motion.

41

Smitty

'Would Madam care for some white wine or red wine with her *Spaghetti alle vongole?*' With a flourish, Tyler whips the pale cream napkin that sits in a fan shape next to my fork and spoon, and lays it gently and expertly across my lap. With an equally elaborate flourish he indicates to the wine bottles in the middle of the table.

He has pushed most of the low coffee tables away and has moved a circular dining table into the middle of the darkened café. Along the counter there are small tea lights in crystal holders, whose flames come together like embers from the Olympic flame to create a gentle wall of light behind him. In the middle of the table stands a silver candlestick with three arms, holding long, red tapered candles. The entire scene is romantic and thoughtful, and I'm honoured.

Like the lights on the counter, a flame of excitement dances and flickers inside me because this is thrilling and new and, well, thrilling. I can't think outside of those basic, almost teenager-like, terms otherwise the rest of the world where I am adult with adult problems and responsibilities will come gushing in like water into a cracked dam, and spoil it.

Time with Tyler is all about uncomplicated, new, exciting stuff. Time away from him is adult and scary and real. It has been two days since I had to call an ambulance to take my grandmother away and no one from my other 'family' has updated me on her condition. Not even a text to let me know if the worst has happened, if she is hanging on, if the doctors are still working on her. I am clearly not part of them. That has been a stark, adult lesson to learn in the last two days. I haven't been able to concentrate on anything without knowing what is going on. This has also changed everything: the decision might have been taken from my hands, which would be a relief. Or it might have become more pressing, I may need to speed up the deciding process because this is a signal that she doesn't have much time before something happens and she is as helpless as she fears.

Adult stuff, adult fears and decisions, have no place in the teenagery world of being with Tyler. Being with him is all about hoping my hair looks nice, wondering if my dress is flattering enough, choosing the right wine to go with this pasta dish.

'*Vino bianco* is the correct wine to have with *vongole*, I believe,' I say to him.

'Ahh, I see, a woman who is well travelled and well eaten,' Tyler says. 'Which could present a problem for me because you actually know what this is meant to taste like.'

'I do, I'm sorry. It's one of my favourites.'

'Well, nothing ventured, no one impressed by the brilliance I have managed to cram into this dish.'

In front of me, on top of the cork place mat, Tyler places a large white bowl into which he has curled spaghetti, with small, black clams studding the creamy-white strands. It is seasoned with flecks of bright green parsley and tiny, almost transparent pieces of garlic. The scent of a decent wine, which will have infused itself into the food, wafts up to me from my plate as it had been doing from the kitchen. 'You used good wine,' I say.

'Only the best for you, my dear – it was on offer for £2.98 in the local shop.'

'Oh, poor wine,' I reply, 'so cheap they couldn't even get away with charging the extra penny to make it ninety-nine.' I turn my mouth downwards. 'I feel sad for the pathetic bargain-bucket wine.'

Tyler's smile is unexpectedly intimate and affectionate, the beam of someone who has been in love with the person they're in front of for years. I avert my gaze to the silver fork I have picked up and am about to plunge into the stringy depths of my food.

'You're pretty silly, you know that?' he says, an equal amount of affection in his tone. I stop my fork making contact with my food. Without looking directly at him I watch him unfold his napkin fan, lay it across his jeans-covered lap. 'It was one of the first things I noticed about you. Not many people are silly in a charming way.'

I say nothing to him, instead I concentrate on finding a Zen state. On bringing calming breath into my body. On not getting up and walking out. This is not teenager-ish, this is adult and serious and not what being with Tyler is all about.

'That was a compliment, in case you were wondering,' he tries again.

'Thank you,' I mumble into my chest.

Seth and I have split up. It is over between us; we couldn't be together any more. I am not cheating on him. I am not, I am not, I am not.

White wine glugs softly into my glass, and the lights from the candles flicker throughout the café. Outside is black but I know out there is the sea. If I strain, I'm sure I can hear it, shushing the sky, pouring calm over the pebbles.

'Are you not having a good time?' Tyler asks. 'Is this a bit too much after we've only really talked over coffee?'

Brace yourself, I tell myself. *Look up.* He smiles at me, nervously.

'I'm sorry,' I say. 'I'm in a bit of a strange place, my head is a bit fried at the moment. Lots of other things going on.' I open my mouth to start to explain. Then shut it again. Where would I even start with the tangled, knotted mess that is my life at the moment? I open my mouth again and: 'But I'm having a great time. This is all amazing. Especially for someone who makes questionable coffee at the best of times,' comes out.

'Lady, you can insult my cooking and my taste in décor but never, *ever* insult my coffee.'

'I wasn't insulting your coffee, the coffee can't help it, I was questioning your ability to make it.'

'I am wounded,' he says. 'Especially after I imparted my expert knowledge, that is usually only handed down from barista to barista, to you.'

'I'm sorry for wounding you,' I say.

'No, no, nothing short of *loving* my *vongole* will make up for it,' he says.

I grin at him. I slip the fork into the waves of the spaghetti, twirl them into a ball on the end of my fork using my spoon. Tyler watches me slip the food between my lips and chew. 'It's divine,' I say.

'You got yourself out of trouble there,' he states.

'Phew!' I can do this. Honestly I can.

'How about you try to leave all that head-frying stuff to one side for the rest of tonight?' Tyler says. He is suddenly serious, his dark, velvety eyes trained on me so I can't look away even if I want to. 'If it's truly important, it'll still be there to worry about in a couple of hours.'

He's right. All of it: my grandmother, my other mother, Seth, Mum, Nancy, and all the ways they touch and influence my life will still be there in a couple of hours. If I set them to one side, I'll be free to exist, to be a teenager, to even be an adult who has fun. I can almost taste the liberation of that.

The next bite of *vongole* tastes incredible now that I've been unhooked from the rest of my life.

'I thought you said you'd done this before,' Tyler states.

'When, pray tell, did I say that?' I reply.

'I asked if you'd ever been roller-skating along the promenade and you said...'

'I said nothing. I shook my head because I hadn't ever been roller-skating along the promenade or anywhere else in fact.'

Tyler has lent me skates with white boots, red wheels and red ribbon laces. The rubber stopper at the front is red, too. So much

cooler than Hillary Senton's. When he produced them as my designated pair for the evening, I wondered if he probably took all his
dates roller-skating and I would be wearing a dumped woman's
skates. But no, they had the label on and as soon as we'd checked to
see if they fitted me, he removed and binned the label.

'I suppose I should have asked if you'd been roller-skating anywhere, ever,' Tyler states.

'Yes, I think you should have.' I am clinging on to the clammy
sea wall that runs along the promenade outside his café. He'd laced
me into the boots while we sat on this bench because locking up in
roller skates would have been too difficult. Once the last lace was
tied, I'd got up and had promptly fallen over. I had made progress
in the last ten minutes in that I had now managed to go from the
bench to the wall without falling over. I am currently working on
letting go of the wall.

'In my mind's eye,' Tyler says wistfully, 'I saw us skating up and
down here, undaunted by the lack of light, holding hands, showing
off to each other, maybe one of us "accidentally" falling and bringing the other one down with us, landing in a happy heap and...'
His voice trails off.

'Oh, no, don't stop. You were just getting to the good part. You
weren't making me feel at all guilty for not having a clue how to do
this. Not one little bit.'

'Revenge for the coffee dig earlier.' Tyler skates nearer. 'Haven't
you ever been ice skating?'

'Yes. I ended doing this that time, too. I'd completely forgotten
how much I didn't like that out-of-control feeling then, how anything can just go off in any direction it pleases and you can't do a
thing about it.' My left leg, as if to prove my point, decides to slide
away and I have to bring it back sharply while my fingers grope for
purchase on the wall. This is actually worse than ice-skating. This is
a different kind of powerlessness that I'm having to navigate.

Tyler stands in front of me. Slung across his body is the large
black messenger bag containing our shoes and my bag. Despite the
cool night, he's wearing a white T-shirt so his arms are bare – I'm

sure he's wearing it to show off the sleek muscles of his upper body. (I don't blame him, they're pretty impressive arms and I'm surprised I've managed to avoid running my fingers over them for so long.)

'Take my hands,' he says.

'Yeah, I'm not going to do that.'

'Trust me, do it one at a time. Just reach out and take my hand.' Gingerly, carefully, I reach out for him and his hand is there, immediately, clamped around mine, holding me steady. My legs wobble, slip a little, but mostly I am fine, I am upright, I am not sprawled all over the promenade showing myself up. 'Now, the other hand. You'll be fine, trust me.' That's twice he's asked me to trust him, twice he's used the word as though trusting someone is the easiest thing in the world. That when you need to, all you do is close your eyes and believe and everything will be tied up in a happily ever after bow. Trust, blind trust, is easy to give when you're young and naïve and have never been hurt, it's even easy to give when you've met someone new when you're not so young. But when you are older, when you have been hurt, when it seems every incidence of trust you've given to others has been betrayed in some way, you don't become jaded, you become suspicious and mistrustful of every act of trust you're asked to perform – even the most trivial ones. I don't trust Tyler not to let me fall. But there's also a part of me that needs to let go so I can prove that people always, *always* let you down if you trust them.

I push myself away from the wall slightly as I reach for his other hand and it is there. His hand, strong and sure, encircles mine and holds me safe and upright. 'I told you,' he says. His hands tighten around mine. 'First thing, stop looking down,' he tells me. Reluctantly I raise my head. Looking down lets me check what my feet are doing and it prevents me from . . . looking directly at him.

Tyler is like the Sun sometimes – you have to try to avoid looking directly at it because of what it can do to your body. The Sun can damage your eyes if you look directly at it – with Tyler, he'll make your stomach flip several times in a few seconds, and will unleash unnecessarily potent lust throughout your veins.

'Now, I'm going to skate backwards for a bit...' I must look horrified because he adds quickly: 'I won't let you go. I'm going to skate slowly backwards, taking you with me until you feel safe.' He moves while he speaks, carefully but slowly dragging me with him. 'Any time you feel yourself slipping, grab tightly on to my hands.' We continue to move. It's not so bad now. I'm actually enjoying the feeling of passive motion, of moving forwards without even trying. 'See, this isn't so bad, is it?' he asks.

'No,' I reply. I don't want to speak too much in case I throw my balance off and end up on the floor.

'Good, this is good. You're doing well. Keep moving, keep coming forwards. That's it.' He keeps looking behind him, to check where he is heading, but at that time of night there are few people around and the promenade is thankfully hazard-free.

We've moved quite far despite my terror and I am starting to feel comfortable on wheels, as though I could one day possibly, maybe feel like I belong on them.

'Now, I'm going to let go of one of your hands. I'll still have the other one so once I let go, if you feel at all worried, you can just grab my hand again. OK?'

'OK.' I can do this. I remember when Dad sat me down and told me that it was back, that there was nothing they could do, that it was now just a question of marking time on our new calendars, I thought I couldn't do it. I thought I would never get through. But at some point, I don't remember when, I realised I was doing it. I could do it because I was doing it. I had no choice, and because I had no choice, I managed to do it.

At some point, when exactly I didn't notice, my feet have stopped being passive, they have started to move, to be the cause of my motion. Clumsy, clunky and awkward at first, then smoother, easier, nearly a hint of graceful. 'Put your free arm out to balance yourself,' Tyler says. He is beside me now, holding on to one hand as we move. Without hesitation or fear, I put my arm out, and without panic I feel the shift of my weight as I find my centre on the two lines of wheels.

'See? See?' Tyler says. 'You can do it. You're doing it.' I can hear pride in his voice.

I can do it. I am doing it.

Looming right ahead of us is my building. We have skated all the way from Beached Heads to my flat and I haven't fallen over, Tyler hasn't let me down. 'That's where I live,' I say to him.

'Really?' he replies. 'I've always wanted to see inside that building. It looks incredible. Is it authentic on the inside?'

'The communal areas are, and the windows have to be the right style for the planning department, but most of them are double-glazed. And there's a cage lift like you see in old American movies.'

'You do realise that you're talking and skating now?' Tyler replies. 'You've done brilliantly.'

'Yeah, yeah, but tell me, how am I going to stop?' My building is coming towards us very fast. 'Because it seems my only option is to fall over or crash into the wall.'

Turns out that stopping involves hitting the wall with my hands instead of my body, and pulling myself to a standstill. I watched Tyler do it gracefully then did it myself.

Unusually, for that time of night, the car park is virtually empty. Normally it's a bun fight to get any space here because it is free, off-street parking that is exempt from the attentions of traffic wardens. Red, white and shiny, Lottie sits in her place at the far end of the car park, probably loving the view she has of the sea but not loving what the salt is doing to her metal parts. I need to take better care of her, take her out for a drive more.

Now that I've stopped, I feel a little less steady on my feet. 'I think my days of skating are over,' I say to Tyler, who is standing beside me at the wall. 'Maybe I should quit while I'm upright.' His laughter in reply is easy and calming. From the bag slung across his body he produces my flat red ballet pumps. He bobs down as though he isn't on skates and starts to unlace me. Every so often his hands stray to my ankle, and the heat of his touch sends pleasure all the way up my legs. It's a let down almost literally when my left foot is freed from the skate and returned to my shoe. I feel like I have fallen from a great height. Once I am back in my pumps I feel tiny compared to him. The speed with which he changes into his own trainers tells me that he was lengthening the process of taking off my shoes so he could touch me. Which I do not mind *at all*.

'So, that was an experience,' he says, once we are both back to normal height and on solid ground.

'It certainly was.'

'One you might want to repeat?'

This is 'end of the date' talk – we're not only talking about skating, we're discussing whether we're going to 'see' each other again.

'I feel strange not rolling around,' I say. 'I almost feel unsteady on my feet because I'm steady on my feet.'

'Ah, classic avoidance of the question,' Tyler says. He drops the bag, which now contains the two sets of skates, on to the ground.

'More like nerves about what might happen next,' I explain.

'What do you think might happen next?' he asks.

'Well, on any other normal date I might ask you in for a coffee – only instant, I'm afraid – and see once we're inside if I fancy progressing it to something more, tonight or another night…But, right now, I not only have my mother staying with me, my cousin and her daughter are here as well. I have a full house so it'd require far too much sneaking around. And anyway, who's to say you'd want to come up? Drink my coffee? Want to progress things? You might not even want to see me again. I realise those were some pretty big assumptions I was making, which makes me nervous.'

Tyler takes my hand, slowly presses his palm against mine until they are flat against each other like a reflection in a mirror. Staring intently at me, he reaches out with his other hand and slips it around my waist. His body against mine feels different to— I stop myself short. I'm not supposed to be thinking about *him*. *He*'s all part of the stuff that's been put to one side.

Tyler is simply different. I haven't related to another man's body in this way in over a decade. A frisson of excitement at being about to embark on something new tingles down my spine.

'I told you before, you're silly,' he says quietly. 'How could I not want to see you again?'

Our lips are suddenly millimetres apart and then they are together. My body feels like it did when I first stood up on the skates, wobbly and out of control. This is all good, *wanted*, though. This is the kind of out of control I enjoy. Tyler's kisses intensify, he presses me back against the wall, my hands go to his face, and he moves his body so close to mine I can feel the hammer of his heart against my chest. These mouth touches are incredible, they shoot shards of pleasure through me that pool in my stomach, explode in my chest, cause an ache between my legs.

'Get a room!' someone shouts at us from a passing car, and we immediately jump apart. Above the sound of the car engine driving away, we can hear the shouter and his friends laughing loudly.

Tyler lowers his forehead on to mine and chortles. 'That's the sort of thing that would only happen to me when I'm with you.'

'I'm not sure if that's a good thing or not,' I reply.

'It's a good thing. Being with you is a good thing.' He lowers his head. 'Here, let me prove it to you.'

Right before our lips slot together again he pauses as though something is wrong. Tyler frowns, then turns his head towards the sea, towards where Lottie is parked. My heart almost leaps out of my chest when I realise there is someone leaning against Lottie in the otherwise empty car park.

That person wasn't there before. At least, I don't think they were. But I maybe didn't notice much in the excitement of being with Tyler. I had glanced at Lottie, noted how shiny she looked, decided I needed to drive her more, but did I *really* look, take a note of the shadows she cast, the shadows others cast upon her? The shadow stops reclining against my car and stands to its full height.

'Sorry, is there something I can do for you, mate?' Tyler asks. He sounds pleasant and reasonable enough, but the way he has stepped slightly in front of me, has checked over his shoulder to make sure we're not going to be pounced on from behind, suggests he thinks trouble could be about to come our way. It is, unfortunately. But not in the way he thinks.

'No, not really,' the man who was watching us replies. 'Not unless you want to tell me why you're kissing my wife.'

42

Abi

To: Jonas Zebila
From: Abi Zebila
Subject: Sigh
Wednesday, 22 July 2015

Jonas,

Thank you. Thank you for sending me that email. I know it only said, 'I love you, little sister' a couple of hundred times, but it lifted my spirits. It made me feel less alone.

Gran is back in hospital. It's very serious. Seems like last time was just a trial run. I'm trying to make light of it but it's incredibly stressful. A diabetic crisis, a mild heart attack and various other minor things that all added together to put her back in hospital. She's probably going to have a stent put in.

I keep thinking, if I was like Gran is, what would I want? Would I want to be looked after by family, or would I want to be in a place where I get looked after by strangers who are experts? It's not like she and Mummy get on and she knows Mummy's doing it out of love and concern instead of duty and obligation.

Or would I want to be around at all, is the other question I keep asking myself. The thought of not being here, not seeing Lily and Declan and the other people I love, is terrifying to me. The thought of being alive but living this half-life of knowing that I'm never going to get better and will need dozens of different types of medication every day to keep me going is terrifying, too. But then, I'd want to live, I think.

No matter how ill I got, I'd want to live.

No matter how ill Gran gets, how awful she is to me and everyone else, I think I want her to live, too. I just want her experience of life to be better and pain-free. I can't imagine a world without Gran. I can't imagine her carrying on as she is, getting more sick and relying more on others and hating every second of that, either. But what's the alternative?

Gawd, that got a bit maudlin, didn't it? I'm so happy because you actually replied to one of my emails and Clemency came with me to... OH MY GOD! She called the ambulance for Gran and I haven't even told her if Gran's OK or not. Better go.

Abi

xxxxx

43

Smitty

Tyler reacts by moving his confused gaze from Seth to me, back to Seth, back to me. I don't deny what the man from the shadows has said, I don't call him a liar, which means to Tyler…He takes two steps backwards, putting distance between us.

The only real light we have shining down on the car park comes from the flats in the building above, and a streetlight on the corner where the cycle path disappears from view around the building. Standing here, in the near dark, the sound of the sea suddenly seems to have been magnified. Its volume is deafeningly loud all of a sudden, or maybe it is all the blood in my body rushing so forcefully to my head I fear it is about to explode.

This really shouldn't be happening. I'm not altogether sure how it is happening.

'Time I went,' Tyler states.

'Tyler…' I begin. Then nothing more comes out because I've run out of words. What do you say when the man who asked you if you were single before he arranged a magnificent date and was showering you in glorious kisses, discovers you're married?

'Yes?' he asks.

'I…' What do you say? Nothing. Except: 'I'm sorry.'

'So am I,' he replies.

Everyone was in their beds with their doors shut, only the corridor light was on so it was easy to unlock the front door and shunt Seth through to my bedroom without being seen. He walks across the room towards the windows, leans against the sill and folds his arms over his chest. I shut the door, lock it behind me. This shouldn't be happening and I have no idea why it is happening. As it continues to happen, though, I take a couple of deep breaths before I turn to face him.

He's grown a beard. In all the years I've known him, the only time he ever even flirted with facial hair was when Sienna asked him to grow a beard so he could be like Father Christmas. He got to three days before the itching was too much for him. In our separation he has managed to change that, though. It's made up of short brown, neatish hairs, so I'm guessing he trims it but doesn't groom it. His hair has grown as well – the grade-two shave replaced by a shortish back and sides from not bothering to have it cut. The skin under his eyes is a pewter colour, his normally healthy peach skin is pale, almost grey. He's lost weight, probably from not eating properly. How he looks is how I feel most of the time.

'What are you doing here?' I ask him when he doesn't speak, simply stands with his arms folded. 'In fact, how did you know where "here" was, considering I never told you?'

'Your mother called me.'

'*Which one?*' is on the tip of my tongue before I remember he doesn't know the half of what's been going on. And seeing as only one of them knows about him... 'Of course she did,' I reply. I know the exact day she called him, too: the day she met Tyler and decided he wasn't good enough so she'd better make do with the other not good enough one who she at least knew. 'What did she say? No, wait, don't tell me. No, actually, do... Actually, no, don't. I don't think I can bear to know what she said. Actually, d—'

'She said at this time of her life she should be planning on what to knit for her grandchildren, not worrying about whether she should be signing up her daughter for online dating. And that she didn't know how I could stand to look myself in the mirror every day when I'd wasted almost all of your child-bearing years. And that if she ever saw me again she wasn't sure if she could restrain herself enough to not slap me into the middle of next year. Oh, and when you did meet someone else, not to show my weaselly little face anywhere near you as she might instigate said slapping. Or words to that effect.'

'Had quite a lot to say for herself, didn't she, my mother?'

My husband nods. 'Yeah, quite a lot.'

'Erm . . . hang on, how do you get from "slapping you into the middle of next year" to "here's my daughter's address, turn up whenever you fancy . . . oh, and, don't worry, I won't warn her in any way"?'

Seth pushes up the sleeves of his navy blue sweatshirt. On his left wrist he wears his divers' watch and the leather, intricately plaited wristband I made for him at the height of the loom-band craze last year. On his right hand he has the silver cuff that I engraved with our initials in the same design he'd come up with for our engagement party. I keep staring at his arms, the pale skin covered in light hairs, so I do not have to stare at his face.

'I told her that she was right; that I'd thought about it and was incredibly sorry for everything that had happened. That I'd tried to get in touch but you wouldn't talk to me so could she tell me where you'd gone so I could come and beg your forgiveness and maybe get our relationship back on track.'

'And she handed over my address, just like that?'

'Yes. She told me she'd moved with you.'

'Well, it's a good thing I hadn't fled from you in fear of my life, isn't it? I swear, that woman doesn't think sometimes.'

'She was only trying to help.'

'Yeah, that's what she was doing,' I say sarcastically. 'If you and her are such good buddies, why weren't you in here instead of waiting outside? Which, by the way, is a really creepy thing to do. If I'd been on my own I might have died with fright. Especially with your new facial hair.'

Seth raises one of his hands, runs it over the bearded lower half of his face. 'I called your mobile and it was off, so I called your mother and she said you were out, probably working, and would be back later. I decided to sit on the bench and wait.' Even though I'm not looking at his face, I know he is staring at me. I can feel the weight of his gaze on the top of my head. I raise my eyes to meet his.

If I'd been on my own is currently playing on loop in his head. I knew the moment I said it that I shouldn't have. Betrayal and a deep sense of wounding have settled on his face.

'How long have you been seeing him?' Seth asks.

'What?' I know what that note in his voice is implying.

'How long? It's a fair enough question.'

'I didn't cheat on you,' I tell him. 'You know I wouldn't do that.'

'Answer the question then: how long have you been seeing him?'

'I met him a week or so after I moved here and this was the first time we've been out, not that it's any business of yours.'

He opens his mouth to say something and I cut in with: 'I can't talk any more right now. My head is fried about this and so many other things. I am not able tonight.'

'OK, fair enough, but can you answer me this: weren't you going to sort out us before you moved on?'

I say nothing in response because I don't want to talk about this right now, I am not able.

He takes my silence as a green light to ask another question. 'Or have you already "moved on" and this guy is just another step further along the road?'

That is goading enough to get me to bite. 'What are you saying?' I ask. Even though it's obvious, *blatant*, what he's accusing me of.

'You're not exactly shy about sex with different people is what I'm saying. How many of them have there been in the past three months?'

I'm guessing Seth has been examining what should be the wall of photographs he's helped me assemble and disassemble during the various moves of my life and he has been shocked and injured by the way I have edited him out. The only one that remains of him is the one of him with Dad. And yet, on the second row of the wall of my life in photographs that I'm rebuilding, there is Tyler. Melissa is there, too, but I wasn't kissing her a few minutes ago.

What he is saying reminds me of the time I found a bee on the washing in our back garden. I didn't think, just reached out to pick it off, and the bee objected to being moved on and stung me. Seth is like the bee – doesn't like the idea of being picked off, moved on, and has decided to sting me.

'How many were there before me again?' he says. 'Or did you lose count? Have you lost count now?'

His words continue to pump in poison, like the bee's sting did in my hand. The poison kept pumping in until Dad stopped me trying to pick out the sting and brushed it off with a quick, sideways swipe. I remember staring at it, incredulous at how this little sliver of a thing had managed to cause such extreme pain in my hand. I stare at my husband, incredulous that after everything he has done, he is causing extreme pain in my heart. It never seemed to have bothered him that much that I'd once slept around, and I thought in the moments it might have bothered him, he accepted it as part of who I was. I never thought he'd use it against me, no matter what the provocation.

'Fancy sleeping in your hire car, do you?' I ask. My quick, sideways swipe to remove this sting and stop his poison.

He unfolds his arms and stands upright. 'No, no I don't.'

'Are you sure?'

'Yeah, I'm sure.'

'Sure? Sure-sure?'

'I'm sorry,' he replies, finally ashamed and mollified. 'That was bang out of order. I'm sorry. I didn't mean it.'

'Why are you behaving like a dick?' I ask.

His hazel-green eyes flare suddenly. 'Because I *really* hated seeing you kiss someone else. And I really, *really* hate knowing you'd probably be in that bed fucking him right now if I hadn't turned up tonight.'

'But I can do what I like because we're finished, Seth. I made it clear we were over. What part of "we have to split up" didn't you get?' I reply.

'That isn't—'

'Isn't what?'

'That isn't how you end a marriage, OK? You don't just tell

someone you're splitting up and not tell them why. That's the part of "we have to split up" I don't get.'

I drop my face into my hands. If I had told him why, he would have carried on lying to me. He would have told me the truth eventually, but it would have been so eventually I wouldn't ever have trusted another thing that came out of his mouth. 'My head is fried,' I plead. 'I don't want to talk any more – about anything. I just don't.'

'I know, I'm sorry, I'm sorry. A lot has happened.'

'You have no idea,' I say, my voice wrapped tightly in a sob.

'We both need sleep. How are we going to do this?'

'Top to tail,' I say.

'*Really?*' he replies. 'When was the last time you topped to toed it?

'Apparently tonight.'

'Right you are then.'

'And keep the underwear on,' I add.

'I can't do that. I can't sleep with anything on.'

'You'll have to learn, starting tonight. I don't want "it" on the loose in the night.'

'What, you think it detaches itself from my body and roams around in the night?'

'No, I just don't want to encounter it if I roll over in the night and parts of our bodies touch each other. And then we have one of those awkward moments where it responds and I can't get my leg far away enough and you start having to think of your grandmother or something to make it— '

'Yes, all right, I get it. The black jacks stay on.'

We are silent as we undress, but the rustle of clothes being unbuttoned, pulled off, pulled down, fills the space in the room, everything amplified and loud. Each undone button, each piece of clothing folded and placed on my desk, is a noisy reminder that we used to rush through this part almost every night so we could get into bed together, talk and eventually fall asleep wrapped up in each other. We would usually not wake up like that, would be separated as we moved through dreamland, but undressing was always the start of finishing our day together.

Without being asked, he takes the foot of the bed and I throw him a couple of pillows. He accepts them with a small smile of gratitude and slides under the duvet. I do the same. Even though we are on opposite sides of the bed, I'm still aware of him. Of his body, his heat, the weight of history that links us.

He rests his head on his arm and stares up the ceiling and I do the same. Our breathing is deep and synchronised. Seth will probably sleep. He always used to say he hated sleeping without me beside him, and now we're back in the same bed, coupled with the exhaustion of the drive and the adrenalin of the last half an hour, I can imagine he'll probably flake right out. I hate that idea. I hate that he has snatched away the chance for me to have something else on my mind before I go to sleep, something pleasant and exciting, and after doing that, he'll probably just slide off to sleep like nothing has happened.

'I don't think Mum told you,' I whisper in the dark. 'Nancy and Sienna are staying here with us for a while.'

His demeanour is immediately tense. I can almost hear how alarm bulges his eyes, while his body has obviously been dragged away from its slow descent into sleep.

It's mean and awful that I did that, but I'm quite pleased to know that neither of us will be getting much sleep tonight.

44

Smitty

Since first light came creeping in through the open blinds I have been sitting on my desk chair, my feet up on the seat, watching Seth sleep. I had a break to go for a shower and to get dressed, but mostly I have sat here and watched him while the Sun has got higher and higher in the sky.

He doesn't suit his beard, but he looks the same. Maybe a little older, more tired, thinner, but he's still Seth. He's still one of the best friends I ever had. I would have stayed with him forever, I think. I certainly planned to. Our future was set, made from stitching together every day, week, month, year we'd had – each one distinctive, unique and important – until we had the patchwork quilt of who we were as a couple.

'Wake up, Seth,' I say from across the room. We have to talk. I wasn't fair on him. At the time it'd been too difficult for me to even contemplate: after losing Dad, talking to Seth about all this seemed an impossibility when he had kept things from me. No matter what he'd done, though, that wasn't fair on him, he did deserve better.

I move across the room, crouch down beside him and hiss, '*Seth! Wake up!*' into his ear.

He jerks awake, his eyes wide and shocked. 'Whaaa-what?'

'Shall we go get a coffee, have a talk?' I say.

He grunts, tries to turn over. 'Later,' he mumbles.

'No, now.'

'No,' he murmurs. 'Sleep.'

A wave of anger crashes through me. 'OK, you sleep,' I say, irritation in every word. 'And I'll send Nancy in with coffee a bit later, shall I?'

He dresses quickly and efficiently, asks for the bathroom so he can use the toilet and brush his teeth. Last night was the second night ever that I'd known him not brush his teeth before bed (the other time was the night we first slept together). I used to sit on the edge of the bath and talk to him while he brushed his teeth. It was for two minutes, he couldn't reply as the toothbrush buzzed around his mouth, but it was one of our 'things'. Sometimes, he'd sit beside me and we'd have a conversation before we started work. That was another square of the quilt of our life, another bead on the string of our time together.

With Seth, February 2014, Leeds

'Are you sure you don't mind not having anyone here?' I asked him.

He kissed under my right ear lobe. 'Not at all,' he whispered before raising the camera on my phone above us. 'Say "nuptials"!' he said with a laugh.

'Nuptials!' I said, and grinned as he imprinted the image of our special day into the space in my phone. Password-protected so no one would ever know.

I'd heard Sienna in the living room watching CBeebies on her own so we'd had to creep out of the flat so she wouldn't see Uncle Smitty, as she called him. Outside my building, we both stand for a moment and stare at the sea. 'This is such an amazing view,' he says. 'When I was sat out here last night I had a real sense of peace and being connected to something huge.'

'This way,' I say to him. I turn towards the main road, intending to head up towards George Street, the main street in Hove. On that small road there are more coffee shops – chains, independents and local chains – than any other type of shop.

'I saw a café along the seafront. Let's go there.'

'No, let's go up to George Street.'

'Why? That café looked cool. I'm sure it's open now. It'd be nice to talk and see the sea. Ha! See what I did there?'

My face musters a smile. 'No, let's just go to George Street. There are so many more places. Some of them have nice views, especially if you like to watch somewhere come to life.'

'Look, what's the problem with—'

Seth has finally faced me, seen the uncomfortable manner in which I bite at my lower lip, keep my eyes on the uneven black-grey surface of the car park where less than twelve hours ago he watched me kiss another man.

'He works there,' Seth states.

I nod. *Owns it, actually*, I should say. *Makes brilliant coffee in the most brilliant cups.*

'I might have known.'

'What's that supposed to mean?'

'What do you think it means?'

'I don't know, that's why I asked.'

'It means I might have known he'd be someone you see every day.'

'That doesn't even make sense – I see the postman every day, are you expecting something to happen between me and him? Or are you calling me a slut again?'

When he doesn't reply, I say, 'Well, are you?'

He shakes his head.

'Well then, stop saying things that don't make sense or imply you think I'm a slut. I haven't slept with anyone since you. And even if I had, it'd be no business of yours.' I sound far more indignant than I am: I'm single, we're separated, our marriage is over as far as I'm concerned, but guilt is gambolling through me, leaving a sense that I have betrayed him. 'And I don't even drink coffee every day,' I add for good measure.

'George Street it is,' he eventually says.

My unwarranted sense of guilt and betrayal makes every step slow, laborious and painful as we walk together to the place where our marriage is going to end properly.

45

Smitty

We find our places in the café just at the bottom of George Street. It is old-fashioned on the outside with double-bay tinted glass windows, but the height of modernity on the inside: brilliant white walls with primary colour picture panels containing bright, bold prints in each of the picture panels, and white, distressed-wood floors.

It's mainly populated by people who are coming in for a coffee on the way to work, or those who have come early with their laptops to stake out a space to work for the day. Seth pulls out a low striped fabric-covered bucket chair for me at the back of the café, then turns towards the counter.

'The usual?' he asks.

'I suppose so,' I reply. I'm not sure what the usual is any more. Everything feels like it is in flux, nothing set; all that I knew or thought I knew is fluid and changeable. He returns a few minutes later, after I've watched him queuing, after he has constantly looked over at me, as though checking I am still there and won't be running away again. *'Where would I run to?'* I should have called over to him. *'It's not like I have anywhere else to go.'*

He lowers himself into his seat, slowly, dragging the moments out before we need to speak. I have no idea where to start with the process of unravelling. How do we make sense of any of it? It's like a huge, sheer rock face: the summit so high it's not easily visible to the naked eye, and I – *we* – need to climb it without any safety equipment. It's possible, doable, but dangerous, particularly since it is so unknown. Seth and I used to talk all the time. About anything, everything, it was our 'thing'. We talked and listened to each other. Now, I don't know what to say; which words to choose to start the conversation.

'How about we start with this,' he states. From the side pocket of his trousers he produces a rectangular box and slides it across the table to me. I knew I shouldn't have bought him a pair of those trousers. I wear combats and workmen's trousers because it allows me to carry all sorts of things in the various pockets, my own wearable toolbox. He coveted them so passionately I finally bought him a pair. And now look: they've let him bring that thing here without me having a clue he was carrying it. What's that expression about no good deed going unpunished?

I stare at that box, long and oblong with coloured writing and a coloured design. It was the most discreet one on sale, that's why I chose it. Hid it amongst my other shopping and avoided eye contact with the person who served me. Not that they'd care, but I had cared.

'There's only one left in the box,' he states. 'I'm assuming there were two when you bought it.'

My gaze goes from the box to him. Calm. He's calm. That's good.

'Here we go,' the waitress trills. She's that 1950s vintage Brighton-type with her spotted scarf tied in a bow around the front of her glossy black bun, her lips coated in bright red lipstick, her foundation overly pale and her eyes heavily made up. 'One café mocha, extra shot of chocolate, and one double-strong latte.' We each indicate which is ours and continue to stare at one another as she sets the large white cups in front of us. From the corner of my eye I see her notice the box on the table and she visibly winces as it crosses her mind that we're not going to be having a nice coffee and chat. She winces again, gritting her teeth, then quietly withdraws. When the crowd has died down she's going to stand behind her counter, pretending to polish her coffee machine while watching how this story plays out.

'So, one test instead of two?' Seth asks when it's obvious I'm not going to restart *that* conversation.

'I used one just before I came down here.' The box fascinates me. Why didn't I throw it away instead of hiding it? I remember dashing out of the bathroom into the corridor when I heard his motorbike pull up outside. I remember thinking it would be the worst thing in the world to be caught with that box so instead of shoving it into my back pocket with the test, I hid it in one of my packing boxes. Why? And why didn't I take it away when I went back to collect as many possessions as I could? Did I want to get caught?

'What was the result?' he asks.

'I don't know,' I admit. 'I was so freaked out by everything that I stopped down the road from the flat and threw it into the nearest bin without checking.'

He frowns, the action crinkling his forehead, while he calculates something. 'That day at the flat, that's what you were doing?'

'Yes.'

Obviously the more important thought hits him then: 'Have you done a test since?'

I sigh before I'm forced to shake my head.

'So you could be . . . You could be pregnant right now?'

'No, I'm not. Which is why I didn't need to look. I'd know if I was and I'm not.'

'Have you had a period?'

I sigh again. Stupid box. If it wasn't for this stupid box this conversation wouldn't be going this way. I wouldn't be on the back foot and having to think about this again. No, I haven't had a proper period since before I left Leeds, but I was incredibly stressed, grief-stricken about Dad and the break up with Seth. I was moving. My mother decided to move in with me. Any one of those things would normally have stressed me out enough to make a period late, but all of them together? It'd be a miracle if my body got itself right again enough to have a period in a decade or so, let alone three months. I glare harder at the box. This stupid box that's caused all this trouble.

'Clem? Have you had a period since you took the test?'

'I am not pregnant,' I state. I pull the box across the table towards me, drop it in my bag to give me a way to hide my face. 'I will do this test later, if it makes you happy. But I am not pregnant.' I was pregnant once when I was seventeen as the result of a split condom and it felt completely different to this. Admittedly that pregnancy lasted for about two days until nature decided to take another course and spare me having to make the decision that my birth mother made, but my body felt different then to how it feels now.

'Would you tell me if you were?'

'Yes, Seth, I would tell you. What sort of thing is that to ask?'

My husband reclines in his seat, pushing his legs out before he runs his hands over his haircut. 'Have you not been living the life where you left without an explanation?' he says. 'I wouldn't have asked if you hadn't just ended our relationship without talking to me properly.'

'Marriage. I ended our marriage. We're married.'

'I know we're married.'

'But no one else does, do they? And why is that? Oh, yes, because of your "*friend*" Nancy.'

Abruptly Seth's expression changes – worry and fear dance on his features. Now he's the one on the back foot, uncertain where this conversation is going to take us. What I'm going to say next.

'Nothing happened with Nancy.'

Liar, I think. *Liar.* 'Something *always* happens with Nancy. *Always.*'

He tells me I'm right almost straight away. Not with words, but in the way he slides down in his seat and slowly runs the palms of his hands over his temples, trying to massage away the memory of it all.

'Smitty—' he begins.

'I told you what she did to me, Seth,' I cut in. 'I told you how she made my childhood a nightmare, how I couldn't talk to my mother about it because Mum can't see what she's like. And you saw what she was like yourself, how she ruined our engagement party, how she's tried to ruin other stuff, and you still started a secret friendship with her.'

'I didn't start it, it sort of happened.'

'Everything always "sort of happens" with Nancy. That's what she does. She starts turning up when no one is around, just for a chat.'

'She wanted me to help her with her website. That was all. And she kept coming over.'

'Even though she's been doing her website for years and has even designed stuff for other people?'

'It all made sense at the time. But thinking back now, I didn't do much of anything, not even give her design advice. We sat at the computer together, but she did most of it.'

'And then she starts bringing over the joints and the beers.'

'It was only the odd joint and beer.'

'Even though you don't ever do drugs, and you very rarely drink during the day, especially when you're meant to be working.'

He rubs at his temples again. 'But it made sense at the time. We were just hanging out while I was working. And…'

'And then suddenly she's confiding in you about her latest man problem, you're trying to make her feel better by paying her com-pliments because men have been shit to her all her life and it's not her, it's them. Especially Dylan who you're even more disappointed in because he's your friend and he's abandoned his daughter.'

'But—'

'Then, because she's trusted you, it's not long before you're telling her stuff that you wouldn't normally tell anyone.'

'It didn't seem so calculated.'

'Of course it didn't. She's been doing it all her adult life. All *my* adult life. She's tried it on with every boyfriend I've ever had. I told you this.'

'But she just needed a friend. That's what it felt like.'

'I know that's what it felt like. And that's fine. But what isn't fine is that when I asked you about it, you lied to me.'

'How did you find out?' my husband asks.

'Apart from finding her hair in our bed?' He blanches. 'Yes, I know she got into our bed naked and propositioned you, it's part of her repertoire. The other way I knew what was going on was that she was writing stuff on her blog that could only have come from you. I started to read it when I found her hair.' If it's possible, more colour leeches out of his skin and he is now as white as the floor of the café.

'She said she wouldn't tell anyone she'd done that. She seemed more embarrassed than I did when I turned her down and told her to get dressed. She even asked me if I was going to tell you, and when I said yes, she practically begged me not to. I should have known it was too easy when she said she wouldn't tell anyone.'

'That's what she does,' I remind my husband. 'She gets you into a situation where you go against your better judgement and suddenly she's got something over you because you've been keeping a secret with her.'

'You believe that I didn't sleep with her?'

'Yes. Of course I believe you. I knew you wouldn't sleep with her, Seth, but it wasn't about that. It was never about that. I asked you – practically begged you that last night – to tell me. But you wouldn't. I knew if I started asking questions you'd panic even more and lie and I couldn't stand that. I only wanted you to be truthful with me. I have trusted you more than anyone else I've met in my life, and you lied to me.'

'I felt like I couldn't tell you the truth. I wanted to, but I couldn't. You were in so much pain and I didn't want to add to it.'

'You told her we were starting to try for a baby.' That hurt more than her getting into our bed.

'She wrote that on her blog?'

'No. She texted me saying if we were thinking of trying for a baby that I should talk to her about any tips I might need and not to forget the folic acid. On the surface a nice text from one cousin to another, and if I told anyone else about that text they'd all think I was crazy for being upset by it. In reality, it's her way of telling me that you're confiding in her.'

'Oh, God.'

'How could you, Seth? It was *such* a big deal, we have talked for years about it so I could get my head around it. We got married and everything so I'd feel safer about trying for a baby. I didn't even tell my dad in my last few months with him that we'd got married and were trying to conceive. even though I knew how happy it would make him, because we agreed it was something for you and me. There were so many times when I came close to telling him, when I wanted to say that we'd at least got married so he'd feel happy that I'd be settled once he was gone, but I didn't because we'd agreed that no one else was to know. And you just up and told Nancy about us trying for a baby. Her of all people. Why didn't you just tell her we'd got married and be done with it?'

These feelings, bottled up inside for so long, don't feel better out in the open. It's worse. They're raw, like newly scraped skin exposed to salt, it's an indescribable pain. Safety is so underrated, dismissed as being boring and dull in the whole spectrum of a *grand amour* relationship. Passion, sex, grand gestures, romantic meals, big long kisses, swooning... They are what love is meant to be about. They are the things we are meant to crave and revel in, but safety? It's something that apparently signals a relationship has become stale and predictable. Safety is what I need, what Seth always told me he needed. If either of us were to fall, we needed to know that we would have a soft landing place, that we would be safe. He loved his parents but, as he got older, realised how smothering they were and he only felt able to breathe when we had got together. He found safety with me. And safety, trust, is what I'd had with Seth. The safety to be myself. I opened myself up to him, trusted him with my thoughts and fears and the depth of the void inside, and how I could never fill it. With Seth, I was safe. Then, somehow, I wasn't. I couldn't trust him, I couldn't rely on him to not repeat things to the one person who had made my life a misery. Without safety and trust I couldn't be with him any longer. Without safety and trust I have this pain that doesn't feel like it will go.

When Seth is highly stressed he closes his eyes and focuses his attention on the blackness inside his eyelids and takes deep breaths to try to calm his racing heart. I watch him sit with his eyes closed, the rise and fall of his chest slowing and slowing until he is holding his breath for long seconds, releasing it for an equally long amount of time.

When I'm stressed, I want to run. Not jogging or anything constructive like that, I just have an urge to stop what I'm doing, throw down whatever I'm holding and run away as fast as I can, only stopping when my legs and feet are too exhausted to move or I come to an intractable natural barrier. I want to run. I want to leave all of this behind and run away again.

'Can you forgive me?' he asks. He has opened his eyes and is staring at me.

No. That is the answer. *I don't think so, no.*

'I want to,' I say instead. 'I'm not—' I stop. The agony of what I am saying is slashed across his face. His eyes are closed again. He's retreating into darkness, calming his erratic heart with measured breathing. 'I want to,' I repeat.

It's not only about forgiveness. It's forgetting as well. Can you truly forgive someone if you haven't forgotten what they have done? Our marriage won't withstand the need for forgiveness. Together, we can withstand a lot of things: arguments, comments from other people about how we shouldn't be together, disapproval from my mother, poverty, even attempts by Nancy to break us up, but it can't withstand something like a breach of trust that requires forgiveness. We could pretend, we could get back together and carry on, but I know the moment I don't tell him something because I fear he'll tell someone else, will be the moment I'll know I haven't forgotten. And if I haven't forgotten, then I haven't forgiven.

I want to forgive him. I want to move on and get back together, but I won't be able to forget. Without forgetting, forgiveness is meaningless.

Seth wants to walk around for a bit to clear his head. I'd love to as well. But I have another difficult conversation to have, a huge apology to make, and I can't delay it any longer.

46

Abi

To: Jonas Zebila
From: Abi Zebila
Subject: Big news
Friday, 24 July 2015

Dear J,

I meant to tell you something. I'm up the duff again. Yes, big news. It was all planned, which is why Declan keeps going on about getting married. No, Mummy and Daddy don't know and I'm not sure if this is or isn't the time to tell them. *Is* the time because they're so stressed about Gran nothing will seem as bad; *is not* the time because they're so stressed about Gran, telling them now would be incredibly selfish.

Gran is home. She seems better. In fact, this is the best she's looked in a long time but it's still stressful, especially for Mummy. Not only because she does most of the caring, but I get the impression having Clemency around has made Mummy rethink a lot of things about her life. I noticed that the box of artwork she 'disappeared' from the loft is now in the pantry area of the kitchen – she must be going through it again.

Since Gran has been in hospital Mummy's been sketching on random pieces of paper and has got herself a sketch pad now. I wonder if she's going to take her art up again if she gets the chance? I'm not sure she can, because Gran's care is the most important thing in her life and Mummy has to make everything fit around that. The best thing, though, is that if I need a hug, I know I can get it from her now. No, it's not all happy families around here – if it was I'd have told them I'm pregnant – but it's getting there between me and Mummy. Everyone knowing her secret is, I think, slowly turning her into the type of mother I always wanted. So, all a bit strange round here but not terrible.

Love and miss you,
Abi
xxxx

PS I forgot the other big news: Clemency is going to look after Lily-Rose. When I texted her about Gran being in hospital she said she'd take her next week so I can work. Lily will be over the moon as she loves Clemency's niece, Sienna. They've decided they're cousins. So let's see how that pans out.

47

Smitty

'What can I get you?' he asks politely. I've been downgraded. Not only to 'just another customer' but to 'annoying customer who I deal with politely'. If you spend a lot of time in Beached Heads, as I have, you notice how Tyler deals with people, how he categorises them. Loyal customers are treated like friends, he finds things to banter about, he remembers their orders, he assigns them their own special cups. Ordinary customers get the banter and recommendations on new coffees, are possibly assigned a cup if they've been more than once. Annoying customers get a polite greeting where he asks them what they want.

'How about a big cushion to break my fall when I throw myself to my knees and apologise profusely?'

'I don't do cushions,' he says. Politely.

'OK, I'll do it without the cushions, then...' Nothing. No response, no hint that he wants me to continue or to leave. I lower my voice. 'I'm sorry. I'm so, so sorry. I can't even begin to understand how you feel. That wasn't meant to happen.'

He jerks his head indicating that I should come to the other end of the counter, to near the machine where he taught me to make coffee. It's quieter there, more private.

'I'm so sorry,' I repeat, a little more confident now that he's not going to sling me out or ignore me. He does want to hear what I've got to say. 'It was such incredibly bad timing.'

'I don't mess with married women. It's not my thing – never has been, never will be,' he states.

'I'm not married in that sense of the word.'

'That guy wasn't your husband?'

'Yes, he is, but we've split up. I thought he'd got the message that we'd split up.'

'He's stalking you, then?'

'No, not exactly. Or even at all. He came here because he wanted us to sort out splitting up.'

Tyler's lips move upwards but they don't manage to make one of those smiles that I have been feeding my crush on. 'That makes no sense to me. Have you split up or not?'

'Yes.'

'But he doesn't know.'

'He does now. I thought he knew before, but there won't be a scrap of doubt in his mind any longer. That's why it's taken me so long to come see you. We were sorting things out.'

'When?'

'This morning.'

'No, I mean, when did you split up?'

'Nearly two and a half months ago. Although I haven't seen him in nine weeks.'

'In other words, when you moved down here.'

'Yes.'

'Ahh, right. And when did you last speak to him?'

'Apart from this morning?' I ask, jokily, trying to inject some levity into this. He's being altogether too polite for this to turn out well for me. And I hate Polite Tyler.

'Yes, apart from this morning.' Deadpan. He is not playing.

'He's been ringing me and texting, but I haven't replied.'

'Not really split up, then.'

'We had. He didn't want it to be true.'

'Had you started divorce proceedings? Or even seen a solicitor?'

'No.'

'That's not what being split up is. It's fine, you do what you gotta do, but like I said, I don't mess with married women.'

'I'm only a married woman in name. And not even in name because we both kept our own names.'

My feeble attempt at humour is met with: 'Where did he sleep last night?'

Ah, *that* question. He is so convinced that I am married more than in name, whatever I say now will be wrong. 'We slept top to toe.'

'No sofa in your house?'

'I couldn't ask him to sleep on the sofa after his long drive and there were other things. I told you that I had a full house, it would have been too complicated.'

I receive a cordial, disappointed smile. Tyler picks up the nearest cup, the pastel yellow cup with white daisies all over the bowl. Then he takes a matching saucer. The way he picks it up makes it feel like it is no longer my assigned cup, just something he'd give to a customer he could not care less if he saw again or not. 'Coffee?' he asks. 'Cappuccino? Mocha?'

'Please believe me, Tyler. Nothing happened because we're not together any more,' I explain. 'I would have told you about him if we'd been out on another date. It's not really first date talk. But please believe me, I would have told you.'

'I don't mess with married women,' he reiterates. 'And, much as I like you, you're married. You don't think you are, but you are. You couldn't even make him sleep on the floor. You shared a bed with him because you're not done with him. Which is cool, but not something I want to get involved with.'

'It wasn't like that. I—' I stop. This is humiliating. Excruciatingly humiliating. I am begging someone to believe that I'm not still with my husband. I am trying to stop someone from dumping me, rejecting me. I thought I was done with being scared of rejection by men when I got together with Seth. I've been rebuffed so many times in my life, I should be used to it by now. I shouldn't mind too much standing in front of Tyler with him holding my favourite of his coffee cups in his hand, with him poised to make me a polite cup of coffee with which to wash down this huge, rich, creamy dose of rejection.

I wish I'd thought to take a picture of my favourite Beached Heads cup that Tyler had assigned me before this day. It would have made the wall at home. I'd have to take it down along with the picture of him and store them in the butterfly box, of course, but at least I'd be able to look at it occasionally even though I'd never be drinking from it again.

'I think I'd better go,' I say to him.

'Coffee to go?' he asks, his face open and friendly. Polite.

'No, no, I'm fine.'

'Are you sure? I'm making one anyway for the bottomless cup at the back, there. It's no trouble.'

'Oh, go on then, if—' I catch myself. 'No, actually, no.' I'm a little more forceful than necessary but I'm not going to play along with this. He's got every right to reject me but that doesn't mean I have to accept it placidly. 'I'm just going to go. Do some work or something. I'll see ya.'

'Yeah. Drop by any time you fancy a coffee, Clemency,' he says, the politest kick to the guts I've ever had, I think.

Tap, tap, tap. Pause. *Tap, tap, tap.* Pause. *Tap.* Pause. *Tap.*

Seth's secret knock. We came up with our secret knocks and secret codes in texts, in case either of us was ever taken hostage and we needed to let the other one know there was danger. (We loved doing stupid things like that.) He's tapping on Lottie's door. How he knew I was in here, have been in here since I briefly returned to the flat after I humiliated myself at Beached Heads, I don't know. My guess is that he's too scared to ring the doorbell to the flat in case Nancy or my mother answer. They've gone to Southampton for the day. Shopping, eating, hanging out like a family does on their summer holidays.

'It's open,' I call.

He slides back the door and is a bit taken aback to see me splayed out like a starfish on the floor. I hoist myself upright to sitting while he climbs in and shuts the door behind himself, seals us into the place where we spent many hours working together. We reloved Lottie back to this current state of glory. The bodywork was mainly good, but she needed a lot of work – hence the name – and both Seth and I wanted to do it. We housed her in a garage a short walk away from the flat and every night after work and most weekends, we'd work on her. We talked so much while we worked on her. We talked about our lives before we met, about our years in college, about having children, about the engagement party, about deciding to get married. All those important things were discussed, and very often decided, while we worked on some part of Lottie.

He sits on his favourite seat, the one behind the driver's seat that faces backwards.

I take the white test from its place in my bag, push it across the floor towards Seth. He stares at it for a long time in silence. He's disappointed, it's clear on his face, but he doesn't say or do anything except nod while staring at the result. I *knew* I wasn't pregnant. That was why it hadn't been a worry for me. Not a total worry, anyway. I had felt a fleeting nanosecond of disappointment ripple through me, followed by a small wave of relief that things could end properly between Seth and me now – we had nothing to tie us together. Then a huge gut-wrenching sob had escaped me when I realised Seth and I had nothing to tie us together. I wasn't going to have his baby and we were over.

'When are you going back home?' I ask.

'I'm not. Not right away, anyway.'

'What about work?'

He scratches his fingernails through his beard, the sound is dry and unpleasant. 'I resigned.'

'Resigned? Have you lost your mind? What are you going to do for money?'

'I'm still working for them until my notice period expires, then I'll be employed by them on a consultancy basis. I'll tidy up their big projects, help with pitches, etc. Any meetings can be done on video conference calls. I even sold the motorbike. I couldn't bring it so I sold it. I've sublet the flat to Jorge and his girlfriend.'

Slowly I ease myself up on to the seat diagonally opposite Seth. I rest my head against the window and stare into space. There is so much going on, but I keep thinking about Tyler. Every time I try to enjoy the memory of the way he smiled at me moments before we kissed, the expression of betrayal on his face before he left last night washes it away, and leaves huge chunks of guilt moored on the shores of my mind. He was so hurt, last night and today, and that was because of me. He didn't deserve that. No one did, to be honest.

'Have you been to see him?' Seth asks.

I nod without looking at him. I know what Seth does, though: he twists his lips together and nods. Right now, he'll be overtly struggling with himself – his innate, caring response as my friend will be in pitched battle with his instinctive, jealous response as my husband. 'Want to talk about it?' His friend role has won.

'Not with you, no.' He is not my friend. No matter what we might pretend, after a decade of sex and love and exclusivity, and then marriage, he can't go back to being 'just' my friend no matter how hard we'd both like him to be.

'Can I stay?' he asks, probably relieved that he doesn't have to listen to me chat about someone else.

'With me?'

'Yes.'

'The flat is full, where would you sleep?'

'In your bed.'

'*My bed?*'

'Yes.'

'You think that's wise?'

'No. Do you still love me, Smitty?'

Of course I did. There was a hole in my life that was Seth-shaped. But he couldn't step back into it. I knew I'd have to get used to living with that hole in my life because there was too much hurt for us to mend. 'How is that a fair question?'

'It's not. But I don't feel like being fair, not about this. And why should I be? If you can't tell me if you still love me, don't you at least miss me?'

I sigh, avoid looking at him. 'That's not the point. And how is it supposed to work with Nancy around?'

'I don't know. It'll just have to, I guess.' He shrugs. 'You know I can't sleep without you. It's been hell these past few months. Last night was the first night I've slept properly since you left.'

'Seth—'

'Don't you miss me, Smitty?' he interrupts.

I know what he's thinking: *Smitty and he have only been on one date, it's nothing serious, they haven't had sex and, from the look on her face, he clearly isn't keen to keep things going, which means I've still got a chance. All I have to do is stick around and she might be reminded of what we had, what we could have again.*

If I was him, I would be thinking the same, part of me *is* thinking the same. But I have to put a stop to this for both our sakes.

'Yes, you can stay,' I say. 'I suppose if you're around it'll make it easier to sort out the divorce.'

48

Smitty

Mum has been avoiding me these past five days since Seth arrived. She leaves early with Nancy to go shopping somewhere, and they return in time for Mum to put Sienna to bed. By the time she's got Sienna down, I've left to go to my workshop. I do most of my work at night now that I've got more to avoid about being at home. Since Mum has spent the last few weeks almost stalking me, like she used to do when I was in my teens, listening at doors to try to overhear my phone calls and would most likely hack my email if she could, it's been a bit odd to have so much space from her.

I'm sure Mum figures that if she leaves it long enough I won't say anything to her and I'll eventually be grateful that she forced me to get back with him. She's out of her mind, of course, if she thinks that's going to happen but I don't care. I've spent five of the best days with Lily and Sienna. We've been swimming in Worthing and they both encouraged and reassured each other about going down the huge water slide. We went to Lewes to visit the castle but the parking was so atrocious we came back and went to Drusillas animal park instead and managed to rush round before it was chucking out time. We've been to a play park that is crammed with dinosaur sculptures.

Every day that I go to collect Lily with Sienna in Lottie, Abi looks concerned then relieved that I've kept to my word and shown up. 'Are you sure you don't mind doing this?' she asks, and the answer is the same: 'No, I don't.' I love spending time with the girls. They're completely devoted to each other and every day act as if they have been friends since they were born.

Today the forecast was for rainy showers, and I saw how exhausted they were. Super fun overload was tugging at their good natures and shortening their tempers. I decided on a sedate, calm day. We walked into the centre of Brighton and browsed all the bead shops we could find, we even went into a few stationers and newsagents, anywhere that sold beads and charms. Then we headed back to my shop. Last night before I left I had cleared a space in the centre of the shop, laid out two huge tartan-patterned blankets for us to sit and work on. We had a picnic, show tunes on the CD player and all the time in the word to string beads together.

When I was first training to become a jeweller I remember thinking that beadwork wasn't as skilful as the metalwork stuff. It seemed elementary and unsophisticated until I was assigned the task of making an affordable set of wedding jewellery including tiara, necklace, earrings and garter. My eyes were opened when I began to see the beads, how they fitted together, what they made when placed next to the correct colour or the correct texture. Each beaded piece had to be planned, laid out, arranged, thought about again, rearranged. By the time I had finished the assignment I had changed my mind about beadwork. Like most things, it was only as beautiful, intricate and perfect as you allowed it to be.

Sometimes, in the evenings, when I need to tune out for a while, I will string beads for a necklace, or a belt, or to have a really long piece of string with beads.

Lily and Sienna sit cross-legged on the picnic blankets, the tubs of beads in front of them. I have given them each a large velvet bead mat to lay out their designs, or rather to drop random beads on to when they scoop fistfuls out of the pots.

'Why are you doing this?' Abi asked me yesterday.

'I want to,' I said. '*I want to be a part of your family*,' I should have added. '*Mum has her family now that Nancy is here, I want to be a part of mine. It's also the right thing to do.*'

'Auntie Smitty?' Lily has started to call me that too, mainly because

Sienna calls me that and anything Sienna does is perfect. It works the other way, too: Sienna's favourite colour was pink until she discovered Lily's was green and now she sits stringing green bead after green bead after green bead on her necklace.

'Yes, Lily?'

'Why did you decide to make jewels?'

'I don't actually remember,' I tell her. 'When I was a little girl I used to love to play with my mum's jewellery. I would sit on the floor of her bedroom and put it all on. My dad would think it was hilarious then would tell me to put it back because my mum would get upset in case I broke it or lost something. Maybe that was why, because I wanted to make stuff I could play with.'

Lily and Sienna have both paused in stringing their necklaces to listen to me. 'I had to go to university first, though. My mum and dad would not have let me go straight off to make jewellery, I had to do something academic and I had to show my commitment to jewellery making by paying for it myself.'

'What's commitment?' Sienna asks.

'It means being all serious,' Lily says.

'But making jewels is fun.'

'I know. I think Auntie Smitty was doing it wrong.'

'What do you girls want to be when you grow up?' I ask.

'A hairdresser, princess and doctor,' Lily says.

'Me, too!' exclaims Sienna. 'Pinky-promise?' She drops her string, Lily drops hers, and the pair of them leap on each other to hug and pinky-promise best friends forever that they'll be hairdressers, princesses and doctors. From my place on the picnic mat I watch them hug and kick over their pots of beads, the communal pots of beads and the tray of findings, nylon strings and catches. They all ricochet off in different directions. I'm going to be finding these scattered things for years to come.

I have my small black radio that sits on top of the shelves on quite loudly and I almost miss the knock on my shop door. It's insistent but not Seth's emergency knock. I lower the radio volume, listen again. Rat-a-tat-tat-tat-tat. I know the knock, but it couldn't be. I check the time: 22.45 p.m. Not at this time.

Cautiously so the person doesn't see me if it's not someone I would want to see, I peek out of the doorway that leads to the back of the shop and my workshop area. I can just make out the outline of the person who is knocking and it is the right height and shape. 'I can see you, Clemency Smittson, you open this door right now!' For some reason, the timbre of her voice isn't at all muffled by the glass and distance. I swear, the military could use my mum's voice as a weapon.

Once in, she stands in the darkened shop area looking around. Assessing it, wondering if I own it or not. I don't think I ever got around to telling her that I had a shop as well as the workshop.

'How did you get here?' I ask to distract her from the shop. She has spots of rain glinting on the shoulders and back of her black cardigan – no coat I notice – and on her black Bermuda shorts.

She holds up her helmet. 'I cycled, of course.'

'Wearing that? Jeez, Mum, it's raining and it's dark and you have no reflective clothing on. You're a living, breathing unsafe cycling awareness video waiting to happen.'

'Do you have lights in this place?' she asks.

'Let's go through to my workshop,' I say.

'You've been seeing those people behind my back,' she accuses the second we move from the darkness of the shop into the bright light of my workshop. I stand with my back to her, staring at my bench. I'd been about to anneal a piece of silver to make into a ring. I'd set it up: the silver rectangle was in the tweezers-like clamp, I'd turned on the gas from the canister to the blow torch, lowered my daylight lamp so I could see when the metal colour started to glow pink as it reached the right temperature. I'd picked up my lighter to light the flame when I'd heard her knock.

Carefully, I bend down and turn off the gas to the blowtorch, using the valve at the canister, then rise to my full height and raise the daylight lamp so my bench is bathed in artificial sunlight (necessary when you're doing close work, a hindrance when you're in the process of annealing).

'Have you nothing to say for yourself?' Mum asks.

'Abi's grandmother is in hospital, she needs to work so I've been taking Lily out.'

'I only found out because young Sienna was talking on and on about Lily and how they were cousins because you're their aunt. It's bad enough you've been lying to me but to drag young Sienna into it...I'm surprised at you Clemency. Surprised and ashamed.'

'I didn't drag Sienna into anything. Nancy doesn't want to look after her and I do. Lily and Sienna adore each other so I thought there'd be no harm.'

'Well, there is harm, Clemency. When you lie to me there is harm.'

'I didn't lie to you, I just didn't tell you.'

'It's the same thing and it's still unacceptable.'

That's a bit rich coming from you, I think and the fury behind that thought illuminates my nerve endings like a direct lightning strike.

'Why did you call Seth, Mum? Since we're talking about keeping stuff from each other, I want to know why you called Seth.'

'We're not talking about that.'

I face her at last. I haven't looked at my mother in a while, I realise. Since Nancy has been here, I presume, she has had her hair styled – cut into a bob with honey-blonde streaks added, which complement the brown and grey bits really well. They've obviously been going for facials and the sea air has probably done her constitution a world of good because she seems to glow with health. Nancy has been good for my mother – after her bereavement, a good dose of Nancy is obviously what she needs.

'We are talking about that. If you want to talk about the other thing we have to talk about this first. Why did you ring Seth? You were all for me calling the police on him the other week and suddenly you're all buddy-buddy with him, giving him my address. Why?'

'You had a long history together,' she states. 'I didn't want to see that go to waste.' As she speaks, Mum is clipping and unclipping the fastening of her cycle helmet. It punctuates her words with loud clicks.

'Nothing to do with you seeing me flirt with Tyler and deciding you preferred Seth, I'm sure.'

Mum is wilting under my scrutiny, my dogged determination to get her to admit it. She doesn't like to be in that position of weakness so she visibly stands up to me. 'I simply think it will be easier for you if you are with Seth,' Mum says. An end to the matter as far as she's concerned.

'Easier in what way?' I ask. I want her to admit it, to spell it out so she can hear how awful it sounds for me, the one who is on the receiving end of this type of thought process, even from her – my mother.

'People will accept you.'

'Do you mean the people who look like you will think I'm all right and safe to be around because I've got Seth with me?'

Mum's face tightens, the muscles seem to sew themselves together in quiet disapproval, even though that is exactly what she's saying. 'That is not what I meant.'

'That's what you said, though.'

'You're being wilfully difficult.'

'That's what you were saying, though, Mum. And what about black people, will they accept me because I'm with Seth instead of Tyler? Aren't they people whose opinions should count if I'm taking comments on who I should be sleeping with? Shouldn't I worry about what they think, too? And what about nice Mrs Khan from the Middle East, who lives upstairs? Or what about lovely Mr Suki who runs that Japanese restaurant in the Lanes? Should I worry about who they think I should be taking to my bed?'

'Don't be crude,' she says.

'Mum, don't you see how ridiculous it is for me to care what other people think about who I'm with?'

Another tightening of her facial muscles. 'I'm other people, am I? That's how you see me now you've been secretly seeing those people.'

That's not going to work at the moment. She won't distract me by marking out my wrongdoings like lines in the sand. 'I'm really sorry to tell you this, Mum, but you're racist.'

I think for a minute she's going to throw her cycle helmet at me.

Bop me right in the face with it in response to what I have said. Instead, her upper lip curls back, exposing the pink of her gums and the grey-white of her ex-smoker's teeth as she snarls: 'How dare you! How dare you! How can I be racist?'

'Really easily. It's not like you do it on purpose, but that doesn't mean it isn't true.'

'You dare!' Her snarl continues until it has taken over her face.

'I dare because you spent the whole of my childhood apologising for me. Who does that? Who can't see how they are damaging their child by making their very existence something to be sorry for? Dad never did that.'

'Your father was not perfect, Clemency. In your head he was this perfect being but he was not.'

'I know he wasn't. And he made mistakes, and he upset me, but he loved me no matter what. He didn't say sorry to other people all the time because I wasn't blood and he couldn't pretend I was. You did.'

'I am *not* racist. You take that back.'

'No.'

'Take it back, Clemency.'

'No, I won't, actually. Not until you take it back.'

'I have no idea what you're talking about.'

'All of it, Mum. You take it all back and I'll take back what I said. You acknowledge what you were like when I was growing up and I'll take it back.'

I don't know where this has come from. Maybe I've reached my limit. Maybe it's got to that point where the pressure is so much, so heavy, pressing down so relentlessly on my head, my shoulders, every part of my being, that I cannot be who I was any more. The old me, the one who had to be so appreciative and scared and unable to speak for fear of being branded ungrateful and told I should be happy that I even got the chance at life, has cracked. And the other me, the one who was submerged under the waves of gratitude and desperation to make everyone happy, is spurting out through the cracks.

'I didn't do anything wrong. And I am not a racist.'

'Well, that's fine, then. If you didn't do anything wrong, then that's fine. But, Mum, be honest with yourself about why you called Seth – someone you never really liked. Be honest, accept that it's because he only became good enough in your eyes when the alternative was me being with a black man.'

'That is not true!'

'Yes, it is. You know it is. Just be honest with yourself and with me for once in your life.'

She is silent, her sneer replaced by the defiance she has whenever she is dealing with me. It's only me who encounters defiance, her obstinacy and determination to get what she wants at all costs. With everyone else she is conciliatory, apologetic. After all, she is the woman who couldn't get it right and couldn't have a baby the 'natural way', and then when she managed to get a baby by other means, it didn't look right. It didn't blend in so her family always stood out. The shame of that, of not being like everyone else, was a millstone around her neck and she could never apologise enough, do enough to make it right. But with me, she was always strong, stubborn and ultimately a parent. A hardline one, but still a parent.

'Maybe I simply didn't like Tyler,' she states.

'You didn't even know him, Mum. You met him for all of five minutes and he was nothing but genuinely welcoming and friendly towards you.'

'That doesn't make me racist,' she says. 'It just makes me picky about who my daughter spends her time with.'

'But it's not up to you. I'm not an extension of you. If I want to sleep with half of Brighton that's my business. And I like Tyler. He's a great person.'

'He's not right for you!' Tears seep into her tone.

'Why not?'

'I am not a racist,' she replies.

I shrug. 'If you say so.'

'I am NOT!' I don't remember the last time she shouted at me. She's hardly ever needed to. Quiet words and disapproving looks have always worked on me. I am stultified by her shouting, genuinely frightened because she never loses control like this with me. 'I AM NOT, NOT, NOT A RACIST!' she continues to shout. Her face is puce with rage, every line heightened. 'HOW CAN I BE WHEN MY OWN CHILD IS HALF BLACK!'

Mum slams her hand, with its beautifully manicured nails over her mouth. But it's too late to trap the words that have escaped. She is not talking about me, of course. And she can't even pretend that she is because I am not 'half black'. Mum had a child, a 'real' child that is biologically hers.

For the second time in five minutes I look properly, carefully, at my mother. I see her now. I see her in sharp focus: the hidden facets of her personality, those parts of her blurred under the things she does, the way she speaks, how she relates to me, are suddenly vivid, clear, apparent. Now I know why she is the way she is.

I wonder if she is finally seeing me or if she has always and will always see her other child, the one that I am the replacement for, whenever she looks at me.

There's a point when it's enough. When what you feel is too much, there is too much inside for you to handle any more. I am there. I am at that point. Like the banks of a swollen river, I am too full: another deluge and it will be too much; another drop and I will spill over and out, my being trampled and drowned as everything inside begins to disappear, the less secure bits washed away, the rest submerged. Drowned.

This is the final drop and I am drowning. Among everything, everything that my mother and I went through, I always knew it would be all right because she had chosen me. Out of everyone else, she chose me. But now I know it was only because I was a reminder, a replacement for her other child. And I know, from the look on her face, that her first child, her 'real' child, didn't die, she had them adopted.

I take huge breaths, my chest expands to the limits of my ribcage and then rapidly contracts as I drown, submerged under the torrent of my tears. I can't even raise an arm, pretend I am waving not drowning. More than anything, I want to make believe that she hasn't told me that I am a replacement for the one she really wanted. That like everyone else, I wasn't 'real' to her. I drop my face into my hands, try to contain the tears.

'Oh, Clemency, love,' she says. I feel her come towards me, her arms out ready to offer comfort and love. Ready to be my mother.

Is that even my name or is it the other one's name? I wonder as I shrink away from her, prevent her from touching me.

'Clemency, I'm sorry, I never meant to tell you. I was so young—'

'I'm going to the toilet,' I say to her as I try to stem the flow of tears. 'I'd like you not to be here when I get back.'

'Clemency—'

'Just go, OK? We can talk another time, but just go. *Please.*'

'I love you, Clemency,' she says. 'With all of my heart. From the moment I saw you, I fell in love with you.'

I nod to appease her, to get her to leave. 'I know,' I say. 'I know.' It's all very well loving someone, but does it matter if they're merely a replacement? Does it count if they're second best, not really what you actually wanted?

49

Smitty

I am my mother's daughter. I am pretending that the conversation we had last night didn't happen. I have slept top to toe in the same bed as Seth, like I do every night. And this morning I am up making breakfast for everyone. Toast, cereal, tea, milk, coffee, jam, Marmite, marmalade, butter – all in the middle of the table for when every-one arrives.

Surprisingly since she's almost always up at first light, Mum, not Sienna, appears first. I set the marmalade jar down beside the butter dish, look up at her and switch on my smile. 'Morning,' I say.

She probably hasn't slept very well, but I can't see for myself because I don't look at her for too long. I can only do this if I don't look at her for too long. I can only sleep in the same bed as Seth if I don't dwell on our past for too long. I can only be in the same city as Nancy if I don't remember all the things she has done and will do in years to come for too long.

I go to the toaster, take out the latest pieces to pop up.

'Clemency,' Mum says.

She's meant to tell me everything right now. My mother is sup-posed to unburden herself and let me into the secrets of her past: what she did, why she did, how she did. I am supposed to listen and let her explain the unvarnished truth of who she is, what she is capable of doing. She did this thing that was done to me. I cannot listen to that. I cannot stand to hear that she did it to someone else for their own good. I'd love to have the luxury of being unconnected, unaffected by the choices she made back then that kept her making certain choices all of my life. I would love to be able to sit here and be as unconditionally sympathetic as any stranger who hasn't been shaped by Mum's choices can be.

'Yes, Mum?' I say. 'Is everything OK?'

She says nothing, so I have to turn to face her. And then I switch on another smile. Grin at her because I am her daughter. I don't have a handbag to root through, but I know how to pretend, how to forget and act like something isn't happening. 'Not fancying toast this morning?' I ask. 'Do you want scrambled eggs instead?'

She wraps her pink dressing gown around herself, pulls out a chair. 'No, no, toast will be fine.'

'Great,' I say.

50

Smitty

I've brought her flowers and fruit and magazines.

I chose pink carnations, plump, green-flesh white grapes and a selection of magazines filled with fictional stories, and was reminded as I vacillated over every decision that I don't know this woman. Despite the time I spent with her, she is a virtual stranger and I have no idea if any of these are to her taste.

My grandmother by birth is propped up in her bed, frail and unhappy. Dad felt how she looks: frustrated, angry, defeated. We're alone, as she's requested. My other mother looked unsure, uncertain that I should be left alone with this woman. She flitted from fixing the pillows behind my grandmother, filling the water jug, fixing the cushions behind me on the seat, arranging the flowers I brought in a vase – constantly leaving and returning, fussing and fixing, until there was nothing left for her to do. She's worried about secrets being shared, created; concerned that I will find out something I shouldn't from a woman who obviously has form for twisting the truth. It probably never occurs to her that me being a virtual stranger to both of them would lead my grandmother to make the request she has.

Dad's parents died when I was a baby; Mum's parents never really took to me. It was nothing very personal – they never really took to Nancy, either, when they were alive. They sent Christmas presents – birthday presents were an indulgence that no one should have simply for being born – and they tolerated us if we showed up for a few hours' visit. Although, admittedly, they showed that blood did

321

in fact influence how much they didn't take to me by not leaving me anything in their wills. Nancy got some jewellery and some Premium Bonds. I got nothing, as Nancy reminded me at various points over our teenage years, because I was not real.

I wonder if this woman realises that I don't want anything from her, that I don't expect anything from her will, but she will still be leaving me something no one else in her family will have – the memory of witnessing her death because I am not real, having not grown up in this house with the rest of her real family. That's why she's asking, of course. Because, to her, I am not real enough to be considered part of the family she would not ask this of.

'How do you want me to do it?' I say. No polite small talk or meaningless words. She doesn't deserve to have a slow, lingering death if she'd rather it was over now, and the irony of her condition means that what is killing her is preventing her from killing herself.

Her tremors are pronounced today: she is sitting still, her frustration evident, but her body shakes uncontrollably. Her eyes, though, can stay focused on me. I have pulled one of the chairs from by the window closer so she can look at me without having to turn her head. Something like a smile comes through the strained lines of her face. 'You...you will help me?'

'I don't want to,' I state. 'But, yes.' I sigh; push breath out loudly, resignedly. This is wrong. It's the wrong thing to do. 'Yes, I will do it.'

My grandmother by blood is suddenly lighter, freer in how she holds herself. For her, this is the right thing, what she wants.

'You have to speak to your doctor and your nurse, though,' I say. 'Tell them this is what you want, make them understand that you've thought this through and it's your choice. And then I'll help you.'

Her body still trembles, but she is back to being pensive, unsure.

'That's the only way I can help you. That's my only condition.'

She says nothing for a time. Eventually, so eventually I think she is not going to speak to me again, she states, 'Agreed.'

'Right.' I'd been hoping she wouldn't agree. It would have given me an easy out then. I only have her word that she will do it. But I have to trust her. She trusts me enough to ask me to do this for her, so I have to trust her back. Anyway, who wouldn't do something that could possibly prevent the person, the *granddaughter*, who has risked everything to help you, from going to prison?

'How...' I can't quite believe we're going to have this conversation. 'How do you want me to help you?'

Slowly, haltingly, she explains it all to me and she starts by telling me where to find a key to the house.

Part 7

51

Smitty

I am counting down time until I have to do this thing. The key burns a hole in my pocket, and the 'plan' burns a hole in my mind.

In the workshop at Karina's Jewels, I used to have a clear glass jar that I would fill with beads when I was counting down to something. It lived at the centre of the first shelf, between the plastic drawer set of different wires and the drawers of different sandpaper grades, and I would drop a coloured bead in every day. Karina said that I should be doing it the other way round, that I should put the same number of beads as number of days into the jar and take one out each day. That way, I could see the days until D-day (whatever 'D' happened to be) getting closer and closer. I explained, though, that I needed to see how patient I had been, how many days I'd survived without D-day. Doing it my way was as a visual reminder to myself that no matter how long it seemed until something arrived, it would always come;

I've been trying to fill up the days until this D-day arrives. She has a specific day in mind – it will give her a chance to get her affairs in order, she said. It will be soon, but not that soon. Until then I have to get from here to there without the benefit of a bead jar.

Now that I'm not looking after Lily and Sienna I can work during the day again, but I can't face it. Being in the workshop during the day makes me claustrophobic and scared. I keep wondering what's going on outside, what I'm missing out on. If I do this thing, there's every chance that I won't have the ability to walk around whenever I want during the day. I need to enjoy it as much as I can.

Working at night fills up those sets of hours, keeps me away from the flat and Seth and Nancy and Mum. Seth doesn't speak to Nancy at all. She gave him a look the first day he was there, to try to gauge what was happening. 'I've told Smitty everything, Nancy,' he said. 'No more secrets, no more lies, OK? Leave me alone now.'

He works a lot at the kitchen table, sometimes he walks up into Portslade to work in a café, but we make polite conversation and I generally avoid him because if I'm around him too long I dwell on our past.

I want to tell someone. I want to tell someone what I've decided to do and I want them to tell me that it's the right thing, or the wrong thing, or that it's *some*thing. I just want to share the knowledge, the decision that has become the weight of the world and is pressing down on my shoulders.

My feet have walked me all over Brighton and Hove these past few days and here I am outside a church. It is a little deeper into Hove and seems welcoming. It is a large bright-red brick building on a junction and the way the building stretches out along the side road and main road, it reminds me of someone offering a hug, standing still with their arms outstretched in hopeful expectation. To the side of the building that sits on the main road there is a large arch and at the end is a huge tower, topped with a green steeple that reaches right up into the sky, as though attempting to touch the heavens. The doors are open and I step into the church.

I'm going to light a candle for Dad, see if I can sit in the quiet and talk to him. Maybe it'll be the same as telling someone else. A glass wall with double doors set into it greets me when I enter the church. It separates the main area from the entrance and, I'd imagine, must have significantly cut down on their heating bills.

There is a mass going on so I move towards the noticeboard to wait patiently for the service to finish. I stare at the flyers pinned to the corkboard, the handwritten welcome note from the priest, the signs asking for volunteers to help them with various activities.

A whoosh and the glass doors are open, and the priest leaves first. His white hair looks almost unrealistically perfect and, I suspect as he walks past in his green vestments, that he might curl his hair. Wouldn't that be something – a priest in rollers! I watch the people leave, quite a few for a Wednesday morning mass. Some people have got out their Sunday finest but most of them are dressed as though they do this as part of their normal daily routine.

The steady flow slows to a trickle and I am about to step into the church but have to stop because there is someone I wasn't expecting to see about to leave the mass. Quickly, I step back in case the person – Tyler – sees me.

I risk another look and notice he isn't alone. He is pushing a wheelchair in which sits an elderly woman who wears a red and black hat that is an elaborate design of lace and netting. I move back to my space beside a pillar where hopefully I'll be out of sight.

Who is the woman? His mother? Grandmother? Great Aunt? They are the last to leave and, as they approach, it's obvious Tyler's going to find it difficult to open the doors on his own.

I step forward, my fingers close on the metal D handle and pull it open as far as it will go. Then I step across and open the other door.

'Ahh, thank you, thank you,' the woman in the wheelchair says with a strong Jamaican lilt. 'You've appeared like an angel to save my feet being bashed on yet another door.'

I smile but keep my head lowered to avoid looking at the man who is pushing her. I can sense him staring at me, willing me to raise my head. Technically, we've not had a falling out and we can still speak to each other, but realistically, I'm far too humiliated and guilt-ridden to face him. Once they have cleared the doors, Tyler says a heartfelt, 'Thank you,' but still I do not lift my gaze.

I don't even glance at them as they move towards the doors to the outside. I close the door I am holding on to, and shut the other one behind me as I enter the church.

The church has white walls and cream pillars that flank the pews all the way down to the altar. The pews are in a light-coloured wood, while the altar and pulpit are carved from white marble. It seems an effort has been made to create a bright, light space. When I was younger I used to think that Heaven was a bright, white space that was also warm and comfortable. It would be filled with clouds and gentle soothing music. You could have whatever you wanted, you could be alone or with people, you would never get tired but you would sleep if you wanted to. You would never be hungry, but you could eat anything you wanted. It was the most amazing place in the world and you would always feel wonderful.

Yet, in every thought or imagining of Heaven I had, I didn't really want to be there. Because I couldn't come back here when I wanted, I wouldn't have the people I loved around when I wanted. What was the point of Heaven if I couldn't be with the people who I wanted to be with and for that to happen, they'd have to die. And I wouldn't want that.

I haven't been in a church since Dad's funeral, before that it was probably for Karina's wedding, before that probably Sienna's christening. I don't make a habit of going to church, even though we went every week when I was a child.

This church has the serenity of silence. I remember to genuflect before I slide into a pew. I close my eyes and try to tune in. Try to link myself with the serenity and hush of the building. I want to climb on to that other reality and stand there, looking, searching. If I manage to do that, to be there, to ground myself in that other reality, I may find him. I may feel Dad's presence.

The quiet comes slowly, unlinks itself blood cell by blood cell throughout my body until every part of me feels it. I am not here. I am not there. I am everywhere and nowhere.

'Hi, Dad,' I whisper. 'Can I talk to you?'

Tyler is leaning against the wall beside the church door. His arms are folded across his chest, and although it's a cool day, he's in one of his seemingly never-ending supply of bright white T-shirts that show off his sleek, beautiful arms.

'Hello,' he says when I spot him.

'Hi,' I reply. 'Bye.' I don't want to hang around, having awkward conversations with him, so set off in the direction of home. Maybe Seth has gone to work in a café and Mum will probably be out with Nancy and Sienna. Maybe I will be alone in the flat for a while. If Seth isn't out, I'll ask him to go—

'I'm sorry,' Tyler calls at me.

I stop and, confused, turn back to him. 'What are you sorry for?'

'I didn't behave very well the last time I saw you,' he says. 'I was shocked, humiliated, and a little angry, so I behaved badly. I'm sorry.'

'You didn't behave badly at all. And even if you did, I think you were entitled.'

'No. I had the right to be angry, but not to be condescending and downright rude. I apologise.'

'Apology – as unnecessary as it is – accepted. I'll see you, Tyler.'

'Clemency,' he calls.

'Yes?' I ask without bothering to turn around.

'Are you all right? You seem so sad.'

'I know.' That's the simple fact: I am sad. About Dad, about Seth, about Mum, about my mother and father and sister and brothers and grandmother. About what I have to do for my grand-mother. I am sad. 'I've been sad for weeks, though, have you only just noticed?'

'No. Before, though, you looked sad, which is understandable since your dad had recently died, but now you seem bereft. As though nothing will make any of it any better.'

I turn to him. 'I don't look that bad,' I say with a smile.

The concerned look on his face chokes the laugh in my throat. He steps closer. After another step, he reaches for my hand. 'You don't look bad at all.'

I like the feeling of my hand in his, the touch of his skin against mine. He steps closer and the smell of him – sharp tangy citrus, woody notes and, of course, coffee – fills my senses. I inhale deeply, breathe him in. I exhale, push him out again. This is a distraction, a way to escape my complicated, sad life. His hand is on my face, warm and reassuring. He fills my senses on my next in-breath, leaves again as I breathe out. My hand is on his face. Another inhalation that draws him in, an exhalation that pushes him out. His lips are on mine, my lips are on his. We stand in the middle of the pavement of a busy street kissing, as though it's the most natural thing in the world.

In the park around the corner from the church, we sit on a bench and watch parents play with their children. I find children fascinating. They seem so free, easy. One girl has sleek pigtails that bounce as she swings arm over arm from one end of the monkey bars to the other. A four-year-old boy with a curtain of blond hair 'Wheeeee!'s his way down the largest slide in the park, stands up and runs around to climb back up the steps. A little girl, tall but probably younger than she looks, is on the climbing frame, confidently making her way to the top, while a woman who looks like she could be her mother waits fretfully at the bottom of the equipment. They could be mother and daughter – but like me and Mum. The woman is a pale white with light brown hair, the little girl is a warm, dark brown like me.

Tyler and I haven't really spoken. We stopped kissing after a couple of minutes and then were completely awkward and embarrassed. I was surprised, not only because we were standing on a main road and it was broad daylight and we were outside a church, but also because, well, I'm a married woman and he was very clear that he didn't mess with married women.

I rest my head on his shoulder, he has his hand on my leg. We sit like an established couple spending precious time together, doing not much.

'Who was the woman in the wheelchair?' I ask.

'Manma,' he replies. 'My grandma. I take her to church every other Wednesday, my brother does the other week. My mum sits outside and waits for us to load her into the car then drives her home.'

'She waits outside?'

'Yup, my mum isn't setting foot in a church. Her and Manma have had some spectacular rows about it, but my mum isn't having it. She takes Manma there and takes her home, but she won't step inside.'

'Any particular reason?'

'Lots of reasons, none that I completely agree with or understand to be honest, not that I completely agree with Manma's arguments either, but that's my family for you – they're always on the verge of falling out and then straight back to normal.'

'It must be so strange, growing up in a big family. I had no siblings and only really had my cousin Nancy who was my age. How many siblings do you have?'

'Six.'

'Wow! It must have been so noisy.' Envy is oozing out of me so fast I'm surprised Tyler can't see big, green globules of it. 'It must have been brilliant. Not that only having Mum and Dad wasn't brilliant because it was.'

'It drove me mad. There was never any peace and quiet, no privacy. My mum and dad kept trying until my mum got her girl in the end, that's the main thing.'

I laugh. I've heard of people doing that. It took me a lifetime to get my head around the idea of having a child. Seth and I talked and talked and talked about it and I was still uncertain. When I had got my head around it, I had been so excited about the prospect of having a baby with him. I knew he'd love the child and I would, too. And I would have someone who was not only linked to me biologically, but would link me to him, too. The fact he had told Nancy about that still breaks my heart.

'A lot of thinking going on in that head of yours,' Tyler says. He's looking down at me. His eyes are a shade of brown that I've only ever seen on a pebble pendant I bought on holiday in Lisbon. It wasn't quite a dark chocolate, it was a colour in between that and mahogany. I'd stripped the pendant of its chain and jumprings, then set it into a little silver tray and strung it with little cream beads as a belt. I'd sold it for £125. The most I'd ever got for something so small and unrelated to a wedding.

'I was just thinking about a conversation I had the other day. I thought I knew what I felt about most things, but in this instance, once the subject was raised, I realised I didn't have any opinion on it at all. Has that ever happened to you?'

I wonder if I can sound him out in a theoretical sense, if he'll be able to tell me what I need to hear. Talking to Dad was good, but I'd had no response. I didn't have him tell me if it was the right or wrong thing to do. I'll still be doing it, because no matter what my grandmother is like, she does not deserve to live the rest of her life in fear of being trapped, but I need someone else's opinion.

'I'm not sure what you mean,' Tyler says.

'I mean, let's say, for example euthanasia or assisted suicide. It came up in conversation the other day, and I realised I can't even have a proper conversation about it because I don't have a fully formed opinion.'

'Ah, but that's usual. I don't think anyone knows what they think about something like that until they're actually touched by it.'

'What do you think about it, then?'

'I don't know.' He grins down at me and then slowly strokes his thumb over my cheek.

'You are such a wind-up merchant.'

'A wind-up coffee merchant, thank you.' He strokes his thumb over my cheek again. 'My grandmother, Manma, has been in a wheelchair for a long time. Osteoarthritis that's particularly bad in her knees and ankles. She can't be upright for long periods. Her hands, elbows and wrists are bad but not like her knees. It's been really hard for her over the years.'

'And she wanted someone to help her die?'

'No! No way. She's determined to outlive us all. But other people don't think she has any quality of life so subtly and sometimes unsubtly they tell her she would be better off dead.'

'You're not serious!' I say that like I haven't been told all my life subtly and unsubtly, I should be grateful my birth mother didn't abort me and had me adopted instead.

'They don't often say it outright, but you know the pitying looks, the "How can you stand it when you used to be so active?" and "I suppose you live through your children and grandchildren now" comments are all saying the same thing – because she can't do what they think of as "healthy", "normal" things, they assume she must feel bad about it, too.

'And we've had some close shaves in the past – Manma will have been ill enough to be hospitalised and more than a few times we've had to ask the doctors to speed up or do everything they can to keep her alive. Not all of them, obviously, and not every time, but there've been enough who you can see aren't working as fast as other doctors have. In their minds, I guess, she's old, she's had her time, she's in a wheelchair, her quality of life isn't up to the standard they'd like to live at so it's fair enough to let her fade away. It's really scary, having to stand up to the professionals who you're trusting to do their best. And for them, their best is to let people like Manma die.

'After all those times, she's still around, still being who she is. The thought that someone else would have euthanised her because she didn't fit their ideal of what they want from life is very upsetting.'

'But some people want to die. Not like your grandmother, but other people in the same situation as her would rather not be kept alive, they'd rather just go,' I say.

'And that's fair enough. That's their choice. But someone taking that choice away is just wrong. And putting pressure on people by implying their life isn't as great as it is for someone young or able-bodied is even more wrong.'

'But what if they can't do it themselves and they need help? The person who helps them could get into trouble.'

He focuses on me with such intensity the air in my chest stops. *Does he know? Does he know what I'm waiting to do?*

He changes his line of vision to across the park and takes his hand away from my cheek. 'It's a pretty complicated subject,' he says, his words are bathed in frostiness.

'Where has the sudden drop in temperature come from?' I ask.

'Pardon?' he asks.

'Why have you gone all funny?'

He is silent for a few moments, although his face reveals plenty: he's struggling with whether to say what he wants to say or to keep his counsel. When he looks at me again, he's obviously decided to speak. 'It feels like I'm being led down the path to agreeing with something I don't agree with. I mean, you see my grandmother and suddenly you're asking these questions. I know it's not popular and people should, if possible, be allowed to decide when they go, but I also think we have a responsibility to others. Not just to people we know, but to people we don't know. It's not popular, no, but we should think about other people and how the choices we make impact on them. I don't want to be led into an argument where I'm forced to agree that if you want to die you should be allowed to. That's not something I necessarily disagree with. I think if it becomes the norm, though, so the people who "help" don't get into trouble, it will lead to potentially vulnerable people like Manma being in danger.' As he speaks his words gather momentum and power and volume. 'On paper my grandmother hasn't got this glittering lifestyle where she lives without pain and drugs and a huge loss of what people call "dignity", but it's her life. She lives it. I don't want her, or people like her, to feel that assisted dying is the only option for them, even obliquely, when the rest of us don't have to deal with those pressures.'

'I wasn't leading you anywhere. I was talking – that's all.'

'With subjects like that, people don't often "just talk", they always have an agenda.'

'Not always...I don't have an agenda. And it has nothing to do with seeing your grandmother. I just wanted to...Remember, I said about how you don't realise you don't know what you think about a subject until you start to think about it? Well, yeah, that's what this conversation was about.'

'Sorry, sorry,' he says. His apology seems genuine, heartfelt. 'It's one of those subjects that people have such strong feelings about and I've had some humdinger rows. Things get said that can't be taken back...'

'I can't remember ever having a conversation with anyone about it.'

'Apart from the person the other day, obviously.'

If only you knew what that conversation was really about, I think. 'Yes, well, apart from that person. You've honestly had more than one conversation about it?'

'Occupational hazard.'

'What, people turn up in a coffee shop and start spouting off about euthanasia? It's all fun and games in your café, ain't it?'

Tyler kisses me, presses his mouth on to mine and slowly opens me up with his tongue. His hand is on my face and the kiss is delicate but firm, exciting and sensuous. I close my eyes and fall into the moment, tumble right into it and forget. I forget about everything that's gone before, everything that's to come. I allow myself to be free and unburdened for just a minute or two. Then it's all back. All of it, everyone, and what I have to do is at the front of that. I need to tell someone. Mid-kiss I pull away from Tyler.

'I'm sorry, I'm sorry, I, erm, need to go.'

'Go? Go where?'

I inhale a few times, calm my nerves, prepare myself to upset him. I don't deserve him anyway. He's far too nice for me. All that stuff he was saying was right, it's absolutely what I believe, too, and I couldn't tell him what I'm going to do. I couldn't burden him with that when I hardly know him.

'I need to speak to my ex-husband,' I say.

'Are you serious? I kiss you and you have a sudden need to speak to your ex?' He seems offended and confused in equal measures. 'Was it that bad a kiss?'

'No, no! Of course it wasn't, Tyler. I could sit here kissing you all day. I have something I need to tell him and I need to do it now or I'll bottle out of it.'

'Fine,' he says.

'It really isn't anything you've done—'

'Spare me, Clemency. If you've got to go, go.'

'I'll see you?' I ask him hopefully.

'Not if I see you first,' he replies before he gets up and marches away.

He's sitting barefoot on my bed, headphones on, book open on his lap, television on in the background. This is how Seth preps himself for a new design project. He immerses himself in all different types of media, blending them together in his mind until he comes up with a new concept.

When he looks up and sees me, he grins. I feel like I'm about to shoot him, if I knew what shooting someone was like. I feel like I am about to damage him in a deep, fundamental way. I need to tell him though. I need to say the words aloud so I can know how bad it is, how final. He's the only person on Earth that I can tell.

The smile slowly disappears from his face and he pushes the headphones off his head, switches off the television and lays aside the book.

'Do you want me to leave?' he asks.

I shake my head. 'I need to tell you something. And I need you to listen to me. And then I need you to tell me the truth about what you think. I'm still going to do it, but I need you to be completely honest with me about how bad you think it is.'

Frowning, he climbs over the bed, slips off and then sits on the floor, resting his back against the bed. He indicates to the space beside him, which I take. 'Tell me,' he says.

'In ten days' time, I'm going to have to kill somebody,' I say.

The relief of being able to say it out loud, the horror of what it means, and the fear of having to do it, cause me to break down and sob in the arms of my husband for the next two hours.

Part 8

52

Smitty

I am standing in my bedroom in front of the huge windows which look down over the promenade, which runs like a thick black marker line under the constantly undulating blue-grey waves of the sea.

Since I moved in here I have been drawn to the windows, to staring out at the sea, to losing myself in the constant motion of the water. Even when the sea is calm it moves, shifts, reshapes itself. I stand here and think about Dad, about life, about my grandmother.

Seth doesn't want me to do it. I probably shouldn't have told him, it was selfish to burden him when we are as we are. And the more people who know, the more it will look like premeditated murder, not privately fulfilling her wishes. Even if she leaves a note, it could be argued that I pressurised her into writing it – that I influenced her to reach the decision and then carried it out. It could be argued that since she has not asked anyone else to help her other than me, a relative stranger, I could have made up the whole thing simply to kill her.

These are the things that Seth has been telling me. His fear is that I could go to prison, possibly for the rest of my life. We talk about it constantly, whispering about it behind closed doors, sometimes arguing because he doesn't want me to do this, so much so he offered to do it instead. I can't let him do that. She asked me, and I have seen just a small fraction of her suffering and I know she doesn't want to be here any more.

I have to do it. I've said I will. And I will. There are three days left.

53

Abi

To: Jonas Zebila
From: Abi Zebila
Subject: Call me
Monday, 10 August 2015

There's a sound I love most in the world, more than any other, and it's the sound of my daughter laughing. It comes out of her in easy waves and spreads throughout the house. That's always the best part of my day, when I let myself into the house and hear her giggling, loudly and freely.

J, I have something important to tell you and I don't want to do it by email, but I tried your phone and you've changed your number. Call me. It's important.

Abi
xxxxxxx

54

Smitty

I love seeing Abi.

It's not simply because she is a younger version of me, and after years of not seeing someone who looks like me and often thinks like me, it's amazing to have that. I like her. She is open and friendly, incredibly welcoming. I have not had many close female friends over the years because from an early age Nancy managed to instil in me a fear of getting too close to anyone, and women in particular, in case she disapproved and told them things that put them off me.

I'm overjoyed when I open the door to my shop after hearing a knock and Abi is standing there. Her face is solemn and her eyes are a scarlet red. Something has happened. She doesn't have to tell me what, I know. Of course I know. There's only one thing that would make her turn up here out of the blue with that look on her face.

I'm cold. Suddenly, unexpectedly, I am cold. I can't feel my fingers, nor my toes, nor any of my limbs. It's not usual to be aware of them, but I'm now conscious that I can't feel them because I am so cold.

'Come in,' I say to her. I have to make a real effort to move my cold, numb body aside to let her in. I pull the shop door shut behind her, the little brass bell tings. I need to focus on making my hands do what I want them to do when I lock the door again.

That's what it was like for my grandmother: she had to focus, use incredible strength to do the tiniest things because her body did not always obey the usual commands. Her body did not listen when it was meant to carry out the simplest of tasks. That is why she wanted to go. Her body and soon her mind would not be under her control and she wanted it to be over before that happened totally. She wanted one last chance to assert control. This is only a small moment for me, but it is a reminder of what every-day tasks were like for her. Of why she thought it would be too hard to find out how bad it would really get.

Abi stands near the entrance to my shop. She clutches her black leather satchel to her chest like a child's comfort blanket while her fingers pick at the stitching.

'Do you want to come through to my workshop?' I ask. I am trying to delay the inevitable. When she tells me it'll be true and I do not want it to be true.

'I had to tell you myself. I couldn't call or text,' she says after a head shake at my offer of more comfortable surroundings. 'It's Gran.'

I face her properly, ready to accept the news I already know head on.

'She...' Abi closes her eyes and steels herself. This has never happened to her before – at least not in a way where she was old enough to understand. The pain, it comes and goes, undercut with moments of denial and disbelief. The disbelief, it blossoms suddenly and winds itself around your heart like a protective shield that allows you to relax and forget for a few precious minutes before it cracks apart and falls away and leaves you with the pain and reality. 'She...She...'

'She died?' I say.

My sister nods then crumples. Without thinking I gather her in my arms. 'Oh, Abi,' I say into her hair. 'I'm so sorry. I'm so, so sorry.'

My grandmother didn't think this bit through. Why would she when it was her life, her death, that she wanted to control? That was her focus, that was her goal. She wanted her life back under *her* control when that control, that ultimate feeling of being in charge, had been slowly eroded by the various illnesses that had taken over her body. What she wanted was paramount – this bit, the part after-wards for the people left behind, hadn't really featured.

She was ready to go, but were the people who loved her, the ones who wanted to get to know her, ready to say goodbye?

55

Abi

To: Jonas Zebila
From: Abi Zebila
Subject: Your brother!!!!!
Friday, 14 August 2015

Jonas,

Ivor is pissing me off. After weeks of pretending she doesn't exist, he's back on his obsession about Clemency but it's so much worse than before and now he does it front of Mummy and Daddy. Thankfully, he doesn't do it in front of Lily-Rose. If he did, I think I'd take his head off.

'It's her, she killed Gran. It's got to be. Gran was all right till she showed up.' He says that about a million times a day. All right, not a million but you get what I mean. He just won't let it go. Mummy is having none of it. She keeps telling him to stop being so wicked and to stop saying things that aren't true and couldn't possibly be true. Will he listen? No.

Daddy's not talking much. He mostly listens to Ivor as though he can't really hear what he's saying. For all his not liking cuddles, whenever Lily goes to him, climbs on his lap and puts her arms around him and her head on his chest because he looks so sad, he doesn't go all rigid and uncomfortable like usual. Now he just lets her sit there and I think it's comforting to him.

I wish Ivor would stop. Yesterday, he'd been going on and on once Lily was in bed, about how Clemency had a lot to be angry about and 'this is the way she starts to get revenge on the people who were there at the time. I'm telling you, Abi, she did it. Or she made Gran do it.'

'Oh, right, yeah,' I said. 'Since when has anyone ever made Gran do anything, ever?'

'She was ill. Illness does all sorts to people. It messes with their minds, changes who they are. She was old and she was ill and this so-called sister of yours got to her.'

'Right, when we've always been around? How did she get into our house if we've been around all the time?'

He thought about that one, then he said, 'It's really easy to steal someone's key, get a new one cut and then put it back before they've even noticed. How many times has she been in the corridor, huh? All alone, all the keys to the house right there hanging up in the key cupboard. Does anyone ever lock it and put the key to it somewhere safe? Nope.'

I felt really bad cos he had a point. But still. 'She didn't do that. She's not that sort of person. I've got to know her really well. She wouldn't do that.'

'You only know what she wants you to know. I'm telling you, she did this. And she's not going to get away with it – I'm going to make sure of that by going to the police.'

What do you think? From everything I've told you about Clemency, our sister, do you think she could have done something to Gran, or worked on her to get Gran to do it herself? Gran was too ill, though. Most times Mummy or I had to feed her because her hand shook too much to hold the spoon or fork. She couldn't have done it herself. At least that's what the police are saying now. The way she died, with her Parkinson's, she must have had help. Was it Clem? What do you think? Let me know. Talk to you soon.

Abi

xxx

P.S. Are you going to come back for the funeral or are you going to stay away?

56

Smitty

It's been six days and there's been no news about the funeral.

Apparently, Abi says, they have to do an autopsy because, even after the seriousness of her last hospital stay, our grandmother shouldn't have gone so soon. They may start to treat her death as suspicious. I wasn't expecting her to die so soon, either.

I've been cut off by the rest of my birth family. It was always going to happen if they ever found out what I had agreed to do, but it's happened anyway. 'Thank you for the call,' my other mother said on the phone when I asked if I could visit, 'but that is not necessary.'

'I just want to see you,' I said. 'I know there's not much I can do but it'd be nice to see you.' To hug you. To be with you like families are at times like this. I'd wanted nothing more than to have Seth hold me after Dad died. I'd wanted to do the same with Mum but she didn't want to be touched and she didn't sit still long enough for me to get near. It never occurred to Mum, of course, that I needed her to take his place as the parent who hugged.

'No, that's not necessary.'

'I know it's not necessary, but it'd be nice to see you all. See you.'

'You do not want to be around here,' my other mother said, quietly, gently, but with finality. 'This house is full of sadness. You do not want to be here. When we meet, Clemency, it should be about happiness, enjoying each other's company. Not sitting around crying and talking in hushed voices. We need to be happy together.'

'*No, we don't,*' I wanted to say. '*We just need to be real with each other. And that means sharing the good and bad bits.*' 'OK,' I replied instead.

Mum sent a card and flowers, I think she put my name on it but I didn't ask so I don't know for sure. It's like when my grandmother was in hospital, but worse. I don't even have the right to think about her and miss her or anything because although I'll never speak to her again, I didn't know her long enough to feel her absence from my life.

'How are you?' Seth asks. He enters the room and shuts the door behind him to give us a bit of privacy from my eavesdropping mother.

He has been working in the kitchen while Mum reads in her room. Nancy is off into Brighton with Sienna to see a friend, and I sit on the sofa alternating between staring at the television and staring at my phone. I should be working, but since it happened I haven't been able to. Everything seems too much right now for me. Melissa, who I'm turning a locket into a watch for has been in touch twice asking if I fancied a drink or if I had received my adoption papers. I haven't called her back and I haven't applied for my papers – it didn't seem important any more with everything that's going on and I couldn't face going anywhere.

'I don't know,' I admit to my husband. 'I don't know how I feel.'

He smiles sadly. 'I can't pretend to understand what you're going through, but I am here if you need me.'

'Don't you find it weird being around me when we're not together?' I ask him.

Seth sits back on his haunches and observes me coolly, as though I've slapped him across the face and is wondering the best way to respond. 'No, not really. I was around you for years when we weren't together.'

'But this is different, surely?'

My husband, my ex, examines me carefully for long, contemplative seconds. 'Are you trying to start a fight?' he asks. 'I'd understand if you were. And I will happily oblige because there are loads of things I'd love to row with you about, but I just need to be sure where this is headed before I come out all guns blazing.'

Mollified, chastised, I look down. After pulling himself up, he sits beside me on the sofa. Without waiting for an invitation, he reaches out and tugs me towards him until I'm sitting on his lap. He wraps his arm around my waist then reaches up to wind one of my curls around his forefinger. 'This must be so hard for you.'

I shrug, which of course means yes. Hard doesn't seem the right word, a big enough word, really. It needs a word that has all the letters in the alphabet – every single one – so that it can show how all-encompassing this feeling can be.

'I'm sorry for trying to pick a fight with you,' I say to him. 'It wasn't very fair of me when you've been nothing but supportive.'

'Apology accepted,' Seth replies. We glide easily into a moment. A snippet of time where it's easy to forget all that water that still has to flow under our particular bridge. Where we could be together and remember the good times. How easy would that be? No divorce, no separate lives, talking, having sex, laughing, back to who we were. Maybe Tyler was just an aberration, a momentary thing I needed to get out of my system; maybe Nancy was the friend Seth thought he needed when I wasn't around to be there for him. *Maybe I'm deluding myself.*

'I know you don't want to hear this,' he begins, the words as ominous as his tone.

'Don't say it then. If I don't want to hear it, please don't say it.'

'I love you.' He releases my curl. 'It's incredibly difficult being around you when we're not together, not least because I know you're sort of dating someone else and I hate the idea of that, but I love you.'

'I... I'm not dating Tyler,' I say. 'We had a date, which you showed up on, and then I bumped into him the other day and I ended up leaving to come and talk to you about the stuff with my grandmother. I haven't seen or heard from him since.'

'Clemency!' my mother says sharply. As always, when she interrupts us, we react like teenagers caught about to undress each other in my parents' house. I leap off Seth's lap, stand guiltily staring at the now open door, and he is up and halfway across the room, lurking in the bay window in record time. '*We never touched each other, honest,*' are the expressions we always wear for my mother.

Her eyes glint with disapproval as she glares at me and then at Seth. Or maybe it's not disapproval, maybe it's anxiety. Worry and concern brought about by the presence of the uniformed police officer who stands behind her. His uniform is dark, and he appears so large he seems to block out any light from the corridor.

I used to watch *The Bill*, I used to watch *NYPD Blue*, I still watch re-runs of *Law & Order*. In all that time I don't think it's ever crossed my mind that a police officer would one day show up at my house to arrest me. Because that must be what he's here for. There are some things you just know and that is what I know: he's here to arrest me in connection with my grandmother's death.

When the policeman has entered the room, a second officer appears. He is not uniformed, he is wearing a navy blue suit with a matching blue tie and a beige rainmac. He clearly thinks he's Columbo. A cop show Dad regularly watched. 'Clemency Smittson?' he asks.

I nod.

'We would like you to come down to the station and answer some questions in relation to the murder of Soloné Zebila.'

My no-longer-watched phone, which was knocked into the folds of the sofa cushion when Seth pulled me on to his lap, lights up suddenly. The ringtone – 'Come As You Are' – trills through the room. Abi's ringtone. She must know. She must be trying to warn me.

Too late, I think. *Just too late.*

57

Smitty

I didn't do it. I was going to, but I did not. There are two very good reasons why it wasn't me: first it happened two days earlier than planned; second, I didn't do it.

I should say this. Explain so they stop this process of bringing me in for questioning, which feels a very small, pigeon-type step away from being arrested.

'No!' says Mum loudly. In two steps she is by my side, and her hand clamps on the arm of the uniformed police officer. 'She didn't do it,' she says. 'It was me. It was me. I did it. Not her.' The plain-clothes officer stares at the lady with the honey-blonde streaks in her greying hair, who is about to start wrestling with a man twice her height and probably five times her strength. 'It was me. I did it.'

The uniformed officer plucks my mother off himself like she is an annoying but insignificant insect, and places her a little distance away.

When I was a child I had nightmares that someone was going to come and take me away. I wasn't 'real', I didn't belong here, maybe I would be taken somewhere else. Sometimes it was the police, sometimes it was a big faceless monster that lived in the bright, blinding spaces that made up my pain. Sometimes it was my 'real' parents; people I didn't know who wanted to steal me away from the only life I'd ever known and force me to live in a strange place, away from the people I loved. In these dreams, when this would be happening, my mother would be shouting and screaming that they couldn't take me, that I was hers and they should take her instead.

This is my nightmare: I'm being taken away and my mother is screaming.

'Mum, please don't.' That stops the uniformed officer: he looks at me, looks at Mum and then looks at me again. The other officer obviously knows the score since he doesn't react at all. 'Mum, just don't.'

'But it was me,' she says. 'I did it. Arrest me, it was me who did it.'

This is my mother's nightmare, too. The thing she has feared more than anything is happening: someone is taking me away from her. It isn't my original parents as she probably always thought it would be, but the police.

'Nobody is under arrest,' the plain-clothes officer states. 'It's merely questioning.'

'Please.' She turns to him, hands linked together, begging, pleading. 'Please, please. I did it. I know exactly how it was done and when. It was me, please. Take me.'

'We have your daughter's fingerprints on the murder weapon and other parts of the room where they shouldn't have been. There are no others that haven't been accounted for.'

That stops Mum. She focuses on me. 'When did the police get your fingerprints?' Mum asks.

My gaze flicks to Seth, who is standing in the bay window, rooted to the spot with horror. He knew this would happen if I did it and this is the reality he doesn't want to deal with.

'We were arrested once on a protest march,' Seth says after clearing his throat of the fear that has clogged it up. 'We...we accepted a caution even though we didn't do anything.'

My mother swings towards him. 'You! You did this? You're the one who got my daughter's fingerprints on record so now she's being treated like a criminal?'

'Mum, it's not his fault. And you can't stop this. It's all a big misunderstanding. I didn't do it and the police will find that out as soon as we get to the station.'

'I know you didn't do it. I did.'

I return to looking at my husband. '*I didn't do this*,' I mouth at him.

'*I know*,' he mouths back with a nod.

I move my head slightly, nodding towards my mother. '*Please*,' I mouth again.

'Mrs Smittson.' Seth comes to life and goes to my mother. 'Mrs Smittson, please, come. Come.' He gently takes her arm and she struggles against him, wanting to come back to where I am. 'This isn't helping Clem,' he says to her. He moves his head, trying to get her to focus on him so the police officers can take me. 'Please, come here with me and I'll drive us both to the police station.' She finally looks at him. 'Yes? OK? OK?'

'They can't take her,' Mum says to Seth. She's begging him.

'It's only questioning, not an arrest. We'll get her back. And when we do, they won't be able to take her again,' Seth says. 'OK?'

He's making sense to her: her body sags in resignation, and she doesn't look at me. She probably can't. Seth nods at me and the police officers.

'We'll see you later,' Seth says. He takes my mother in his arms and holds her close as the plain-clothes officer asks if I'm ready to go.

I nod instead of speaking. I'd love to pretend that the reason I don't speak is so it can't be used against me at some point. In reality, my mouth barely works, my throat feels like it is fused shut because I am scared. I am terrified of what is going to happen next. I am thirty-seven, I have lived long enough to know that people get sent down all the time for crimes they have not committed.

To prove I'm innocent I'll have to tell them that I was going to do it but I never got the chance. Is that intent to kill? To prove I'm innocent I may have to confess to what might amount to another crime, which may or may not get me into just as much trouble.

I'm staying silent, not saying anything because I'm scared that I am going to get done for something I never got the chance to do. Is this the Universe's way of telling me that the decision I made was the wrong one? That I shouldn't have even thought about committing the ultimate crime, even if it was what the victim wanted.

58

Smitty

I have been in this interview room for a long time on my own. I thought I would be shown to a cell but I have been put in here and a police officer stands in the corner of the room, acting as if I am not here. If I tried to leave, I'm sure he'd notice me then, but as long as I sit in this seat and do not move, he can pretend he is all alone.

My heart almost leaps clean out of my chest when the door opens suddenly. The plain-clothes officer who asked me in for a chat earlier enters the room.

'There is someone here who claims to be your solicitor and would like to see you,' he says.

I have a solicitor? Mum probably got one, but so soon? It's not as if I've even been properly arrested, we're all still pretending I am sitting here waiting for a nice informal chat.

The solicitor who walks in probably didn't jump at the chance, but I do get to my feet. I can't help myself. It's an automatic response to someone who carries themselves with an innate sense of authority; my knee-jerk reaction to being in the presence of my father.

'All of us know that this man isn't really your solicitor, but I'm going to let him talk to you if he encourages you to tell us the truth. It's the best way forward.' 'Tell the truth' to this thin, mean-looking man with his ill-fitting suit and pitifully uncombed hair means 'confess whether you did it or not', I'm sure. 'Unless you've got any objections?' the officer asks me.

I shake my head, quickly.

'I'll be back.'

My father extends a hand to encourage me to sit. He seems taller than I remember. Still as stately, imposing. He sits on the police side of the desk when I cautiously lower myself to the seat – the real ordeal will begin the moment I'm properly braced in this chair. The 'being brought in for questioning' and my mother's reaction were nothing compared to being questioned by this man about the death of his mother. From his briefcase he produces a well-used A4 pad of yellow paper. He's a busy man who makes a lot of notes, the stubs at the top of the page that look like the frayed edges of a badly hemmed dress tell me this. His hand slips into the inside left pocket of his expensive-looking suit and removes his pricey black Montblanc pen.

'Hello,' I say. That is how you begin a conversation with someone, whether they're a stranger or not. No matter what the situation, you should at least greet them. 'Hello'. The words of the Lionel Richie song unspool in my mind like a long thread of words, woven with a melody to become a symphony, a song that could have been describing parts of my life of late. Hello.

My father, Mr Julius Zebila, seems startled by this. He does not look up from his yellow pad, which is being slowly written upon by the expensive pen as he notes down the name my adoptive parents gave me, but he does stop writing for a moment.

He has paused at the second 's' of Smittson. That's my name, who I am, but is that how he thinks of me, refers to me now in the private space of his mind, his memory, his heart? Or will I be forever Talei Zebila? Can he divide himself in two like I do sometimes? On the paper he has written my adoptive name, the name I grew up with, but maybe inside he has written Talei, and when he looks at me he sees Talei. Maybe on the outside I am Clemency Smittson, and on the inside, to him, I am Talei Zebila. That's how it seemed to be with my biological mother.

Maybe I am ascribing thoughts and feelings to him, when in all honesty, to him, I am nobody special. I am Clemency Smittson, a person who was born in Brighton, who grew up in a small house in

Otley, who is sitting in a police station accused of a terrible crime committed against someone he actually loved.

When we met last time (the first time), he wouldn't look at me. He let my mother, my sister, my brother and my grandmother talk, but he said nothing. Like Ivor, he looked in my general direction and stayed silent.

'*Why won't you look at me?*' I ask him in my head. '*Am I that much of a disappointment?*'

When my first father pauses again, this time while writing the date, I know I've said that out loud. He stares at the pad. He's going to get up and walk out. He's not going to stand for being questioned, not by me.

'Mrs Smittson is very upset. She is outside with a young man. They are *both* very upset. I told them I would make sure that you were not being ill treated. Have the police treated you well?'

So that's how it works: I talk, he ignores me; he talks, I am expected to answer. 'Yes, they've been fine.'

'Can you verify where you were seven days ago?'

'Working.'

'Alone?'

'Yes, I work alone. I was in my workshop for most of that day and night.'

'Did anybody see you there?'

'Maybe, I don't know. They might have looked in through the shop window and seen a light on in the workshop. Or seen me walk past from one end of the workshop to another. I don't know what other people saw.'

'This is a very serious matter.' Stern. My father is being stern, almost harsh with me. I wonder if he is like this with all of his children or only the ones who are 'brought in for questioning'.

'I know it's serious. And I didn't do it,' I reply. 'I probably can't prove that I didn't do it, either. I don't know how she died so I don't know what the murder weapon was and if I touched it. I keep trying to remember what I touched when I was in her room so I can work out what it was that did it, then I have to stop that train of thought because I can't imagine anyone actually doing that to her or any object I might have touched doing that to her. But I can't stop thinking about it because I need to remember what it was I touched and why that might have the police thinking it was me.'

The man opposite me has the same colour eyes as me; the same kink in his left eyebrow as me, too. We have similar shape noses, but mine is more like my other mother's. The first time we met, my eyes scoured their faces like a miner panning for the gold pieces of similarity between them and me.

'They believe she died of a massive overdose of insulin and a combination of other drugs that became a lethal cocktail.' That was how she wanted me to do it. To sneak into her house when it would be empty and give her the mixture of drugs she'd made me write down. By the time I got home I had memorised them, even though there were so many, and destroyed the piece of paper so that I wouldn't have those names hanging around, ready for anyone to stumble across.

'Because of her condition,' my father continues to say, 'they know that she did not take them herself. Someone else administered them.'

This is his mother he is talking about. The strain of that shows in the tense lines in the deep, dark brown skin around his glossy, black-brown eyes, in the way he holds his mouth when he is not speaking. He's only twenty years older than me, my biological mother is only seventeen years older than me. He seems older, though. That's what losing a parent can do to you.

'I didn't do it,' I state.

'I am certain you didn't.' He still refuses to look at me while he speaks. 'I would not be here if I believed for one minute you did. No child of mine would commit such a crime.'

In one hurricane-like rush, my breath leaves me as my chest is almost crushed by being legitimised by him. He is my father. I am his child. He accepts me. Really, it shouldn't matter. I am his daughter, it shouldn't matter whether he accepts me or not, what he says and what he doesn't, whether he looks at me or keeps his eyes averted. It shouldn't matter, but this small crumb of acknowledgement means another part of me has been made real, made here and present. I have another little anchor that says I am from somewhere. I am from here.

'Would you like me to stay with you while they question you?' he asks. 'I can't step in or act for you legally, but I can stay if you wish me to.'

I nod. I want him, my father, to stay.

The door to the room opens and he stands to come over to my side of the table. Still he doesn't look at me. My gaze, however, is drawn to him, mesmerised. I am panning for more gold, desperately seeking more similarities while the police officers enter the room.

It shouldn't matter, I shouldn't need him to accept me to be able to further define myself, but it does and I do.

59

Smitty

They keep asking me the same things over and over: 'Why were your fingerprints on her medication?' 'How many times were you in Mrs Zebila's room?' 'Where were you the day she was killed?' 'Why did you kill her?'

I keep answering in the same way over and over: 'She knocked them over once and I picked them up.' 'A few times, I can't remember exactly how many.' 'I was in my workshop, working.' 'I didn't kill her.'

My father for the most part says nothing, does nothing, simply allows them to question me.

Suddenly, the questions are different: 'Why did you track down the Zebilas?'

'I didn't, I met Abi Zebila by accident.'

'A pretty big "accident", wouldn't you say?'

'I suppose.'

'Did you know before you met them how wealthy they are, especially the deceased Mrs Zebila?'

'No, I knew nothing about them. I haven't even applied for my adoption papers. I didn't even know their name.'

'Do you have money worries?'

'No. I make enough to get by.'

'And your inheritance from your deceased adoptive father, Mr Smittson?'

'From my dad, you mean, yes.'

The man next to me in the expensive suit, who hasn't reacted to anything else I have said so far, reacts to that: he sits up in his chair and lays down his expensive pen at a perfect perpendicular angle to the lines of his yellow legal pad.

'Did the death of your adoptive father inspire you to look for the Zebilas?'

'No. I told you, I met Abi by accident.'

'How did your adoptive father's death make you feel?'

'I wish you'd stop calling him that, he was my dad. My father. My dad. You don't have to add the other word on.'

The detective looks at the man beside me and I can sense that the man beside me's whole body is as stiff as a totem pole. I'm guessing he expected me to take his feelings into consideration when answering these questions.

'How do you think his death made me feel? I was devastated.'

'Were you a little disorientated by his death?'

'Yes, I suppose so.'

'Maybe a little angry at the world that someone you loved was taken from you?'

'Maybe, I suppose.'

'Maybe a little keen on some cosmic payback because if you hadn't been put up for adoption you wouldn't have had to lose this wonderful man you grew close to over the years?'

'No. I wouldn't do anything like that.'

'Can you explain why your fingerprints were on Mrs Zebila's medication?'

'I told you, I was there once and she knocked a lot of them on to the floor. I picked them up.'

'No one else in the family mentioned this happening. Who else was there at the time to verify your version of events?'

The detective has open pores on his nose. I'm not sure what that says about him apart from the fact that his nose looks like the crater-covered surface of the moon, but it's a piece of information that lodges itself into my brain. I'm trying to work out how to tell the truth without sounding like I am guilty.

'No one,' I eventually say.

'You were alone in the house with Mrs Zebila at the time that you say you picked up her medication?'

'Yes.'

'How many other times were you alone in the house with her?'

'I'm not sure.'

'Can you estimate? More than two, less than twenty, say?'

'About ten,' I state. I feel the man beside me grow still. He does not know this, no one does.

'Was it during one of these ten or more times you were alone in the Zebila house with the victim that your fingerprints came to be on her jewellery?'

'I looked through her jewellery a few times, yes.'

'It's an impressive collection, isn't it?'

'Yes.'

'How much do you think her collection is worth?'

'I don't know.'

'You're a jewellery expert, you must have worked with thousands, if not hundreds of thousands of pounds worth of items over the years. Can't you even estimate?'

'No, I don't do valuations. It's a very specialised skill.'

'Well, if you can't estimate, which I'm surprised by given the length of time you have worked with jewellery, I'll tell you. It is upwards of two hundred thousand pounds. Could be closer to half a million. Does that surprise you?'

'Yes. She just had it in a box in the bottom drawer. I looked at it and sorted it out but I didn't realise it was worth so much.'

'Really? I find that hard to believe when you're such an experienced jeweller.'

'It's true,' I insist. Who knew my obsession with looking at pretty jewellery and hearing stories about people would result in this line of questioning?

'Just out of interest, did you have a key to the Zebila house?'

The police rarely ask a question they don't know the answer to. I learnt that from watching all those cop shows. They know I have a key, or they suspect I have one and they want me to confirm their suspicions. Do I brazen it out or tell the truth?

The man next to me now looks in my direction, disturbed that I haven't answered already and that he didn't know I was alone in the house with his mother several times. That I went through her very expensive jewellery collection.

'Yes,' I say. And my father's entire body swings towards me.

'How did you come by this key?'

'My grandmother, Mrs Zebila, gave it to me.'

The policeman visually logs the reaction of the man next to me.

'Why would the victim do that?'

'Because she wanted me to have it? Because she thought it might make me feel part of the family?' *Because it would make slipping in and doing what she wanted easier. And what she wanted was for me to kill her.*

'But neither of you mentioned it to any other member of the family, is that correct?'

'Yes.'

'Did you kill your grandmother?'

'No.'

'Did you feel like killing her when you found out that it was her who called Social Services to have you put up for adoption before you were born and pressurised both of your parents to give you away?'

'No, because I didn't know she did that.'

'Are you sure?'

'Yes, I'm sure. My birth mother hinted at it, but I didn't know my grandmother called Social Services or that she put pressure on my parents.' My father should probably be bowing his head in shame but he isn't. He is still staring at me, stuck back at the revelation that I have access to his house whenever I want.

'Did you put pressure on your grandmother to end her life?'

'No.'

'Did you make her believe that she would be better off dead as payback for what she did to you?'

'No.'

367

'Did you think that after you killed her you could let yourself into the house and help yourself to her jewellery whenever the mood took you?'

'No.'

'Did you want her dead?'

'No.'

'We have evidence that since you came into their lives, Mrs Zebila started to express thoughts of suicide and ending her life early. Do you know anything about that?'

Over the years I have collected old-fashioned tools to help me craft my metalwork jewellery and one of my favourite things is an old steel screwdriver. It looks like a wooden-handled whisk with a turning handle at the side. Where the whisk blades would be, there is a gap where you insert the different screw bits. The first ring I ever used it to make, I secured thick pieces of silver and copper wire into my metal clamp then fed the ends into the open end of the screwdriver. I turned the wheel handle, wound it slowly but consistently, twisting the wire into something new, unrecognisable from what I started with. This police officer is like that steel screwdriver with the metal strands of the truth – he is twisting what nearly happened between my grandmother and me into something new and shiny and unrecognisable; a version that will make me look guilty.

'Do you know anything about Mrs Zebila's sudden thoughts of suicide?' the officer asks again, showing me the twisted, reshaped strands of truth.

'Not in the way you mean,' I reply. *Not in the way you've twisted things.* 'She told me she was tired and old and ill and that she wanted to die.'

Another visceral, shocked reaction from my father. Him staying with me was a spectacularly bad idea. It seemed wonderful before, that my father was willing to publicly acknowledge me, that it was a chance for us to bond. Now he is finding out things he shouldn't know, in ways he shouldn't have to.

'You were more than willing to help her out, I take it?'

'No. I told her to talk to her doctor or nurse. I thought if she talked to them, they'd make her see her condition wasn't as bleak as she thought. They'd give her hope and comfort, show her that with the right medication she could live a comfortable life for her remaining years.'

'She did talk to her doctor and nurse, as it turns out,' the policeman says, 'but had a different take on what you've just said. She told them both that she was thinking of ending things and that someone had come into her life who had not only made her feel it was possible, but had eagerly agreed to help her.' *That woman*, I think. *That woman*. 'Judging by the look on Mrs Zebila's son's face, I am guessing this is the first time he or anyone else in his family has heard of her plans to end her life.' *That woman. That woman.* 'I think it's safe to assume, Miss Smittson, the person she was referring to, was you.'

They've let me go without charge. But I'm not to leave the area, and I'm not to think for one second that any of this is over because they are continuing the investigation against me. They will be going through my home and place of business looking for evidence that I carried out this crime; that I had maybe helped myself to her jewellery and had convinced her to kill herself to cover it up. The police officer told me if it was true that she did want to die, it would not be any better for me – that they take cases of assisted suicide very seriously, because even supplying the means for someone to kill themselves is a criminal offence. 'We all know Mrs Zebila was not capable of carrying out the act herself,' he said, 'especially not injecting such a huge dose of insulin let alone the other medication, which means someone else would have done it for her.'

Mum's face, small, extremely pale and scored with fretful lines, is the first one I see. A little behind her is my other mother, her face as worried and concerned as a mother's would be. To Mum's right stands my husband, a full head and a half higher than both of the women.

'I think it's best that you stay away from my family from now on,' is what my father says to me when we leave the interview room and are shown out into the reception area. Mum has reached for me, pulled me towards her and hugged me tight. I wonder if that is what causes him to say that. I called Dad 'my dad' in front of him and he hadn't been happy, and Mum is the person I go to for comfort. Or is it the shock of finding out all those things about his mother that he probably would rather not know?

'Julius!' my other mother says, horrified that he is doing this.

My father glares at my other mother, and when he does, I see *his* mother, my grandmother: her sternness in his forced-together lips, her stubbornness in the frown on his brow, her determination to get her own way in the set of his jaw.

'What are you saying?' my other mother says. Even though less than a week ago she put me off coming to see them.

'This is for the best, Kibibi.'

'It is,' Mum says. 'I was about to say the same thing.'

I release myself from her hug like a toddler releases themselves from their buggy they've outgrown and push myself free. 'Mum, don't—'

'No, Clemency, this has gone on long enough. I have watched them welcome you with open arms, then cast you aside when it suits them. And now this.' She shakes her open hands upwards, to emphasise the place we're in. '*This*. It's gone too far. You're to stay away from them, do you hear me?'

'I'm not nine,' I tell her.

'I think Mrs Smittson is perfectly correct. We welcomed you into our home and you have violated our trust by not being honest with us.'

'I thought you said no daughter of yours could do such a thing,' I say quietly. I'm sure he's sat next to innocent and guilty people before, did I sound like a murderer, a killer to him?

'That was before I knew *all* of the facts. You are to stay away from us or I will have the police charge you with harassment.'

Is this what that woman wanted? To have me out of their lives at any cost? Even at the cost of her own life?

'I didn't do it,' I say.

'I will be telling Abi to avoid all contact with you also,' Mr Zebila, as he has morphed into in the last few minutes, states. 'Ivor has always had his doubts.'

'Come on, Clemency,' Mum says. 'We are leaving.'

'I didn't do it,' I say to my other mother.

She looks incredibly, heartbreakingly, sad. Her features are soft, her face a little downcast and her eyes are a liquid brown that swim with soon-to-be-shed tears as she stares at me. Her hair is so neat – each strand is glossy, black, smooth and perfect. I'm sure she never has tangles in her hair. She most likely has them in her mind, her heart, but not in her hair. I have them in all those places. The hard Sussex water is playing havoc with my hair, and the complicated Sussex life is playing havoc with my mind and heart.

'Please tell Abi I'm sorry I won't be seeing her,' I say to my other mother.

She doesn't reply.

'And Lily. I'll miss her, too.'

'Come on, Clemency,' Mum states.

I grab my other mother and hug her, hold her close. She relaxes for a moment in my arms, and I'm overwhelmed by how comforting it is to hold her. If I had known it would feel like this, I would have done it a million years ago. A second or two later, she stiffens and retreats. That moment is enough – it tells me she believes me. She believes me that I didn't do it.

'You must promise me you will not see those people again,' Mum says in the taxi home.

Seth does not turn from his place in the front seat to look at us, but I know he's listening, wondering what I will say because he knows how 'complicated' my mother can be. How despite the effect she has on me, when she makes me promise something, I always do. Except, Seth knows this is different. *I* know this is different. Mainly because I am different and 'those people' are my family, too.

'Promise me,' Mum insists when my silence is her answer.

'I promise,' I say. In my flat black ballet shoes, the only shoes I could put on in a rush, I have, obviously, crossed my toes.

60

Abi

To: Jonas Zebila
From: Abi Zebila
Subject: Please reply. PLEASE!!!!!
Monday, 17 August 2015

It's all gone a bit batsh*t around these parts. Which is why I am plotting my escape. I think it's going to have to be Declan. I make him sound like the terrible option but he's not. He's simply the commitment option and I'm not ready for commitment. But, there are times in your life when you have to sh*t or get off the crazy pot, and I am getting myself off the crazy pot quick smart.

Daddy actually thinks Clemency killed Gran. He truly believes it. He came back from the police station and informed me I wasn't allowed to go near Clemency again. I was so taken aback I actually said, 'I'm not nine, Daddy.' And he told me I would do as I was told while living in his house. Like I don't pay rent, like I don't do chores, like I didn't help feed, clean and take care of Gran. Well, that's it, I'm done. I've texted Declan that he needs to start looking for a bigger place for us all to move into. He's over the moon.

Mummy didn't say much during all of this. She kept looking at Daddy with resentment in her eyes. When he'd finished she said, 'I'll never forgive you or your mother for what you've done. You took my first child away from me. My eldest son is rude, unpleasant and talks to me like I am beneath him because that is what your mother taught him to do. She drove away my second son. I suspect my second daughter is already planning on leaving and never returning. And now you have taken away my first child again because of your mother. I will never forgive you, Julius.' And then she left the room. Daddy just stared after her and Ivor looked terrified. For the first time in Ivor's life someone had told him he wasn't the be all and end all of everything. He'll miss that about Gran, I think: not being her golden child any more. That sounds mean, but when I think of some of the things Gran said to me and about me just because I wasn't male or Ivor . . .

I feel so angry right now. It's like Ivor doing this thing and Daddy ordering me about has made the scales fall from my eyes. Or allowed me to be honest with myself for the first time in years. I feel like I've been part of this conspiracy that let Gran get away with anything she wanted because she was ill. I was so scared of losing her, I moved in to be with her, to help take care of her, and she never really had a kind word to say to me. I didn't want gratitude, just for her to treat me nicely. How she treated Lily-Rose, how she treated Ivor. She wasn't even that nice to Daddy if I think about it. She was a mean old woman.

Yes, yes, Jonas, I know you worked it out all those years ago. I'm sorry that I ever made you feel guilty for not getting in touch with her. And I am so, so sorry for what she did to Meredith. I'm guessing because you haven't told me otherwise that after the miscarriage Meredith still can't get pregnant again? I feel so awful for being a part of Gran's world. I really hope you can forgive me.

I'm sorry, you probably don't want me dredging all this up. It's like the floodgates have opened and I can't believe how under her spell I was. I hope I don't end up with only negative memories of her, that would be bad for me more than anything.

Will you talk to me now, Jonas? Now I can see everything so much more clearly, will you talk to me?

I love you.
Abi
xxxx

61

Smitty

Someone killed my grandmother. And they want me to be convicted for her murder.

These are the thoughts that accompany my every waking moment, every step I take, every time I leave the house to go and meet someone who wants their jewellery reloved or something special made. Someone killed my grandmother and they hate me enough to let me be accused.

They'd have to know me and they'd have to know her. They'd have to have access to her house or my key, and knowledge of when it was safe to get into the house to do it. There aren't that many people with all that information, all that access. If I didn't know me, I'd think it was me, too. But it wasn't.

The only person who I know who could hate me enough is the person who would call Social Services before I was even born to make sure I never set foot in her house. I'm still smarting at the idea of that. She sat there and pretended that she had wanted to see me, that she regretted it, when all along she never had any intention of seeing me. And then she manipulated what she told her doctor and nurses to make it sound like I had been the driving force behind her decision to die. The only person who would hate me enough and would want her dead was *her*. My grandmother. Even if she did, though, there was no doubting that she couldn't do it herself, which means someone had to help her. Which means they must know I am being investigated for their crime.

Somebody killed my grandmother, and they're going to let me go to prison for it.

I let myself into the flat, kick off my shoes, stop by the bathroom to wash my hands and then head straight for the kitchen. I had a message from Melissa earlier, asking how it was going, whether I'd got any closer to applying for my adoption papers and saying she'd come with me or be with me while I read them. I remember the first time we met, her saying that it was important to have them even having met her birth mother. I need to call her back, I felt such a connection with her, like she had lived so many of the things I did in a similar way. But I am barely functioning at the moment. All that keeps going though my head is that someone killed my grandmother and they're going to let me be convicted for it. I can't engage with anybody about anything else beyond that.

I can hear the others in the living room; I caught a glimpse of them on my way to get a drink. Mum and Nancy are on the sofa, the TV is on, Seth and Sienna are by the window watching the world go by and shouting 'Bingo!' every time they see a dog.

On the worktop nearest the kitchen door, the foil, wire top and cork of a bottle of champagne sit discarded, as if someone had hurriedly opened them. Champagne at 4 p.m. Mum and Nancy are becoming ladies who lunch clichés. Nancy was gutted (Mum probably was, too) when I stopped taking Sienna out with me every day.

In the fridge I reach for the orange juice, which is too large a bottle to fit in the fridge door. Next to the orange juice is a champagne bottle-shaped space, from the bottle I've stored since I arrived here. I leave the fridge door open and return to the foil, wire and cork on the worktop by the door. Snatch it up. The metal cap that sits between the wire and the cork is the same brand, same vintage, as the one I had in my fridge in Leeds for more than a year and then brought here. It was very expensive and the same brand and year as the one Dad had given Seth and me after we'd cancelled our engagement party. He'd scrawled a note saying how sorry he and Mum were about the party but how pleased they were that we were together and happy. The bottle and note were from him because he'd known what had really happened, he wasn't as blind to Nancy as Mum was. When I told Dad I'd almost saved up enough to open my own shop, he'd bought me another bottle of the same champagne to keep for that day. The bottle lived in that part of the fridge. I go back, check it hasn't been moved, shunted along to make room for something else. It's not there. It's not there ... but they wouldn't, they just wouldn't.

Slamming the fridge door shut, I dash out into the corridor then across into the living room.

'Clem, go back into the kitchen and grab yourself a glass, we're celebrating my good news,' Nancy says. On the low coffee table in front of them, a coffee table Mum and Nancy ordered and had delivered without consulting me after one of their shopping trips, sits the condensation-soaked bottle of champagne. I snatch it up, look at the bottom right-hand corner of the label where Dad had written *Love, Mum & Dad, 2014*. Nancy and Mum would, they did.

'This is the bottle that my dad bought me,' I say, the first time I've spoken directly to Nancy without her having asked a question first.

'Seth did mention that, but Auntie Heather didn't think you'd mind much since I've had such brilliant news,' Nancy says. Her brow is a little creased, she probably wonders if she has said it properly or if I have a hearing problem. Even after everything, she still thinks I care about anything good or bad that happens to her. 'My blog has been shortlisted for an award. The inside word is that I'm a shoe-in to win. Isn't that wonderful?'

My attention moves from the bottle to Nancy. That's it; done. She has at last succeeded in taking everything from me. Even in our most desperate-for-a-drink moments, Seth and I wouldn't open that bottle, not even when we got married, because it was special, it was for when I opened the shop. It was a promise between Dad and me. Since Dad died it's become more than that promise, it's also the last thing he ever gave me to complete the important task I needed to fulfil.

'You need to pack up and leave,' I say to Nancy. She's done it all, she's taken everything from me. She can go now.

Her glass pauses on its journey to her mouth, her smile becomes a rictus mask of what happiness should look like on her face.

'Sienna.' Seth is on his feet. 'Would you like to come for a walk on the beach with me? We can play dog bingo and maybe get an ice cream in Marrocco's.'

'OK, Uncle Smitty.' My niece, who is really my second cousin, gets to her feet as well. 'Is Auntie Smitty going to tell off Mum?' The emotion in the room is heavy, potent enough to be real, touchable. Sienna can sense it and isn't about to pretend that she can't.

'I'm not sure,' Seth replies, as honest an answer as Dad would have given, 'but I think it's best that neither of us is here right now.'

'OK.' She shrugs. Makes no difference to her whether she's here or not, plus she gets ice cream.

Minutes later, when Seth has gathered his keys and wallet from the shelf in the corridor, when they have debated and decided on which shoes to wear, whether to take coats or not, a click – quiet and discreet – tells us we are alone.

'You need to pack up your stuff and leave,' I say to Nancy again.

'Clemency, love,' Mum says, 'I know that bottle meant something to you, but I didn't think you'd mind sharing it with Nancy when she'd had such good fortune.' Mum is now by my side and she rubs carefully at my shoulder. 'You're just going through a run of bad luck. Things will pick up for you soon, I know for certain they will.' This is how my mother has reworked the last couple of weeks – a run of bad luck. Not another of my family members dying, not me being investigated for a serious crime, not me being cut off from my other family members on *her* say-so. Just a run of bad luck.

Nancy, meanwhile, hitches her eyebrow briefly, warns me that she knows too much about me for me to simply throw her out, to even complain when she has robbed me of something so precious.

My gaze rakes over Nancy with her perfect hazelnut hair that tumbles down towards her shoulders, the 'kooky' blonde patch at the front she had done when we were fourteen, the unsymmetrical lay of her features that have always denied her the chance to be a model. Her plan from an early age (when she was constantly told by her parents that she was beautiful and her cousin – me – wasn't) was to be a model. She was going to take the catwalks of the world by storm, and earn buckets of money. That's why there are so many photos of her on her blog/Twitter/Facebook/Instagram – she wants the world to see what the talent spotters and model agency folk missed: she was a natural model. She is hoping still that someone will 'spot' her. She knew she would have been perfect for the catwalks and the magazine covers and shoots. She might not be tall enough, or – to them – have a beguiling enough face, but they were wrong to deny her. She has the body – neat torso, slender limbs, always stylishly, quirkily clothed. She has, too, her most important asset of all – her unwavering sense of being entitled to whatever it is that she wants, whenever she wants it. Life may have dealt her merely a comfortable (instead of rich) upbringing and denied her the career she dreamt of, but she hadn't let that hold her back. And one of the many ways she gets what she wants is to have things over people, to manipulate them into doing her bidding.

I stare at her as I ask my mother: 'Do you want to know why I hate Nancy?'

'You don't hate her, love. Of course you don't. You're like sisters.'

'We are not like sisters. It's only ever been you who has thought that. She has been hideous to me most of our lives.'

A shake of the head from my cousin Nancy – I was obviously suffering from false memory syndrome – she had been nothing but delightful to me during our childhood. Nancy's lip twisted ever so slightly at the corner, reminding me that if I dared to say anything different, she would be doing her own remembering and what she recalled would be things I would not want my mother knowing. No matter how old, independent and adult I am now, there are things no one wants their mother to know.

'When I was nine Nancy knocked over your mother's ashes from the mantelpiece at her house and you and Uncle Colin blamed me, remember?' I say to Mum. 'I said to her that when I was older my real parents would come for me and make everything OK. I was nine. I didn't even have a concept of what a "real" parent was except Nancy and her parents had been telling me all my life that I wasn't real. So, I said it and Nancy held that over me for years – saying she was going to tell you and Dad what I said.' *There you go, Nancy, that's one thing you've got on me gone.* 'When we were ten and those boys kept calling me names at school, she joined in. She said it was all true, and I couldn't tell you because she'd tell you what I said when I was nine. When we were twelve, she blackmailed me into smoking cannabis and then used *that* to blackmail me into having no friends and doing whatever she wanted all through our teens because I knew how much it would hurt you that I'd done drugs and had said that thing when I was nine.' *Another one gone, Nancy.*

'When I was fifteen I had sex for the first time with a lad I was seeing at school. Nancy tried it on with him a few days later. When he wasn't interested she spread rumours at school that I was a slut, that I'd slept with loads of people, and that I'd given him an STD. I got bullied and called names that whole year. But I couldn't say anything because I didn't want you to know I was having sex.

'When I was seventeen I had a pregnancy scare due to a split condom. I don't know how she found out but I suspect she'd cosied up to my boyfriend and he was just as panicked as me so he told her. She tried to get him to dump me before we could get enough money together to buy a test. When he wouldn't she said she'd tell Dad, who would beat him up. My boyfriend dumped me, just as she wanted, and I had to go through the stress of the test on my own.' (I have never told anyone the real result of the test nor what happened two days later when I had a miscarriage, and I wasn't about to tell these two.)

Mum's face has grown paler and paler with every word, her features frigid with shock. 'Oh, I forgot, every time we met someone new, she would tell them that I'd been found in a cardboard box on the steps of an orphanage.'

Mum looks at Nancy then because that's shocking to her, it seems.

'And do you know what, Mum? I don't even hate her for all of that, and I don't hate her for ruining every single significant event that's ever happened to me.'

'That's not true!' Nancy states. She has to find her voice now that

379

her three biggest pieces of leverage over me have gone and Mum is starting to look at her with new, un-rose-tinted eyes.

'Clemency—'

I thought Mum was listening but she isn't. She is desperately trying to rearrange every word that filters into her brain so that they don't tell the story of my experiences with Nancy, but instead hold the key to how I have got all of this wrong. 'Mum,' I almost scream, 'just listen to me. Please! For once, just listen. She has ruined almost every single significant event in my life. I wasn't allowed to celebrate getting ten high-grade GCSEs because Nancy only got five low-grade ones.'

'Her father was awful to her about that, she felt so terrible,' Mum says, patently not listening. But I don't care and plough on. It's liberating getting all of this out there, off my chest.

'The same thing with my A levels – she does badly because she didn't bother to work hard, I'm not allowed to celebrate. And my graduation – you almost didn't come because she turned up the night before having broken up with her boyfriend and you were suddenly the only person in the whole world she could turn to. You do realise, don't you, Mum, that the only reason you came was because Dad put his foot down and said he'd never speak to you again if you missed it?'

Mum's face draws in on itself, her body tenses, she's been remembering it differently all these years, obviously.

'Every time something good happened to me, Nancy was there to ruin it.'

I think Mum is still back at being reminded of those conversations around my graduation with Dad. I heard him asking her if she wasn't glad she made the right choice in the end. *How could you have even thought of missing that, quine, for Nancy of all people?*' he'd whispered when they thought I was asleep in the back of the car.

'Nancy even ruined my engagement party by pretending to be mugged on the way there by a gang who were prowling the area because the thought of me being the centre of attention for once in my life was too much for her.

'Like I said, I don't hate her for any of it. And I don't hate her for the fact Seth and I had to get married in secret last year because I knew, no matter how small the ceremony, she'd have somehow made the occasion all about her.'

A small, shocked, distressed gasp from my mother. She covers her lips with her hand, and immediately her eyes are laden with tears. It is now such a part of mine and Seth's background, the tapestry of who we are as a couple, I forget how significant it is to your family, to your parents, when you get married. I am so used to doing things in secret that to me it isn't the big deal it is to have gone off and done it alone and not told anyone about it afterwards.

Mum's pale blue eyes look at the rings on my fingers, trying to work out which one it is. When we got married, I stopped wearing the rings I'd made on my hands and wore them on my chain necklace, except my amber engagement ring and my silver wedding ring. I wore my engagement ring on the fourth finger of my left hand – as everyone expected – and my wedding ring on the fourth finger of my right hand. When we split, I swapped: the engagement and wedding rings went on to the chain and my other rings returned to my hands. Seth still wears his wedding ring. I remove the rings, nestling under my top on the chain I wear as well as my butterfly pendant, and show them to Mum.

'This is my wedding ring. I made it and I made one for Seth and we got married in Leeds Registry Office and we advertised on the internet for two people to come and be our witnesses. About twenty people turned up.' I sound defiant, and I don't mean to. I want to sound calm and rational. Plus, I need to not get sidetracked by Mum's reaction: the hurt on her face reveals I have torn a strip off her heart, that I have denied her something she was looking forward to.

'I can see you're upset and shocked, Mum,' I say. 'And I should be upset for you, but I know pretty soon your upset is going to turn into annoyance at me. Everything I've said will become part of my imagination, the way everything does when it comes to Nancy. Because, let's be honest, Mum, she's the daughter you've always wanted, isn't she? She's the one who looks like you, and who's got so much in common with you. And that's all fine.'

'*That is not true!*' Mum cuts in. She is more horrified by that than the time I told her how racist she was being about my dating Tyler. '*You must never say that, not ever!*'

'OK, it's not true,' I concede. I don't want to get into this with Mum. It's not about the things I've said and done, it's about Nancy and how Mum needs the chance to see her for who she really is. 'But what is true is that I dislike Nancy for all she's done to me in my life, but I *hate* her for using the last few weeks of Dad's life and his illness... to... to first of all make a move on my husband.' Mum slowly revolves to face Nancy again. 'That's why Seth and I split up. She kept going over there, pretending to offer comfort when all she wanted was to sleep with him and get information. She even got into our bed naked. Worse than that, though, is that she was using Seth to get information about Dad's illness, his final weeks and days, so she could write about it.

'She pretended to the whole world that she was living it, that she was helping and suffering just like we were. She took something private and personal, something we were barely struggling through, and made it public. That's what her award nomination will be for, because she convincingly used our pain to make a name for herself and to make money. I'm sure the only reason she's here now is to get more material for her blog.' The guilt that crosses Nancy's face tells me I'm right. 'That's why she's taken the last thing that Dad ever bought me. And that's why she needs to go. She has everything she's ever wanted now. She's taken everything from me, there is nothing left about my life that is special that she can ruin, so she has to go.'

Mum's body is rigid: her arms are at her sides and her fingers are spread and held so tight that they are trembling. For a moment I think she's going to throw back her head and roar, she looks so incensed; fit to burst with a rage I've never seen in her before. Instead, she orders: 'Leave us.'

Nancy moves, relieved that she's got away with it. Again.

'*Don't you move,*' Mum snarls so viciously I'm not surprised Nancy freezes. She looks as terrified as I was the time Mum started scream-ing at me in my workshop. '*Clemency*, leave us.'

I collect my bag from its place in the corridor and leave as instructed. It doesn't matter. A few tears, a few hollow apologies, and Mum will be back to loving Nancy like the daughter she is to her. It won't be long before the real issues that need discussing will be me not telling her I got married, me having sex at fifteen, me doing a pregnancy test at seventeen, me saying one time in my life when I was very young that they weren't my 'real' parents. All of this will be used to take me apart while telling me I should be kind and understanding to Nancy. That's how these situations always pan out.

Outside the building, I stand beside Lottie and then lean against her, propped up by my biggest reloved project. Exhaustion is pulsing through my body. Journeying through the shittiest parts of my child-hood has taken all the spirit out of me. If all of those memories were laid like beads on the bench in my workshop, waiting to be strung together, I wouldn't know where to start. It would make a hideous piece with its dangerously sharp edges and blinding snatches of bright-white pain – no amount of reloving and redesigning would change that.

But my life hadn't been all like that. No way near like that. The sharp-edged moments were interspersed with so many smooth, well-rounded, luscious, warm-coloured beads of moments and memories. I had a good childhood. My teenage years were as fraught and des-perate and fun as any of the other people's around me. Like I told my mother, my biological mother, I had been OK. Mostly.

It's the reliving all the awful bits in such a short space of time that has drained me. Thrown me, too. Was it really that bad? Even though I can call up some of the best moments without too much trouble, they don't seem as tangible and real as the bad bits did.

I need to forget. I need something that will put all of that right, right, *right* at the back of my mind so I can concentrate on something else.

I take my phone out of my pocket.

The person on the other end picks up on the second ring. I was expecting it to take longer.

'Are you free right now? Do you want to meet up and maybe go for a drink or something? My treat.'

I should feel guilty when I hang up the phone after we've planned where to meet and where to go so we aren't seen, but I don't. It's far too late for feelings of guilt. Like everyone else, I'm going to do whatever I want, simply because that is what I want to do.

As I head off to my meeting, I can't help thinking: somebody killed my grandmother and they're trying to lay the blame on me.

62

Abi

To: Jonas Zebila
From: Abi Zebila
Subject: Hello
Saturday, 22 August 2015

Dear J,

Thank you for saying you don't hate me and that I did nothing wrong. I really wish it hadn't taken me so long to see it. Now that you've started replying to my emails, I'm hoping that you'll move on from a few words.

Clemency called me out of the blue earlier and I went to see her. Daddy asked me where I was going and I said that I was seeing Declan. I know, right? Suddenly him thinking I'm seeing the man responsible for me not finishing uni is better than seeing Clemency. I only lied because Declan hasn't found us a new place yet.

She told me everything. She was open and honest, told me that Gran had asked her to help her die but Clemency didn't do it even though she agreed to. I believe her. I think she was actually quite brave to agree to help Gran like that. It was like all the stuff I was telling you about what Gran actually wanted. What she wanted was for it to be over. I can't think about that though. The thought of going into nothingness completely terrifies me and I have to think about something else. As Clemency said, though, if she didn't do it, then who did?

That's the most terrifying thought of all. Someone did this to Gran, or someone helped her. And we have no idea who.

Right, it's late, I need to sleep.

Love,
Abi
xxxx

63

Smitty

Thankfully, the flat is in darkness when I return. I took the time to walk as far as possible around the building to see if any lights were on. They were all out so it was safe to come inside. I don't really call it home – I had started to, then all sorts started pitching up to stay and it became 'the flat'. Opening the front door, I see they've turned off the corridor light, which we usually leave on for Sienna.

I pause for a moment after shutting the door behind me, trying to make out shapes in our entrance hallway so I can map out where the potential obstacles are in the dark.

If I can creep in, not turn on any lights, I can probably slide quietly into bed, and I won't have to deal with trying to erase guilt from my face about who I've been with, nor explain to Seth what had been said earlier.

'I've been waiting up for you,' Mum says in a whisper, at the exact moment my eyes decipher through the darkness that there is a human-type form at the end of the corridor. My heart spirals into my throat with fright, and I have to clamp my hands over my mouth to stop myself swearing or crying out in shock.

Who does that? Who stands in the dark, waiting for someone? I almost ask her if she's literally been standing in the dark corridor all night waiting for me, but I'm not sure I could handle her answering yes to that question.

'Hi,' I eventually manage, and flick on the light.

She is dressed for bed in her pink silk dressing gown and her tartan slippers. I was always surprised Dad allowed her to wear those slippers since fake tartan enraged him like very little else did.

I've reached that part of the exhaustion spectrum where it hurts to breathe, it's painful to blink, and I know I can't withstand a barrage of explanations, questions and recriminations. Although the questioning has already begun: when Mum says 'I've been waiting up for you' she actually means, *'Where have you been?'*

'It's very late,' she whispers. *'Why didn't you call me and ask permission to stay out so late?'* she means.

'I know,' I say.

'You look tired,' she continues in a whisper. *'Have you been with that man? In his bed? Is that why you look so tired?'*

'I am tired.'

'I was getting worried.' *'You have no right to do this to me.'*

'Mum, can we do this tomorrow? I need to sleep.'

'I need to talk to you. Come into the kitchen, I'll make us both a cup of tea.'

'I don't want tea, I do want my bed,' is what the me who I am in my head, the person she got a glimpse of earlier, says. 'Fine,' the person I am most of the time says.

In the kitchen I pull out a chair, trying to avoid scraping the legs against the black slate tiles, and sit where I always sit – with my back to the window, to the sea and the promenade. I didn't even realise until this moment that my seat in the flat has become the worst one since Nancy and Sienna moved in. The first few weeks, when it was Mum and me, I used to love sitting in here, a cup of coffee on the go, the radio on low, watching, through the multiple panes of the kitchen window, the world outside shake off the night, open its eyes, and carefully stretch itself awake.

Mum flicks on the lights under the wall units, casting a quietening glow over the kitchen. Once the lights are on, she moves to shut the kitchen door before returning to the chrome kettle. Beside it she has placed her favourite emerald green mug and my white 'Jewellers Do It With Links' mug. I stare at that mug. I'd had to put it right to the back of the cupboard when she moved in with me – she glared at it with such passionate hatred I feared it'd crack under the weight of her disapproval. Once, when she was out, I'd gone to look for it and found she'd moved it right to the back of one of the lower cupboards where the tinned black beans and peaches lived, in other words, somewhere I wouldn't be finding it in a hurry. Its resurrection tells me she feels guilty about something.

I close my eyes when I realise that it's probably because Nancy has been forgiven, welcomed back to the bosom of my mother after what must have been, for Nancy, a scary minute or two out in the cold. If I'm honest, I knew nothing was going to change. I knew in that place in my heart where knowledge comes from that Nancy was going to get away with it. Her type always...

Mum is sitting opposite me when I open my eyes. There are two cups on the table, both have steam rising from them. The taste in my mouth and the heaviness in my eyes, the stiffness of my neck, the tingling in my arm upon which I rest my head, tell me I was asleep for longer than it took Mum to boil the kettle and make tea.

'You fell asleep,' she says.

'How long for?' I ask.

'About an hour,' she replies.

'An hour? And you sat here watching me for an hour?'

'Yes. And making tea so you'd have a fresh cup when you woke up.'

'You seriously sat watching me sleep for an hour?'

Mum smiles at me. 'I used to do it all the time when you were a baby. It was one of my favourite things to do. It made me feel like a real mother. I could watch you sleep and no one could stop me. I used to look at you and think...' The smile on her face changes, becomes wistful and sad as she looks down into her cup. 'I used to think, "I'm allowed to keep this one. This one is all mine and no one can ever take her away."' The corners of her mouth turn up, even though she is so sad I can feel it in the air around her, like it is fizzing outwards from the centre of her being and slowly dissolving into my skin. Soon her sadness is my sadness.

'Do you truly believe Nancy is the daughter I wish I had?' she asks.

Of course I believe it. Everything she has ever done has shown me that. Nancy has always come first and that is something I've grown accustomed to, like I've grown accustomed to crippling period pain the months I don't consistently take my fish oil – it's a consequence of who I am, a result of my biological make-up. If I was different, if I looked like Nancy, Mum might have found it easy to be with me. And for her, being my mother might not have been an ordeal where she felt that ignoring huge parts of who I am and what I look like was the best thing to do.

'Of course I don't, Mum,' I reply. I can do this. I can look her in the eye and say this. 'I was just upset.' I can say that to her because even though I am not Nancy, I am not the daughter she dreamt of when she was given that baby in the butterfly-covered box, I still love her. She's still the woman who brought me up, who tried her best even when her best was downright agony at times, and I can't hurt her, no matter how many times she's damaged me.

Mum's fingers spread themselves on either side of her cup. Her melancholy is almost painful now, I am reaching my limit of how much I can stand.

'You're lying to me,' she says quietly. It is the gentlest of accusations, the saddest of rebukes. 'That's why you're the daughter I always wanted, you would do that for me even though I have...' A lifetime of secret aching seems to unfold on her face and it is stark and raw and visible, even though she continues to hang her head. 'When you were about four or five your father bought a Polaroid camera from a man he met down at the pub – if you can believe it. Down the pub, I tell you!'

I remember the camera well. It was white with a rainbow stripe down its body. I've been tempted so many times to buy a second-hand one online but I've never gone beyond the thought. Maybe because it reminds me of all the pictures I was forced to pose for with Nancy. I love my Polaroid camera because it's nothing like that one. I want that vintage one, but it carries with it painful reminders.

'I loved that camera,' Mum continues after a final shake of her head at how they came by it. 'I used to take pictures of you all the time. It drove your father bonkers. "Have you seen the cost of those films, *quine*?" he'd say, half cross. "And you're taking the same photographs of the bairn doing nothing every five minutes!"' She shrugs. 'I didn't care. I wanted to photograph everything you did even if you were doing nothing. I liked to hold the photos in my hand as soon as I had taken them, they felt more real somehow. I couldn't be doing with taking a week to get them back.'

'I wasn't lying, Mum,' I say.

'You know, I haven't heard from Colin or Marcia at all since your father's funeral. They weren't interested in helping me rent out the house, nor in the fact I was moving. Even Nancy was only in touch once before she showed up – I didn't even realise that until you started talking earlier.'

'Oh, Mum.'

'I did so many things wrong. I was ... I was so scared of what my brother would do. When your father lost his job down in Lewes, I was so scared that we wouldn't be able to cope. I begged my brother to put in a good word for your father at the power plant back in Leeds. I knew I didn't need to, your father would have got a job without too much trouble, he was a good worker. But I was so scared, Clemency. I thought if anyone found out that we didn't have a regular wage packet coming in they would come and take you away from me. I couldn't stand to lose you. I couldn't even stand the thought of it.

'And I knew as you got older Colin could at any time tell you about my first, try to make you believe that you were a replacement instead of someone I loved with every fibre of my being. I put up with whatever my brother said and did because I didn't want to risk having you hurt in that way. There always seemed to be someone around the corner who would be able to take you away, take you back, tell me they had more claim over you than I did. Or someone who could damage you by telling you my secrets. My brother knew how scared I was because he could remember how I was when they took my first baby away, and he used that against me. I think that's why I've ignored the things I don't like about Nancy for so long.

I grew used to putting them first so as to not rock the boat.' She shakes her head.

'I can't believe he treated you like that for all those years. Uncle Colin is a horrible, racist little man.'

Mum openly winces at the R word. 'Mum, you don't have to flinch when I say that, it's not wrong to say he's horrible or racist when it's the truth. It's what he is.'

'You thought that of me, too,' she says quietly.

There are lots of things I want to say to comfort her, but I can't say them without sounding disingenuous, or without lying. And she's just pulled me up for lying. It's not like she's racist in the way that Uncle Colin is, Mum doesn't even realise she's doing it. She seems so scared of simply admitting I'm different to her and that I'll get treated differently and sometimes badly because of that difference. She's desperate to pretend that everything will be all right if she doesn't acknowledge she and I aren't the same. And she's so unhappy about the fact that I look like sets of people she's never known, has never really taken the opportunity to know or understand, and that looking like them may translate into me being closer to them than I am to her. Mum seems terrified of 'other' because other is who I am to her and who she's not, and it's too frightening and beyond the realms of what she's comfortable with doing to try to get to know what this 'other' is all about. Like the hair thing: Dad didn't care what he had to do, where he had to travel to, who he had to talk to, to stop me from crying when my hair was combed. Mum just pretended it didn't matter because the thought of going to 'other' people, admitting that I was different, was too much for her.

She prefers Seth to Tyler for surface things: Seth looks like her, Tyler doesn't. Being around Seth is comfortable to her because she can relax with him. She doesn't realise that Seth goes to a black barber to get his hair shaved, he listens to 'black' music, he spent his youth travelling to 'black' clubs and that he studied Race and Resistance for his MA, and it's only his terror of what I'd do to him that stops him from discussing her white privilege with her.

She has no clue that Tyler listens to the middle-of-the-road 'white' music she does, he likes the same tea as her and I've even seen him working through the same crossword puzzle magazines that she does. Tyler and Seth are both full, rounded people who like things that are considered 'white' and 'black', but if it came down to it, if an analysis had to be done, between the two of them, Mum would have more in common with Tyler than with Seth – but she's unlikely to realise this because she only sees the colours of their skin and would probably find it hard to believe me if I did try to explain it to her.

The worst part is that after all these years of raising me, knowing me, because I don't look like her she still doesn't realise that no matter what, first and foremost, she is 'Mum' to me. She means the world to me. Nothing will change that.

'You're nothing like Uncle Colin. Or Nancy.'

'Oh, I don't think Nancy is like that,' Mum says, her default setting kicking in. 'If you heard some of the things your uncle said about my... about my first boyfriend. What he threatened. I can't imagine Nancy ever saying anything like that.'

'Nancy's more subtle about it but she is racist, just like her dad. Only, if anyone ever calls her on it, she doesn't get angry like her dad, she bursts into tears and claims people are bullying her.' Few people continue to tell off a popular girl when she cries about being bullied, no matter what she's done. I learnt that lesson from Nancy, mistress of manipulation herself. 'And what about Sienna, eh, Mum? Despite all the blonde hair and paleish skin, you know she's part black because of Dylan – is it really any good for her to be hearing all that stuff? What kind of mother continues to let her child be around people who hate a fundamental part of who she is?'

Mum's gaze snaps up to meet mine. I didn't mean it like that. I honestly didn't. I felt unshackled, free at last to be honest about how I felt about Nancy and her family, so I hadn't sent what I was saying through the filters of 'how this would sound to Mum' and 'how much it would hurt her' before I said it.

'A mother like me, I suppose,' she says, each word is brittle, frosted over with indignation.

'I didn't mean it like that, Mum. I'm sorry. I'm really sorry. You've explained why you did what you did, and I'm ever so grateful that you put yourself through that to protect me.'

'That's what parents do for their children, so there's no need to be grateful,' Mum's voice is positively Arctic now. 'Unless you don't feel I'm your real parent and therefore I somehow need the gratitude you'd show to a stranger.'

'You know, Mum, I think I've got quite a talent for saying the wrong thing and then making it worse by not being quiet straight away.'

Her reply is straight from the Mum book of glowers.

'If that's all, I'm going to leave my foot in my mouth and hop to my bed.'

'What did you wear to get married?' Mum asks. I haven't even had a chance to swig from my mug of lukewarm tea as a show of the type of gratitude I would give to everyone – parents included – before I depart. I'd forgotten that she knew now, and it didn't occur to me that she might be curious about it.

I remove my mobile from my pocket, and type in the passcode. These are the only significant photos I haven't printed out. I couldn't risk anyone finding them in my butterfly box or seeing them on my wall. It was a private thing that I knew would upset my parents and would be trashed by my cousin.

I hold the pictures of my wedding, suspended as they are in the world inside my mobile phone, out to my mother. She plucks her glasses from the top of her puzzle book, slips them on to her face. Her hand trembles as she takes the silver phone from me. I watch her face as she scrolls through them: her gaze darts to every corner of the screen, taking in every detail, then her eyes mist over behind her glasses. *Swipe.* Another image. This one probably of me grinning at the camera, the burgundy of my lipstick highlighted by a dab of gold at the meeting point of my lips, pastel-coloured confetti littering my hair, and pieces of it dotted on the lattice tiara I made from silver wire and tiny silver roses each with a diamanté at its centre. *Swipe.* She doesn't linger on that one so it's probably Seth dipping me backwards as he kisses me, his hand prominently placed on my bum. *Swipe*. Seth standing behind me with his arms around me, while we both grin at the camera. *Swipe*. Our hands linked, showing off our matching rings, made from the large hoop silver earrings I was wearing that New Year we got together.

I annealed – *softened* – them with the blowtorch, dipped them in pickle, ran them through the roller to flatten them, and then individually twisted them on the mandrel. Twisting, plaiting where I could, having to be careful to keep the shape. When I made them, especially Seth's, they felt like the most important pieces I'd ever create. Every hammer, twist of the roller, smoothing with the wire brush, run over with the blowtorch, felt like an act of love, a way to tell Seth how much he meant to me. How much our life together meant to me. I want my mother to swipe on. It hurts. When I remember the effervescent excitement that bubbled through me, the unbridled pleasure I got from thinking about being his wife, and how that all came to an end, it's a physical pain. *Swipe, Mum, swipe.* I can't stand that photo being seen by someone, when it's gone. All that excitement and joy and anticipation and expectation and pure happiness has come to an end. *Swipe, Mum, swipe. Please.*

A tear escapes Mum's eye, travels slowly down her cheek. I'm on my feet, moving towards the sink with my mug. Coffee. I need a coffee. It's about two o'clock in the morning but I need a coffee. I've been coping by not thinking about it. Even if we get back together, all of that innocence, that ability to feel without barriers that I had with Seth, has been extinguished and it'll never come back. There'll always be something damaged about our relationship. About any other relationship.

'You both look so happy. Is there really no hope for you and he?' Mum asks. I hear her carefully place the phone back on the table.

The brown granules of coffee rain into the wet cup and form uneven peaks at the bottom, some of them already dissolving to create a shiny brown-black sludge. 'No.' I have no hot water. 'I don't know.' Her eyes are watching my back. I should face her. Be honest with her so I can start to be honest with myself. 'I don't . . . I love him.

Still.' I rotate towards her. 'I still love him, of course I do, but I can't trust him any more.'

'Nancy swears nothing happened. She admits she tried but he wouldn't even look at her.'

'I know it didn't. It's not about that. I trusted him with everything and he became friendly with *her*. Told her deeply personal things. She damaged me and hurt me for years and he— I can't trust him.' I should flick on the kettle, boil the water. Make the coffee. 'And anyway,' I say to pull myself away from that particular artery of pain that runs through my life at the moment, 'I really like Tyler.'

Predictably, Mum bristles, holds herself a little tighter, her disapproval evident in each tensed muscle in her body and face.

'I know you don't want to hear it, Mum, and for whatever reason you don't think he's right for me, but I really like him. He's nice and uncomplicated and I don't know him so I don't have to worry about whether I can trust him or not. And I've hurt him. He probably won't even speak to me again so he's not really an option, but I still like him. But then there's Seth and it's not like I can stop loving him even though I can't trust him. And even though we're not together he was there for me recently when . . . So, I don't know, Mum, if there's any hope.' I just know I'm muddling through this thing in the best way I can.

'I wish I had the answer for you.'

'Did Dad know about your first child?' I ask.

'Of course,' Mum says, 'your father knew everything about me.'

'Can you tell me why your first baby was adopted?' I ask. I thought I didn't want to know but now I do. Now it'll let me know if it's me or the other baby she sees when she looks at me.

She stares at me, really scrutinises me. 'Because I was fifteen and pregnant by the boy I wanted to marry in my class. I didn't know then how much other people would have a problem with us being different. And I have a horrible, racist little man for a brother and I had a horrible bully of a man for a father, and I had a mother who would never stand up for me.' She speaks quietly but firmly. 'I wanted my baby, and so did he, my first boyfriend, but my father said no.

My mother cried about the neighbours. I said I would run away and my brother said he'd break my boyfriend's legs – maybe even kill him – if I didn't do as I was told.'

'Oh, Mum.'

'I did as I was told, I went to the home for girls like me, and I cried and cried every time they took him from my arms. I called him Aaron. Every day, Clemency, I think about him. He was a beautiful boy and they took him away to live in America and I'll never find out what happened to him.'

'You should have told me about him, Mum. I would have been supportive. I freaked out the other day because you seem so dead set against me having anything to do with my birth family and yet you knew how it must have felt for them. Well, for my birth mother at least.'

'I knew how she must have felt and I was jealous. Because if he came back into my life, I would never want him to leave. Of course I wouldn't. I'd want to hold on to him and I'd want him to stay with me and forget about the other people who brought him up, so I was jealous and scared that all my years with you would mean nothing. And my first child has never contacted me or even tried. I was so envious of Kibibi and Julius. I was also worried what would happen if they rejected you. After losing your father, breaking up with Seth, I wasn't sure how much more you could take.'

'I wish you'd just told me all this. I would have understood.'

'I know. But there's a part of every parent that never stops thinking of their child as a child. All these things are for adults to talk about. I sometimes forget you're an adult with adult choices to make.'

'I'm sorry I kept things from you,' I say.

'I'm not surprised you did. You learnt it from the expert.' She grins at me, conspiratorially. 'After they took him away, I could never get pregnant again. The doctors didn't know why, there was nothing physically wrong with me or your father. I thought it was my punishment for the sin I had committed. Then, when the social worker showed me your picture, I knew why I could never get pregnant.' She smiles at me again. 'It was so I could have you. You're the daughter I always wanted and the child I was meant to have. And I'm sorry.

I'm sorry for how I am sometimes, I'm sorry I have hurt you so many times. And I am sorry for not being a better mother.'

'You're a great mum,' I say automatically. It's true, she is. She has her moments, she needs to address her fears about how different I am to her and stop driving me crazy with how she is, but she is a fantastic mum. She's my fantastic mum.

'Kibibi is, too,' she says. She is challenging me now. Does she want me to agree, to confirm that I do prefer her, or is she just making conversation? I'm not sure and probably look terrified at the thought of what I'm meant to say. 'I'm not trying to trick you,' she says. 'Kibibi is a good mother. Apart from that one time when she turned up unannounced, she has let you set the pace, has she not?'

I nod.

'When I saw her she was desperate to be with you, it was clear in her eyes, in everything she said and did. But she's not pushy like me. She has held back and let you decide everything.'

'Apart from when my grandmother died and she didn't want to see me.'

'When your father died, did you want to see anyone? Did you want anyone near you or around you? Even the people you loved, let alone someone you are desperate to get to know.'

'I suppose not.'

'She made a difficult choice in difficult circumstances. Was it the right one? We'll never know, but think of the decisions you made when you were seventeen. Think about what was going through your head when you took that pregnancy test at that age.' Another thing about me that Mum now knows. 'She was barely finished with childhood and she made a choice that she's lived with every day.'

'Like you,' I state.

'Like me.' Mum looks at the large kitchen clock. 'Clemency Smittson, I can't believe how late it is! Where have you been all this time?' It's incredible how quickly she can become 'Mum' again. She doesn't want to talk any more, and I suppose there's not much left to say. We have no answers for each other, only the hope that the other will do the best they can.

I shrug. 'Out.' It's just as incredible how I can become 'Child' again in a flash.

'That's no answer. Now you get to bed.'

'I'm thirty-seven, Mum,' I say.

'Does thirty-seven mean you don't need sleep?'

'No.'

'Well, then, get to bed.'

'What about you?'

'I'm going to sit here and think for a little while longer,' she says. 'I have a puzzle I need to work out.'

'Tyler likes puzzles,' I tell her, in the hope that she'll see that he and she do have something in common. Not that it'll matter since he won't be coming near me again. I just want her to consider that beyond what he looks like, he may share common ground with her.

She looks me up and down then says, 'I'm not at all surprised he does.'

It's not until I'm creeping into bed that I realise she actually meant me. I was the puzzle that she wasn't surprised he liked.

64

Smitty

The last thing that Mum told me before I went to bed was that Nancy was going home in the morning. She'd already started to pack, and they'd be gone by lunchtime. I'd nodded my head and hadn't said, 'I'll believe that when I see it.'

Here she sits, curled up in the corner of the sofa, still in her dressing gown, hair hooked behind her ears, picking at her nails like a smoker who is desperate for a cigarette. My cousin doesn't seem like someone who is leaving in less than six hours.

I watch her for long minutes from the doorway of the living room before she even notices that I'm there. When she sees me, she sits up straighter, rubs the tears from her pale face, pretends she wasn't staring into space.

Nancy has been such a nemesis in my life for so long, I'm not sure if they are real tears of regret and worry or fake ones of manipulation. If they are fake, then she's wasting her time; if they are real I don't know why she's bothering – we both know that she's going nowhere. The poisonous bond between us is broken now. She has nothing on me, I have no reason to speak to her again – not even to tell her to go, so if she stays, no one will challenge her.

'Can I talk to you?' she asks quietly.

'No, I can't face it,' I reply. I shouldn't really be talking to her. After last night, the emotional toll that having an open conversation with my mother took on me, I should conserve every last drop of energy I have. I won't be getting much more sleep today, and I need to sit down and work out who it was that killed my grandmother.

'I just want—'

'That's the problem, Nancy, it's always, *always* about what you want. I can't face it.'

Miserable, dejected, she rests her head on her hand and starts to cry again. I can't, I just can't. My keys are in my bag in my bedroom, which is a no-go zone because I'll wake Seth if I go back in. I need to get out of here. I need fresh air, and I need to be away from the woman crying on my sofa. Since moving here, out of the city, I like to be outside. No matter the weather, unless it is torrential rain, I like the air on my skin, the sounds of the world filling my ears. Walking along to Beached Heads was one of my favourite parts of the day before I ruined that experience.

In the corridor, I slide my feet into my trainers and let myself out of the house as quietly as possible. Nancy's face is worming its way into my head, the tears, the quick, quick wiping motion she made to hide them. I try to shove away her tears, her sorrow, because I've cared enough about her over the years. At some point, surely, I am allowed to not automatically worry whether her tears are real or not.

Of course I want her to be all right, she is Sienna's mother after all, if she isn't well, then Sienna will be impacted. However, there comes a time when a person has to say no more. She has to put on her shoes, and leave her flat with no means of getting back in without pressing the buzzer, wearing her blue fleece pyjamas with the white stars, that she's taken to wearing since she started sleeping beside her husband again.

Outside, I start to relax, unclench, unwind. Outside is a big expanse and it becomes my space when I exit the gate and shut it carefully behind me. I need to escape, to get out of this place, and here I am, doing just that. I could walk along to Beached Heads, sit outside and wait for Tyler to arrive. Beg him to serve me coffee and explain why I left him after he kissed me.

'You have to listen to me.' Nancy. She's had the audacity to follow me and speak to me and make me jump out of my skin.

She's wearing her thigh-length nightshirt and has replaced her dressing gown with my chunky-knit cardie that she'd unhooked from the coat rack by the door, and my favourite red ballet pumps. She wants to talk to me and because of the way Nancy sees the world, I will jolly well listen.

I take off, racing away from her towards the promenade. I don't look back, not even as I turn the corner on to the seafront proper, but I'd imagine her face is a picture of disbelief and incredulity. 'Oh, no, you don't!' I hear her shout at me before the wind whips her words away.

My feet pound the uneven black tarmac, every stone, pebble and uneven surface, shaking my bones through my thin trainers. 'COME BACK!' she roars at me. She's chasing me. I don't look back but she is pursuing me as though I owe her my time, my listening ear, my anything.

'Come back!' she shouts. Her words reach me then are whisked away by the strong breeze that twirls the sea into angry-looking peaks.

'I only want to talk to you!'

No. I keep that word in my head as I run. Each step of my run coils a tight length of high-tension rubber around my already tight chest, my side is agony – as though a poker is prodding at it – and my feet and legs complain and ache. But, *no*. Not this time. She doesn't get what she wants. *No! No! No! No! No! No!*

The poker finds its mark, the soft, vulnerable bit below my ribs, and spears itself into me. My body halts. My mind is still running, still screaming 'No' inside but my body can't go on. It has to stop.

I am doubled over, clutching the stitch in my side, willing my body to move, to keep me away from hearing what she has to say.

'I only want to talk to you!' she screams when she reaches me.

I clamp the hand not pressed over my stitch on to its corresponding ear and push my shoulder up to the other ear. 'LALALA! NOT LISTENING!' I shout in reply.

Frustrated, angry, probably also embarrassed, Nancy shoves me. I stumble. My stitch is suddenly forgotten, cured by my outrage that she's laid hands on me. I stand upright.

'Don't you touch me!' I shout at her. 'Don't you ever touch me!'

'Listen to me, then!' she yells back. She moves to do it again but I have my hands up and shove her back. Her bony body is no match for my push and she staggers backwards, too.

'Don't push me!' she shouts, affronted. Shove. She's done it to me again.

'You started it!' Push. I return the move to her.

'I only want to talk to you!' she bellows.

'I don't want to hear it!'

'I only want to say sorry!' she cries. 'I'm sorry, I'm sorry, I'm sorry.'

'That's a great way to say sorry: shove someone about and then shout at them.' I rest my hands on my knees, winded again. 'I bet everyone loves being apologised to by you.'

'I am sorry.'

I eye her up. 'You look ridiculous. And your apology is even more ridiculous.'

'Why am I even bothering?'

'I don't know, Nancy, I really don't. You don't mean it, so why bother?'

Her hair has been thrashed about by the wind and she uses both of her hands to smooth it down. She's shocked. Not an emotion I've seen much in Nancy before. No, there was one time. After she had been off for three months, leaving Sienna with Seth and me, not caring how we were going to fit work and our lives around this new, unexpected responsibility, Nancy waltzed back in expecting a warm reception.

Seth and I had been positive, excited and supportive to Sienna about Nancy's return, as we had been the whole time she was away – following a band on tour (and screwing their drummer) for her blog – so that Sienna wouldn't feel abandoned. When Nancy had walked in Sienna looked her up and down in disgust and had gone right back to playing. Nancy had been deeply shaken. She'd looked wide-eyed from me to Seth then back to me again, shocked that Sienna hadn't been interested in her. It took three days to convince Sienna to go home to her mother. That was the first and last time

Nancy had ever been shocked because it was the first time anyone had held up the mirror of consequences to her behaviour and had refused to be taken in by Nancy's reluctance to accept what sort of person she truly was.

'I...I mean it,' she stammers, her brow furrowed. I'm sure I read something on the *Guide to Femininity* that said pulling fun faces at the camera was feminine and desirable because it showed your kooky side, but frowning was forbidden as it gave you wrinkles in uninteresting places.

'Do you bollocks mean it. You've never meant anything that wouldn't benefit you directly in your whole life.'

'I...I...' she begins, completely thrown.

'Oh, poor Nancy, isn't this going the way you expected? Aren't I accepting enough of your bullshit apology?'

'It's not bullshit.' Nancy trembles. Probably from the cold, maybe from shock at her apology not being accepted. Her shaking reminds me suddenly of my grandmother in her better moments. *Who did it?* Wisps across my mind again. *Who did what I was going to do?*

'I didn't realise until you were telling Auntie Heather about it how much I had done to you over the years.'

'Right, you didn't realise you've bullied me and been a complete bitch to me pretty much our whole lives?'

'I...I mean, I knew, but I didn't realise it was so much.'

'Bullshit, Nancy. Bull. Shit.'

'I wasn't trying to hurt you.'

'You just did, without trying.'

'I didn't...Everything comes so easily to you. And, growing up, it—'

'I DON'T CARE!' I yell at her. 'Haven't you got that yet? Haven't you worked that out by the fact I've barely spoken to you since you pitched up here? I don't care about you and what you do or what you say. None of it. I don't care if you apologise or if you don't. You're nothing to me. I care about Sienna but not you. It's that simple.'

'But...'

'I didn't always think like that, if it makes you feel any better. There were so many times I was *desperate* for you to be my friend again, to treat me like a cousin, like a sister, as we used to be. Later on, I wanted you to apologise, to say sorry so we could move on and maybe try to be friends. Then I realised that nothing you could say would make it any better. It would mean nothing because the damage was done, the hurt was caused, I couldn't get any of the things you ruined back so why hang around for an apology that would be disingenuous at best. And do you know what? The second I did that, the moment I accepted that my life wouldn't be transformed by an apology from you, things got magically better.' I wave my hands about to illustrate my point. 'I was set free by realising I didn't need you or your bullshit apology. So there, no apology needed.'

She is petrified by what I've said, unable to move because this has never happened to her before.

'You don't have to go home today,' I tell her. 'You and Sienna can stay as long as you like because truly, I don't care what you do, say or think.' I take a huge puff of salty air into my lungs, slowly release it. I feel so much lighter, freer. 'Now, please leave me alone. I don't want to talk to you any more.'

We return to the flat, Nancy about ten paces behind me. Seth answers the door to us.

'Don't ask,' I say to him and his quizzical look as I march in wearing my pyjamas and Nancy closely follows in her nightshirt.

'OK, I won't,' Seth says, although I'm sure he's dying to.

65

Smitty

Light comes through the whited-out windows and I stand in the middle of the shop with my eyes closed. I am trying to visualise what the shop should look like. The outside is olde worlde, with teal-coloured panels and triple-bevelled frames. The door has a brass bell and the wood is sombre, ancient. When I first saw it, especially with the wonderful workshop space that could have been made for me, I knew I had to have it.

Now, I realise it is too old-fashioned for me, for what I want this place to be. I want to do something different, new, not play it too safe. That is what I have done throughout my life: I have played it safe, done what others want and expect me to do, while trying to do what I want to do. I have tried for so long to fit myself around the shapes of other people's desires, I am not sure who I am, what I want, what I need most of the time. Then, when what the person asked of me turns out to be wrong, I feel slighted and hurt; bereft and unwanted.

I need to stop that. Now.

When the police went through here and the workshop and the flat, they left a trail of disorder. They took apart everything I had built up in the last few months. I'd sat in the wheelie chair in my workshop, gawping at the mess they had made: every drawer – over a hundred in different shapes and sizes – had been emptied on to my bench and then, when there was no room, on to my chair and the floor. Every folder and box file, sample board and notebook, had been removed from the shelves and left scattered and open on the benches and floor. They had taken the protective oiled cloth off the rollers, they'd opened each pickling jar, they'd taken the lids off my pickling warmers. They'd even emptied the barrel polisher, which is packed with ball bearings, on to the sink's draining board, and several of the small, metal balls which give an extremely shiny finish to textured metal that can't be filed have rolled down into the plughole. Every shelf and wall cupboard had been cleared in the kitchenette and the contents left on my worktop or floor. Everything under the sink had been pulled out and left in the middle of the kitchenette floor.

In here, the devastation had been worse. They'd emptied every box, left the contents on the floor, some knocked over so findings and beads had obviously rolled away, like the ones Lily and Sienna spilt, never to be seen again. I'd felt violated, as if someone had marched into my head and emptied the contents all over the place for me to see how trivial and frivolous my life would seem to some. They had poked and prodded around to make sure they hadn't missed anything then had withdrawn with nothing.

After the violated feeling I started to think about it – all of it, and realised I needed this. I needed someone to come storming into my work life and shake it up, force me to take stock and consider doing things differently. I had tacked pieces of my old ways of working on to this workshop. It was ordered and staged like the small space I had at Karina's place up in Leeds and the spare bedroom at my flat. The ideal would have been to rip it all up then start again.

The police had ripped it all up, now I need to start again.

This place needs to be nothing short of what I want. It needs to remind me that I can do something right, I can put down roots and I can create something that grows and becomes successful. I have to stop being so passive in all of this. In my life. If I want to stop being from nowhere, I have to find myself somewhere to be. That somewhere is here.

I revolve slowly on the spot, trying to see the shelves, the cases, the stands, the area where I'll sit and talk to people about their designs. Glass or wood or Perspex? Blond wood or mahogany? Stainless steel or white? Primary colours or pastels? I need to open the shop, I need to forge ahead, put all the stuff of the last few days behind me and go forwards.

I tip my head back, open my eyes. The ceiling is deceptively high for a shop that is quite small. Maybe I can suspend something up there. Some of my old tools I don't use any more? Photos of my designs? I lower my head to look at the wall opposite. It is a large blank canvas. My photos. I'll put my photos there. I will ask those who I make jewellery for if I can put up photos of them and their jewellery there as well as on the internet.

In front of that wall I will put two armchairs and a small table where people can sit while we chat about the jewellery they want made or reloved with the backdrop of others' pieces behind them, and in front of them in an album.

I turn towards the window. I will display some of the pieces I sell on white velvet trays, in front of photos of people wearing them. I rotate on the spot, look at the wall which currently has heavy, dark wood shelving from one end to the other that reaches high up the wall. I can move them into the back where they'll be helpful for organising my equipment. I will replace them with a wall of Perspex drawers, so customers can easily see the jewellery.

The floors will be white tiles, even though they'll need cleaning every day, and the counter can be Perspex, too, but the front will have long thin tubes filled with different coloured beads, standing like test tubes of coloured liquid waiting to be experimented on in a science lab.

I can see it. I can actually see it. The images come to me in a rush, flashes and colours and panels, shades and displays. If I were able to sketch like my mother, I would be putting these images on the page, instead of storing them in my head. When it is finished I'll have a launch party, I'll invite all the clients I have down here, I'll even invite my first family. Surely that won't be seen as harassment? Surely they will, by then, have decided that I couldn't possibly have done it and they will accept me back?

I'm deluding myself, I know. But I need hope. I need something to cling on to. I need them to realise that I can be a part of their lives. Not the be all and end all, just a little sliver of it. Just someone they would like to be around every now and again.

Part 9

66

Smitty

Today I am on a double mission. First, to find another out-of-the-way place for Abi and me to meet. Second, to sit down and try to work out who did what I was going to do.

The answer is nearly there, I can feel the fingers of my mind groping for it, nearly clasping it and then having to give up as it twirls itself out of reach. I'm sure, if I come away from everything and everyone, I will work out what happened, who did it and why. What I'll do with that knowledge I don't know since the police are hardly likely to believe me and I would have heard by now if they were pursuing anyone else in connection with the death instead of just me.

Also, if they had moved their attentions on from me, Abi and I would not be having to sneak around still. Even though I sorted out a lot of things with my mother, I'm not sure how she would really feel about me meeting Abi. The jealousy and worry won't have dissipated like dry ice now we've talked; conversation can't erase worries and anxieties and fears, especially irrational, illogical ones. From what Abi said the other night, even though her mum, my other mother, had told her dad, our father, that she'd never forgive him for sending her child away again, she hasn't outright sanctioned or approved Abi seeing me. Until other people are comfortable with it, we're going to be having a sibling affair as Abi called it.

This café seems perfect for our purposes because it is one of those out of the way but 'in plain sight' places. You can only get there by foot and you have to be pretty determined at that: crossing a concrete lock that I'm convinced wobbles when you walk on it, or driving down to the desolate area of huge, ominous-looking nearby power plant and then getting out to walk the rest of the way once you run out of road.

The café should, with its place right on the water, be a glass and chrome affair but it isn't. It is made up of low, pebble-dashed buildings that look suspiciously as if they were once outhouses and the outside ambience comes in the shape of white plastic garden tables and green plastic chairs. It would be perfect, though, for illicit meetings with my sister.

I order coffee from the waitress, take out my notebook. At the centre of the page I write the initials SZ (for Soloné Zebila) and draw a circle around them. Inside the circle I cram a question mark next to the initials but away from the curve of the circle. Somebody killed my grandmother, SZ, and I can't work out who. To do it, they would need access. I scrawl down the people I know who that applies to: AZ (Abi), IZ (Ivor), JZ (Julius) and KZ (Kibibi). To be thorough, I add LZ (Lily), too. Maybe JoZ (Jonas), my other brother who no one talks about. Not even Abi will talk freely about him beyond saying he lives abroad. Whenever I ask about him she glosses over him or outright changes the subject. It doesn't take a detective – qualified or not – to work out there was some kind of falling out. And with my father issuing decrees to me the other day, it's likely to be him that Jonas fell out with. Actually, with my grandmother the way she was, how manipulative she was, it could have been her also. I draw lines between JoZ and SZ, JoZ and JZ. Question marks go along those lines.

I have access, well, had – pretty sure my father will have changed the locks by now. I write down CS (Clem). Seth knew I had the key, so his initials, SC, go down too. He didn't want me to do it and he offered to do it instead. Each of these factors earns him a circle around his name. I have the same number. Who else? Mum? (HS).

She knew where they lived, but the access is out. My other mother, she has access (one circle), she and SZ didn't get on (second circle) and she knew all about the medication (third circle). So did I. (Another circle for me).

I look at the page again. I have the most circles.

'Here you go.' The waitress, with her pristine white apron, rolled-up sleeves and peach lipstick, places my coffee beside my notebook then stops to gawp at what I've written and a deep frown forms between her unplucked eyebrows. She stares at the initials, the connecting lines, the question marks, the circles. I see them as she sees them: a load of rubbish, fanciful nonsense from a person who has watched one too many cop shows. A wave of embarrassment flows through me. I wonder if she's guessed what I've been trying to do, what I've convinced myself I can do. She frowns again, then leaves me to it.

I snap shut my notebook, embarrassed that I seriously thought I could work it all out over a cup of coffee in an out-of-the-way café.

I pick up my coffee, move to take a sip. Except it's tea. Tea. I don't drink tea. I pretend to Mum that I do to make her happy, but the reality is, there's something fundamentally flawed about tea in my mind. It's flavoured water. Not like coffee, coffee is something *made* with water, it is a real drink.

For a few seconds I toy with the idea of drinking the tea, forgoing the coffee just this once. I can't, I just can't.

I hook my bag over my shoulder, pick up my notebook and pencil and stand to return the tea that should be coffee. In the café there is a queue for service even though it hadn't looked that busy outside. I stand behind a tall, wide man who wears clothes that are too small for him. The teacup clatters because my bag wants to slip off my shoulder, and I can't quite get the correct angle with the notebook and pencil in one hand and the cup in the other, so I am playing a sort of balancing act that rattles the cup and saucer.

I should put the whole lot down at the nearest unoccupied table and reorganise myself so that I'm not in imminent danger of dropping something. I shouldn't be looking around the café, scanning as

I always do, for a face I recognise in the crowd. In the time before I met my biological family, I used to do this all the time. I used to look at people to see if I knew them, if they looked like me, if I looked like them, if *they* were that familiar stranger I was connected to by blood. I still do it. A habit of a lifetime cannot be broken in a few short months, after all.

I spot it. I see a face that I recognise. And another. I see two faces I recognise, sitting right at the back of the café, in that hidden, private nook all the best cafés have. Those are the areas where I conduct my business with new clients who don't invite me into their homes, the places Abi and I would probably sit so we won't be easily seen as we conduct our sibling affair. This pair, this couple, obviously do not want to be seen. They have come here, to this secret café, and they have taken up a private space. And they are sitting with their heads close together as they make their plans, probably discussing how they're going to tell me about their relationship. Or maybe they're chatting about how much longer they're going to keep me and everyone else in the dark about them. The jangling of the crockery in my hand is now out of control – I'm going to shake the cup off the saucer altogether at this rate because I am so horrified by who I have seen together.

My eyes dart around looking for a clear surface, but my gaze keeps returning to the couple in the corner because if I look away for too long, they might disappear, I might realise I have imagined it, imagined them. I choose the table in front of me to set down my burden. It's occupied by two people who probably mind having a half-full teacup and tea-flooded saucer placed in front of them, but would probably concede it's better than it being dropped beside them.

I stare at the couple at the back. I can't believe what I am seeing. My Paddington Hard Stare is so firm, immovably fixed, one half of the pair glances up in my direction, looks away then immediately swings back when they register that they've seen me. The other one notices their companion is staring and looks in that direction too. That half of the couple is more openly horrified at being caught.

'*You should have drunk the tea,*' I tell myself. '*If you had, none of this would be happening.*'

Without noticing them properly, fully, I move around the other people and tables in the café until I am in front of the couple in the back, waiting for one of them to speak. They stay silent. They sit and watch me: one is wide-eyed with alarm, the other impassive; the only clue as to their shock is the way their eyes keep darting to the door, waiting to see who else will arrive and catch them together.

I look first at Mum, I look second at Julius, my father. The pair of them together, so close they're . . . *Surely not.*

'We have to tell her, anyway,' says Mum when the silence has gone on long enough for them to know I won't be speaking first.

'But—' begins my father.

'Just tell me,' I say.

One remains mute, the other fixes me with their pale blue eyes, eyes that are used to hypnotising me, making me stand still while I'm about to be told off or insulted.

'We did it,' Mum says. 'We're the ones who helped your grandmother to die.'

67

Julius & Heather

Julius with Heather, two weeks ago, Brighton

He opened the door to the woman who looked, frankly, deranged. She had seemed demure and respectable when he met her, a woman who had class and a certain amount of breeding.

'We need to talk,' the woman said loudly, dispelling all thoughts about her being the type of person she appeared to be. Even her accent was different from when they first spoke. The woman walked straight past him and into the house as though she belonged there.

'Kitchen that way, is it?' she asked.

He was working at home because he was waiting on some very important documents and it would be quieter to work there. Kibibi had taken Lily-Rose out so he could get some work done in peace. Kibibi had even prepared and administered his mother's medication to ensure he would not be disturbed.

In the kitchen, the woman looked around, examining their home as if she didn't think they were good enough. 'Who do you people think you are?' she said. 'How can you even think of doing that to my girl? Who do you people think you are?'

'Why are you here?' Julius asked sternly. He had no time for this woman. He was grateful that she and her husband brought up the girl, turned her into a polite young woman, but he had no time for this woman. The girl... Seeing her again had been a reminder of a part of himself he did not like to admit existed. He had been ashamed for most of his life. Back then, in 1978, he had been scared of what doing the right thing might entail, what hardships they would all have to endure. When his mother made the call, made the decision, he had been relieved. He could show Kibibi how hard he was fighting, but ultimately, his mother, his father, they would have their own way. They always had their own way. He was ashamed of not being man enough at the time to take responsibility for his mistake. Seeing the girl in the present had brought that mortification back to the front of his mind.

'How dare that woman ask my daughter to do that?' the woman in front of him repeated.

'What woman? What are you talking about?' *She is my daughter, in all actuality*, he thought. He wanted to remind her of that. She was his daughter even though he did the wrong thing back then.

'That woman! She wants my daughter to help end her suffering. What about my daughter's suffering? She's in bits, trying to work out how to do it. And she will do it. Because Clemency will do anything for someone who is family. How dare *she* do this to Clemency.'

'I do not know what you are talking about. I might understand if you calm yourself down and explain to me what you are trying to say.'

The woman's nostrils flared like an untamed horse's, her body was like that of an animal ready to pounce.

'Sit, sit. Sit. Tell me.'

'Your mother,' she said when she was seated. 'Asking my Clemency to help her to do *that*.'

'Help her to do what? What suffering?' He didn't fully understand, although he feared that he did and was too cowardly to face it.

'I knew it. I knew she wouldn't be brave enough to ask one of you, it would be my daughter because she sees her as second best.'

'Mrs Smittson...'

'Don't you dare Mrs Smittson me. Don't you dare! She wants Clemency to help her to die. She is suffering and she wants Clemency to help her. What about Clemency's suffering? Just because she didn't grow up in this big house with all these expensive things, and didn't go to private school, it doesn't mean she doesn't know right from wrong. It doesn't mean she would do that.'

'You think she would ask Clemency to...I don't think so. My mother is very religious, she knows killing is wrong.'

'And yet she has still asked Clemency to do it.'

'She has spoken to Clemency twice as far as I know. No one would ask someone they have spoken to twice to do such a thing. Certainly not my mother. You must be mistaken.'

'She's the one who is mistaken if she thinks I would let my daughter do that.'

'Maybe Clemency misunderstood when my mother was discussing the pain she feels with her conditions.'

The woman's eyes became wide and staring, fuelled by anger and outrage. 'Let's ask her, shall we? Then we will all be in a better position to understand what is going on.'

'We talked to my mother,' he says. 'As she talked, explained as best she could what she'd asked and why, slowly I began to understand. I had left the care of my mother to Kibibi because I could not stand to see her like that.

'I did not want to accept the reality of what was happening to her. I had been hiding from the truth. This disease, it had altered who she was. I wish you – both of you – had known her before. She was a formidable woman. Not always right, and she did some terrible things, but she was also remarkable and capable of such generosity.

'Talking to her, I realised she was no longer the woman she used to be. She was always so strong and in charge. These diseases – the Parkinson's, the diabetes, the heart problems...they made her feel weak. She could not care for herself, she could not be who she was, and it was going to get worse. She could not do the most basic things and the humiliation of that was more than she could bear.

'I began to understand, for the first time, what her condition actually meant. I have lived alongside her for years, but I had not taken the time to speak to her, to find out what she wanted. Kibibi had been telling me for years to talk to her. I had been too afraid. I did not want to face what was happening to her. I did not want to accept that her mental pain was as acute as her physical pain.'

Julius with Heather, two weeks ago, Brighton
'I could not ask one of you,' his mother explained. 'You are too close. Too much has happened. A virtual stranger might be able to. She might not have the emotional attachment of you others, especially you, Julius.'

'Mamma, you should have asked me. This isn't something for a stranger to do. You should not have done that to my daughter. What we did to her all that time ago was wrong. What you did to her now is wrong too. You should have asked me.'

'You do not have the strength, Julius. That is why I had to take control all those years ago. You have never had the strength to do what you must do.'

'She was underestimating me, of course. She always has done. She has done outlandish things to protect me. None of them have been necessary but she has done them regardless. I could not watch her suffer now that she had explained.'

Julius with Heather, two weeks ago, Brighton
'Clemency is not doing this.'

'No, she isn't. I will,' he said.

'It has to be a stranger.'

'You do not think I am a stranger to her? That by not engaging with her all these years, I have not lost all idea of who she is? I am her child, I am the one who should do this.'

'I won't let you do this alone. We can both be there. Anything to stop Clemency from doing it.'

'Yes, anything to stop her having to be the one.'

68

Smitty

'We talked to her. Discussed the options, came up with a plan,' my father says.

'Did that plan happen to include me getting practically arrested?' I ask.

'I told the police it was me,' Mum says. 'I told them. They wouldn't believe me. Even when we got to the police station. I told them again but they thought I was just trying to protect you. That's why we're going to confess.'

'Oh, right, *after* I was "brought in for questioning"?' I turn on my father. 'And you just sat there next to me and let them accuse me when you knew it was you all along.'

'I was in shock – I did not realise how far along the process you were. That you had been to my house so many times to see her and how close you came to carrying out her plan. I could not confess, either, until I knew what Mrs Smittson was going to say. I did not want her to get into any trouble when this was my task to complete and she merely stayed to hold both our hands.' He pauses, waits to see if I have understood. 'I told you to keep away so that you would not be further implicated.'

'This is the first chance we've had to meet. And Mr Zebila has been trying to contact his other son, heal the rift caused by your grandmother before he potentially goes to prison.'

Mum's last sentence clarifies for me what my mind has been grasping for: the other night she was talking like someone who was mending fences before they left. 'Is that why you tried to convince me that Kibibi was a good mother?' I say. 'You thought she'd be able to take over from you if you go to prison?'

'No, Clemency. I simply wanted you to remember that even though she doesn't know you, she loves you, like a mother or father should.'

'How did you even know?'

Mum is unusually abashed all of a sudden.

'You might as well tell me now you've told me everything else,' I say.

'Little things all pointed to it: the look on your face when we left their house that first time. The question you asked about your father and if he felt he was a burden. What you said reminded me of the look on your face the day you met your grandmother and how I felt when your father asked me the same thing. Telling me she'd been in hospital...' Mum seems incredibly uncomfortable and even squirms in her seat a little as though being interrogated. 'I got confirmation from eavesdropping on your conversations with Seth. To be fair,' she adds quickly, 'I thought you might be pregnant because of the way you two were suddenly so close and were off whispering all the time.'

I blink at her because I don't understand why she thinks this is such a heinous thing to have done, considering she's been doing that most of my life, and considering what she actually did do with my biological father.

'Mrs Smittson was a great comfort to me,' my father says. There's a strange formality between them considering what they did together. I would have thought that would have made them incredibly intimate, closer than friends. 'She cycled over to the house on the day my mother had chosen. Kibibi was out early with Lily-Rose, Abimbola and Ivor were at work. I left the house to go to work as usual, and when they had gone, I returned. We sat with my mother, we held her hands and we talked with her the whole time while the medication took effect and afterwards when she slipped into a coma.' A wisp of a smile haunts my father's face. 'I had not held my mother's hand since I was a small boy.'

'Was she, my grandmother, was she...' '*OK*' or '*all right*' seem inappropriate considering the outcome, but was it still what she wanted, is what I want to know.

My father, who I look a lot like, understands what I am trying to say. 'It was what she wanted and how she wanted it to happen. It was one last act under her control, as the person she used to be. She was...' '*Fine*' seems the wrong word for him, too. He nods, conveying his understanding of my question and the answer I wanted. 'She was.'

'We are going to tell the rest of our families before we go to the police,' my father says.

Mum is looking at me. That's nothing new, though. She's always done it. From the earliest age I can remember her staring at me – the multiple photos she used to take were just an extension of that, I suppose. I used to look at her, a lot, too, especially when I realised that apparently, according to other people, the liquid that flowed in our veins was water because the connection between us was meant to be weak. I was always desperately trying to do as Dad had told me back when I was four, to focus on the things that made us similar, to find a point of contact that made water and blood and their thickness irrelevant. Our greatest similarity is each other, I've come to realise. We love the other so much, we're willing to do anything for them.

My father is looking at me, too. I had been upset and more than a little curious as to why he didn't look at me before, didn't seem to see me even when his gaze did stray in my direction. Our eyes meet over the table.

He reaches into his jacket pocket, pulls out an envelope and places it on the table in front of me. 'These are for you. I was going to give them to Mrs Smittson to give to you, but now I can give them to you.'

It is an unassuming brown A5 envelope and on the front he has written *For you*. When I reach inside, my fingers feel photographs. I pull them out and place them on top of the envelope. The first picture is a strip of four black-and-white photo-booth pictures. In them, a man holds a baby. He has a small neat Afro and he is so incredibly handsome. The baby in his arms is wearing a light-coloured bonnet and a white towelling Babygro. The baby looks nonplussed, obviously enjoying being held by the man in the photo but not sure what's going on. I turn another photo over – it is a professional colour photo, the man sits on a chair, holding the baby in a swaddle of blankets, the same bonnet in place. The other four photos are colour, too, but faded from age. They are of the baby on her own in the butterfly box, without her bonnet. And in each picture she is a little older than the last, and each time her face is confused but delighted to have this man around.

I stop staring at the photos of myself and my father, and look at him. 'Mrs Stoner, your foster carer, let me take you out a few times. I didn't want to forget what you looked like. I had never seen a baby so beautiful. I wanted to take so many photos of you. Every time I saw you, you had changed. Kibibi never knew that I came to see you. She still does not know. I wanted . . . I wanted to be a better man but I could not.'

'I don't want you to go to prison,' I say suddenly. 'Either of you. I want you to stay with me. It feels like I'm only just getting to know both of you and now you might be taken away from me.' I can't stop the avalanche of emotions that cascade down my face. 'This isn't fair. None of this is fair.'

They each take a hand, my 'Mum' and my 'father'. Then they tell me as many times as they can in the time they have left that it's all going to turn out for the best.

69

Abi

To: Jonas Zebila
From: Abi Zebila
Subject: S.O.S
Thursday, 27 August 2015

Jonas,

I need you to call me. Please, just call me. I know Daddy's been trying to get in touch with you and you haven't replied, but it's really important you call me. Mummy and I have spent the last few hours sobbing and if you lived near enough, you'd probably see Daddy and Clemency's adoptive mother on the local news.

70

Smitty

They're probably in the police station right now. Telling their story, starting the process to see what will happen to them for what they did. They've each been home, have told the people who need to know and now they are telling the authorities so that they can find out what comes next. Mum wanted to tell Nancy and Seth on her own and she didn't want me anywhere near the police station in case I was asked to have an informal 'chat' before they have told the police everything and given them their evidence. I didn't even bother asking my father if I could come with him because I knew what his answer would be.

They did it for me.

I have walked the length of the beach – from Portslade to Brighton Pier – repeatedly since I left them. I have been bashed and buffeted by the wind, nearly run over by idiot cyclists who think they have a right to ride on the main promenade, and sworn at by people I've accidentally bumped into. Now I am sitting on a bench, where my body has finally collapsed from the exhaustion of trying to walk off my anger, being lashed by the rain.

I am angry. I'm not supposed to be, but I am. I am so incredibly angry I could explode. They did it for me, to stop me from doing it. They have probably sacrificed their freedom for me, but my God, it's like the adoption all over again.

It's someone making decisions that fundamentally impact me and not bothering to consult me. When I was a baby they couldn't consult

427

me, but I am an adult. When are any of my parents going to start seeing me as an adult? As someone capable of being talked to, reasoned with, considered, *consulted*. Is this what being a parent is about, or is that what being *my* parent is all about? At every stage, my parents – all three of the ones I have alive – make decisions that impact me as though I am still that baby in the butterfly box. When do I get to make a decision in the open and have it stick?

'You're getting wet,' he says. I am too numb to jump out of my skin at the sudden sound of his voice. From the fat drops of summer rain, from the events and revelations of the last few hours, from walking about sixteen miles back and forth, my body is too shut off to feel much more. 'I've been watching you walk back and forth all afternoon. At first I flattered myself that you might be working up to coming in to see me, then I realised you were just walking, *then* I noticed you had stopped on this bench. And *then* I noticed, after locking up and everything, that you were still on this bench even though you're getting very wet.'

Suddenly I am no longer being showered upon. I look up to find I am being sheltered and covered by Tyler's large, blue golf umbrella.

'Did it occur to you that I might like getting wet?' I say. 'That I am adult who has made the decision to become soaked by the rain, and should therefore be allowed to live with that decision and all its attendant consequences?'

He sits beside me on the bench, which is equidistant from his café and my home. From the sound of him as he moves, I guess he's wearing a rainmac as well. 'Don't be like that,' he says.

'Like what? What am I being like? Someone who has had people make decisions for her all her life, who has reached her limit? Is that what I'm being like?'

'Yes, I suppose that is how you're being.' He waits a few seconds before daring to speak again. He may have worked out I'm not feeling particularly rational right now. 'Come back to the café, get dry or not if you like being wet, have a coffee and we can talk.'

'Not a good idea.'

'It's a great idea.'

'Tyler, if we go back to your café, with the level of emotion rampaging through me right now, I will probably make a pass at you. Right there in the middle of the café.' I steal a glance at him from the corner of my eye. 'And we both know that would be a bad idea. And possibly unhygienic if you respond in the way I hope.'

'You can't stay here.'

'I can. And I'm going to.' *There's no place I'd rather be, actually*, I decide. It's one of those decisions you make when you're so drunk you know that you won't mind sleeping on a park bench; in fact, it's the best place you've ever slept, and if someone tries to stop you sleeping there you will take very big issue with them. I am not drunk, I am simply making a decision like a drunk person. Like an adult who wants to be allowed her choices, no matter how rubbish they may be.

Tyler's response to my confession is a silence that extends and expands, grows and magnifies, until it starts to feel so wide it could cover the sea in front of us. I guess he is struggling with himself. He doesn't want me to make a pass at him, but he does want me to come out of the rain.

He wants to talk, to be friends as we should have been all along. I wish we had stayed friends. If we had, though, I wouldn't have had those giggly, wobbly moments on the white roller skates with the red wheels that he bought me. We wouldn't have shared those wonderful kisses. 'I don't want you to feel uncomfortable, Tyler. Anything to do with me is so messed up right now and I'm still married, too, so I'm not sure being around me is a good idea.'

'Come back to the café,' he eventually says. 'And if you make a pass at me, I'll decide how to deal with it if and when it happens.'

In his office, which is up a set of wide stairs, Tyler 'deals with it' by kissing me back. He deals with it by allowing me to start to take off his clothes before he responds by removing my wet clothes while covering my neck in long, sensual kisses. He handles it by guiding me to the sofa, letting me sit astride him while I roll a condom on him, tugging me on top of him until I am filled by him and he is groaning with every move I make. He copes with it by seeming to enjoy every moment from the first kiss to the last orgasmic thrust.

Right now, I'm not thinking about him even though we're reclined together afterwards on the sofa under a picnic blanket he has mag- icked up from somewhere. I'm thinking about where my life will go from here. The map of my life seems to have left Nowhere and navigated us to Thiswhere. In this Thiswhere I am a sister to a sister, a sister to brothers, a daughter to a mother and father couple who are both alive. I am a sibling and a daughter to people who look like me.

It's all gone, now, of course. My brothers and sister and mother will hate me. If my father goes to prison they will blame me for coming into their lives, for bringing Mum into their lives, who made him talk to his mother, which made him decide to do that thing I was going to do.

'Coffee for your thoughts?' Tyler asks.

'There isn't enough coffee in the whole of Brighton and Hove, let alone this café, to know my thoughts right now,' I say.

'We're not going to talk about what's going on with you, then?'

'I'm sorry, but I can't, not at the moment.' *Maybe never.*

'You know this sofa on which we recline is actually a sofa bed,' Tyler says, expertly changing the subject.

'Are . . . are you, *like*, asking me to sleep over?'

'I, *like*, totally am.'

'But, *like*, what about your mom and pop?'

'Oh, they're, *like*, totally cool with me having my GF stay over.'

'So, I'm, *like*, your GF now, am I?'

'Stay,' he says, seriously, quietly. 'We may even get around to talking like we were meant to.'

Stay. It seems like the easy, natural thing to do when you're naked with a good-looking man who you like in so many ways.

'We can worry about all that other stuff tomorrow.' My husband, Seth, is what Tyler means. He has no idea about the rest of it, about the reason I was walking back and forth along Brighton seafront, about why I almost threw my phone into the sea earlier to stop the ringing because even though it was off, I could still hear it ringing, vibrating with people who wanted to talk to me.

'Please don't call Seth "other stuff". He's a person. It's not comfortable to talk about him, especially when we've just...but please don't dismiss him like that. People did that to me so many times over the years because I was adopted and I didn't know who my "real" parents were. Being negated and dismissed even unintentionally is horrible. Please don't do that about Seth.'

'Sorry. Stay over. We'll talk about where we are with you and me and you and your...'

'Ex. He's my ex.'

'We'll discuss the situation with your ex tomorrow.' His hand moves over my waist, slides down until it rests on my bare bum and he brings me closer to his body. He trails his fingers over my hip, moving them slowly until they brush the hair between my legs. 'And if you're not going to talk to me...' He slips two of his fingers deep inside me, enough to make me gasp and arch my body towards him, aching for more, wanting the feel of him inside me again. His lips cover my nipple, his tongue teasing at it. When I gasp again, he moves to kiss me.

'I suppose my clothes *are* probably still wet.' I didn't notice earlier how good it felt to kiss him with his warm, naked skin next to mine. My mind had been too focused on escaping the other part of the day, not on enjoying these moments with Tyler. Now, I concentrate on him. I gasp louder against his lips from what his fingers are doing to me. I shove everything else out of my mind and concentrate on getting to know Tyler without talking to him.

71

Smitty

Tyler hands me a cup of hot black coffee – made from the jar of instant he keeps beside the kettle in his office – and returns to his place on the other side of the sofabed.

'You are such a fraud,' I say. He's put in four sugars, even though I didn't ask for them. 'I cannot believe you drink instant coffee when you spend all day pushing the good stuff on others.'

'You think a Michelin-starred chef doesn't eat takeaway burgers?' he replies.

'Michelin-starred chef? OK then,' I say with a laugh.

'Hey! What are you saying?'

'Nothing, nothing.'

Our 'morning after' silence returns, full of sharp, awkward edges that jut like angry elbows into what had been tender moments between us, leaving huge, unsightly bruises.

'I'll need to be opening the café soon,' he says. 'Thankfully there's a shower here, you're welcome to use it, too.'

'Thanks, I suppose I had better be making a move as well.'

'All right, since you're clearly not going to bring it up, where do we go from here, Girl From Nowhere?'

Tyler settles his cup on the floor on his side of the sofabed. He climbs up on the bed until he is close to me.

'This sofabed was quite comfortable as sofabeds go,' I say. 'I only dislocated one of my shoulders on that metal frame.'

He says nothing, waits for a non-evasive response. I place my cup on the floor, sit up to face him properly. 'I've behaved badly,' I say.

'Don't be so hard on yourself, you were quite good actually,' Tyler replies.

'Oi, you!' I go to tickle him and he catches my wrist, pulls me towards him. His physicality is intoxicating as we tumble down on to the bed.

'What I'm asking is: is this a one-night thing for you?'

'I'm guessing by the fact you're asking that it'd be a problem if it was,' I say.

'Yes, it would be. I like you, I think you like me, but I'm not interested in anything casual. Laidback, yes, but "just sex" is not my thing.' He strokes his thumb over my cheek. 'Is it just sex you want, Smitty?'

'No. I don't know. I just know I like you a lot. Even more so after last night. I'm really confused, I suppose, about you and lots of other things.'

Tyler's beautiful eyes with their long eyelashes regard me for several elongated seconds. Frustration and disappointment emanate from him. 'You need to be honest with yourself, Smitty. Ask yourself what you really want. I've been stupid, I've let you stampede all over my boundaries because I like you. Last night shouldn't have happened. It was great, *really great*, but this isn't my thing at all. So, you know what, I'm putting an end to this in all its forms. When you're sure of what you want, when you've been brutally honest with yourself, maybe we can talk.'

He's right, of course. I need to be honest with myself about what I want from him. What I want from Seth. What I want from my parents, my family, life, but most of all, what I want from myself. I keep ducking out of that – being honest about what I truly want from myself. 'So, there's no chance of a quickie before I head off, then?' I say with a smirk.

His laugh ripples through me and he tickles me as we giggle. His hand works its way inside my stiff, radiator-dried clothes, and rubs seductively over my nipple, while his lips brush against mine in a soft, brief kiss. 'Not a chance in hell,' he says. He kisses me again – longer and slower, but with his hands outside my clothes.

It's a goodbye kiss, no doubt about it, but it's wonderful all the same.

72

Smitty

We've been waiting out here for what seems like forever.

After leaving Tyler's I decided to go to work, to forget about everything and get on with the commissions that had been backing up. The workshop is a different place – it is complete and whole, how I want it to be. I have found a space for everything and the shelves from the shop have been perfect for creating room for everything to be labelled and easily accessible.

The shop is still 'coming soon' but there is progress that I am happy with. I need to fine-tune the images in my head, but the basic outlines are there, I simply need to sketch them in and make them real. I reached the shop and stood outside, unable to unlock the doors and enter.

I had to deal with what had happened the day before. The walking, the sitting in the rain, being with Tyler, were all delaying tactics from having to face what my parents had done.

Seth was already there, sitting in Lottie. We didn't speak when I opened the side door and sat down, watching the building. He sat in the driver's seat, I sat on the side watching. Waiting.

My other mother arrives soon afterwards. She stands outside the building, trying to decide if she should go in or not. She decides not to enter, then sees me sitting in Lottie, walks across the road and sits down next to me. She doesn't speak to me, she sits down next to me, on the floor of my campervan, watching. Waiting. Abi arrives next. She doesn't have Lily with her, but she does have a noticeable bump because she's not wearing baggy clothes. I wonder if she's told them or if they've noticed. She comes to us and lowers herself between us. Her space is between our mother and me. Unusually for her, I suspect, she doesn't speak, she simply sits. Watching. Waiting.

The four of us sit and watch and wait for what seems like hours. Eventually, after what feels like the whole city has entered and exited the building, the glass doors slide back and Mum steps out first. She stands very still, wearing yesterday's clothes, looking around as if she is surprised it is daytime, and that she is out there at all. We all move, drawn towards her across the road that is now lousy with closely parked cars and vehicles. She sees us coming and does nothing. As we reach the bottom step, the doors slide back again and my father steps out.

He stands a little way away from Mum, marvelling, too, that he is out, he is free. No one speaks, we all simply reach for each other. I go for Mum, but find my other mother there, too, nestled in the crook of my left arm. In my other mother's other arm is her stiff-backed, uncomfortable husband, and in his other arm is his daughter Abi, in Abi's other arm is her sister's mother, Mum. We pull together, closing the gap between us until we are together properly, creating the strangest group hug I've ever been a part of. While we hug, I realise that someone is missing. Someone who should be there with us has kept himself apart, even though he is part of the family.

73

Smitty

'I think I'm going to drive around,' Seth says. 'Clear my head.'

We dropped the others at their place and then he has driven us back home. We've all barely spoken, but instead communicated with our silence how bonded we were. This thing had tied us together and it was too huge to chatter about, too incredible to speak of.

'Thank you, Seth, for the lift last night and the lift home,' Mum says to him.

'No problem, Mrs Smittson,' he replies.

'You must call me Heather,' she says.

He can't help his side eye to me, wondering what's got into her – after more than ten years he's finally being initiated into First Name Basis with Mum. 'I'll try,' he says. 'But it's not that easy to call people older than me by their first names.'

'You make me sound ancient! Just how much older than you do you think I am?' Mum retorts.

She giggles at the way alarm widens his eyes. 'She's messing with you,' I tell him. I'm not sure when Mum started messing in general, especially with Seth, but that's what she's doing. Maybe it's another way of making sure I have someone if she does end up in prison.

'I will see you later,' she says. With ease she climbs down from her place beside Seth in the front and makes her way into the building.

'I'll see you later,' I say to him.

'Yes, I'll see you later.' He can't look at me because he's probably worked out where I was when I didn't come home last night. I look at him though: clean-shaven again. Back to being the man I married, the man I lived with, the man I fell in love with, the man I met all that time ago. Except is he? He's changed, I've changed. We all of us only vaguely look the same, we're probably only vaguely the same people on the inside.

I watch and wait until my red campervan, driven by my husband, my ex, disappears from sight when it blends into the traffic heading along the road into Brighton. He was the one missing from the group hug. He is part of my family.

Nancy, who by all accounts didn't handle what Mum told her very well, has taken Sienna to London for a few days to stay with friends and the flat seems empty without Sienna. Mum has spent most of the afternoon asleep in her bedroom. She doesn't want to talk and I don't blame her. We will have to talk properly, comprehensively, at some point; we'll have to get her a solicitor and brace ourselves for what comes next, which includes the very real possibility of prison. The little she has said about what the police told her has been enough for me to know that it's likely to go to court; at the very least it will come before the Crown Prosecution Service for consideration for trial. If convicted they could get up to fourteen years. She knew this, but she was still willing to help a relative stranger die to stop me doing it. After our brief chat, Mum disappeared into her bedroom and hasn't emerged since.

When Seth returns to the flat he tries the kitchen first, then the living room and then my bedroom. 'There you are,' he says. 'The door was shut which is why I didn't try in here first.'

I have been sitting on the floor, waiting for him. He comes in and manages about three steps across the room before he stops, halted by the wall in front of him. The wall, which had felt so empty, has been refilled with images of him again. That's what I've spent the past few hours doing. My wall is now *With Seth, With Seth, With Seth, With Seth, With Seth* again. He's a huge part of my family, whether we're a couple or not.

'Come sit down, please,' I say to him.

Cautious and confused, unable to completely take his eyes off the wall, he comes to sit opposite me, attempts to cross his long legs, thinks better of it and sits side on instead.

Between us on the floor is *that* picture, it used to be his favourite one of me.

'I wanted to thank you for all you've done for me,' I say. I sound formal and I don't mean to. 'Remember this?' My fingers slide the photo towards him. He nods contemplatively. *With Seth. (Finally!!!)* 'I don't just mean the photo, I mean those few days. Do you remember them?'

He looks like he did earlier: agonised. He went out to clear his head, to process the fact I'd been with someone else, and all I'm doing is dredging it up again, raking his feelings over the red-hot coals of our separation and the drift between us. But it's necessary. We have to look at all of it before we can move on, together or apart.

'I remember those few days, yes,' he says flatly.

'It felt like nothing could touch us. I never wanted those four days to end, I just wanted us to stay together without the rest of the world barging in,' I confess. 'I was trying to telepathically get you to ask me to move in with you so I'd never have to leave you.'

'I didn't want you to leave, either. I didn't want you to leave the first time you stayed with me, and after those few days I wanted you to stay for ever.'

'I look at this photo and I can't work out what went wrong.'

'Neither can I,' he replies sombrely.

'Then I look at that photo,' I point to *Seth With Dad, February 2013*, 'and I have a clue.'

Seth is confused.

'I'm sorry, Seth,' I say to him. 'I'm sorry for shutting you out when Dad was dying. I was so mired in it, I didn't even notice. I just didn't think.'

I did a terrible thing to him. It didn't even cross my mind that he'd need to be there. I just focused on what I needed to do because Mum needed me, Dad needed me, I didn't think that Seth needed to be a part of it too. I remember how he sounded, how he would talk to me when I couldn't speak, how he would listen when I could talk, how utterly broken he sounded every time I told him what was happening next. I didn't notice that a lot of his pain was because he wasn't there, too. It wasn't intentional, cutting him out, but I did it. In all our years together, whenever we stayed over at my parents' place, Dad and Seth would go round the corner for a few drinks in the pub, then more often than not, Seth and Dad would sit up into the small hours talking with a bottle of whisky while Mum and I would be in our beds.

We were a family, a close family, and I didn't even notice that Seth, one of our members, wasn't there when he needed to be. No wonder he turned to Nancy, someone he thought had been cut out in the same way.

'You and Dad were good friends but I didn't think you might need to be there, too. Part of me was trying to spare you the pain of seeing him like that because it was awful, and part of it was selfish – not thinking of anything or anyone else except how to get through each day, even though each day was bringing us closer and closer to the end. You must have been so hurt. And so *angry* with me. I'm so sorry.'

'I wasn't angry with you. I was scared and hurt. But not angry. That came later.'

'Are you still angry with me?' I ask.

'No. Not at all. I was angry with myself, too, for not saying something. For not talking to you and letting you know I wanted to be there. I should have known you were too preoccupied to take my feelings into account.' He picks up the photo. He grins at Clemency circa 2004. 'I remember I wanted you so much, then and in the years leading up to that night,' he says. 'I've told you this, but that's why I came to talk to you and Dylan that day. I was never sure what it was about you, but I remember looking at you across the bar and just wanting to be with you. That New Year's Eve, I thought I'd made a mistake inviting you over because my feelings were out of control. Everything you did drove me crazy with lust. I kept telling myself that the feelings would pass – all I had to do was get through the night and I could go back to being your friend.

440

Thankfully it didn't quite work out like that... Are you still angry with me about Nancy?'

'No. I'm still a little hurt that you lied to me when I asked you about her, but that will pass.'

Seth continues to grin at the photo of my younger self. 'Listen,' he looks up at me, 'I know you're angry with Heather and Julius for what they did, how they took over.'

'How do you know that?'

'I know you – twenty-odd years of sharing secrets, remember?' His grin is genuine but fleeting. 'Don't be angry with them. You never would have done it.'

'I...'

'You wouldn't, Smitty. Not for her. You might do it for me, for your mum, but not for someone you don't love more than life itself. You couldn't. Julius could because she was his mother, Heather could do it because she would do anything to protect you. You didn't have that connection with your grandmother and you couldn't have done it. In this instance, what they did was the best thing for you.'

Seth is right. I couldn't have done it. It's not in me. Whether it was something she wanted or not, it is not in me to do something so personal, so intimate, for someone I barely knew – I didn't even realise how little I knew her despite the time we spent together until I was questioned by the police.

I look over my wall, how he has featured in it for so long. 'Seth.'

'Yes?'

'Nothing. I was just reminding myself how the word felt in my mouth. I haven't done that in a while.'

Seth's smile spreads right across his face – he's grinning at the memory, at the photo, at this moment where we're sharing something as special and unique, simple and ordinary, as a talk. Talking is what we were all about. 'Ahh, vintage Smitty, I haven't had that in a while.'

'Stick around, matey, there's plenty more vintage Smitty where that came from.'

74

Smitty

Grand Opening!

You're invited to the opening night launch of

Smittson Designs

on Friday 27 October, 2015

At my new Brighton shop, there's jewellery to suit every taste, plus commissions and redesign work undertaken.

RSVP to
07760104876
for details

See you there!

75

Smitty

'I'm still not sure about this dress you're wearing,' Mum says. She stands in my bedroom doorway, sizing me up as though if she decides what I'm wearing isn't suitable, I'll be changing it.

'Well, it's a good thing you're not wearing it then, isn't it?' I say.

My silver dress that I wore to my engagement party has been brought out of Purgatory, where I stored it after the debacle that unfolded that night, and I am reloving it. It's entirely appropriate for tonight and Mum has no say in that.

'Kibibi and I were saying that you'd be suited to something more blue, like sapphire. Or even a ruby red dress.' Mum and my other mother are besties now. They're how I imagine Lily and Sienna will be in sixty years or so – hanging out, giggling, pinky-promising each other things. (I can't say with certainty that Mum and my other mother haven't done the pinky-promise thing at some point, either.) My other mother has bought herself a trike and the pair of them go for days out in the countryside. I think, sometimes, from the way they talk, that Mum even told her about her first child, and that has been an additional bond. It's odd, seeing how the two of them are together, but I know it's been good for them both. Especially Mum, who has discovered through all this that 'other' isn't scary, and she does have lots in common with people who don't look like her. 'This dress is not suitable.'

'It's entirely suitable since this is my dress and my opening night and the colour of my favourite precious metal.'

'Is that how you speak to me nowadays, Clemency Smittson?' Mum says. She hasn't changed. For some reason I thought after everything we'd all been through that there would be some miraculous transformation where she would be more tolerant, more understanding, less likely to drive me completely round the bend. Today has been like that drive from Otley last May. Every opportunity she has a chance to stick her oar in or tell me what to do, she seizes with both hands: there's too much food, check; the start of the party is too late, check; there's too little food, check; there won't be enough room for everyone, check; are you sure you should be opening a shop in this current climate, check; this dress you're wearing is not suitable, check, check, check, check, check.

'Mum, I like this dress. I am going to wear this dress. If you have issues with this dress being on my body, then I'm sorry, but there's nothing I can do about it because I am going to keep wearing this dress.'

Mum's mouth becomes a tight circle of disapproval. 'I know what your father would have said if he was here now,' she says tartly.

'What?'

'Leave the *wee bairn* alone, *quine*. She knows what she's doing.' She sounds so much like him, with the same intonations and the same England-flattened Aberdeen burr, I have to catch my breath. 'Oh, he said it all the time,' Mum says to my shocked face.

'You sounded just like him,' I say. The tears sting my eyes, squeeze my throat.

'Of course I did,' she says dismissively. 'You don't spend nearly forty years hearing the same thing and not know how to repeat it, accent and all.' She steps forwards and gathers me in her arms. 'He would have been so proud of you,' she says when I have nestled my chin on her shoulder. 'He was always so proud of you.' She pulls me closer and the smell of her – vanilla, lavender, citrus and talc – fills my senses. 'I am so proud of you, too. I am so incredibly proud of you, I can't find the words.' She stands back, holds me at arm's length and looks at me all over again, a big grin of pride on her face. 'I think you're right about the dress being perfect,' she says. 'It's your hair that's all wrong.'

Nancy and I pass in the corridor as I go towards the front door with my keys for Lottie. We acknowledge each other as we always do, a brief glance in the other's direction and, if we're feeling particularly friendly that day, we'll offer the other a brief nod. Other than that, we both know there is nothing that could make us friends or even give us anything to speak about. She and Sienna are moving to a small house a bit further up in Hove soon. Sienna started school six weeks ago and, after the initial trauma of discovering Lily wasn't at the same school, she has settled in and is enjoying herself. 'Enjoy your night,' Nancy says suddenly. I pause in putting on my shoes and rotate until I am facing in her direction.

'Thanks,' I say cautiously. 'I'll see you and Sienna later?'

She nods and offers me a small smile. I surprise myself by offering her a small smile in return.

The shop has filled up a lot in the past hour, which has eased my anxiety and made me believe properly, completely, that this will work. It looks exactly as I imagined it because with help from Seth and Melissa, I've managed to make the thoughts in my head a reality. Melissa is grinning good-naturedly at Mum even though Mum has ordered her to take another plate of food around and to make sure no one takes more than their fair share.

Through the square pane of glass in the door, I see a figure start to open the door then change their mind and step back. With a glance over my shoulder to where Seth is – over by the counter, chatting to Bernice Giles, one of my earliest customers – I move towards the front door and open it to step out.

'Hi,' I say to Tyler, who has stepped back to let me out.

'Hi,' he says simply.

The door tings rather loudly in the moment I tug it shut behind me. Seeing Tyler gives me a sudsy feeling as usual, and the spectrum of feelings I had for him foams up in my bloodstream, in the well of my stomach, and I'm suddenly breathing a bit too fast, my heart beating a little too erratically.

Tyler moves across the cobbled street to the other side of the road, where the pavement is a little wider and we have the glow of a streetlamp on us, while the light from the shop across the road acts as a grounding beacon of where we are, which significant person is standing inside.

'I've been walking around for a while now, wondering if I should actually go in or not,' he says.

'I wasn't sure you'd come or how you'd take me sending you an invite.'

'I took it in the spirit I assume it was sent – as an olive branch extended in friendship?'

'And also as an apology for not getting in touch.'

He nods while keeping his gaze lowered and his dark eyelashes flutter against the skin under his eyes. 'And a thank you for giving you one of the best nights of your life?' he says, grinning cheekily.

'Well, of course,' I say. He doesn't hate me, the relief of that is like leaping into a cool pool of water after a long hot, sticky walk.

'Where are you getting your coffee nowadays?' he asks, able to face me again now his joke has broken the atmosphere between us.

'Erm, nowhere,' I say. I place my hand over my stomach by way of an explanation. 'I've given it up since the pregnancy.'

His whole body reverberates in shock and his eyes, wild and scared, find mine. 'What?' he asks. 'You're . . . Is it . . . ?'

'I'm sorry, I'm sorry,' I say with a laugh. 'I'm not pregnant. Just messing with you.'

He puffs air out of his cheeks a few times, presses his hand over his heart, visibly tries to calm himself down. 'Don't do that to me.'

'Ah, I had to – it'll teach you not to make jokes about the best night of my life. The look on your face was priceless.'

'That's extreme.' He puffs more air out of his mouth. 'Remind me never to fall out with you – you'd bring a nuclear weapon to a fist-fight.'

'I haven't been getting my coffee anywhere except the homemade stuff, by the way. I wanted to come into your café, but thought it best to give us both some space.'

' "Space" you say?' he replies. 'Your "space" has made a huge dent in my profits. I don't think that's fair, do you?'

'I'm sorry, I'll recommence buying coffee from you forthwith.' I smile at him. 'I did want to see you, I just wasn't sure how you'd feel about seeing me.'

'Conflicted, probably. But that's no reason to run away from stuff, is it?'

'No, it's not.' I've learnt that over the last few months.

'Are we done?' he asks.

This autumn night seems completely appropriate to be having this discussion. It's cool but muggy; the babble of people down on the shingle and promenade mingles with the soothing soundtrack of the sea in the distance. This is what the words to 'Summer Lovin'' used to conjure up in my mind. I'd never had a summer romance, but that song always made me feel like I had loved and lost over a few short weeks. Now, I sort of had been through it – the weather was colder and that's where it ended.

I nod. 'I suppose we are.'

'Not that we ever really got started.'

'No, I suppose not.'

'Are you trying again with your . . . with Seth?'

'I don't really know,' I admit. 'We still sleep top to toe and nothing beyond a few hugs has happened between us. But we do spend a *lot* of time together and neither of us has started or even mentioned divorce proceedings. So, who knows?'

'Ah, Smitty, as clear about what she wants as always.'

'Watch it, you, remember the nuclear weapon?'

'Oh, yeah, yeah. I almost forgot.'

Across the road a well-dressed couple, the woman taller than the man, who I think I made wedding rings for, walk up to the shop, clutching the silver invite for the opening.

'I'd better get back. Are you coming in?'

'Yes. I have to celebrate with you, don't I?' We cross the road and the shop comes into proper view, glowing like an amber gem against the dark background of this street. I push open the door and the bell announces our arrival. 'Let me introduce you to Melissa. She was one of my first customers down here. She helped me to sort the shop out and she's a great person.'

With a neutral expression on his face, Seth watches us cross the room, heading for Melissa, who has escaped being Mum's skivvy and is standing in front of the wall of photos. Both Melissa and Tyler, framed in the white box of a Polaroid photo, with words scribbled underneath, are up there. Melissa's locket-cum-watch is up there, too. 'Melissa,' I say, 'I'd like to introduce you to Tyler. He is the owner of Beached Heads on the seafront, where we first met. Tyler, this is Melissa. As I'm sure you'll notice, you're both up on the wall of fame, even though I haven't finished making Tyler the cufflinks he didn't ask for and will probably never use.'

My mouth babbles at them, but they're not interested in me. They're both virtually starry-eyed at each other, matching grins on their faces – fireworks going off all over the place for them. I'm more bothered by that than I should be – not enough to begrudge either of them the chance to be together but it niggles at me. 'I think you'll get on like a house on fire.' They will, as well. They're both such great people. I predict a summer wedding. Platinum matching rings made by yours truly.

Superfluous to them now, I retreat and find myself next to Seth. He has a bottle of Prosecco in his hand and a white cotton tea towel folded over his forearm. He's been circulating the room, filling glasses, chatting to people, starting conversations with anyone who is on their own. And watching me go outside to talk to a man I had a one-night stand with. We're not together, we're not apart – we're nowhere right now. Tyler is right that it is ridiculous. I want to change that, I want us to give us another chance. Even if it doesn't work out, even if too much has happened for us to find each other again, I want to be somewhere certain with Seth. I open my mouth to say I'd like to talk to him about it later, but Seth speaks first. He lowers his head until his lips are by my ear so he can murmur: 'So, is tonight the night I finally get to have you in this luscious silver dress of yours…then take it off you and have you all over again?'

'Depends how lucky you're feeling,' I say.

'I am feeling very, very lucky indeed.'

I'm just saying goodbye to a couple of people when I see Abi and Lily, who seem to come dancing up the road. Lily executes elaborate ballet steps, Abi moves in the wobbly dance gait of a heavily pregnant woman trying to keep up with her daughter.

'Auntie Smitty, Auntie Smitty!' Lily calls as she arrives in front of me. She is wearing a pink dress with folds and folds of netting and lace. She has a pink bow topping her mass of sleek, shiny black plaits. If I hadn't known better, I'd have thought she and Sienna had been on the phone co-ordinating what they would wear tonight since she is wearing exactly the same thing.

'Hello, you,' I say. I stoop to hug her. 'And hello, you,' I say to my sister. Her stomach is full, ripe and in ten weeks she'll be giving birth – she has asked me to be her birthing partner.

'Declan is just parking the car. Insists on driving into town because taking the bus or a taxi is slumming it, apparently, but doesn't have a clue about parking. We drove around six times before I got him to drop us at the end of the road so he can go find a space. Well, good luck with that, eh, matey?' On the fourth finger of her left hand glints her engagement ring. I conspired with Declan to make the twisted platinum band studded with diamond chips. He proposed, she said yes. '*I have to give him a chance now that he's proposed properly instead of just talking about it,*' Abi said when she told me about it.

'Lily, Sienna is in there somewhere. Do you want to see if you can find her? I think Uncle Smitty has some cake pops with your name on, too.'

She squeals, and I hold open the door for her to dart inside.

'How are you?' Abi asks.

'I'm fine.' I know what she's really asking me. I don't want to talk about it any more. I've talked and talked and talked about it with her, with Seth, with my other mother, and nothing has changed. I can't change anything that has gone before, I can only change the future. I've even made enough peace with myself to be seeing Mrs Lehtinen on a regular basis, working on her wonderful jewellery box.

'Sure?' Abi asks. I think sometimes she forgets that I'm the older sister and I'm the one who should be checking she's OK.

'Yes, I'm sure.' I open the door again. 'There are cake pops with your name on too, plus your picture is on the wall. All in all, I think you've pretty much hit the big time.'

'Enough with the pregnancy jokes, matey,' she replies before she steps in through the door.

I'm about to return to the shop when a Brighton green and white registered taxi pulls up outside. The door opens and out steps my other mother. She doesn't pay the driver, but does shut the door behind her. She smiles at me, grins like she is pleased to see me, Clemency the adult, not Talei the baby. She grins at me and opens her arms to me. Turns out that she's the parent who hugs. Every time I see her I am swamped by them, as I was with Dad. She also spends a lot of time drawing Abi, Lily-Rose and me for her part-time art foundation course.

'Hello,' I say. I'm still working on what to call her. In my head she is still 'my mother' and 'my other mother'. In reality, in the words that come out of my mouth, I avoid calling her anything to her face. 'You look so lovely.'

'Hello, Clemency,' she says, clinging on to me for just that bit longer, then she squeezes just that bit tighter. She's doing that to make up for my father. To make up for Ivor. They're not coming. Ivor blames everything on me and wants nothing more to do with me. My father... He is complicated. He does not want to see or speak to me. Despite giving me those photographs and confessing to seeing me after I was born, he doesn't want to be around me. I am a painful reminder of what he did back in 1978 and what he did more recently. I wasn't even invited to the funeral because neither he nor Ivor wanted to see me. My other mother reckons once he and Mum have been on trial and they know whether the future holds prison or not, he will change his mind.

I try to hide my disappointment at not seeing my father or brother but it is plain on my face. I really thought that this opening would give them the chance to be in touch without doing much. They could have just stood in the corner, talking to the parts of their family they did like.

'Give them time,' my mother says. She takes my hands, holds them out and looks at me. Pulls me in for another hug. Holds me close and the smell that is my other mother – vanilla, citrus, cinnamon and talc – takes over me.

The taxi pulls away to reveal a tall man in a dark grey suit and beige overcoat. He could be Ivor but he is taller and younger. He steps on to the pavement and waits politely for my mother to let me go. When we are unlatched, he offers me his hand, which is big with long, rectangular fingers. Much like mine.

'I'm Jonas, your brother,' he says. 'Abi has told me a lot about you, mainly via email, then by phone, but that's been enough for now. I'm incredibly pleased to meet you.'

'You too,' I say. He left because of my grandmother, because my father and mother wouldn't stand up to her. He stayed away because he couldn't stand to pretend when she had been awful to all of them for so many years. But he's here. He has flown all the way over from Montenegro to be here. He didn't even come back for the funeral.

'I was so desperate to get in touch with Abi when she told me about you but I knew the second I did, it would mean getting sucked back into all . . .' He shakes his head. 'I can't believe you're real,' he says. Unexpectedly, he's hugging me. Holding me close in his big arms, like he thinks I might disappear. 'My sister. My *big* sister. I can't wait to get to know you.'

'Me, too,' I say laughing. 'Me, too.'

With me, later, here

This is somewhere.

This is where I am from at last. I used to be from nowhere, but now I am from here. Thiswhere. This somewhere. Inside my shop there is a big, disjointed, mishmash of people I am linked to by blood and by circumstance; some are called relatives, others are called friends, but they're all *here* for me. Even without them I would be somewhere, I realise that now.

I have a shop and it is filled with people who are unique, precious, flawed, and all mine. They're my jewels. They're my family.

With Mrs Stoner, March 1978, Brighton

'Goodbye, little Talei. Precious one, your first mother said it meant. I wish so much we could keep you, but we can't. You're going to your new parents now. They'll look after you and I can tell by the way they look at you that they'll love you.

'I'll miss your little box, too. All those pretty butterflies. I hope you keep it all your life. It'll be a reminder of how much your other mother loved you. I know your new parents will love you, but I'm sure Kibibi, your first mother, loves you, too. I see it in her eyes every time she looks at you. And so does your first father, Julius.'

She gathered up the box with the baby. She had grown so much she wouldn't be able to sleep in the box for much longer. Kate Stoner had tried to get her to sleep elsewhere but she didn't seem to want to. She cried in the Moses basket, in the cot, on the big bed. Nowhere settled her like the butterfly box. The foster mother composed herself, she was almost blind with tears.

The baby didn't look like the new parents, but she could tell they would care for her. She had been fostering for many, many years and you got a sense about people. The sense she had about the Smittsons was that they wanted nothing more than someone to love and bring up as their own. And the sense she got about Julius and Kibibi, the first parents, was that they wanted nothing but the best for their baby – even if it meant doing this.

With the box in her arms, Kate Stoner descended the stairs, ready to send baby Talei on to the next stage of her life.

THE END